Black Web

By

James Leonard

Sequel to Silent Screams

First edition published September 2022
Annecy, France

ISBN 9798842148752

Cover Image by Art Guzman
art.photography

CHAPTER 1

East Berlin

February 1985

Without warning, a white beam of light shot across the gap in the wall. Meticulously, it searched the crevices of the old ruins. Lieutenant General Petro Marchenko dropped to his knees. He ignored the snow's icy sting and glared at the hovering light.

Behind him, three shadows pressed against the stone wall. Terrified eyes peered from beneath thick woollen scarfs. They did not move.

"Traitors!" the freezing wind howled through jagged windowless openings.

Petro expected the worst: dogs pulling at tethers; soldiers charging; shots fired… But the only movement was the flurry of snow swirling aimlessly in the night.

For the umpteenth time he questioned their decision.

Did we walk into a trap?

What if…

Stop!

It was too late for regrets. If a trap, he would be solely to blame. That was the simple truth. Fuelled by anger, convincing them had been easy; they would have followed him into hell.

But would it be that easy to watch them die…?

It did not bear thinking about.

Recalling the Politburo chairman's words, he crunched his fist into the snow as if squashing a vile insect. The rasping voice of the bastard still rang in his ears. "Your son's cowardly act was an admission of guilt. Best you forget him. He was a traitor to the Motherland. I spit on his grave!"

These words Petro could never forget, nor forgive.

Enraged, he watched the light linger.

Slowly the minutes ticked by…

How many are waiting, ready to pounce? he wondered.

Finally, darkness.

Squinting into the storm, he wiped the snow off his brow and grey beard.

Where are you?

His hand touched the pistol on his hip. If betrayed, he would spare his family a slow and painful death. Once more he shifted his weight, easing his numbed toes.

Fifty metres to his left towered the concrete wall with its guard towers. In front of it the three-metre-high chain-link fence topped with coils of razor wire marked the restricted zone. An area littered with anti-personnel landmines and rows of anti-tank barriers. It was a brutal scar drawn across the face of Mother Earth. Attempting to flee over the wall would be madness.

A red blip caught Petro's eye.

A second blip…

His fingers inched along the wall. He glanced at the guard tower. It was quiet.

Squeezing his wife's hand, he whispered, 'Get ready.' Without another word he vanished into the dark.

Waiting underneath the dilapidated roof of the porch, Olena, Karina, and Danylo joined him. He turned towards Captain Abramovich. Dressed in his Soviet military uniform, the captain's cold eyes studied them. 'You're ready. Let's go!' he snapped.

Petro fully understood the absence of a salute by the young officer as dictated by military protocol. Regarded a

2

traitor like his son, he was no longer respected. To them, he was a disgrace to the uniform he wore. But his tall frame remained erect. He felt no shame as he followed the captain.

For two hundred metres they struggled through the blizzard, unsure of their destination. Reaching a pile of snow, they stopped. Abramovich did not hesitate to clear a path and disappear down the flight of stairs.

One by one they followed. At the bottom of the stairs, they found themselves waist-deep in a pool of filthy, icy water; the putrid stench of fermented waste was unbearable.

Forcing herself through the muck, Karina cried out, 'Mama, it's freezing!' She shook uncontrollably. 'Papa, I can't, it's…it's-t-too cold,' she moaned through chattering teeth.

'Shut up! You'll get us killed,' Abramovich barked.

Behind her, Danylo whispered, 'Sssh… You'll be fine.' Gently, he guided her by the shoulders through the water.

Inside the third room the crack of a blue night-light exposed four mould-covered walls and a concrete platform. Quickly they scrambled out of the icy water on to the dry surface.

In the next room their moods plummeted. There was no exit! The room was empty except for an old tarpaulin draped over a large object against one wall. It was a dead-end!

Petro drew his pistol and aimed at the captain's head. 'What's this?' he demanded. At less than three paces he would not miss. His ears perked up, listening for men rushing through the filthy water behind them; their executioners.

Is this where we are to die…

'Don't be a fool, old man. Put it away and help me move this,' Abramovich hissed. Ignoring the pistol, he pulled the tarpaulin to one side, exposing four large wooden crates.

Behind the crates was a steel door. Abramovich opened it and said, 'Hurry, you have forty minutes.'

'Is that enough time?'

'Yes General. Show some faith. Now go,' Abramovich replied, and entered a narrow passage leading into the bowels of the earth. As his gloved hand gripped the metal rail of the rickety spiral staircase it rattled alarmingly.

Familiar with all routes to the West, including Checkpoint Charlie and the underground train tunnels, Petro had opted for this secret tunnel being the safest option. It was also one of the last still used by the Soviet Security Forces for covert operations.

Nine storeys below ground they faced another steel door.

'This is as far as I go. From here, you're on your own. Now the rest of the money,' Abramovich said.

With the money in his hand, he swung the door open. The overhead security camera blinked. They could not tell whether they were being watched or not.

'Remember, you fled through the underground rail tunnel after bribing your way through. If the Americans discover this route, we'll know. And believe me, we will find you.'

He handed Petro a key. 'Take this and leave it in the trapdoor's lock. It's at the end of the tunnel. We'll retrieve it later.' Abramovich glanced at his watch. 'You have thirty-three minutes to reach the security gate before it shuts. If you don't make it, then the only way out is back this way. And you don't want that.'

Petro did not miss the nervous twitch in the captain's eyes. Something was wrong. Suppressing an urge to punch him, he switched the flashlight on and led his family into the musty tunnel.

Setting off at a brisk pace, his 1.9metre frame was oblivious to the fifty kilograms strapped to his back. Burdened down by the heavy packs, his wife and daughter struggled to keep up. They carried everything they thought necessary for a new life in the West.

After three hundred metres, Petro stopped, giving his family a chance to catch their breaths.

'I don't trust Abramovich,' he whispered to Olena.

'Yes, I know. Neither do I.'

He turned towards his nineteen-year-old son and gave him the key. 'Danylo, take your mother and sister to safety. I'll wait here to make sure we are not being followed. When you reach the gate, you stay five minutes and not a second longer. If I don't show by then, you leave. If you hear any noises, you run. You don't wait. And you don't come back. Understood?'

'Yes, Papa.'

In the dim light, Petro's grey eyes shone as he reached out and held his wife. His lips touched hers. The taste of her tears filled him with remorse.

Will I ever see you…our children again? Forgive me.

'Remember why we did this,' he said. Released from her embrace, he hugged and kissed his two children. 'Now, go.'

'Petro, come with us,' Olena pleaded.

'I'll only be a few minutes. Promise.'

Taking cover behind a wooden prop, he watched his family stagger deeper into the tunnel, their bodies framed by the soft light. Gripping his pistol with both hands, he aimed at the unseen enemy.

With every twist and turn, Danylo became more disoriented. Are we heading to safety, or back into Abramovich's arms? he wondered. Once more his water-sodden shoes got soaked. Rushing forward he slipped and crashed into the tunnel wall.

Gunfire!

He froze.

His mother turned around and cried out, 'Petro… Petro!'

She started to run.

'Mama, no!' Danylo shouted. Storming past his sister, he grabbed his mother's arm. 'Please, you heard what Papa said. We must continue.'

'No, you go. Take Karina. Take care of her. I can't. Not without him. Please, Danylo, let me go.'

Not releasing his grip, he said, 'No. We need you.'

Shots!

More claps…

Too many!

Danylo knew his father would not survive. He would perish deep underground… And alone. Shunning his fears, he shouted, 'Papa will be fine. Go!'

They rushed through the water.

At last dry ground.

The floor of the tunnel rose steeply.

Behind them, silence…

Danylo shook his head, dismayed. He now fully grasped why no one chased after them. With the security gate locked, why would they? And the key? Lying bastard. There never was to be an escape. Forced back, they would die just like their father. He shrugged off the idea of failure. They'd come too far to give up. He would break the gate open if need be.

The tunnel levelled out, becoming firm underfoot. Concrete. To Danylo's surprise the security gate stood open. With Olena and Karina through, Danylo placed his backpack underneath the metal frame, preventing it from closing in case his father was still alive.

Karina crouched slightly and felt her way in the dark. A wall blocked her path. 'It's a dead-end. I can't find a door.'

Danylo shone the light from side to side. They were inside a chamber – four walls cut into solid rock. He swept the beam over the low ceiling.

The trapdoor.

He tested the handle. It turned with ease. He inserted the key and sprung the lock. Something weighed the door down. Using his shoulders, he shoved it open. Attached to the top were two large drums.

'Mama, Karina, go. Leave your backpacks,' Danylo said. Having hoisted them into the room above he passed the bags through.

Peering out of the hatch, he pointed the beam of light at two short timbers. 'Quick, hand me those.'

With a loud clatter the timber joists hit the chamber's floor. He grabbed one under each arm and disappeared down the tunnel. At the gate he propped them under the bottom bar of the frame. He scraped some dirt off the tunnel wall, spat in it, and rubbed the mud over the security camera's lens. Having retrieved his backpack, he hurried to join his mother and sister.

'I suppose this is the "Free West"? Or it's the waiting room for the train to the gulag,' he said, climbing through the hatch.

'Don't say that!' his mother snapped, not appreciative of his glib comment. Stubbornly, she stepped over the clutter of timbers and boxes, ready to face whatever lay ahead. If she gave up now, Petro's death would have been in vain.

Like his mother, Danylo had also suffered the loss of a loved one. And for what? He seethed and kicked at the filthy rats loitering on the steps. Ignoring the wail of sirens in the distance he opened the basement door, letting in a gush of freezing air. With the way clear he climbed the icy steps to the road. On his left, as if choreographed, floodlights danced over the graffiti-covered concrete wall of West Berlin.

At last they were safe.

Huddled together, they staggered into the night, through the snow and deserted streets. After twenty minutes, Olena sagged to her knees, unable to bear her anguish any longer.

Danylo bent down and cradled her protectively. His courage waned. He was too young to lead them into a world he knew nothing about.

Caught up in their grief, Olena, Danylo, and Karina did not see the tall figure approach. Without a sound a hand reached out. Touching Olena's cheek it wiped away a tear.

'Shhh…it's alright.'

Olena turned her head towards the silhouette towering over her. 'Petro!'

Petro ignored the burning pain in his side and lifted his wife into his arms. Clinging to each other, they shut out the world around them, oblivious to the scarlet stain seeping into the snow at their feet.

Two red dots crept towards the four figures huddled together in the dark, guiding the snipers' telescopic sights. The orders given to the snipers had been simple: "Kill anyone who survives the tunnel."

The trap set for the Marchenko family was about to snap shut. They would join the other delusional traitors who had tried to flee the USSR. Assisted by dissidents inside the Russian military, these defectors never survived. For them the road to freedom always ended the same. No one lived to tell their tale.

Horrified, Danylo watched the two red dots crawl up along his parents' coats.

He jumped up, shouting, 'Mama, Papa, get down!' With all his strength he crashed into them.

Two shots split the night.

Skilfully, the snipers aimed their lethal rifles and found new targets…

CHAPTER 2

USSR Military HQ
Wünsdorf
East Germany

Forty kilometres south of Berlin, Klaara stirred in her bed as the soft winter hues washed over her bedroom walls. Long, laced curtains draped on to the polished parquet floor.

I can sleep all day she thought and yawned, stretching lazily. With a mischievous giggle she realised it was half-past nine. But comfortable in bed she intended to remain there for as long as she could. Dreamily she peered out through the snow-framed window. In the distance, young conscripts struggled to maintain their footing on the icy parade ground. She shivered in sympathy.

Surrounded by her creature comforts, and thirty thousand trained men armed to the teeth, she felt as secure as an unborn baby in its mother's womb. Thus, lying in bed amidst a clutter of stuffed animals and dolls, French white furniture, and prints of her favourite ballerina, Maya Mikhaylovna Plisetskaya, she banished with ease all unpleasant thoughts. The toys a reminder of her parents' endeavours to fulfil in her every childhood dream. To them she would always be an innocent child.

9

But if they only knew, what would they say…?

Having lost her innocence not that long ago, she wriggled deeper in under the duvet, safe from the blizzard battering the window. Swept away by fond memories of last night she snubbed her good intentions. Monday's assignments could wait. Her heart fluttered, recalling his feather-light kisses, his whispers of undying love, promising to never leave her. She sighed contently and closed her eyes and dreamt of the night ahead, to be seduced by the man she wanted to marry. There would never be another.

Soon she succumbed to sleep, oblivious of the ferocious storm sweeping the base, blotting out the impatient wail of sirens.

They had first met nine years ago in junior school. Shy by nature and diligent in her studies, her peers had regarded her a snobbish nerd. Someone uninterested in boys and in having fun. They were wrong. Like them, she nurtured girlish fantasies of someone special; of him, who was blissfully unaware of her adoration.

Keeping her distance, she had witnessed his transformation from awkward teenager to a tall, handsome young man, wrestling with ease every obstacle in his way. And so her admiration had grown. It seemed nothing could stop his effortless stride to adulthood. His silent confidence had been intoxicating. Frequently, she had caught herself daydreaming, scribbling his name over and over in her workbook. Although somewhat distracted by this, she had successfully enrolled in medical school, at which stage she was also hopelessly in love. In love with a man she had hardly spoken to.

Only much later, with fate's divine intervention, did their paths finally crossed.

In the student canteen at Humboldt University, turning around with her lunch tray laden with food, she had crashed into a cadet. While wiping the food from the soldier's uniform, a hand had stopped her. Hearing her name, she had looked up into the smiling blue eyes of the soldier. Into the eyes she had adored for so long.

'Wake up, Klaara. Wake up. Something terrible has happened,' her mother said, shaking her by the shoulder.

'What… What's going on?' Klaara asked confused. The expression of dread on her mother's face made her bolt upright. Suddenly the room felt cold. She pulled the duvet tight around her slight frame.

'Lt Gen Marchenko, Olena, Danylo, and Karina are missing. People say the KGB took them. Shot them as traitors,' Riina Luik said.

'Mama… Mama, what are you talking about?'

'Sorry, Klaara. They are dead. They all are.'

'Nonsense! Mama, do you even hear yourself?' Klaara said, snubbing her mother's words. 'It's most likely only a rumour. Gossip…'

'I wish it were. But it's not.' Her mother's eyes welled with tears.

Klaara swallowed hard, realising her mother meant every word she said. Stubbornly she spurned the news. 'No, it's not true… Can't be. I would've known if something was wrong. And I did not.'

'None of us did. I'm sorry.'

Finally, Klaara's confidence crumbled.

Seeing her daughter's anguish, Riina stammered, 'Maybe they're okay. Maybe these are only rumours, as you say.' But deep down she knew her words were false; a moth-eaten blanket draped over her daughter's heaving shoulders in comfort. And with the general's quarters sealed off, no one would know the truth.

'As awful as it is, we must prepare ourselves for the worst. Now get dressed, and be quick. They have detained Papa for questioning and will come for you soon,' she warned, trying to compose herself. 'Klaara, I'm so sorry. I know how much you loved him.'

Tucking her knees in under her chin, Klaara clasped her arms around her legs and rocked back and forth. Her large hazel-green eyes stared unblinkingly at the white wallpaper. Remembering the despair in Danylo's eyes before he had turned away the night before, she stopped rocking.

How could I have missed the sadness, the fear…uncertainty?

If she had not been so self-absorbed, she might have noticed something troubled him. She said, her voice firm, 'No Mama, they did not take them. They had fled.'

'What makes you think that?'

'I'm sure Danylo wanted to tell me last night, but he did not want to put me in danger. At least now they cannot charge me as an accomplice or traitor. Also, if I went with him, it would have ruined your lives. So instead, he had said nothing. But his eyes did.'

Riina nodded thoughtfully.

'Mama, remember what happened to his brother, Andriy?'

'Yes, of course. Such a good man, destined for great things like his father.'

'Well, I think planning to defect started with his death. His father had never accepted the reason for his suicide. He had always believed that someone had driven him to it. Since then, he had been a changed man, openly cursing the state, holding them responsible for Andriy's death. He hated those who ran this country and what our society had become. So, I'm not surprised they have fled.'

'I never could understand why Andriy killed himself. Self-pity was not in his nature.'

'No, definitely not.'

'Yes, just thinking of the lavish dinner his parents had held in his honour at the Zhukovsky Air Force Academy. Him beaming from ear to ear having obtained his degree cum laude. Considering all that, then killing himself a few months later makes no sense,' Riina Luik said. 'Wasn't Andriy involved in some secret research?'

'Yes. Aviation technology. Why?'

'Maybe he had discovered something illegal going on.'

'No, that's not it. His father investigated that possibility.' Klaara said and shrugged her shoulders. 'But what really drove him to suicide is still unclear. Declared a traitor during

12

an impromptu hearing, they had decommissioned and barred him from further research. They had accused him of promoting western capitalism, decadence, and democracy amongst his fellow officers. His sentence was to be handed down by military court at some later date. But as a "traitor", he had faced a life in the gulag with no right to appeal. So, he had killed himself.'

'Possibly. But why did he not tell his father? Surely, he would have helped.'

'I asked Danylo the same question. He suspected Andriy was too naïve to see the danger, thinking he'd be able to convince the court of his loyalty to this country.'

'He was very naïve if he believed that.'

'When the general had discovered from Andriy's friends about the events before his death, he had gone to the Politburo, demanding justice. He wanted Andriy's name cleared and the man responsible brought to trial. But the rulers of our "beloved" country did not care,' Klaara sneered. 'To them, the case was closed. Defeated and handed a written warning, they had sent him away to continue with his duties. The general had never forgiven them. Neither the chairman's parting words. So, Mama, do you now understand why I believe they have fled? I just hope they are safe. So, I'll wait for him… I know he'll return.'

'Yes, Klaara,' Riina said, hoping her daughter would let go of Danylo and find someone else. There was no point in waiting. Too many people had tried and failed. Not for one moment did Riina doubt the Marchenko family was dead. No one ever survived the crossing.

But neither Klaara, her mother, nor anyone else would ever know the facts. That died with Andriy.

The reason for him being targeted was very simple.

During the evaluation process of new cadets, the political officer, Capt Kozlov – a man with a personal grudge against Ukrainians – had accidentally stumbled on Andriy's great-grandfather's role in the Ukrainian War of Independence of 1917, resulting in the establishment of a Ukrainian Republic.

Later, the Soviet Union had absorbed most of its territory and renamed it the Ukrainian Soviet Socialist Republic.

Up against the might of the Politburo, and classified a threat to the Soviet Union, Andriy's days were numbered.

After the hearing Capt Kozlov's had made his intentions quite clear, stating that he would destroy him and his family. To him, all Ukrainians were vermin. If Andriy thought his people could infiltrate the upper echelons of the Soviet military and start another revolution for independence, they were wrong. It would never happen.

Branded a traitor and an outcast, he had realised what lay ahead. The gulag; toiling day after day a broken man. That he could endure. But he would not allow his reputation to destroy his family as well. With him out of the way, the government might just spare them the same fate as his.

Feeling powerless, Andriy had taken the only option he thought left. He had killed himself in the middle of the night with a bullet to the head.

The letter addressed to his father, he, or anyone else, would never see. Capt Kozlov had removed the envelope from Andriy's dress-uniform pocket.

CHAPTER 3

USSR Military HQ
Wünsdorf
East Germany

'No more, please... No more... I don't know anything... Please,' Klaara begged, her voice barely audible through her cut lips. The twenty-four hours of sleep deprivation and beatings had broken her spirit. Her head flopped forward; her body numbed.

Ignoring her cries, the burly man's meaty fist pummelled her face. With a sickening crack her head snapped back, ripping her free from the men's grip holding her. The veins bulged in Egor's neck as he grabbed her hair and shoved his nose into her battered face.

'You lying bitch! Six months, and you expect me to believe he didn't tell you anything? How long do you want me to continue? Estonian whore,' he hissed. With disdain he stared at her naked breasts, stained with fresh blood. Slumped in the chair she did not move; her eyes swollen shut.

Egor straightened up, rubbed his chin, and nodded. 'That's enough, let's go!'

As he turned away, he paused, swung back, and punched her in the stomach. Her flaccid body doubled over and fell on to the grime-smeared floor, unconscious. He stomped off, resisting the temptation to kick her in the head.

15

'Clean the slut and get her out of here,' he growled at the two wardens gloating in the doorway. With his work done, he was certain she would never whore again.

Eager to obey, the wardens rushed forward but with no intention of wiping the young woman clean. What was the point? She'd be dead soon. Their long nails dug into Klaara's arms. Like a lifeless doll, they dragged her out of the cell and through the empty corridors. Helplessly, her body swished across the floor behind them as their spine-chilling cackle bounced off the prison walls.

'Rot in hell!' the one warden shouted as they dumped her on to the pavement.

Comatose, Klaara did not hear their curses, nor did she feel the freezing cold. Under the glow of the streetlight, they glared at her sprawled out in front of them. They did not care if some street dog ripped her apart. The more gruesome her death, the stronger the message would be to other whores who thought of sleeping with the enemy.

In disbelief, Riina Luik's hands shot up and covered her mouth, stifling a scream. Powerless, she watched from across the road as the horrible scene unfolded. By her side, Colonel Jakob Luik did not hesitate and charged at the wardens. He wanted to tear their limbs, piece by piece, from their haggard old bodies. Ignoring him, they scampered back to the safety of the military prison.

'I'll kill you!' he yelled.

Reaching Klaara his heart broke. He removed his coat, stooped down, and draped it over her naked body.

Riina crouched down beside him and cradled Klaara's battered head in her lap. She wept softly and stroked her daughter's blood-caked hair.

Jakob steeled himself and searched for a pulse. Nothing. Stubbornly, he shifted his fingers, refusing to give up.

A faint tremor…

Again, a soft pulse.

Gently, he lifted Klaara into his arms and vanished into the night, oblivious to the blank stares of the few bystanders. He cursed himself for having allowed this to have happened to his child. Why did he not stop them? But he only deceived himself. No one could have spared Klaara the beating at the hands of the KGB.

Twenty-seven Days Later

He's still alive, Klaara repeated to herself, not wanting to believe her punishment had been for nothing. She shunned the daily gazette's words, claiming that the "traitors" Lt Gen Marchenko and his family had been shot by the capitalist pigs. Annoyed, she flung the newspaper on to the floor.

Of the twenty-seven days since her ordeal, she had spent ten in ICU and a further eight in the hospital. The remaining days she had recuperated at home under the watchful eye of her mother. Today was the first time she had been left on her own.

Fed up confined to bed she craved fresh air. As much as she liked her room, she started to hate it. Except for reading, eating, and sleeping, her mother had restricted her from doing anything more strenuous; treating her like an invalid. She had to do something or she would go mad. The anguish of not knowing what had happened to Danylo only made matters worse. If he were still alive, then where was he?

She needed someone to talk to. Confide in. Share her fears and hopes with. But who? She trusted no one. Not even her parents with their patience at an end, insisting she must forget him. No, they would not be interested in her rambling. They even failed to understand why she still dreamt of him, of a future together. How could they? She did not blame them.

Oh, to touch his face, look into his eyes again, she pined. Being separated from him was unbearable.

The chime of the doorbell made her jump.

No, not them… Please, not again.

She covered her head with the duvet and waited for the inevitable crash. The splintering of the front door. The stomping of boots…

Nothing.

Petrified, she hardly breathed.

After what felt like an eternity she peered from under the duvet, slipped out of the bed and sneaked into the hallway. The few neatly arranged ornaments and pieces of furniture were untouched. On top of the doormat lay a nondescript brown envelope. She scooped it up.

Addressed to "Kallim" her heart leapt. Worried someone was watching, she quickly tucked the envelope into the folds of her gown, glanced at the door, and hurried back to bed.

Safely under the covers she opened the sealed envelope. With trembling hands, she withdrew the handwritten pages and immediately recognised Danylo's slanted style of writing.

Savouring his every word she read the letter for the third time. His vow to return to her as soon as possible filled her with joy. It was exactly as she had believed. Indifferent to her own pain she yearned for him.

He had insisted she must destroy the letter, but how could she? To part with it was unthinkable. Instead, she hid the neatly folded pages inside her pillowcase, laid her head on the pillow, and closed her eyes. For the first time since he had left, she relaxed. It was only a matter of time before they would be reunited.

CHAPTER 4

Ramstein Air Force Base
West Germany

The late-afternoon sun spilled into the sparsely furnished bedroom. Beneath the window stood an old wooden desk with the names of previous tenants etched into it. On top lay a blotter covered in scribbles, assignment papers, textbooks, a fountain pen, desk lamp, more stationery, and a framed photograph of Klaara. Books neatly filled the four shelves next to the desk. A chair, a single bed, a wardrobe, and a rug completed the rest of Danylo's possessions.

Two photographs of Klaara and one of them holding hands on the banks of the Großer Wünsdorfer See adorned the egg-white walls. Nothing else.

He found it impossible to concentrate. Ignoring his studies, he shifted in his chair, hoping his plan had worked.

Smuggling the letter past the ever-vigilant East German State Security Service (Staatssicherheitsdienst, SSD) would never be easy. However, if it did somehow slip through unnoticed, Klaara should have received his message by now.

Eight weeks; an eternity since he had last seen her. He would give anything to hear her voice again. How much longer do I have to wait? he wondered. Away from her, from his soulmate, everything had become meaningless. Worried

19

sick about her, he prayed for her safety, and in the same breath, cursed the day he had left her behind. The day he and his family had nearly died on the empty streets of West Berlin.

He had shoved his parents out of the way too late. The bullets had found their targets. Scrambling for cover, his wounded father had returned fire, felling one assailant. Fortunately, the other assailant's second bullet had slammed harmlessly into the masonry wall, only grazing his father. Two more shots fired in return had seen the assassins flee to the safety of East Berlin.

Rushed to the hospital by the West Berlin Police, Lt Gen Marchenko was treated for two splintered ribs, a punctured lung, and a ruined shoulder. And his wife, for a bullet wound to her upper left thigh.

And so, they had survived the devious assassination attempt by the KGB.

Once Allied High Command had established the family's identities, and with their defection confirmed, they had been escorted to Ramstein Air Force Base. And as the Bauer family they had begun their lives in the Free West.

Neither the West nor the USSR had acknowledged their successful escape. Instead, the shooting incident on the night had been reported as the murder by USSR security forces of a Ukrainian family attempting to reach the West. Subsequently, with the *bodies* cremated, and the ashes delivered to the Soviet Ambassador in Germany, their existence as the Marchenko family had been concluded.

Under their new identities they had settled in Bavaria as Ernst, Anna, Thomas, and Susan Bauer.

The Allied High Command employed Ernst as a military adviser. And Thomas, aged nineteen, had joined the German Bundeswehr Intelligence Corps to complete his law degree.

The first letter to Klaara, expressing his undying love, and explaining why he had left without her, Danylo had written the day before the defection. His close friend, Yakov

Grachev, had delivered the letter as soon as he had received word of their safe crossing.

Under the alias of Johan Schmidt, Danylo had posted a second letter from Kempten in Bavaria. The letter was brief and to the point, imploring Klaara to be patient, to wait for him. He would come to her. Under no circumstances must she try to escape the USSR. The wording was in a simple code, contrived between two friends. Klaara would only be referred to in passing as Ekaterina, Yakov's older sister.

The real Johan Schmidt, an old school friend of Yakov, was unaware of his role in this deception. He and Yakov had met ten years ago when Yakov's father had been stationed in Bonn as the USSR Ambassador.

As expected, the East Berlin Stasi had intercepted the letter. With the origin, contents, and recipient's authenticity confirmed, it had finally reached its destination. The harmless enquiry by a school friend regarding Yakov's well-being did not raise any concerns. But as it involved a Russian citizen, the junior officer's report plus a copy of the letter had been delivered to the desk of officer Mikhail Semenov.

Mikhail, a veteran of twenty years in the service of the KGB, was a man whose hawk eyes and suspicious nature had led to the capture of many traitors. And undoubtedly would again.

I'll keep an eye on you. One foot wrong and you'll regret the day you were born, officer Semenov thought, toying with the letter in his hand. Diplomats. One could never tell when they'd turn. Especially their brats who had lived in the cesspool, their heads filled with propaganda.

CHAPTER 5

USSR Military HQ
Wünsdorf
East Germany

'Bye, Mama… Papa. I love you,' Klaara said, kissing them on their cheeks, ready to board the train for East Berlin.

'Glad you're your jolly old self again. But remember, they're watching you. Any odd behaviour, and they'll start asking questions,' her father cautioned.

Her mother had her own concerns, noticing Klaara's pale complexion. 'Are you alright?' she asked.

'Mama, I'm fine. Just nervous… And a bit scared. I've missed a lot of class and I'm not sure I'll be able to catch up,' she said. But to be honest, she wasn't feeling quite herself lately; the queasiness at all hours was becoming more prevalent. This she put down to some kidney or liver disorder, a result of the beating at the hands of the KGB. And for having missed her period. Or was it?

'Are you sure everything's okay because it doesn't look like it,' her mother stated bluntly. 'Please, go to the doctor on campus. You've been through a very traumatic experience and if something is wrong, it won't go away by itself.'

'Yes, Mama, I will…'

'And if anyone troubles you, call me immediately. I shall not let them touch you again, I swear,' her father promised.

'Papa, don't worry.'

Three days later, her condition had not improved. Something was wrong. She had to speak to someone.

Going to the surgery on campus was too big a risk. Being watched, the doctors would undoubtedly report her visit to the KGB. Although there was one lecturer she had befriended who might be prepared to help. Someone she could trust.

Dr Anna Kuznetsova's raised eyebrow spelt nothing good. 'You are pregnant,' she said.

Klaara's shoulders slumped. Her face crumbled. Why now? 'How long do I have?' she asked nervously.

Dr Kuznetsova busied herself for a few moments, and said, 'One week and seven months.'

'Oh…'

Dr Kuznetsova did not approve of the morals of some girls on campus, sleeping around and getting themselves pregnant. Klaara was different. She had principles, and that's why she liked her. She made a mistake and needed help. 'Do you love the father-to-be?'

'Yes, I do.'

'Will he be happy to be a father?'

'Definitely… But he's gone. I don't think he'll ever see our child… Or me again,' she whispered, unable to hold back the tears.

'Oh, dear. What do you mean?' Dr Kuznetsova asked. She sat down and draped an arm over Klaara's heaving shoulders.

'He and his family had fled to the West, and—'

'Shh…' Dr Kuznetsova stopped her. 'Not a word more. If so, then I think it is wise to end the pregnancy,' she said in a conciliatory tone. 'Come back tomorrow and—'

'No. You misunderstood. There is nothing I want more than this baby, believe me,' Klaara interrupted as her face lit up, knowing a part of him was growing inside her.

Arriving home for the weekend, Klaara let herself into the third-floor apartment and quietly entered the kitchen. She crept up behind her mother and greeted, 'Hello Mama. I would also like a cup, please.'

Deep in thought, her mother nearly dropped the teapot. 'How many times have I told you not to do that! You'll give me a heart attack one day,' she scolded good-heartedly.

Klaara did not reply, smiling mischievously.

In silence, Riina looked at her daughter. Something was different? 'Come here, my beautiful child,' she said, and with a hug steered Klaara to the nearest chair. 'Sit down and tell me about your week. Did you—'

'Danylo is alive!' Klaara blurted out, ignoring whatever her mother was about to say.

'Please, not again,' Riina moaned and banged the teapot on the table with a loud clunk. She guarded her tongue and looked at her daughter; this time more intently. Yes, she's positively radiant. What a remarkable change from five days ago. But what nonsense, claiming Danylo is alive. Getting herself excited over nothing. The best for her, and us, is to forget him.

'Klaara, we've spoken about this many times. Please, for your own sake, let it be. We also loved him and would have wanted nothing more to see you two—'

'No Mama, he's not dead,' she said defiantly. 'He wrote to me. He's in the West. They all are. I want to—'

'Stop!' Riina cut her short. 'They may be listening.'

Klaara got up and pressed her lips against her mother's ear and said, 'I'm pregnant.'

'What! No...' Riina stammered, unable, unwilling to believe what she'd heard. 'When did this happen? Who's the father?'

'Sorry, Mama. It did. Danylo is the father and we love each other.'

'I... We thought you were cleverer than that. Why were you so careless? You have your whole life ahead of you.'

'Yes, I know.'

24

Riina's legs felt weak. She sat down. 'What are you going to do? I honestly can't believe this is happening.' She was livid. If the KGB found out their world would become a living hell.

In the background the clock on top of the fridge ticked softly. Facing her daughter, the distraught mother shook her head, disappointed, while Klaara's eyes searched hers for understanding. For support.

When Riina finally spoke, her voice did not waver. 'You must abort the child.'

'No. No, Mama. Please don't ask that of me...'

'I understand how you feel, but you cannot keep the baby. If it's true that they are still alive, the KGB will use you and the child to find them.'

'They don't need to know.'

'And how are you going to keep it a secret?'

'I can stay with grandma...'

'I'm not sure. She won't approve of your behaviour... And people talk.'

'Please Mama, ask her. Please. Only until the end of the summer holiday, or till the baby is born. I can go to her as soon as I've sat my exams.'

'And then? Once the baby is born, where will you go? How will you be able to look after the child?'

'I'll find a way.'

'Are you sure about this?'

'Yes Mama, I am.'

'I'll ask. But I can't promise anything. And I'm sure your father will also have something to say.'

Giving her mother a peck on the cheek, she said, 'Mama, I'm so happy.'

As much as Riina wanted to share in her daughter's joy, she could not. To her this was a big mistake, one which would undoubtedly end in disaster.

CHAPTER 6

KGB HQ
East Berlin

And congratulate Ekaterina. Delighted for her. You know, I would love to see her again. Pity the father-to-be turned out to be a swine. If it was me, I'd do anything for them. She doesn't have a suitor by any chance? Will you put in a good word for me? That's if you approve.

Write soon and good luck with your studies.

Your buddy,

Johan

Comrade Mikhail Semenov finished reading the letter and toiled with it in his hand; it was the fourth in less than three months addressed to Yakov Grachev. This sudden interest in each other after so many years stirred his curiosity – something didn't add up. But what exactly he could not tell. Not yet.

'Grigory, I smell a rat.'
'Why?'

'This loose talk. Drivel not to draw attention. Flowery stories. Innocent questions. Rubbish. What punk wants a broad with baggage unless she's a stunner?'

'Maybe she is?'

'How would he know? He hasn't seen her for years. She may look like a horse by now, and pregnant, too. Nope. It's a lot of tosh. What does he hope to gain stuck in the West? Or does he plan to sneak in here and rescue her from the *evil communists*? Nope, I don't buy it.'

'Yes, I think you're right, boss. Looks like a big smokescreen. Must admit, always impresses me how you can see through a sham,' Grigory grinned. 'But you're way too neurotic. A bit like an old woman. You keep this up and you'll never make sixty.'

'Watch me, funny man. That's why I sit behind a bigger desk than yours, dumb shmuck,' Comrade Semenov shot back jokingly at his right-hand man.

'Yeah, yeah. And you're full of it. Anyway, who's this Johan Schmidt?'

'A friend. And surprise, surprise, he really exists. That's just it. It's too perfect. The information checks out. They were at school together in Bonn; used to be friends. Possibly he's just another horny Westerner lusting after our sexy broads,' Mikhail replied.

'But?'

'I suspect Johan is an agent with German Intelligence, and he has recruited Yakov. These letters are far more sinister than what they seem. Thing is, they're all clean. No code, no microscopic or electronic messages. Nothing. So whatever intel there is, is in the text. Well, time to start digging. Grigory, pick a team. I want twenty-four-hour surveillance on Ambassador Grachev's children,' Mikhail said.

He pushed his chair back and put his feet on the desk. Pensively, he looked out of the window where a tiny sparrow flapped its wings in the fresh morning air. Leaving the safety of the windowsill, it flew up into the grey sky. That's right, my little birdie, fly away, and bring them to Papa. We'll uncover the truth soon enough, he thought, and threw the resealed envelope addressed to Yakov into the out-tray. Content, he folded his arms over his sizeable belly.

CHAPTER 7

USSR HQ
Wünsdorf, East Germany
Saturday Evening

Another two hours, Klaara sighed. The suspense between letters was killing her, never knowing if they would reach her or not.

'Do you want anything, Mama… Papa?' Klaara asked and got up off the settee. There was enough time till the nine o'clock film, a re-run of the popular, "Moscow does not believe in Tears".

'A shot of vodka, thanks,' her dad replied.

'Nothing for me,' her mother said and stole a glance at her husband who reclined in his favourite armchair.

An hour later, Col Luik got up, stretched lazily, and stifled a yawn. 'Yadi-yadi-ya. Women, always the same, yearning for love, for mister perfect,' he complained good-humouredly. 'Okay, I need some fresh air. Anyone for a walk? Klaara?'

'No Papa. I'm quite comfortable right here.'

'I'll keep her company, Jakob,' his wife smiled.

It was a smile which had drawn him to her many years ago, one that still filled him with endearment. He was a lucky man. But above the playful turn of her lips, her eyes simmered with anxiety.

Aiming for the cluster of trees and shrubs fifty metres up ahead, Jakob fell into a brisk walk. He wanted to get this over with; get to the bottom of his daughter's somewhat predictable behaviour. Now and then he glanced over his shoulder. Reaching the heavy foliage he stopped, bent down, and prodded some object in the undergrowth. The next instant he disappeared in amongst the trees.

Right, let's see who delivers these letters you so eagerly snap up.

It had not taken him long to recognise the pattern. Every third Saturday around eleven, Klaara would casually linger near the front door.

On cue, at precisely 10:55 PM, a young soldier carrying an envelope entered their building. Jakob broke cover and sprinted after him. Quietly, he let himself in and raced up the stairs. One floor below theirs, he peered through the banister and saw the envelope pushed through the door's letter box. Quickly, he returned to the dim-lit ground floor lobby.

As the soldier stole outside, Jakob barked, 'Halt! Your name and number!'

The unsuspecting soldier froze in his tracks. Confronted by a senior officer, he blurted out, 'Private Smirnov, 84434111N, Sir!'

'I think we better have a chat, Private Smirnov. Come!' Jakob ordered.

Jakob peered into the lounge. His wife was on her own. 'Where's Klaara?' he asked.

'In her room,' Riina said, also eager to learn what these mysterious letters entailed.

'We'll be in the kitchen. Please make sure she does not disturb us.'

The two men faced each other across the table. Jakob reached out and moved the single vase with its arrangement of flowers out of the way. He smiled genially, and asked, 'A drink?'

'No, Sir.'

Jakob ignored him and poured two glasses of vodka. He put one in front of the soldier. 'Drink.'

Before Jakob replaced the bottle's cap, Pte Smirnov had swallowed the clear liquid.

'I thought you said you didn't want one. You're either very thirsty or just plain scared,' Jakob said and refilled the young soldier's glass. 'Drink up. Good, your colour is returning.'

He allowed the alcohol to take effect as he stared in silence at the young man opposite him. After the private's fourth glass, he said, 'So, enlighten me. What is your interest in my daughter?'

'Nothing, Sir.'

'Don't take me for a fool!'

'Yes… Of course not, Sir.'

'Right, then try again.'

'I don't know your daughter, Sir. I swear. A guy I met in the mess yesterday asked me to drop the envelope off as a favour. It's a love letter. He claims he's too shy, and he's worried someone may spot him,' Pte Smirnov said unconvincingly.

'Don't try my patience, Private. Or I'll throw your arse in that ugly square block on the other side of the base. It'll be your home till you decide to tell me what's going on. Is that clear?'

'Yes Sir. I'm sorry. But I've told him—'

'It's your honour or the cell. Your choice,' Jakob cautioned.

'My friend asked me for this favour,' he admitted with his head down.

'So, this guy is now a friend. His name.'

'Yakov Grachev, Sir.'

'Address, damn it? Must I drag everything out of you?'

'74 Wilhelmina Strasse. Please, Sir, don't tell him I told you.'

'I won't. But here's what you're going to do. First, you never set foot near this apartment again. Second, you never discuss these activities with anyone. And lastly, not a word about our chat with Yakov. No warning or telling him I know who he is.'

Klaara's run-in with the KGB, which had nearly killed her, was still fresh in his mind. On that night while carrying her naked body home, beaten to a pulp, he had vowed it would never happen again. He stood up and growled, 'Go!'

Jakob's loud voice, accompanied by the bang of the front door, and followed by her mother placating him, interrupted Klaara's thoughts.

Wonder what's going on? she thought. Ignoring the raucous she returned her attention to jotting down the details of the letter; the nonsensical girlish gibberish in her diary would make no sense to anyone else. Again, she recalled the contact names, places, and schedules for her escape in case she misplaced the diary.

Klaara hated tearing up his letter. It was especially hard, this being the last communique until she would be safely outside the reach of the dreaded Stasi and KGB. As she flushed the toilet, she watched until the last scrap of torn paper disappeared into the spiralling eddy.

Fulfilling his promise to his friend, Yakov's embittered hand had dutifully laboured in decoding Danylo's letters. As each word had flowed with ease from his pen on to the thin paper, they had also conveyed his own feelings to Klaara; that of love and devotion.

Thankfully, the first phase of the plan was completed, and with no repercussions.

And now, my dear, to get you out of here safely. He sighed, torn between his love for Klaara and his loyalty to Danylo.

Despite the mild satisfaction of being the architect of Klaara's escape, one flawed with ifs and buts, he was deeply resentful. The last day of the academic year would mark the beginning of her perilous journey into the unknown. She would travel to the country to live with her grandmother, and from there to the West. The fact was, he would most probably never see her again.

If only roles were reversed, Yakov thought resentfully. It was not the first time jealousy had reared its ugly head. But his devotion to her had kept him on course in continuing his allegiance to Danylo.

Sorry, my friend, I love her. Can't help it… Maybe I can persuade her not to go. I can become the father of—

'Yakov, you have a visitor!' his mother called from downstairs.

For a moment Yakov hesitated at the top of the stairs, wondering who the visitor was. Shunning this concern, he skipped down the stairs. And sliding his hand along the polished dark-wood banister, he ignored his ancestors' stern looks in the row of oil paintings lining the wall.

'Please to meet you, Yakov. I'm Colonel Jakob Luik. Is there somewhere we can talk in private?'

'Of course, Colonel. This way, please.'

Yakov shut the lounge door behind him and offered his guest tea, which was declined. The visitor unsettled him.

'Yakov, I won't be long. I guess you know the reason for my visit?'

'I guess I do.'

'Good. Then explain what these letters are you're sending Klaara. Are they yours?'

'Yes, Colonel, they are.'

'Why don't you deliver them yourself? There's no reason for you to be shy. If you're old enough to court, then you're old enough to act like a man and introduce yourself. Or is there an ulterior motive behind all this secrecy?'

'No, Colonel, there is not,' Yakov replied, his voice light, friendly. 'It's just that I'm not sure whether she's over Danylo. I don't want to cause her anymore distress. With women, one can never be too careful.'

'True. But you'd tell me if there was another reason, won't you? For instance, if they were from someone else.'

'I don't understand?'

'I think you understand perfectly well.'

'No Colonel, I don't. There is nothing underhand going on. They are mine,' Yakov said, oozing charm.

'Right. And you stand by that?'

'Yes, Colonel. As you are here, I ask for your permission to court Klaara?'

Suppressing the urge to clout Yakov for his impertinence and for lying, he got up and said, 'You have my permission.' He had learned enough. Yakov was a liar. And considering who he was, an extremely dangerous one. Whose side he was on, who he worked for and his connections, only time would tell.

Jakob shut the garden gate. Pausing on the pavement, he glanced left and right. No traffic. About to cross, a black V8 GAZ M23 parked thirty metres down the road caught his eye; the much-loathed transport favoured by the KGB. Two dour faces stared at him. Ignoring them, he kept his composure and hurried to his car.

Who are you watching, and why? Or are you guarding the ambassador?

Worried that he might be the target, he slipped in behind the steering wheel. With his eyes on the rear-view mirror, he pulled out on to the road. The black V8 GAZ M23 did not move.

Nervously, Yakov paced his bedroom floor. He knew his lies had not convinced Klaara's father. They were so close, and now this. Well, it did not matter whether the colonel believed him. He had far bigger concerns to deal with than his friend's love life. Having helped Danylo annoyed him. But it was too late for regrets. Klaara had to be warned.

Not trusting the house phone as it was most likely tapped, Yakov raced outside in search of a public phone. In his hurry, he failed to spot the car pull away from the kerb. Slowly, it followed him at a discreet distance.

Five minutes later, out of breath and with trembling hands he fed a coin into the slot. It rang.

Come on, pick up… Come on!

On the eighth ring, a youthful voice answered. 'Luik's residence, good morning.'

'May I speak to Klaara, please?'

'Speaking. Who is this?'

'*Johan's* friend. Are you able to talk?' Yakov asked.

'Yes, but people could be listening.'

'Understood. I'll keep it short. Your dad knows about the letters. I told him they were nothing more than love letters from me to you. My name—'

'No names,' she stopped him. 'Please, continue.'

'Of course. You may remember me. We met a few times.'

'Yes, I do.' She remembered him all too well. How could she forget the adoration in his eyes the second time they had met? Even with Danylo present, he did not take his eyes off her. As much as it was flattering, so was it embarrassing.

'Then you must convince your father that what I've told him is true. Tell him I am, and always have been, madly in love with you. That I can't stop pestering you with my ridiculous letters. Hopefully that will do it. And if he's not happy with that, then best we cancel our *picnic*,' Yakov said.

'No. Under no circumstance do we cancel it.'

'Then, we must move it forward. Meet me tomorrow, lunchtime, student canteen.'

Leaving the phone booth, Yakov glanced up and down the street. It was a typical Sunday morning: quiet, with hardly any traffic. But the parked car with two passengers, its engine purring softly, seemed out of place. A nauseating fear gripped his stomach. He turned and walked home, fighting the urge to run.

He was under surveillance, a fact which could jeopardise everything. He dreaded being taken in for questioning, as he would talk if tortured. All that he could do was to leave the USSR. Whether Klaara would approve was irrelevant. He would go with her.

Yakov opened the front door and looked over his shoulder. The black car pulled up opposite their house. The engine fell silent.

Col Luik arrived home, convinced the men had been watching Yakov's home. Why was a mystery? He knew they would report and investigate his visit. And if they discover he'd visited the son and not the father, he would have some explaining to do. It seemed he had inadvertently walked into something much bigger.

The warning received during his interrogation by the KGB had left him under no illusion of what would happen if he got caught doing anything they did not approve of.

What are you up to, Yakov? If you are using Klaara, I'll kill you.

'Papa, I don't care for Yakov. I find his letters amusing, that's all. He doesn't stop going on about how much he loves me. Apparently, he has been in love with me since the day Danylo introduced us. He wants to marry me and take care of the baby,' Klaara said, sounding sincere and fed up. Her father's questions made her uncomfortable as she made up lie after lie. But she was a terrible liar. Lying was not in her nature.

'Were they good friends?'

'The best. Imagine that.'

'I'm not surprised. My dear, you still have a lot to learn about men. More than anything else, you must be very careful. To be frank, I don't trust Yakov. I think he may be involved with things he should not be. My advice to you, stay well clear of him.'

'Don't fret, Papa. I'll tell him to stop.'

'Good. Now I'll leave you to rest,' he said.

Shutting the bedroom door, he knew she was lying. If Yakov was involved in anything underhand, it would be in his and his family's best interest to know as soon as possible. Therefore, a visit to the KGB in the afternoon would be a wise decision. They may provide him with some much-needed answers.

Chapter 8

Monday Morning
KGB, East Berlin

Satisfied that his instincts had proved correct yet again, Comrade Mikhail Semenov drummed his fingers on the file; a document substantially heavier than the one placed on his desk a few months ago. Thank you, Colonel. At last, we know who these letters are for. And more importantly, the source, he thought, reflecting on Klaara's father's statement of the previous day.

Some important pieces had been added to the puzzle. Early in the investigation, they had established that Yakov's sister, Ekaterina, was not pregnant. But the name of the mysterious girl in the letters had eluded them until now.

Grateful for his co-operation, he had assured the colonel that nothing would happen to his daughter – Yakov and his band of subversives were the target. Not Klaara. The colonel was also instructed to refrain from any interference in the ongoing investigation. He must permit Klaara to play her part in whatever they were plotting. She would be used as bait.

Their enquiries had exposed a far more damning matter than Klaara's romance with the traitor: the newly formed Russian Freedom Party. An ultra-left organisation of radicals currently recruiting members amongst students. Yakov was one of its ringleaders.

'Grigory, if we're wrong about this punk, we can say goodbye to all this,' Mikhail warned and pointed at the walls. 'Don't forget, his dad's a senior member of the Politburo.'

'This comes from sending our kids to the capitalist. If he had not been, he might have been a good citizen today. Instead, we've got a rebel on our hands who's disloyal to the Motherland. And shows no respect to his father or the Party,' Grigory volunteered.

'Damn his father. The Party is all that matters,' Mikhail swore. 'As from this minute, every person linked to this worm, anyone who as much as breathes in his direction, is a suspect. When I present this file to the boss in Moscow, there can be no mistakes or it will be my arse in a sling and not the pretty boy's. Remember, Grigory, if I go down, so will you. So, no mistakes.'

Humboldt University, East Berlin, Monday Morning

'Good morning, Klaara. What a miserable day,' Hilda complained on entering the medical faculty. 'You're ready for the exam?'

'Not really. But I suppose as much as I can be. And you, how're the nerves?' Klaara asked, pulling her green-hooded raincoat off.

'Like steel. Ready as always,' she laughed, and studied her friend. 'You look nervous. Are you worried?'

'I think I missed too many classes. Though I may be lucky and scrape through.'

'I'm sure you'll do fine.'

No, I won't. Not while they are watching me. Especially not today.

Leaving the dormitory fifteen minutes earlier, she had noticed the woman loiter in the near-empty foyer looking at her. She was under surveillance.

Having no intention of facing an executioner's rifle, she had adhered Yakov's advice: "From now on, regard yourself a fugitive. Keep your eyes and ears peeled. Trust no-one.

Always expect the unexpected. Listen to your instincts. Remember, nothing will be what it seems. If caught, you'll face the gulag, or worse, execution."

As calmly as possible, she had walked to the faculty and made two detours. The woman in the grey raincoat had followed her. For a fleeting second she had been tempted to call things off. But aware there might not be another chance, and knowing Yakov would be with her, she had persevered.

Hanging up her dripping raincoat, her eyes glared at the woman sheltering from the rain outside the faculty's entrance.

Bavaria, West Germany

As the sun disappeared below the Alpine ridge, the sky turned a murky grey. Frustrated, Danylo paced up and down the pavement. For five hours he had guarded the phone on the outskirts of Kempten. No one dared venture close; his intimidating size and aggressive posture deterred even the most courageous. For the umpteenth time he looked at the phone. Not a sound.

The last contact with Yakov's men had been late last night. It was a call which had left him furious; her schedule had been advanced to today. It was a big mistake. But his objections had been in vain. The matter was out of the caller's hands. It was Yakov's decision. Sorry.

Klaara, where are you?

The expected telephone call from Czechoslovakia was already three hours overdue.

Her escape plan worried him greatly; relying on strangers was far too risky. After his family's narrow escape, he would never trust anyone again. And now Klaara was walking the same tightrope, putting her faith in some custom officers – members of Yakov's resistance group – to sneak her undetected into Czechoslovakia. Armed with fake diplomatic passports and student-visas, she and Yakov were travelling to West Germany by train and bus to take up employment on a farm outside Regensburg for the summer.

Unstoppable the minutes dragged into hours.

Still he waited.

Nine o'clock…

The phone remained silent.

Inside the booth, insects buzzed around the flickering light. No longer could he ignore the hollow sensation in his stomach. Something was wrong.

Ten o'clock.

He felt powerless. She must be okay or someone would have called… Maybe they were being delayed by the unreliable USSR rail service?

Logic cautioned otherwise. Considering all eventualities, the journey to Prague should have taken only five and a half hours. They left Berlin at midday; therefore, they should have arrived by six o'clock at the latest.

Or could maintenance work be underway on the track?

Were they transferred on to a bus to complete the journey?

Unlikely…

Klaara, where are you?

Tired, he sagged to the ground, his back against the glass booth. There was nothing else to do. Staring into oblivion he continued his vigil, waiting for the call.

Czechoslovakian Border Control

So far, they had encountered no surprises, except for a long delay at some station in the middle of nowhere. Everything had gone according to plan. Only the border crossing remained. The last obstacle.

Klaara and Yakov watched the customs officers scrutinise their documents. The one mumbled something incoherent to his colleague, who nodded his head in return. With an abrupt, '*Spasibo*,' the two officials thanked them and handed back their stamped passports.

As they turned away, Klaara whispered to Yakov, 'Thank God that's done.' At last she was free to leave the USSR. She sat back, ready for the last leg of the journey to Prague.

'No, don't thank God. Thank my friends,' a jumpy Yakov said. 'Best we don't jinx fate. We're not home just yet.'

'Okay. But forgive me for being excited. I can't wait to—'
Her words faltered.

Behind them, three men rose from their seats and blocked the aisle.

KGB!

'Yakov,' she said and squeezed his arm.

Looking up, he stared into three pairs of cold, heartless eyes set in faces of granite.

'Get up!' they ordered, pointing their weapons at them.

Klaara tried to stand, but her legs gave way. Again she tried. It was no use. Hands grabbed and hauled her into the narrow aisle. Twisting her arms in behind her back, handcuffs locked around her wrists.

Faintly, as if far away, she heard a voice shout, 'Move!'

Struggling to obey, a rifle slammed into her back.

None of the fellow travellers looked at her. In a daze she stumbled on to the platform and shuffled towards the brick building. To her left, the two handcuffed customs officers were also being marched away under guard. Their heads hung low; their faces filled with dread.

With their arrests documented and shoved into separate cells, the KGB did not waste any time to interrogate Yakov. Inside the cell next to his, Klaara heard every word.

'Yakov, if you want to live, you'll give us the names of your so-called Russian Freedom Party members. Start talking!'

'Never heard of it.'

A sickening thud.

Yakov screamed.

With the beating at the hands of the KGB fresh in her mind, Klaara cowered in the corner of her cell.

'Let's try again, shall we? Who are your co-conspirators?'

'You are confusing me with—'

Another loud blow followed by a drawn-out squeal like a dying mouse caught in a trap.

What party? What's going on? Klaara wondered.

Then it dawned on her why Yakov had insisted on accompanying her. Refusing to delay her escape for one more day had nothing to do with her father learning about Danylo's letters. That was just a convenient excuse. Yakov was in trouble and had to flee. And because of him, she got caught.

The monotonous blows continued. Klaara covered her ears, trying to block out Yakov's cries of pain. Trembling with fear she waited her turn; she would be next.

His confession made amidst the punches confirmed their claim. The Russian Freedom Party existed. And worse, he was one of its leaders. Yakov rambled off the names of those involved.

Klaara did not want to hear more. Even if he told them she was innocent, they would not believe him. Not when caught fleeing as his companion. No, they would also regard her as a revolutionary. To be shot like the rest of them.

Forgive me, Danylo… I have failed.

She wept. Her heart reached out across the vast plains of Europe to where she knew he waited for her.

Bavaria, West Germany

'What? Oh,' Danylo mumbled to himself, confused by the persistent ringing somewhere close by. He jumped up and snatched the phone off the hook. 'Where is she?' he asked without giving it a second thought. A call in the middle of the night to this lonely booth could only be for him.

'They got caught,' a frightened voice said.

'Is she alive?'

'I don't know, sorry.'

Danylo did not reply and hung up. It was four in the morning with not a soul in sight. The next instant his fist smashed against the booth's door, shattering the glass panel.

Czechoslovakian Border Control

'You can thank your father. If not for him, you would now face a firing squad like your friend Yakov,' Comrade Mikhail Semenov said, leaving Klaara bewildered. 'Luckily for you, we realise you're not involved with him. But why did you risk your life for a man who had left you behind and pregnant? Are you that dumb?'

'My dad…? No, you're wrong. He knows nothing about this.'

'No, you're wrong, Missy. He knows all about Yakov acting as a messenger. He wanted it stopped and reported it in to protect you. And running away is how you repay him? Well, so much for gratitude. Shame on you.'

'No, no, no…' she cried.

Papa, why did you not try to stop me? Why did you betray me to them?

She was confused, hurt. Gradually, her pain turned to anger, eroding the love she had felt for her father.

'Unfortunately, you'll not be going home as I've told your *dear* daddy. So, don't be too hard on him. He'll be upset enough when he finds out,' Comrade Semenov said, having vindictively set out to destroy the relationship between the father and daughter. On her own, she would never survive what lay ahead.

'As a traitor, you'll be going to your new home in the foothills of the Urals. So, chin up and smile. You're alive, are you not?' His eyes filled with disdain as he laughed at the wretched girl in front of him.

What were they thinking, such a ridiculous plan? Mikhail mused. Did they honestly think they could just walk out of the USSR with their fake documents? Amateurs. But the bitter defiance in Klaara's eyes surprised him. Unable to stand the sight of her for another second, he ordered his men to take her away.

You'll soon lose that stubborn streak of yours. Perm-36 will teach you manners, guaranteed, he smirked to himself.

CHAPTER 9

Perm-36, Ural Mountains
USSR

The early seventies had brought another wave of suppression to the USSR, especially to those found guilty of being unsympathetic to the Motherland. It was a period when suspicion amongst families, friends, and neighbours had spread like wildfire. Trust had become a dangerously expensive commodity, often resulting in one's demise.

For those political activists and traitors caught and spared execution, Perm-36 on the bank of the Chusovaya River in the foothills of the Ural Mountains served as a special treatment facility, and had changed accordingly to receive them.

A new perimeter fence of reinforced timber, double barbed-wire, and an alarm system secured the camp. Reinforced boarding separated the living quarters from the work area. A new brick structure had replaced the administration's old wooden hut, and a new boiler and central heating system, the wood-fired one – this was not to increase efficiency but to stop prisoners conceal contraband inside the wood piles and stoves for exchange.

Further "enhancements" included the addition of a centre for special treatment constructed on the spot where an old wood-workshop used to stand twenty years ago. This was to detain released prisoners, rearrested for similar crimes. The so-called "especially dangerous repeater criminals" were isolated in these cells day and night.

This most severe detention centre in the USSR subjected its inmates to the worst possible conditions. State propaganda glowingly referred to this incarceration as "Advanced Socialism". To maintain the secrecy of the camp's purpose and location, the government code-named it VS-389/36; the last special-treatment camp for political prisoners in the Soviet Union. Soon it became known as Perm-36 amongst political activists.

Arrested for trying to flee to the West, Klaara shared the same fate as those imprisoned for espionage, or simple political crimes such as promoting dissidence inside the Soviet Union. Punished with the minimum sentence of seven years as a first offender, Klaara arrived at this high-security "labour camp". For her, a second failed attempt to escape to the West after her release would result in a minimum sentence of ten years spent in isolation in the "special treatment centre".

The sun was low. Through the van's side window, Klaara saw the wide river meander peacefully through an uninhabited countryside of grasslands and forests.

On the opposite side of the road, an unimposing timber and barbed-wire fence, straddled by a few watchtowers, hid a vile reality far removed from the tranquillity of the surroundings.

Entering through the dreaded gates, Klaara cast her eyes for one last time over the desolate world she was leaving behind.

Will I ever set foot outside this place again?

With her mind reeling, quarantined since her arrest, she did not know where she was or what had happened to Danylo, or her parents. Despite their betrayal she missed them. They must have meant well. Why else would they have done what they did?

45

The van jerked to a stop.

The back door flung open.

Dolefully she climbed out and put her foot on the ground.

Welcomed by a line of unsmiling faces, Klaara was escorted into a redbrick building. In a daze she entered a cramped office. Behind the desk, covered in brown files, sat a dour, middle-aged woman. Registering Klaara's details and reading out the camp laws, the commissar did not look at her once.

Next, they marched her to the camp barber. Five minutes later she exited with her head shaved clean.

Entering a courtyard she swallowed hard. In the middle stood a wire cage of three-by-three metres. Three pairs of eyes stared despairingly at her. Two women and an old man.

Stopping at the cage, a guard bellowed, 'Strip!'

She hesitated, not sure she heard correctly.

A fist hit her in the face. 'I said strip,' the man repeated. 'I'm not telling you again. Take everything off, whore!'

With blood pouring from her nose, Klaara obeyed. Shivering, exposed to the cool breeze, she handed her meagre bundle of grey prison clothes to the guard. He let it fall to the ground.

'I did not ask you to give it to me, did I?' he snapped, and with his foot, trampled her clothes into the dirt. 'It will be here for you in the morning. Now get inside!'

The stench inside the cage was unbearable. In one corner the earth was covered in excrement. Shyly she covered her modesty and looked at the others. Also naked, they averted their eyes.

'I am—'

'Ssh!' the old man whispered under his breath and shook his head for her to be quiet. The punishment for talking would mean another night in the cage.

No one spoke as the night dragged on. The sky glittered with stars. The temperature plummeted. Her legs ached. Finally, she sat down on the filthy ground.

As the cold breeze cut through their bodies, they huddled together for warmth. By now the guards had left, allowing them to whisper encouragement to each other, hoping to survive the cold. No one dared divulge any information about themselves: why they were there, who they were, or where they were from.

It was the longest night of Klaara's life. Also, the most humiliating, having to relief herself in front of the others, even with their backs turned. The old man kept reassuring her not to worry as they all had suffered the same fate.

As a slither of gold lit the horizon in the east, a guard unlocked the cage and let them out. Exhausted, Klaara crawled to her bundle of dirty, damp clothes. Dressed she followed the guard.

Klaara scooped up another spoon of hot *Shchi* – cabbage soup with potatoes – and swallowed. With her world ripped apart, succumbing to the drudgery of prison, the days had become unbearable. The comforts and love of her family home were by now only a distant memory. That she would never be able to grant her child the same happiness haunted her.

She was not well. Her skin was pallor pale with her stomach protruding awkwardly from her slight frame. And with every centimetre gained to her girth, her caricature body invited more vile jibes from the prison staff. Carrying a traitor's child only exacerbated matters: her pregnancy warranted her no special privileges.

In silence she tried to wish away the long days of suffering as a child would wish away the memory of a violent beating by a drunk father. But it was not possible.

As usual she sat by herself. The nine hours of hard labour stacking timber under the scorching sun had sapped her energy; the flimsy headscarf failing to protect her shaven head from the sun's harmful rays. She dreaded the daily heat for fear of losing her child. If that happened, she would die.

The rectangular dining hall with its worn-out wooden tables and benches constructed of rough timber planks – as was the floor – felt bare. Five clerestory windows cast a dim light on the white-washed walls, decorated with three framed

47

objects: a Soviet flag, a hammer and sickle, and a picture of Secretary-General Konstantin Chernenko.

Eating her dinner she blocked out her fellow inmates' suspicious stares. Protectively she placed her hand over her stomach, unsure whether they would allow her to keep her child.

'Don't fight it. It's no good,' a voice said. She glanced up from her half-eaten meal. Across the table, a pair of murky-grey eyes in a wrinkled face studied her. 'Four weeks I've watched you. Some advice from an old woman. If you want to survive, then stop pitying yourself.'

Klaara ignored her and kept on eating.

The old woman pushed a piece of bread towards her, got up, and walked away.

The next day, the same old woman sat opposite Klaara yet again. This time she remained quiet and when she left, pushed another piece of bread towards her.

On the fourth day, having repeated the same routine, Klaara whispered, 'Thank you.' It was the first time she spoke to anyone since her arrival.

The woman did not reply.

Two days later, carrying a bundle of planks, Klaara slipped, fell, and dropped the planks on the ground. A sharp pain shot through her side as the guard's foot hit her in the ribs. Ignoring the dreadful cursing, she scrambled to collect the few pieces of wood. Staggering to her feet, and about to lose her balance, a hand steadied her by the shoulder. The same hand which pushed a piece of bread to her at every dinner.

'Leave her,' the guard warned.

The old woman said nothing and withdrew her hand. The standard punishment for disobeying them was two days and nights in the filthy wire cage. Once had been enough; she would not survive another night.

In the evening, sitting opposite each other in the dining hall, she introduced herself between mouthfuls of food. 'I'm Klaara.'

'Nastya.'

'How long have you been here?'

'Six years. How many years did they give you?'

'Seven.'

'By the way, be careful who you talk to. They reward prisoners for telling on each other. Now, not another word. We don't want to spend ten days in isolation,' Nastya whispered, pitying the pregnant girl.

With their heads down they continued their meal. No-one showed them any interest.

Three weeks later, returning from work, Klaara paused outside the women's dormitory, frightened by the leers of the three guards. She averted her eyes, rushed inside, and slammed the door shut.

'Why are the guards gawking at me? Did I do anything wrong?' she asked Nastya, who was resting on her bed.

'No, you did nothing wrong. And you know why they're staring,' she replied. 'No one is that naïve. Well, that took them a while to start on you. Even in these rags, and as thin as you are with your enormous stomach, you are very sensual. And your face... Prepare yourself. And when it happens, don't refuse them or you will not survive. They won't take no for an answer.'

'Are you saying...'

'Yes. You must be strong. Think of the baby you carry and nothing else. Block out whatever happens next.'

Fleeing the vulgarity, Klaara stumbled out of the guardroom. Two months had passed since Nastya's warning. She had lost count of the number of times they had raped her. How much more she could endure she did not know. But her biggest concern was picking up a disease which could affect her unborn child.

Having scrubbed herself clean she fell on to the straw-filled mattress, yearning to sleep and never wake up.

A powerful kick inside her made her open her eyes. The young woman lying next to her was staring at her. Thirty centimetres separated their beds, each constructed with two broad planks.

Polina placed her hand on Klaara's. In silence she shared in her agony. Subjected to the same abuse, Polina understood her pain.

Haunted by Nastya's words, she had waited four weeks before befriending the twenty-year-old Polina who had arrived at the camp three months before her. The reason for Polina's incarceration did not differ much from her own. While attempting to flee to the West, they had killed her fiancé.

'Ouch!' Klaara moaned.

'What's wrong?' Polina asked.

'Please help me up.'

A powerful cramp made her arch her back. As the pain eased, and supported by Polina, she reached the bathroom. Suddenly, a gush of water ran down her legs. 'It's too soon!' The baby was only due in three weeks' time.

Moments later, Nastya and two other women joined them and took control. It was not the first baby to be delivered in Perm-36. With the continual rape of inmates, pregnancies were common.

Klaara wept softly, propped up in bed with her two-week-old baby resting against her full breasts. What is to become of you? she wondered. The past days had been hard, trying to feed her, ensuring she was breathing properly and free of infection. Fortunately, having to nurture her child, they had spared her hard labour and given her extra rations.

'You're such a cutie,' Nastya cooed by her side. And as her stern eyes fixed on Klaara, she reprimanded her. 'Now wipe away those tears. The worst is over. She'll be fine.'

Polina sat on her bed and smiled at the mother and baby. Despite their circumstances she felt elated. She would only be twenty-seven when released from this horrible place. Still young enough to have a child...

'Thank you, Nastya... Polina, for all your help.'

'That's better,' Nastya said and patted her hand, pleased to see her young friend's spirit lift. 'And how is Nadezhda (Hope)? Did she behave today?' Nastya asked.

'Yes. Like an angel.'

As they spoke in subdued voices, Klaara shunned the thought of the many dreadful years ahead, allowing herself to dream of a future reunited with Danylo.

One week later, forced to return to prison routine, Klaara submitted herself to the harassment by the guards who were set on breaking her will, her rebellious nature. Adamant to give her child the best chance possible, she obeyed.

Maybe they would allow Nadezhda to live with her parents. But just the thought of her baby living somewhere else frightened her.

At two months, it was too soon to tell the true colour of Nadezhda's eyes. But the hazel-green tint like hers was unmistakable. They twinkled with delight as she gurgled happily, sucking on her mother's breast. She was healthy and happy, oblivious to the torments her mother endured daily.

'Well, your daddy will just have to live with it. No blue eyes like his,' Klaara said and tickled the tip of her nose. As Nadezhda fell asleep, she placed her on the roughly crafted cot next to her bed.

About to close her eyes, she realised Polina was missing. Concerned, she walked over to Nastya. 'Do you know where Polina is? I haven't seen her since dinner.'

'They've taken her,' Nastya replied, her eyes damp with sadness.

'Who… Where?'

'To the woods.'

'Why?'

'Don't you see what's happening around you? This?'

Klaara did not reply.

'She is to be their sex slave. She won't be back.'

At the end of yet another day of agony, Klaara ignored the pouring rain and ran to the nursery, eager to hold her child. Her hair was plastered to her face. Futilely, she tried to tidy herself and straighten her clothes. Again, she would be late – rubbing the guards' stench off would have to wait. All she wanted was to be with Nadezhda.

She opened the nursery's door. Her heart sank. There was no sign of Nadezhda in the sparsely furnished room. 'Where is she?' she asked, petrified.

The sinewy guard – in her mid-forties – regarded her with contempt, and snapped, 'She's gone.'

'What do you mean "gone"? Gone where?' Klaara asked, confused.

'To the orphanage,' the woman scoffed. 'She's not yours. Never was. She belongs to the people of the Soviet Union. You go back to your whoring and forget her. Now get out of here!'

'No. Give her to me!' Klaara screamed. Driven by months of hell she launched herself at the dreadful woman.

The other guard jumped forward and grabbed her by the hair, screeching, 'You bitch!' Her fist hit Klaara, sending her reeling back, blood pouring from her nose. Pulling her by her flailing arms she propelled her outside and shoved her face into the mud.

Drenched, covered in grime, Klaara did not move.

A faint moan spilled from her lips, growing louder like a rolling crescendo of drums in tune with the beat of the rain on the nursery's roof. It was a drawn-out death wail filled with rage and grief.

CHAPTER 10

June 1986
Bonn, West Germany

Danylo slumped over the steering wheel; his spirits crushed by the minister's words. Twelve months wasted. He did not know where Klaara was, whether his child had been born, or if they were even still alive. During this time, he had fought the temptation to contact her parents. But it would have been a huge mistake.

No, not good enough. I will not give up till I find them, he vowed.

An hour ago, welcomed by the genial smile of the West German Minister of Foreign Affairs, he had been hopeful; the first time in a year. But listening to the minister's excuses, his hopes had evaporated within a blink.

'Believe me, Danylo, I understand your problem. However, I'm in no position to help. We have no say or influence in the USSR. Sorry. The best I can offer is to make subtle enquiries. See if anyone is prepared to help find them.'

'So, you're telling me there is nothing you can do?'

'Yes. Diplomacy won't work. They will question why this woman when there are who knows how many others just like her? And, you of all people know we can't divulge the real reason as it would endanger your whole family. Also, if the child were born, which you can't be certain of, it belongs to a Soviet *traitor* who died trying to escape. Therefore, you can't even claim to be the father.'

'I understand. But there must be something we can do?'

'Maybe there's another way. Do you have any resources? Money. A sufficient sum to bribe a senior official in the Politburo and buy their freedom.'

'How much?'

'Thirty thousand dollars should do.'

'No, I don't.'

'Sorry Danylo, unless you can come up with such an amount, there would be no point in pursuing this option.'

'I can't leave them there. I'll see if I can raise the funds,' Danylo had said, knowing it was unachievable.

'Good. When you do, let me know and I'll start enquiries.'

The hollowness of those words had irked him immensely. He knew nothing would happen. For starters, he did not have access to such a fortune. This door had been firmly shut in his face.

Bugger you! I'll do it my way and on my own. I don't need your help, Danylo decided.

It was time to end his futile existence, clinging to some hope of them being alive somewhere. He'd find them himself. But how, he was not sure. How does one enter the bear's lair unnoticed?

Then it came to him. Images of a new sport in the Alps. What he had in mind was outright crazy.

West-East German Border

Sitting on the edge of the field, Danylo waited for the sun to set. He stretched his legs out in front of him, mulling over his plan.

In the distance the few dark roofs of Isaar village were barely visible in the fading light. Higher up, at the top of the hill, the wind rustled the leaves of the heavy woodlands. Beyond this natural barrier were the ever-prying eyes of the border patrols and the sweeping binoculars in the concrete towers.

The town of Hof in East Bavaria had been handpicked. At an altitude of a hundred and forty-five metres above the frontier – four kilometres to the north – this was as close and high as he could get to the East German border to launch his flight.

For three days he had delayed his journey, hoping for perfect conditions. But continuously thwarted by the unsettled weather, he had decided; it was now or never.

On the horizon, beneath the heavy clouds, the last hint of red glow vanished.

He jumped up and meticulously spread the canopy and network of lines out on the grass. After one last check, he gripped the lines draped over his shoulders and ran down the hill into the evening breeze, into a forward-launch. Behind him the canopy billowed and rose above his head. The earth dropped away, leaving his feet dangling in mid-air.

For two months, at every given opportunity, he had practised to master the skill of taking-off in soft winds from low altitude. Now, swooping through the sky, he knew the hours of training had been worth it.

Slowly, he ascended into the late August night. With every metre gained his fears of not reaching sufficient height to cross the border undetected eased. And entering the first thermal his confidence of success grew tenfold.

During training he had reached altitudes enabling him to fly for up to three hours, covering distances in excess of fifty kilometres. He had also perfected take-offs at night with an additional payload of seventy-kilogram.

High above the rolling hills of the East German countryside the black sky swallowed him as if he were a tiny insect. The sudden loud rumble and dancing flashes of light amidst the tall cumulus clouds filled him with dread. Frightened, he concentrated on his flight, on her gentle eyes to guide him into the unknown.

Descending from the second thermal into the next, the wind hissed in his ears. Swiftly he cored and climbed another few hundred metres. He pulled the wings of his paraglider in, assisting his thermalling.

At thirty kilometres per hour he glided east.

The dim glare of the guard towers manning the Iron Curtain far below looked like a string of broken Christmas lights. Thankfully, no javelin of white streaked up from the ground to impale him in mid-air.

Resolutely, he continued to the drop zone: twenty-five kilometres inside the USSR, safely beyond the border sector. He had picked this specific location while analysing the topographic maps and military positions on file at the Bavarian Military Intelligence office.

The minutes ticked by.

He willed himself on, wanting to believe his efforts had not been in vain. Every new day may also be Klaara and the baby's last.

Before embarking on his rescue mission, he had prepared every step to the finest detail. To find them, return to the border, and fly them out in tandem would never be easy. Any plan could easily fail. But he had no such intention. Under no circumstance would he leave them behind. Never. If he failed, they would die in each other's arms inside the USSR.

Once more the sky lit-up. A terrifying clap. Icy raindrops stung his cheeks. 'Nearly there, just a few minutes more,' he whispered, his youthful confidence waning.

Eight hundred metres above the ground he checked his position. The lights to the south had to be Plauen in the Sachsen province of East Germany. That was if the wrist compass was correct – his only navigational equipment.

Gradually he dropped altitude. Below him was his target zone: the dark shape of Lake Talsperre Pohlnorth. An image seared into his mind.

The woodland half a kilometre east of the lake rushed towards him. Reaching the centre of the sprawling forest, he pulled the strings of the paraglider in and threw himself into a steep spiral-dive. Free-falling at fifteen metres per second, and not to end his journey in a fatal crash, he controlled his descent by twice levelling out. At fifty metres' altitude he stopped the dive and turned towards Plauen.

He whooshed over the carpet of green leaves, confident no-one had noticed the paraglider plummeting to earth, especially on a night like tonight. A tall tree loomed up, its branches threatening to snatch him out of the air. Just in time he jerked the glider sideways.

Overhead the wind rushed through the canopy's two layered skin, billowing convexly. At the edge of the wood he floated ten metres up and circled slowly, his eyes searching the field for movement. Confident he was alone he broke free of the treeline and dropped to the ground. Touching down in the ploughed field he ran a few paces and stopped. He crouched down and glared into the dark. He was alone.

As the first large drops of rain struck the dry earth around him, he reeled the canopy in and store it inside the stuff-bag. With the bulky pack slung over his shoulder he sprinted for cover.

Thirty metres into the woods, Danylo stopped and shone the torch's light in an arch, searching for a suitable hiding place. At the base of a large oak tree he made a clearing with his boot and unstrapped the military spade. His helmet and suit he stowed inside the backpack. He also transferred some travel clothes, identification papers, and food rations for him, Klaara, and the baby into a soft travel bag.

Barefoot, dressed only in his boxers, he got to work.

The one and a half metre deep hole took two hours to complete. Covered in sweat and dirt he straightened up. With extreme care he pulled the backpack into the pit, avoiding the snapped roots. He could not afford a ripped chute; it was their only way out of the USSR. He had no back-up plan. With the sealed soft bag safely placed at the bottom, he climbed out and filled the hole.

A pile of randomly placed stones concealed by dead leaves marked the spot. Thunder rolled across the umbrella of trees. As the rain poured down, he walked around the sizeable tree and carved "D & K" into its bark. The spade he strung up high in the branches, out of sight.

At exactly 00h30 he re-emerged from the woods.

Putting down the travel bag and set of clothes wrapped inside a raincoat, he stripped naked and stepped clear of the trees. He turned his face up into the rain and rinsed himself clean. With the muck removed, he rushed back to the shelter of the trees.

Dried and dressed, he fell into a brisk walk, heading towards the nearest village. The first leg of his journey had been a success, having crossed the militarised border between West and East undetected.

So much for your guards and fences, he thought, pleased with himself.

His solo flight had rendered the USSR's Iron Curtain defences obsolete. A border watched every minute of every hour, day, and night. All their precautions had failed: the double razor-wired fences, the strip of landmines, the guard towers, the tripwires, the ribbon of sand for border violation tracked by German Shepherds. His lightweight paraglider had remained undetected by radar. He had planned and carried out his daredevil stunt with military precision.

Now to find Klaara and his child. Undoubtedly, they were still alive; it was merely a matter of finding out where they were being held. His first port of call would be Klaara's parents. They would know.

Armed with his nondescript travel bag, some Marks, and Rubles, a false *trudovaia knijka* – the indispensable workbook required by all – and USSR papers for Klaara and him, he strolled into the hamlet of Helmsgrun.

The simple clothes of a poor East-German youth suited him perfectly; a student travelling the countryside looking for work. Leaving the sleepy hamlet, he followed the empty road to Gangsgrun and Plauen, whistling softly.

Thankfully, the electric storm had passed. But for the odd clap of thunder in the distance, the night was quiet.

On the outskirts of Plauen he saw a lean-to roof clumsily attached to a barn. It should do till the morning.

USSR Military HQ, Wünsdorf, East Germany

Colonel Jakob Luik tried the polished brass handle. The door did not budge. He retrieved the key and turned to his tearful wife, her delicate features marred by stress and uncertainty. Side by side they walked down the stairs to the taxi.

Ahead of them lay an arduous journey into the hinterland of Russia. To discover the truth of what had befallen their daughter and grandchild. Jakob patted the folded piece of paper tucked inside his breast pocket, bearing the unpalatable news.

Ever since the letter, he had plagued Comrade Mikhail Semenov of the KGB. Finally, he had arranged for them to visit the prison. Apparently, a favour he owed Jakob for helping to snare the traitor Yakov.

Seated in the back of the taxi, Jakob put his arm over Riina's shoulder. Behind them, inside the locked apartment on the third floor, their phone rang.

Danylo did not give up. At seven in the morning they had to be in. He redialled their number.

Come on, answer. He silently willed them to pick up the phone. Maybe they were too busy getting ready for the day. Twenty minutes later he tried again, but was unsuccessful. Annoyed, he stared at the phone, realising finding Klaara might not be easy.

After the third unsuccessful attempt he changed tack.

Familiar with military protocol requiring all officers going off base for twelve hours or more to log a detailed itinerary of their travel plans, he phoned the guardroom.

Having introduced himself as Endrik Luik from Tallinn, youngest brother of Colonel Jakob Luik, he expressed his need to find his brother. There had been a death in the family. His wife Darja had passed away during the night, having suffered a heart attack.

After a few minutes, his call was transferred to the officer on duty.

'Capt Schneider speaking. I understand there has been a tragedy in the family and you are trying to reach your brother, Colonel Jakob Luik. Is that correct?' a subdued voice asked.

'Yes Captain.'

'Before I can give you any information, please answer the following. What is the name and maiden name of your sister-in-law? The birthday of your brother. And in which town was he born?'

Danylo quickly rambled off the answers.

'The colonel and his wife are currently in transit. They left for the Urals this morning and won't be back for ten days. Best is to contact the Ural Park hotel in Perm, Perm Region where they'll be staying. They are scheduled to arrive there in three days' time. Is there anything else I can help you with?' Capt Schneider asked.

'Is that their final destination?'

'No. They will also visit camp VS-389/36 in Kutchino, the Permskaya Oblast region, to identify the bodies of their daughter and grandchild. I am surprised he did not tell you—'

Danylo stood motionless; the blood drained from his face as the words of Capt Schneider hammered in his head, over and over: "to identify the bodies of their daughter and grandchild".

He always suspected Klaara must be in a labour camp. But dead, and both gone? No. He sighed, defeated, not knowing what to do next.

East Berlin, USSR

Seated in the back of the taxi, Jakob hugged Riina's frail body. Their eyes met. Hers brimmed with tears. In silence they read the letter again:

"We regret to inform you that your daughter, Klaara Luik, and your granddaughter, Nadezhda Luik, had made the ultimate sacrifice while in the service of their beloved motherland. Killed in a most unfortunate accident on the 4th August 1986, you should be…"

Unable to finish the message, Riina pushed the piece of paper away. 'Klaara, what have they done to you...? Why?' she cried.

'They're lying,' Jakob said, rejecting the official version yet again. 'They have killed them. We will find out what happened.'

CHAPTER 11

Perm-36
Permskaya Oblast
USSR

In horror, Riina stared at the remains of her beautiful daughter; a charred body, burned beyond recognition. She clutched her husband's arm for support. Hesitantly she addressed the medical officer. 'This could be anyone. How do you know this is our child? And where is our granddaughter's body?'

'These are her dental records and that of the corpse. They match,' the man said unsympathetically and handed her two sets of X-rays. 'Unfortunately, the fire had consumed the child. Her ashes are all that's left,' he added, shrugging his shoulders. He pushed his thin wire glasses perched on his nose back towards his stone-cold eyes.

Riina studied the X-rays and shook her head in disbelief. The hope that her daughter was still alive had been in vain. Faced with the facts she lowered her head and turned away from the body. 'Come, Jakob, there is nothing more for us here.'

At the door the camp commander blocked their path. 'Her belongings,' he said, handing them a shoebox.

Jakob lifted the lid and picked up two black and white photographs. The one of Klaara holding a healthy baby struck him the most. Her eyes shone with contentment. He replaced the pictures, closed the box, took Riina's hand, and left. Neither looked back at the body on the table.

The mere thought of their child having spent her last days in this place sickened them. She was an innocent child persecuted by an abhorrent system, having done nothing to warrant such a fate. Her only sin was her desire to be reunited with the father of her child.

Riina and Jakob always knew about Perm-36, but never in their wildest dreams did they imagine Klaara becoming one of its victims. They would give anything to see their country freed from tyranny, and places such as Perm-36 wiped off the face of the earth.

During the eighty kilometres journey from Kutchino to the city of Perm, they hardly spoke. Reaching the city's outskirts, Jakob ordered the driver to pull over and drop them off; they needed privacy. Standing next to the road, they watched the noisy vehicle sped into town, clouds of black smoke billowing from its exhaust.

Alone, Jakob turned to his wife and said, 'I don't believe them. Not for a moment. That body is not hers.'

'I agree... But what makes you so certain?' Riina replied, neither shocked nor infuriated by his comment.

Jakob slipped his hand inside the box and pulled out the two photographs. 'This. Does she look suicidal? Like she was about to douse herself and her child in petrol? No, absolutely not. I think she escaped, and they can't find her... Their story is a coverup. She is somewhere out there, waiting for—'

'Or they murdered them and burned the bodies. And what we saw were them,' Riina interrupted, her voice filled with loathing. 'Although, I agree with you. I honestly believe she...they are alive. Jakob, we can't go home. We can't leave here without them.'

'Of course, we'll stay. Remember our promise.' Jakob smiled, the first smile in months. With her delicate fingers entwined in his, they walked the four kilometres to the hotel.

Perm, the capital of the Perm Krai Province, on the south bank of the one-kilometre-wide Kama River, served as the unofficial gateway to Siberia. Producing a huge number of arms, an industry which employed nearly eighty per cent of the inhabitants, the city's security was far more stringent than they would have liked. Fortunately, Jakob's colonel's uniform spared them harassment by over-zealous patrols.

The scrutiny of their papers at hotel-reception once more confirmed they were in the heartland of a KGB controlled province. Their hotel was one of the four in the city; all state owned. Exiting the escalator, they nodded a greeting to the sour woman monitoring visitors to the floor. Their every move would be reported. Back in their room they did not dare discuss Klaara, aware that someone could be listening. They were strangers in a city awash with informers.

In the early dusk, the melancholic voice of Alla Pugacheva singing "A Million Scarlet Roses" resonated from the speakers strung along the main street. Enthused by the lyrics of a trampled love, Jakob and Riina clung to each other, their eyes filled with devotion.

Someone bumped into Jakob as they jostled the crowd. In no uncertain terms he expressed his annoyance and focused on the surrounding faces. As a senior military intelligence officer, he remained vigilant, trusting no one. Quickly he checked his inside pocket; the documents were still there.

Two hours later, seated next to the window in the relative comfort of the restaurant, the couple finished their meal. Jakob put his cup down, called the waiter, and fished out his wallet. With the other hand he reached for his handkerchief in his side pocket.

'And this?' he said surprised and pulled out an envelope.

Reading the note, the crease on his forehead deepened. His mouth tightened into a bitter sneer. 'Really,' he hissed, stabbing angrily at the piece of paper.

He's here in Perm, begging forgiveness, wanting to meet. Rubbish! These fools are so obvious. It's a bloody trap, nothing less.

'Jakob, what's wrong?' Riina asked.

'We're in danger. We must leave. Hurry!'

64

Outside the restaurant, they turned towards their hotel and nervously walked past two police officers. For the rest of the way Riina clung to Jakob's arm.

Jakob knew what was unfolding. Certain officials had not appreciated their insistence on finding Klaara. Therefore, the bastard Mikhail Semenov had it all planned. The letter and visit to Perm-36 was merely a ploy to bring them to the hinterland of Russia and kill them, just like their daughter and granddaughter. Buried in the vast forests of the Ural Mountains, no one would ever find their bodies.

One hundred metres up ahead the Hotel's lights beckoned. They increased their pace.

'Good evening, Colonel, Mrs Luik,' someone said behind them.

Jakob froze, expecting a gun barrel jabbed into his back, and to be marched around the corner to a KGB car.

'It's me, Danylo. Please keep walking and don't turn around. Two men are following you.'

'Thank God,' Jakob muttered under his breath, unable to believe his own ears. 'What a relief to hear your voice.'

'Sorry I gave you a fright. Can we meet?'

'Of course. Where?'

'Statue of Lenin, Central Park, 10:45 PM Use the north entrance and wait ten minutes. If I don't show, leave. Then I'll be at the lion's enclosure at the zoo, 9:00 AM tomorrow.'

'Agreed.'

'You'll have to lose the KGB. Two males, mid-forties at 5 o'clock fifty metres on your right. One bald, 1.8metres tall, well-built, round glasses. The other, medium-built, blond. Jackets over arms, white shirts, grey trousers.'

As Danylo's words hung in the air he disappeared down the side street.

With no alternative left, Danylo had plucked himself up from the abyss of defeat and raced to Perm to intercept Klaara's parents. For seven hours he had loitered near their hotel before following them to the restaurant.

Shielded from the park's streetlamp by the 150-year-old spruce tree, Danylo appeared relaxed in its deep shadow. To passers-by he was just another young man waiting for his girlfriend. With his eyes alert, he pulled the anorak tight around his chest, fending off the late-August cool air.

A couple deep in conversation, their tempers fraying, entered through the north gate of the park. The man tried to placate his partner, dabbing at the corner of her eyes with a handkerchief.

Twenty metres behind them, two couples shared an anecdote and laughed.

The number of people visiting the park at such a late hour surprised Danylo. He had hoped it to be deserted; the fewer people to witness the meeting the better. Anyone of them could be a KGB informant.

Four minutes later, Klaara's parents arrived arm in arm with their heads huddled together. As Danylo retreated deeper into the shadows, a young couple behind the Luiks caught his attention. But they headed in a different direction. They were of no further interest.

Danylo did not move, patiently biding his time. No one else followed. Another five minutes passed with no sign of the two KGB agents. Certain Klaara's parents were on their own, he raced towards the statue of Lenin.

Reaching them, Riina embraced him like a long-lost son, her face lit by a warm smile. Her eyes welled with tears. 'Danylo, I am so happy to see you.' Her show of affection touched him deeply.

'Come here, young man,' Jakob said and hugged him.

Composing themselves, Danylo warned, 'Best we keep moving in case the spooks discover where you've gone. If circumstances were only different. I just hope you'll find it in your hearts to forgive me; for everything. I'm sorry…'

Riina squeezed his arm. She had suffered enough, and so had he. In the soft light of the streetlamp she noticed his sunken eyes; the anguish etched on his face. He looked much older than his twenty-two years. 'Danylo, you are wrong. You are like a son to us. One we never had.'

'I cannot tell you how much that means to me. Just wish I could have saved her.'

'Well, you still may.'

'What do you mean, Colonel?' Danylo asked, surprised.

'Look at these. Tell me what you see?' Riina said, and showed him two black and white photographs.

In the dull light, Danylo defined every detail of the woman who had stolen his heart. His hands trembled holding the photographs. He touched the image. 'Klaara... She looks happy. How can they be dead, and—'

'Exactly,' Jakob interrupted. 'They claimed she killed Nadezhda and herself. We disagree. See the glint of happiness in her eyes? And your child's name meaning hope. Doesn't that speak for itself?'

'Yes, it does.'

'Not once did she want to terminate the pregnancy. So, why commit suicide? She either escaped and is in hiding. Or they have locked her up somewhere else for some strange reason. We believe they are both alive and intend to find them. You being here is a godsend. Will you help us?'

'Of course, that's why I'm here. But I think it's best I do this on my own. No one will suspect me. They know you and asking questions is not a good idea. You may also "disappear". Best you return to Berlin and live as if they are dead,' Danylo said, his face filled with renewed vigour.

While discussing a plan of action, curiosity got the better of Jakob. 'Sorry to digress, but I'm dying to know how you sneaked across the border?'

Danylo smiled. 'Colonel, it will have to wait till we're safely back in Germany. I don't want to jeopardise our chances getting out in case the KGB interrogates you.'

Chusovoy, Permskaya Oblast

Twenty kilometres east of Perm-36, the soulless town of Chusovoy with its twelve thousand inhabitants sprawled along the banks of the Chusovaya River.

Ideally located to begin his search, Danylo had found employment at the local freshwater fish farm as a cleaner. But because of the limited number of leisure venues, mixing with locals was difficult. Therefore, after a frustrating four weeks, he had made no progress in finding Klaara and Nadezhda. But he persevered.

Not in a hurry, he sipped his beer and listened to the conversation. The hostess serving Russian pints was a dour woman in her mid-fifties; her face swathed in bright make-up. The white-crowned headgear, coat, and apron stretched tight over her ample bosom completed the picture of Stalinist "proficiency".

She fit the role perfectly, Danylo thought, seated in the men's bar. It was his first outing with his colleagues.

After two hours of consuming beer and vodka, the five comrades' tongues loosened up. Their initial suspicions of him had dissolved in the heavy smoke. To blend in, he forced himself to puff on a cheap cigarette, hating its vile taste.

The thirty boisterous voices bounced off the walls with politics on everyone's mind, discussing the change in the country's political structure. New party officials were being appointed in areas of economic hardship and where corruption prevailed. More freedom of speech, and the curtailing of alcohol excesses – a fact deeply lamented by his companions – were policies strongly promoted by the newest member to the Politburo, Mikhail Gorbachev.

Much to the men's dismay, this man was already running the country.

'Pity our honoured General Secretary Yuri Andropov has fallen ill, allowing this troublemaker to ruin our country,' Victor, the leader of the group, complained.

'Imagine if this man takes over. We'll have to queue up to by liquor,' another moaned, taking a large swig of his beer.

'Let's drink to him. May syphilis strike him down before he destroys Mother Russia,' Victor proposed amidst loud laughter. 'A thousand deaths to him. *Na zdorovie*,' he blurted out, raising his glass, a gesture replicated by the others.

You're very bold, Danylo thought, surprised by their reckless cajoling of the new man. Being in the heartland of old-fashioned communism, he must tread with extreme caution. People were content with their lives and fearful of change.

Glasses slammed on the table, ready for another round. Two uniformed men entered the bar. Victor nodded in their direction. 'Those worthless swines will also have to find new jobs if Gorbachev has his way. Their "holiday" camp will be shut down first,' he hollered.

Danylo leant forward. Careful not to raise any eyebrows, he asked, 'Which camp?'

'Perm-36,' Victor replied.

Suppressing his excitement at having found someone who might know where Klaara could be, he said, 'Yes, of course… I hear it's a rough place to be.'

'That's putting it mildly. Believe me, you don't want to end up in there,' Victor said, got up and shouted, 'Dimitri, over here!' Under his breath he whispered to Danylo, 'Let's hear the latest gossip; always good for a laugh.'

After some back-slapping and more drinks, the guards shared the latest events in the camp. Speechless, Danylo listened to the horrors committed behind the fence. There was nothing remotely funny in any of it. And to imagine Klaara had been subjected to that…

Another hour of alcohol and cheap talk shifted the topic to delusional encounters with the opposite sex. Ridiculous bragging which stirred their loins, making the need for female company imperative.

'Damn the bloody laws! Why they don't allow prostitution is beyond me. Do they want us all to die with bent backs, crippled old men?' one complained, unable to hide the lust in his eyes.

'Yeah, and I won't find any skirt this time of the night. My old hag will have to do,' another said, and laughed.

Victor, not defeated by such a trivial matter as the law, turned to the guard next to him. 'Dimitri, the broad your friends got in the woods, is she still available?' he asked in a low voice.

'Yes. You want to visit her?'

'Dumb question. Is the price the same?'

'Same price.'

'Bloody rip-off. They should pay us to screw her. She's no better than a corpse.'

'So, you don't want to go then?'

'Are you nuts? Of course, I'm going.'

'Must say my heart bleeds for you,' Dimitri mocked. 'I don't have to pay for a screw. The whores in the camp are free and there for whenever I have the need. Which I may add is quite often.'

Victor ignored his boasting and got up, pulled out his wallet, and counted his cash. 'Right, I'm set. Let's go. Who's coming?' He gestured for Dimitri to follow. Along with two others, Danylo joined him.

The group of men piled into Victor's car. Within minutes, they sped through the outskirts of Chusovoy and along the quiet lanes to Kalino, heading twelve kilometres west. Danylo squashed in the back, hoped whoever this poor girl was, she might be able to tell him something about Klaara.

Filthy green moss stained the basement wall. The constant trickle of water dripped on to the floor, across the raw-clay bricks and pooled in the corner. Slowly, it seeped through the cracks into the earth. The air in the room was musty and cold.

The blanket wrapped around the young woman's shoulders did not alleviate the shivers. Another bout of raking coughs burned her lungs. She struggled upright to ease the pain; her body riddled with disease. She knew she would not survive much longer. Her pleas for help had been in vain. They did not care. She had served her purpose.

In the room above, the drone of male voices and laughter filtered through the wooden floorboards. Chairs scraped across the floor. The flickering lightbulb dangled precariously from the ceiling. The conversation ended. She knew what was to come next and doubted she would survive the ordeal. To give up would be so easy.

She did not know how many days, weeks, months she had been captive in the cramped room, having lost track of time long ago. With no window to the outside world she did not know whether it was day or night. Nothing mattered anymore, least of all time. She was dying and nothing could change that.

The routine was always the same. Visitors arrived. A deal struck. Loud stomping. The mechanical turn of the key. The gloating eyes watching her remove her tattered clothes. If she hesitated, they would rip her rags off her body.

This time would be no different.

The man named Victor moved monotonously over her. She did not respond. He did not care.

The young woman turned her head sideways, towards the stained wall. Her hollowed eyes watched the water drip and trickle into the dirt. As it vanished into nothingness, it threatened to take the last grain of her sanity with it.

The man grunted, stopped moving, zipped his trousers, and left.

Soon another man mounted her, indifferent to the previous man's stains.

God, please end this, she moaned and stared at the wall.

The pig grunted...

Void of any feeling, any hope, she closed her eyes. She heard the door open and close. Footsteps approached somewhat cautiously. She waited for the next one to have his way with her.

Nothing happened.

'Can you hear me?' a concerned voice asked.

She turned her head, too tired to speak. The tall, haggard-looking stranger proffered a photograph and said, 'Do you know this girl?'

His words faltered.

'Klaara?' the voice said, unsure.

'Yes…' Then she remembered who the voice belonged to. 'Yes, Danylo, it is me,' she whispered, coughed, and moved her hands to cover herself.

Danylo bent down and lifted her heaving body into his arms. Holding her, he tried to stop her coughs. She gave a feeble smile. Her sorrow-filled eyes gazing at him were like drowning lilies in a dark pond, sinking helplessly into its murky depth.

Her arm slipped from his.

Her head rolled back.

Through tears he watched her exhale softly.

There was nothing he could do.

He had been too late.

PART TWO

Chapter 12

December 2019
Cuba

'You're fifty-three? Well, let me tell you, you don't look a day over thirty,' Niall McGuire said light-heartedly. In reality, the guard portrayed a figure much older than his years. A soul with no ambition, destined to serve prisoners till the day he died and buried penniless like most on the island.

'*Si*, you good joke make.' Alvaro's round face cracked into a smile.

Progress at last, Niall thought.

'I bet with your looks you must fight off the ladies.'

'Another good joke. No, me married many times. Now I forget wife… Visit *prostituta*. Much a better.'

'Seeing we're talking man to man; I also need a woman. You get me one and I'll pay you well,' Niall said smilingly, aware that this would never happen. 'I've heard the Cuban ladies are the best.'

'*Si, si,* friend. But you'll know, never.'

'I'll give you lots and lots of pesos,' Niall persevered.

'And you get pesos where?' Alvaro grunted, bored with the Irishman's twaddle. But the mention of money got his attention.

'You contact my friend Karl; you'll not be disappointed. I guarantee.'

'*Si, si.*' And with that he slammed the hatch shut.

A smile. This was the fifth time he had managed a conversation with the guard. Progress, and about bloody time. *Alvaro, my friend, you'll get me out of here. You just don't know it yet.*

Niall's eyes lingered on the locked steel door. He wrung his hands, aching to settle a score with "Dearest Irina". Or, rather, Svetlana, having vowed to hunt her down wherever she would be. No border or Russian army would be able to protect her. The mere thought of her filled his mouth with bile.

It felt like years, but the fact was only five months had elapsed since that fateful day. The day she had entered his study in Dublin.

Unprepared, he had crumbled under the power of the ever-alluring Venus; like a meek little lamb with vacant eyes staring into approaching headlights. She had toyed with him, snared him with the ease of an experienced hunter. She had been a vision: full lips, perfect nose, unblemished white skin. Eyes mysterious, vulnerable, and exceptionally bright… For the first time in his forty-eight years, he had fallen in love.

And the price for this weakness was to spend his remaining years in solitary confinement. In a cesspit at the Maria la Gourda State Penitentiary in Cuba.

At the time of his incarceration four months ago, he was the head of the most powerful underground organisation in Ireland, controlling a vast network of drugs, weapons, and sex traffickers. Thanks to her meddling, it was all blown to hell, rendering him a nobody. To the Irish and the criminal world, he no longer existed.

The image of her exquisite face drifted across his mind's eye, taunting him. A suffocating tension gripped his chest. He sat back, relaxed his hands and arms, and breathed slow and deep.

Damn it, she'll be the death of me… Like my Russian friends most probably are, he thought, convinced his arm-smuggling partners, Nicolai Baranovsky and Gen Andreyev, had been executed. Well, he would not succumb that easily. He had plans and dying was not part of it.

What lay ahead, having to start all over, was of no concern. Prudent by nature, he had known a day of reckoning might come. He would either be caught or the virtual Celtic bubble in Ireland would self-destruct. Therefore, he had skilfully hid most of his funds in an array of offshore companies and bank accounts around the world where no-one could ever find it.

And if you don't get out of prison, neither would you, Mr McGuire, Niall cautioned himself. With no heirs, friends, or partners, these riches would be lost forever.

Driven by this desire for revenge, and to enjoy his hidden treasures, he had started on Alvaro. Of all the guards to help him escape, he had seemed the most likely candidate. The only one who spoke some English.

He leaned forward and picked up the one item he possessed; his late-sister Maura's diary – a parting gift from Irina. Her jibe still irked him. "My dearest Niall, you'll have a lifetime to absorb the truth, to repent. So, enjoy."

The first few weeks in prison had proven her words correct while reading his sister's childhood scribbles. The diary filled with emotion-laden words described how Maura, aged fourteen, had slain their father for repeatedly raping her. It revealed his mother's selfless act, taking the blame for this murder to protect her daughter and paying for it with her life in prison. Niall, who now understood his mother's reasons, wanted her forgiveness. Though it was too late. She died seven months ago.

Sixteen at the time of his father's death, Niall had sworn revenge for the brutal murder of the man he used to idolise. Thirty-two years of sordid revenge wreaked on unsuspecting young women, had left sixteen dead by his own hand. Added to this were the countless girls *erased* by his henchmen, having outlived their usefulness in his brothels. Not forgetting the multitude of men who had challenged him, begging for mercy before they had died with a bullet to the brain.

77

Self-reproach, mulling over his sins, never lasted long as it served no purpose. It could not bring any of them back. What was done was done.

How could he have known when his mother had kept him in the dark? And why did she not stop his father from abusing Maura? Surely, she had known what he was doing. All considered, her continued silence made her just as guilty.

She was responsible for all his iniquities, for all the deaths; he was not to be blamed. Therefore, she owed them all an apology. And mostly to him, Niall argued in his deranged, psychotic mind. In solitude, he easily passed the blame and exonerated himself. If it had not been for her stupidity, he would have lived like everyone else. No one would have died.

Well, that's history, he thought.

One thing which cheered him immensely was the deaths of Vera and Sinead. The whores who had stolen his diamonds, sixty-five-million-euros' worth. His men had tracked them down and killed them under the scorching Mykonos sun.

However, liking them both, he did regret their deaths, especially Vera. She—

The hatch slid open with a grating noise. Alvaro's stubbled chin appeared above the egg-filled breakfast plate.

'Good morning, *amigo*. Did you organise a Latina for me?' Niall chirped from inside the cell, facing another day of boredom. Another day, starting with the same filthy breakfast. But he never denied his body the sustenance it needed, no matter the muck they served.

'Cannot… Too much trouble, not possible…'

'Damn shame. Think of all the pesos you could have had,' Niall replied.

'*Negativa.* No woman. You like something other, *si*?' the guard replied expectantly.

'Okay. How about some good old Irish whisky? It will keep me warm. And some bloody ointment for these bites.'

'*Si, si.* First money.'

'No problem. Contact my friend Karl. He'll give you whatever you like. You tell him where I am, and he'll pay even more. You tell him.'

'Where's your friend?'

Two Months later

Niall sat on the mattress. Trying to ease an itch, he accidentally scratched a fresh scab; the cheap anti-septic cream was of little value.

He glared at the walls shutting him in. He could not wait to get out and flee the damp heat and prison stench. Thankfully, the never-ending vermin which had shared his mattress and crawled on all surfaces of the cell had ceased since securing Alvaro's help.

Trapped and at their mercy was raw acid on his nerves. Filled with disdain, he looked at his thin arms and legs, the result of six months' malnutrition. If not for his "arrangement" he would have starved long ago.

He craved a decent meal, but even more so his freedom. To breathe fresh air without a rifle pointed at him. To smell the sweet fragrance of honeysuckle drift across his vast estate. Swim in the clear blue sea. Feel the sun's warm rays on his back... The crunch of sand under his feet, sprinting along the pristine white beach of his Caribbean Island.

Ah, such fond memories, he groaned longingly; moments he would enjoy soon again. But such frivolous pleasures would have to wait; far more pressing matters required his attention.

Not having seen Alvaro for three days was worrying. Did the Cuban take the down payments, resign from prison, and relocate somewhere safe on the island?

Damn it, man. Where are you?

Stuck in this hellhole, his life would end as Irina had predicted, "...until the last breath escapes you." Niall seethed and glared at the plate of gunk left inside the hatch. His dinner. Sticking out from beneath the plate was an envelope.

Having read Karl's letter for the second time, he shook his head in disbelieve.

They're alive! Impossible!

But there was no mistake. They had lied to him. The two whores, Vera and Sinead, were alive, running free, rejoicing in his "death".

With his fingertips, Niall massaged the throbbing veins in his temples. He did not need this, not now. His mood plummeted further, convinced Alvaro would not show. His expectations of being free were blown to hell.

Furious, he threw the plate of food against the steel door and smashed his fist into the flaking plaster wall.

They had planned his escape soon after Alvaro's first smile. Alvaro had fulfilled his role on the inside as a messenger and recruiting collaborators. On the outside, Karl, his old faithful pilot, had orchestrated matters.

Not to scare the guard off, Niall's first steps in manipulating him had been extremely cautious. But as their rapport had grown, the wheels had started to turn smoothly, very smoothly indeed.

He had received a laptop with an internet connection. And with his cell disinfected, a bed and mattress. Ointment to heal the badly infected skin. And as a special favour, the warden had granted him an hour excursion daily on the terrace reserved for dangerous inmates. This privilege had come at a hefty price. One he had gladly paid. With the aid of bundles of pesos greasing the right palms, his living conditions had steadily improved.

When first venturing on to the terrace, faced by the open sea, his spirits had soared as an escape plan had manifested itself.

The white-walled fortress was on a headland with sheer cliffs of granite dropping to the sea fifty-five metres below. All that stood between him and the deep blue waters was a low wall and a two metres high rusty chain-linked fence draped with coils of barbed wire. There were no heavily armed guards, patrol dogs, metal railings, or electrified fencing. Two guards armed with a rifle each had paced the battlement above the yard. Nothing else stood between him and freedom.

But then again, if he did jump, the fall would most likely be fatal. Overcoming that obstacle was up to Karl.

Having enlisted the help of Niall's long-standing business partner and friend, Bill McConvey, all was in place. Bill was a senator on Capitol Hill and a close friend of the vice president. Using his contacts in the US defence force, the VP had recruited a few SEALs to carry out Niall's extraction. With the guarantee of mind-boggling financial rewards, the SEALs had jumped at the offer of a "special weekend break".

Currently, these men were "fishing" off the Cuban coast. Their involvement was minimal and therefore the risk. Their mission involved scaling the cliff the night before the escape, secure a rope below the terrace, conceal a pair of wire-cutters within reach next to the rusty fence, and mark the spot.

On the day of the escape they would return at sunset and remain underwater at the bottom of the cliff. As soon as Niall would slip into the ocean, they would assist him into scuba gear, float the decoy, and swim him back to the "fishing" boat.

And as for Alvaro, he would take care of the guards positioned on the battlement. Each would receive a few wads of pesos to look the other way.

But there was one problem: the exact time of Niall's next hour on the terrace. This rota changed daily. Therefore, Alvaro's role was vital, ensuring Niall would get tomorrow's slot at sunset. And notify Karl the instant he would step outside. From that moment the extraction team would have one hour to get into position.

All their efforts would culminate in one risk-filled venture tomorrow.

And where was Alvaro? Nowhere!

With or without your help, I will go tomorrow, even if it kills me. Not a day longer shall I stay in this dump, Niall vowed to himself, convinced the rope and cutters would be in place. But he would be on his own. An easy target for any guard.

Chapter 13

2020
Athens, Greece

The nurse hurried into the semi-dark ward and whispered excitedly, 'Doctor, please come quickly. I think Sinead is awake.'

'You're sure…?' Dr Papadopoulos asked, surprised.

'Yes… Well, I think so. I was straightening her bedding when her left pinkie moved. I first thought it was only my imagination, but then she moved the other fingers and made a fist. Her face came alive.'

The suntanned Greek did not respond. He merely turned to the door and left with an unconvinced frown on his face.

For eighteen months, he and his colleagues had stood by the stunning patient with shiny black hair and a porcelain complexion who had remained in a world of her own. She was the epitome of a childhood Sleeping Beauty. Few at the Athens private clinic harboured any hope of recovery; they have done all they could. If not for her brother Sean, they would have switched the machines off weeks ago. The skull fracture and gun wound suffered on that fateful day had healed perfectly. But the brain trauma was far worse than originally thought.

Five minutes later, Dr Papadopoulos straightened up and probed, 'Sinead, can you hear me? Sinead?'

She opened her eyes and blinked. Finding the glare of the night light too strong she shut her eyes.

'Sinead, don't go to sleep,' Dr Papadopoulos urged. He lifted her arm and felt the muscles tighten. He stroked her skin and asked, 'Do you feel this?'

She tried to speak.

For twenty minutes they patiently helped her back into the world where she belonged. Bewildered, she finally managed a weak response. 'Where am I?'

'Athens, Greece. In the hospital.'

'Why… What happened?'

'You suffered a terrible accident. Do you remember Mykonos, your holiday?'

'No, I don't…'

But as some distant memory returned, she asked, startled, 'Where are my parents? Are they alright?'

'They're fine, Sinead. You've been with us for a long time. They had to return home,' Dr Papadopoulos lied.

'Thank goodness.'

Poor woman, he thought – both her parents passed away many years ago, but now was not the time to tell her. He continued to question her, trying to establish the severity of the amnesia. What he knew about her past, he divulged, hoping to jog her memory.

Dr Papadopoulos ended his examination. 'Now you'll have to excuse me. I must inform your family that you're fine. I leave you in the capable hands of nurse Helen.'

An hour later the phone next to Sinead's bed rang. The nurse answered and handed it to her. 'It's your brother, Sean. He's calling from Dublin.'

With Sinead in deep conversation, the nurse smiled at her and mouthed, 'Back in a sec.' As soon as she had left the ward she placed a call to Chief Inspector Vasillis Kalifas in Chania, Crete, desperate for news, whether good or bad.

The money offered for her cooperation was three times her annual salary – a temptation too great to resist. Identifying the patient had triggered her first payment. Apparently, the girl was wanted by the police. They had been looking for her for quite some time.

'Great work, Helen. We'll take it from here. The rest of your money will be in your account by tomorrow. And remember, you have never spoken to me. No one has ever enquired about her. You don't want to spend the next ten years as our guest,' Inspector Kalifas warned.

'Of course not. If you need—' she replied feebly as the phone went dead before she could finish her sentence.

Inspector Kalifas did not waste any time and phoned Ireland to share the news. His reward for this information made nurse Helen's pay look like pittance. This would bring Niall's henchmen one step closer to finding the diamonds.

Chapter 14

Present
Trans Adriatic Pipeline
Turkey

In the January cold mist, an orange haze glowed in the distance. Shielded by the lush undergrowth, Colonel Boris Polyakov crouched impatiently and focused his attention on the target: the completed compressor installation of Sector C, a hundred and ninety kilometres west of Ankara, Turkey.

Visibility was down to ten metres, making a detailed reconnaissance impossible. But that was of no concern. After months of gathering intel they knew every detail of the target. The site layout, number of men present, daily schedules, guard rosters, hidden alarms, communications, and defence capabilities.

Therefore, they knew that at this hour the men stationed on the base were fast asleep, except for the few guards manning the towers and guardroom. And having reached the end of their two-hour shift these men were weary, their vigilance at a low. They were young conscripts who could not wait to retire to the comfort of their beds.

Still, they had left nothing to chance.

Deep inside the shadows of the compressor units, their two comrades stood watch, ready to act in case someone spotted the line of advancing saboteurs.

The open field transformed into a shimmering landscape as Boris slipped the infrared night-goggles over his eyes. The terrain was stripped bare and littered with landmines. This did not bother him. Aided by the heavy fog, crossing the field would be no match for his team. Fifteen minutes ago, their two comrades had deactivated the unassailable movement sensors and infrared cameras covering that section.

Boris signalled for his men to fan out. Well-versed in guerrilla warfare, the ten Kurdish rebels slithered across the ground, eager to deal another blow to the Turkish regime. Boris pushed his elbows forward and began his crawl.

A hundred and fifty metres in front of him, a lonely guard zipped up the fly of his pants. Rifleman Abdul Ahmed took his time, ignoring the cold winter weather. Idling at the bottom of the steel ladder, he looked indifferently at his rifle propped against the base of the armour-plated watchtower. He inhaled deeply, savouring the taste of the cheap tobacco with the tip of the cigarette glowing bright red.

At the other seven towers dotted along the ten-metre-high anti-missile security fence, the guards were safely cocooned inside.

Forty metres east of the gas-plant-installation, the barrelled-roof military barracks accommodated a large enough force to repel any attack. Nothing was to interfere with the completion of the Trans Adriatic Pipeline crossing Turkey. A supply line of natural gas via a 1.2-metre diameter pipe stretching from the Caspian Sea across Turkey, Greece, Albania, and the Adriatic to Western Europe. The supply line costing over eighteen billion euro was due for completion by the end of the year.

Destined to replace Russia's completed gas pipeline – the Turk Stream – America was adamant to defend this pipeline at all cost. The Turk Stream gas pipeline, which crossed the Black Sea to Turkey and on to Europe, was another life-feeding artery Russia controlled. One more artery to starve Europe of gas if they failed to bow to Russia's demands.

Rfn Ahmed's gloved hand gripped the ladder. Lazily, his eyes swept the surrounding terrain. Unable to spot the other towers he shrugged his shoulders; how anyone was supposed to see in this fog left him baffled. There were the infrared security cameras and movement sensors which ruled out a stealth attack.

He placed his right foot on the first ring and climbed to the warmth of the armoured shelter.

Standing on the elevated platform twelve metres up, he reported in. Having exchanged a few banalities with the corporal on duty in the guardroom, he signed off with an apathetic 'Roger and out.' He replaced the phone and cast one more blasé glance at the heavy fog, at the impenetrable grey wall. With half an hour to the end of his sentry duty, he stifled a yawn and slid to the floor.

He made himself as comfortable as he could on the hard surface. Concealed beneath his greatcoat, he fished the paperback and flashlight out of his pockets, eager to discover who the murderer was. The novel would help alleviate the boredom till the end of his shift. He looked forward to the comfort of his bunk bed and a blissful four-hour sleep.

By the time Rfn Ahmed finished consuming the drivel of the next page, Boris had already progressed halfway across the open terrain. Guided by the infrared temperature mine-detector attached to his night-sight, the file of men leopard crawled at a steady pace through the myriad of landmines and tripwires.

Behind him at seven-metre intervals, ten armed insurgents followed. Inside the treeline, nine of his men – Russian Special Forces – had taken up their positions, their sniper rifles ready in case of a hasty retreat.

Their designated point of entry was fifty metres to the right of Rfn Ahmed's tower.

Reaching the perimeter fence, Boris scrutinised the area. Satisfied no one had noticed him, he tackled the wire fence with the small Russian-made tungsten cutter. Gradually, the muffled sound clicked an opening in the wire fence. A minute later he rolled away the mesh, allowing the first man to slip through.

With his team inside the compound, he replaced the cut section of wire and sprinted in amongst the compressor units. He checked the time. Thirty minutes remained to complete their mission: plant the Russian labelled explosives, set the timer to one hour twenty minutes, and regroup.

On schedule, each man gave an affirmative nod and retraced their steps through the hole in the fence, instantly swallowed by the heavy fog.

Boris observed the sleepy barracks and grimaced; soon it would be anything but sleepy. This would be the first blow, a blow guaranteed to have severe repercussions. Deftly, he clipped the cut section of the fence back into place, dropped the cutter on the ground and followed the line of men back into the undergrowth.

Thirty minutes left to countdown, Boris and his men piled into the seven 4x4s parked 3.5km from the compressor station. Guided by the blue night lights, the vehicles raced along the dirt track. They planned to be well clear of the area by the time the explosives would detonate.

Rfn Ahmed had just fallen asleep in his bed when disaster struck. The impact of the massive explosion flung him through the air, impaling him on six exposed reinforcing steel bars of the destroyed barrack's concrete wall.

A second series of explosions evaporated kilometres of pipeline leading to and from the plant. These explosives, placed by Boris's Spetsnaz unit, had completed their mission.

Twenty-one days later, the international press gathered on the White House lawn, ready to broadcast President John O'Callaghan's much-awaited response to the destroyed compressor and transmission station.

At 11h00, armed with CIA intel, he presented his arguments and concluded that he and his administration held

Russia, who had sufficient motive, responsible for this attack. Evidence found on the site pointed directly to them as the culprit. He warned that the USA would not tolerate any form of aggression against its sovereignty, no matter where. They would take whatever steps necessary to defend itself, its people, and its interests.

Russia's repudiation of this allegation was met with disbelief by all NATO member states.

And Turkey demanded immediate reprisal for the loss of its men, hoping to further unite its people against the Kurds.

By 16h00, during a special emergency meeting of NATO members, the US had obtained full support for the deployment of ground-to-air and medium-range nuclear missiles in Poland and Ukraine, to be directed at their long-time nemesis. None were under any illusion that this would start a new Cold War. Furthermore, Ukraine would be welcomed as a NATO member.

In the US, many senior senate members cautioned against a repeat of the folly of Iraq. This time, America and Europe would not face a spent third world military power, but a new Russia with China and other BRICS countries in support.

Despite regretting that such steps were necessary, the administration was adamant: Russia's state rhetoric, actions, build-up of forces on the Ukrainian and Baltic States' borders left them no choice.

Incensed, Russia's president Maxim Fedorov responded. Russia would regard such actions as nothing less than a declaration of war. Under no circumstance would they allow the US a first strike opportunity. They had not forgotten the lessons learned during the Second World War, and had no intention of repeating the same mistake twice. Neither would they allow the expansion of NATO to the east.

The installation of any weapons directed at Russia in a neighbouring state would be destroyed.

Behind the public rhetoric of threats and recriminations blasted across the world, government officials worked around the clock to defuse the situation in averting a full-scale war as Europe prepared itself for the inevitable.

Bundeswehr Intelligence, Berlin, Germany

'I think we've covered all eventualities. Won't be easy, Colonel,' Lieutenant General Günther Beck, head of the Bundeswehr and NATO (Europe) Intelligence, cautioned. At sixty-eight, he was tired after weeks of sleepless nights. 'I trust your men are ready, and know what's expected of them?'

'We won't let you down, Sir,' Colonel Thomas Bauer replied confidently.

Not for a moment did the general doubt the colonel's words. Col Bauer was a true soldier. Someone he trusted with his life.

As a young man, Thomas Bauer had joined the German Federal Armed Forces in Munich and soon had enrolled at the Generalstabslehrgang Military Academy in Hamburg. Climbing the ladder of success, he had become a vital player in the Bundeswehr Intelligence Services. Now stationed in Calw, Baden-Württemberg, home of the elite KSK Kommando Spezialkräfte (Special Forces Command), he headed Operational Military Intelligence.

'We'll be wheels up at 21h00,' Col Bauer said, and gave a quick rundown on the planned action, hoping to ease his superior's concerns.

Their mission: establish who was involved in the attack on the gas installation in Turkey. But more importantly, who gave the orders?

Since the explosion, none of NATO's deep-cover agents inside Russia had been able to confirm who had sanctioned the attack. Was it the Russian president, his high command, or both? Or possibly a third force?

'Good, Colonel. Maybe what you'll discover will prove that a group of fanatics orchestrated the attack. If so, then we can still stop this war,' Lt Gen Beck said to his right-hand man. With a nod of his head the general turned away and retreated to the sanctuary of his office.

Col Bauer saluted sprightly, his fingers touching the tip of his beret as he watched his commander, deep in thought, close the door to his office.

It was 16h00. The clock was ticking and the men in Calw were waiting. Like his commander, Thomas wanted to uncover the facts and stop Russia from launching its vast array of weapons on an unprepared Europe. A continent where civil wars simmered, ready to erupt at any given time.

He knew the madness of the Bear, what they were capable of, and what they would do to anyone who stood in their way. Never would he forget what happened to Klaara.

Chapter 15

Major Svetlana Nikolaeva studied the piece of paper in her hand and shook her head, annoyed. It was a translated version of the official death certificate issued by the maximum-security prison in Cuba:

> Prisoner, No. 05341-06-2019
> Name: Niall McGuire;
> Deceased: 01/12/2019;
> Cause of Death: Shot trying to escape;
> Buried: 02/12/2019;
> Location: Penitentiary Graveyard III, Maria
> la Gourda, Havana, Cuba.

'Sir, he died ages ago, and they inform us only now. Incredible!' she exclaimed. 'They should have told us then. Did they think they were babysitting Mother Teresa? Or were they happy to pocket the monthly fee for looking after him? Wonder how long they were planning to continue the charade? Was it not for these murders we most likely would never have known.'

'Doesn't matter, Major. It happened, and the minister of justice asked us to investigate. Seeing it was your case, you'll have to do us the honours,' replied the Deputy Director of the FSB (Federal Security Service) Counter-Intelligence, Major General Ivan Lukyanov.

Svetlana frowned, ready to protest. The last thing she wanted was to relive the past. To be reminded of her time in Ireland with him, believing the episode closed. She welcomed the news of his death. The death of the man she had loathed more than anyone in the world. He was finally gone. Killed. Something which should have been done long ago.

'No ifs or buts,' her superior cautioned with a smile and a raised hand.

He empathised with her unwillingness to comply, fully aware of the emotional stress and dangers she had suffered during her mission. At great personal risk she had seduced the man responsible for her sister's death. If it were him, he would have killed the man on sight. But showing remarkable acumen she had succeeded in ridding the world of the Irishman and his network of criminals. And avenging her sister's death.

'Yes Sir,' Svetlana replied calmly.

The scar on Maj Gen Lukyanov's forehead creased slightly, appraising her. 'Right, you have two days to file a report. Then they can do with it what they want. That will be the last of this Niall McGuire saga. There are far more important matters to deal with than playing detective – a war is heading our way and you're needed here.'

'Understood, Sir.'

He pressed the intercom's button on his desk and spoke into it. 'Marina, please prepare orders for Maj Nikolaeva for a military flight to Havana, 16h00, today.'

On schedule, Svetlana, dressed in an anti-G suit, found herself strapped into a Sukhoi PAK FA T-51D – the two-seater version of the stealth supersonic bomber. Pushed back into the seat, the plane climbed to its service ceiling level of 19 000 metres.

For the benefit of the attractive officer in the cockpit behind him, Captain Vladislav Dmitriev eased back on the controls. He did not need an unconscious passenger, someone most likely more accustomed to airliners' soft ascends of ten metres per second. Tempted to speed up, he thought it might be wise to first check.

'Shall I push her a bit, Ma'am?' the pilot's voice piped in her headset.

'Fine by me. I'll shout if it gets too much,' Svetlana replied, annoyed, addressed as "Ma'am". She always thought the title applied to older women. And old she was not.

The plane shot forward, climbing at the standard operational rate of a hundred and nine metres per second. After a few seconds the pilot asked, 'How you're doing back there?'

'Still here.'

Suddenly, her peripheral vision blurred and locked out as the incline increased rapidly. She knew the danger signs and whispered into the mic, 'Better slow down, I'm having tunnel-vision.'

The next instant the plane dropped its speed and levelled out.

'How's the sight?' Capt Dmitriev asked.

With the blood returning to her head and her vision restored, she said, 'Sorry to spoil the fun. I haven't been in one of these for a while. How many G's were we doing?'

'Ten. The maximum we can operate on for prolonged periods with these new suits.'

'Okay, not for me. What is the top climb ratio with this plane?' she asked, curious.

'Give or take, three hundred and fifty metres per second. I don't think you want to try that.'

'No, I don't,' Svetlana said, and returned her attention to Niall McGuire's file.

Something in the report niggled. Four bodies had been discovered so far, all somehow connected to Niall.

Not a good sign.

The last time she had seen him was nearly twenty months ago, secured in the executive officer's quarters on the Akula II nuclear submarine. Realising his fate, the alarm in his eyes had been comical. The atrocities perpetrated against the people of Russia would never be swept under the rug. No, he had to pay for his sins. But a bullet would have been more appropriate, she thought.

The similarities between Russia's official version regarding Niall's "death" and now Cuba's, filled her with apprehension. The Russian report stated Niall "drowned" while trying to escape arrest. The Cuban report: he was "shot" while trying to escape.

No, it sounded too convenient. Too much like a cover-up.

Well, if you're not dead, then this time I'll end it myself, I swear.

She touched the thickened tissue to her side – a knife and bullet wound. Mementoes from her first assignment under the alias of "Irina", codenamed "Nemesis".

On her return to Russia, they had awarded her with the Hero of the Russian Federation medal; the highest honour reserved for only a few. But amidst all the glory, she remembered one lesson: one's life in the shadows hanged by an ethereal string, to be snipped at any moment.

Therefore, at the young age of thirty-five, she knew every new assignment could also be her last.

Yes, my dear, next time you may not be so lucky, she cautioned herself, ignoring the dull vibration of the plane racing through the cloudless sky.

Shimmering far below in the afternoon sun was the Mediterranean Sea. She recalled her first swim in its warm waters over two years ago. A pleasant memory, however, tainted by the sordid "romance" nurtured in the line of duty. Feigning pleasure as if in her seventh heaven she had sailed alongside a pair of dolphins, snorkelled for hours by his side, and enjoyed romantic candlelit dinners. She had played her role to perfection in the make-believe world of pretence.

Two hundred kilometres west of Gibraltar, Capt Dmitriev reduced their cruising speed of 2 000km/h and manoeuvred the jet in below the IL-78 air-to-air tanker sent from its base at Oka Ben Nafi in Libya. As the plane ascended with its probe extended, it slipped the nozzle into the fuel-drogue.

'Locked in,' Capt Dmitriev confirmed to the tanker crew. With the fuel shooting into the jet's tank, he turned his attention to his passenger, hoping to start a meaningful dialogue. 'Apologies for the pit stop, Ma'am.'

After the initial conversation during take-off, she had responded to his questions with only one or two-syllable words. He had no intention of letting her walk away without a promise of a dinner. He would be stuck in Cuba for a few days, and what better prospect than spending an evening in her company?

First, you make them smile. And if they smile, they'll laugh. And if they laugh, they'll sleep with you. The captain grinned to himself at his tried and tested recipe which never failed. 'But it's either this or we'll have to swim to Cuba. Then we won't make our dinner date.'

'Hmm…' Svetlana pondered, realising the man would not give up. He was a womaniser; she had seen that the minute they had met. Over the years she had fended off enough men like him, so dealing with another sod would be a pleasure. Shuffling the documents on her lap, she asked, puzzled, 'I don't see any instructions for a dinner date on my assignment. So, please, give it a rest.'

Cold bitch! Wonder what flea bit her? Capt Dmitriev thought and returned his attention to releasing the probe from the drogue.

He veered the plane to the left, tilted the wings in appreciation of the help by his colleagues, and shot through the sky to cover the 4 500 kilometres to Cuba. He wanted to say, "Believe me, Missy, you are no match for the girls in Havana". But he changed tact and said, 'Apologies if I offended you, Ma'am. Can't blame a man for trying.'

'None taken,' she replied coolly, not fooled by this sudden charm.

'Quick update. ETA, Havana, 13h00 local time.'

Chapter 16

Kurdistan

Based on the last twenty-four-hours' reconnaissance, a repeat of the previous night's activities were on the cards. The three hundred troops marching past confirmed that.

For three hours the two camouflaged figures did not budge in the undergrowth, watching the road. The sun's rays painted the snow-covered peaks soft-pink as it dropped in behind the ridge. The hazy grey dusk was perfect; a world between two realms with every detail erased, rendering them invisible.

A biting chill set in.

It was Colonel Thomas Bauer's third day in the field.

Guided by First Lieutenant Bernd Schmidt's infrared signal, he and his unit had parachuted into Turkey. The drop-zone had been five kilometres west of their current position.

As part of NATO's surveillance of the Kurdish struggle, the lieutenant's three-man unit had been collecting intel on troop movements and rebel encampments in the Kurdish Mountains. Since the attack on the gas installation, they had focused their attention on the rebel cells operating in the district seventy kilometres north-west of Diyarbakir.

Thomas's unit totalled eleven men. Their temporary tactical base was a cave two hundred metres above, and one kilometre west of the village of Malkaya. From there they could observe all activity in the area. They also had eyes on the makeshift rebel encampment 1.4km east of the village.

Two Kurdish rebel officers approached; their ranks were distinguishable by the cotton insignia stitched to their uniforms. The rhythmic crunch of boots on gravel came closer.

'Get ready,' Thomas whispered to Corporal Johann Müller by his side.

The Kurds strode past.

Thomas listened to the receding strides and craned his neck slightly. He looked to his left, at the straightened backs of the officers heading north. To his right the road was empty. He nodded to Cpl Müller, 'They're alone. Give the men the all-clear.'

'Copy, Sir,' Cpl Müller confirmed and spoke into the mic, breaking radio silence, 'Alpha calling Bravo, come in. Over.'

'Bravo, receiving you, over.'

'It's green for go. Copy, over.'

'Roger. Confirm target, over.'

'Two male officers. Three hundred metres south from your position, over.'

'Got them. Wilco, and out.'

Without a sound, Thomas and Johan rid themselves of the branches and stepped on to the road. Dressed in headscarves and kaftans they resembled two farmers on their way to the village. Staying inside the deep shadows of the trees they followed the Kurds.

The loud drone of an approaching car forced them to jump out of the way. Swallowed by a cloud of dust, they shrugged their shoulders irritably. The Fiat raced towards the village. They increased their pace, hurrying to close the gap with the Kurds.

Thirty metres…

At the fork up ahead, three Kurdish peasants strolled towards Thomas, showing no interest in them or the two Kurdish officers.

Surrounded by mountains and orchards, the settlement of Malkaya resembled a peaceful sanctuary where time stood still and middays were spent sleeping in the shade of poplars. And the evenings toiled away with idle gossip and the re-telling of folklore.

But the preceding days' events had quashed this deception. Kurdish rebels had descended on the village in preparation for a Turkish assault.

Seven days after the Trans Adriatic Pipeline explosion, the Turkish army had obliterated two unprepared pro-rebel villages. The Turks wanted those responsible for the deaths of their men. They would burn them out regardless of the human cost.

Taking up defensive positions in and around Malkaya, the three hundred and fifty strong battalion of men and women in dark olive-green uniforms stayed alert. In the late dusk, their eyes were etched deep in their sockets, their faces lined.

The elders of the village nervously watched the rebels; the murmur of voices questioning their fate. Were theirs the next village to be destroyed by the Turks? The presence of the rebel force left them under no illusions. When the attack would come, the old structures and years of memories would vanish. Most of them and their families would die. Would the rebel force be able to fend off the Turks? No.

Whether they liked it or not, they and the other thirty-five million Kurds under control of the Turks, Iranians, Iraqis, Syrians, and Armenians were as much part of the ongoing struggle for independence as the uniformed rebels. Therefore, they would not be spared.

In the village square, ten boys played a game of football. Ignoring the gathering storm, they enjoyed the attention of a few soldiers cheering them on. Two boys chased after the ball which flew across the road, barely missing the Fiat turning into the square.

The car slammed its brakes...

Eyes turned and glared at the vehicle. Too many eyes, as if they knew. Ignoring the boys' curses the driver sped up. More soldiers turned and stared at the car. Someone spoke into a radio.

Three hundred metres further up the road, two jeeps pulled across the narrow lane, flanked on both sides by buildings, marking the entrance to the village. There was no way through. A dozen men with assault rifles surrounded the jeeps and took aim.

The Fiat's brake lights glowed deep red as it skidded to a halt. The doors flung open. With weapons blazing the driver and his four passengers jumped out, hoping to blast their way through the roadblock. Hit by a wall of fire, the bullets raked their bodies, killing them instantly, except for the driver. Spared, he would share his mission's objective before joining his dead comrades.

Hearing the distant gunfire, Thomas reached for the concealed short-barrelled Heckler-Koch 417 assault rifle strapped to his back.

Up ahead the two Kurds started to run.

In one fluid motion Thomas slipped the rifle from under his tunic and raced after them.

Lt Schmidt and the two men by his side took aim with their silenced pistols. The popping sounds had an immediate effect. The charging rebel captain and lieutenant staggered across the road like two drunks. From behind, Thomas and Johan grabbed the captain. Lt Schmidt took care of the lieutenant.

With the Kurds hooded and unconscious, they carried them into the undergrowth. On cue, a van approached and flicked its headlights twice.

'Our ride. Go!' Thomas ordered, and signalled in the direction of the field opposite.

A shadow clutching a sniper rifle appeared in the long grass and rushed to join the men piling into the van.

With all the men squeezed inside the small space, the van made a U-turn and headed south, away from the ensuing fracas in the village. It was none of their concern. They had their own problems to deal with. HQ needed answers, and fast.

Clearing yet another crest, Thomas ordered the driver to stop and cut the headlights. Something troubled him. There was far too much activity in the settlement below. 'Right, back up… Easy does it.'

The van disappeared in behind the ridge. Thomas, Johann, and Dietrich jumped out, raced up the short incline in the dark, and vanished in amongst the trees.

Lying flat on his stomach, Thomas studied the cluster of buildings through the night-scope. 'Turkish army. Change of plan.'

'Two klicks back is a turnoff,' Thomas said, having re-joined the van. 'Check where it leads. We must find another way around. The Turks are preparing to strike Malkaya. Best we get rid of this van and head for the hills. Road's too busy.'

They drove deeper into the ravine, ignoring the screech of rocks and branches lacerating the van's paintwork. Unable to continue they abandoned the vehicle. Covered by a layer of branches and shielded by trees the van had effectively "disappeared". Unless a herder strayed into the vehicle, no one would ever discover it.

In single file they moved deeper into the ravine, guiding the drugged and hooded Kurds forward. After fifteen minutes of slipping and sliding, Thomas ordered the hoods removed. They were losing too much time.

With the pace increasing, the Kurds tried to delay progress by faking the odd fall. But a few quick blows with the butt of a rifle put an end to that.

Remaining just below the snowline they gradually gained altitude. As the temperature dropped Thomas tightened the scarf around his neck. Above him the sky shimmered with stars. It was going to be a bitterly cold night.

Guided by the glow of the stars they stumbled on to an animal track and picked up the pace. Aiming for the snow-covered ridge five hundred metres up, they hoped to find suitable shelter on the far side.

In the filtered morning light of the cave, Sergeant Major Chris Koch addressed the two hostages in Kurdish. His deep voice rumbled softly, as if speaking to children. 'Right, start talking, my friends. You tell us what we want to know and we love and leave you. If not, we'll still love and leave you, but with one difference: you'll never hug your families again. *Guf?*'

The two Kurdish officers kneeling in the dirt, their heads covered, stayed silent.

'We know your unit was involved in the sabotage of the gas compressor installation plant. But that's not our concern – the Turks can deal with you. What we want to know is who orchestrated the attack?'

The sun was well up by the time the interrogation ended. The Kurds' stubbornness had cost them unnecessary pain. Having cleaned their injuries and bandaged the flesh wounds to their legs, Thomas said, 'Pity. Trust they weren't lying. Lieutenant, prepare a roster. The men need sleep.'

Conversing via satellite with Lt Gen Beck at HQ, Thomas shared the intel. 'Sir, the Kurds believe the Russians were behind the attack. Just as the Americans claim. Aided by Kurdish rebels, a Colonel Boris Polyakov and a unit of Russian special forces planned and carried out the mission.'

After a prolonged silence, Lt Gen Beck replied, 'Not what I had hoped for. We'll try to verify Col Polyakov's credentials. Any idea of his current location?'

'They claim he's at a rebel base twenty kilometres northeast of Tortum, close to the Georgian border. Sir, can you order a sat-recon of the area to pinpoint the base?'

'Will do. I'll contact you when we have them. What is your ETA at Tortum?'

'Midday tomorrow. Too many unknowns to be more precise. We can only move out at sunset. The area is crawling with Turks preparing to raid a nearby village. They may take us for hostiles.'

'Understood. Remember, you're on your own till we know who we're dealing with. Might even be the Turks trying to cause trouble.'

Thomas cut the connection and returned to the cave to catch some sleep. At fifty-five, his body, although lean and fit thanks to a strict training regime, needed rest if he were to lead his team efficiently.

Chapter 17

Cuba

Svetlana stared at the empty chair behind the unkempt desk. She had been waiting for more than an hour. So much for hurrying this investigation along, she thought. Maybe some other pressing matter delayed him, rather than indifference or some childish stalling tactic.

On arrival in Cuba, the warden had been too busy to meet her. He would only be available in the morning.

Well, here I am, Mr Warden, and where are you?

Filled with suspicion, she wondered who called the shots around there. The prison authorities or central government? She wanted to leave as soon as possible. The powerful smell of disinfectant oozing from every corridor and room of the old prison was revolting. It reeked of despair.

So, this is where you have spent your last days... A world apart from the splendours of the Wicklow Mountains and your precious island, she thought, reading Niall McGuire's death certificate again. The memory of the many young women's blood he had spilt, including her sister's, infuriated her. She dropped the certificate on the desk as if it were a snake.

Yes, you deserved what you got. Just a pity it ended so soon.

She tried not to dwell too much on the past and took another sip of the strong coffee.

At least something decent in this dreadful place.

It was her third cup. The way this was going she most probably would die of a caffeine overdose before his highness made his appearance.

At last, she sighed as purposeful steps approached the office.

The door swung open. She got up to greet the warden. But he walked past her and plonked himself down in his worn-out swivel chair behind his desk. She had enough and itched to express her annoyance. Instead, she controlled her temper and sat down.

'Good morning, Señorita. Enjoying the coffee? Good… Um…' the overweight, middle-aged man greeted without looking up at her. He lazily removed a folded piece of paper from his breast pocket and studied it. He frowned, seemingly indifferent to the demands made by the minister of justice.

His chubby hand shoved the files on his desk to one side. That four of his employees were dead was no-one's business. He would have preferred the matter kept quiet. Dealt with it himself. Least of all, get the Russian FSB involved. Best I finish this meeting and sent her packing back to Russia, he thought.

Svetlana bided her time and said nothing. She did not care whether he had manners. She would do what she was sent to do, knowing it would not be easy. Patience, she cautioned herself. Don't act impetuous or the journey would have been a waste of time and money. Which it was, as far as she was concerned. The Cubans could solve their own murders.

But orders were orders.

'What can I do for you…Miss Nikolaeva? Or, more to the point, what precisely do you intend to do for us?' he asked and looked at his visitor.

Confronted by a very attractive female officer in uniform, a smile cracked his dour face, thinking how he would like to get to know her better. Then again, it might not be a wise decision. To play with fire never was. Beneath that charming veneer lay a strength…a steeled determination. A brain not to be challenged. She was dangerous to the extreme.

'Pardon, you were saying?' Svetlana responded. 'And it is, Major Nikolaeva.'

'Apologies, Major, I just remembered something. Nothing important. It can wait.'

'May I continue?'

'Of course. Please do.' His tone bordered on being courteous.

'The police report states all four victims worked in this prison. Is that correct?'

'Not quite. Only three.'

'And the other one?'

'The coroner worked for the prison authorities in Havana.'

'And the rest worked in the isolation wing of your prison?'

'Correct.'

'Roughly, how many guards are assigned to that specific wing?'

'Eighteen.'

'Do you know of any reason why the authorities think the victims were involved with prisoner McGuire?'

'No. Having investigated the matter, I had found no reason why they would even suggest that. There are strict rules. No personnel may interact with inmates. If they do, they're fired, pronto. No relationships may flourish, as that could lead to mayhem in a place like this.'

'Yes, fair enough. That is my understanding as well. Let's move on to my next point.'

'Please do.'

'According to the report, these men did not know each other. They lived separate lives. Never interacted. Worked different shifts. And on the odd occasion, only greeted each other in passing. Is that correct?'

'Yes.'

'So how their murders can be related to prisoner McGuire is a mystery. If they were in cahoots, scheming to either help him escape or squeeze him for money and kill him, they had to meet to coordinate their plan. Someone should have seen or heard something. But no one did. Therefore, it would seem their murders are unrelated. These men might have died for a variety of reasons. Is that not so?'

'Of course! It is in my report. They all gambled, drank, and took risks. Got on the wrong side of someone. Not paying one's debts is unforgivable in Cuba. Someone not associated with the prison must have killed them. I'm sure you agree with that,' Warden Fernandez stated firmly, thinking, maybe she would be happy to finish this investigation and rather join him for a siesta.

'Yes. Believe me, if it were up to me, I would close the file right now and jump in the jet sitting on the runway. To me, it is an open-and-shut case. Unfortunately, I have my orders. I'm not allowed to sign off on this till I've visited the murder scenes, the victims' homes, talked to their families, and the guards in the isolation wing. I'm sorry. Those are my orders,' she said with conviction as a thousand questions mulled in her head.

Clearly, the report had been massaged. And she fully intended to find out why.

Warden Fernandez hesitated for a moment, contemplating how to end this charade. He was on dangerous ground. She was cute, too cute, toying with him. 'Sorry, I can't help you there. It's outside my authority. Except, of course, for meeting the guards. For the rest, you'll need permission from the relevant government departments. And that will take time. Something we have plenty of in Cuba. You may be stuck here for weeks. Are you sure this is necessary?'

She nearly burst out laughing. 'Warden, you have all the authority I need in your pocket. Same as me,' she said. Shifting to the edge of her chair, she took out her copy of the letter from the minister of justice. Her eyes locked on his as a gentle smile tucked at the corners of her mouth.

'Quit stalling. The sooner I do this, the sooner you can return to whatever you have to do. If there's no link between them and the late prisoner, as you say, I'll be gone before you know it. Let me make myself clear. Whatever you and your staff are up to is none of my business. But I shall carry out my orders with your full cooperation, whether you like it or not. Understood? Good. Now that we've cleared that up, I ask you again, nicely. Please arrange for me to visit the crime scenes and the victims' homes.'

Warden Fernandez said nothing. His pupils narrowed to the size of pinheads. Never in all his years of running the prison did anyone dare to speak to him in such a manner.

You insolent whore! he thought.

His first impulse was to grab her by the scruff of the neck, bend her over the desk and teach her a thing or two… He exhaled slowly, struggling to hide his contempt. He knew he had no choice other than to co-operate. He raised both hands in a gesture of defeat, and said, 'Of course, no harm in that.'

Don't cross swords with her. Antagonised, she'll just dig her prissy heels in deeper, he cautioned himself.

The freshly repainted apartment was cheaply furnished. Inside the confined entrance hung a photograph of a young man smiling brightly at the camera. A wreath was draped over the gold-painted wooden frame.

Next to Svetlana the old woman cried and mumbled about her loss as she led them into the bedroom. 'Why would anyone want to harm him? He was such a nice man.' And to prove the virtues of her late son, she shoved a diamond and pearl brooch under Svetlana's nose.

Svetlana shrugged her shoulders and smiled apologetically, not understanding a word. 'Can you please translate?' she asked the interpreter.

'A gift from son.'

'Interesting. Ask her when and why he gave it to her. And any other presents during the past two years?'

Waiting for an answer, Svetlana continued her appraisal of the bedroom's contents, all neatly arranged. There was nothing strange or odd. No picture of a señorita. Nothing. The man must have been an absolute bore. A real mama's boy; never married and living with his mother at the age of thirty-nine.

'No, is only gift. She says… Very expensive.'

'I can see that. Ask her about his habits. Did he have any friends?'

At the second victim's home, and with nothing more to learn, Svetlana walked down the stairs to the car. The circumstances were in total contrast to the "mama's boy". He had been a hot-blooded, messy bachelor.

Of a much younger age, he shared his quarters with a few men. Nude pictures of voluptuous Latinas vied for space on the otherwise barren walls. On his bedside table was a half-empty bottle of tequila, boxes of cigarettes, and an ashtray overflowing with butts and ashes. With the room sealed off by the police, his bed had been unmade – it most likely had never been made.

Apparently, on the night of his death, he had boasted of going to bet all his money. According to his friends, it was a fortune. Fed up with guarding scum, he was to return filthy rich and quit his job in the morning.

That was the last time they had seen him alive.

Her next visit was to the house of a certain Álvaro Garcia. Will this be worth the trip? Svetlana pondered, seated in the back of the speeding car. The few notes she had made so far revealed nothing out of the ordinary. Nothing specific. Although it did raise some questions.

The first victim had been a dark horse and could have met his end at the hands of a jealous lover. He sounded too much of a goody-two-shoes. And the repainted apartment and expensive gift… Interesting? Then again, having been a miser, he might have saved up for several years to afford such extravagance.

The second victim most probably died for reasons as mentioned by Warden Fernandez – too many gambling debts. Or was it?

For the two victims murdered on the same day; that could also just be a coincidence, but unlikely.

The car slowed down, turned into the short driveway, and stopped behind a brand-new Emgrand. The house was like all the others lining the dusty road. A rectangular box with the outside walls covered in bric-à-brac. The grass had not been cut for weeks. Señor Garcia had not been a keen gardener. The file stated he died first. Shot in bed before work on the same day as the other two victims. It had been nothing less than murder.

Again, gambling debts? Svetlana pondered and got out of the car.

Curious eyes watched her. Huddled together inside the safety of their front door, three barefoot girls giggled and waved at her. All three fashioned the same haircuts; bobs with straight fringes. Behind them hovered the mother, staring suspiciously at the stranger. Svetlana nodded a polite greeting and entered Álvaro's house.

The massive flat-screen TV and surround sound system dominated the living room. It seemed out of place. She raised an eyebrow; a new car and TV? In the bedroom, her suspicions were confirmed. The wardrobe was filled with the best Havana had to offer in men's wear.

The bed had been stripped of its linen. Was it not for the bloodstains on the headboard and mattress, no one would have suspected anything amiss. She had seen enough, convinced that if he had hidden money somewhere in the house, it would be long gone by now.

About to leave, she paused inside the front door and spoke to the driver, 'Can you please ask the neighbour if she'd mind answering a few questions?'

'Yes, señorita,' the man replied and hurried outside.

About to follow, Svetlana swept her gaze over the clutter displayed in the glass cabinet. She froze. One photograph of Álvaro and some friends caught her attention.

How did I miss that? Must be half asleep.

She moved closer to study the group of men with their beer glasses raised.

A bullet whizzed past her head.

There was no clap of gunfire. The ping of lead ricocheting off a metal object in the back of the room was followed by breaking glass.

Svetlana dropped to the floor. On all fours she scrambled in behind the settee for cover as the upholstery exploded in a plume of feathers. Harmlessly, the next bullet sailed over her head and slammed into the wall.

A wild shot!

In one fluid motion she drew her pistol, jumped up and ran through the house. She unlocked the backdoor and peered into the garden, wary of gunmen waiting for her.

Somewhere voices shouted.

Footsteps raced across gravel...

She dashed outside into the long grass. Thirty metres to the trees. Too far! She dropped to the ground and slithered feet first towards the trees. She aimed her pistol at the nearest corner.

Two men charged into view, their weapons searching...

Her first bullet struck the one's chest. The next bullet ripped into the other's intestine. She jumped up, sprinted towards the squirming bodies in the grass and kicked their weapons away.

In the driveway, a car door slammed. An engine revved angrily and sped off.

Where's my driver? Is that him leaving?

'Antonio!' she shouted, standing next to the dying men at her feet. She did not expect a reply, knowing she had been set up. But much to her surprise, a white-faced Antonio appeared.

'Señorita... You okay?' he asked, bewildered by what he saw.

'I'm fine,' she hissed and pointed her pistol at him. 'Ask them who ordered this.'

She did not trust the look of shock on his face. Was it because his friends were lying on the ground instead of her? Or because he knew nothing about this attempt on her life? Her aim did not waver as she watched him question the wounded men. One false move on his part and his head would explode.

'They not know who behind this. Say boss sent them.'

'Now why don't I believe you... And the boss's name?'

112

'Alexander Gonzalez. You forget this... You forget him. Come, we leave now,' he whimpered.

'No, we'll wait for the police.'

'Señorita, police big trouble. We go...'

Hearing the wail of approaching sirens, she warned, 'Don't you dare move.' She was confident the matter would be cleared up in no time, allowing her to complete her investigation.

But twenty minutes later Svetlana found herself handcuffed in the back of the patrol car, heading towards the police station in Havana. Her interpreter, Antonio had been dismissed to report the incident to Warden Fernandez. Her claim of self-defence had been ignored. She did not know what Antonio had told them. For all she knew, he could have accused her of shooting the two men in cold blood. That she, as a foreigner, possessed a firearm had sealed her fate.

'Run that by me again. Are you saying she is in prison?' Maj Gen Lukyanov growled.

'Yes, she is.'

'Why?'

'For killing two prison employees.'

Maj Gen Lukyanov was beside himself. And having absorbed the muted reply from Cuba, he warned, 'In my official capacity, I order you to release Maj Nikolaeva at once. If not, you'll have the Russian army there within hours to free her. For your sake, I trust nothing has happened to her. Believe me, if she had shot anyone, she must have had a very good reason to do so. You have fifteen minutes. Got that honourable minister?'

His words were not an idle threat. With his country on a war footing with NATO, it would not take much to persuade his superiors to remove some despot regime in a warm-up exercise.

The Cuban minister of justice meekly reassured him he would, silently hoping that Maj Nikolaeva was unharmed. But knowing his men, he doubted that. The last he needed was to find a Russian gunman stare at him with death in his eyes. He was nervous. Four murders and now this?

'Yes Sir, nothing happened. I'm in tip-top shape,' Svetlana lied, grateful she was to be spared a night in prison.

Across the desk, an anxious commissioner of police viewed her bruised eye and cut lip, suffered during her brief spell in the holding cell.

If he sees me like this there'll be hell to pay. And then this case will never be solved, Svetlana thought.

'Sir, the sooner I leave here the better. Someone wants this investigation stopped. We can expect no cooperation from the prison authorities. The quickest way to resolve these murders is to exhume Niall's body. I doubt it's him in that grave.'

'Why do you think it's not him?'

'All the victims knew each other. One photograph shows them having drinks together; probably celebrating their pay-offs by Niall. Buying loyalties and leaving no witnesses was Niall's speciality. I suspect the prison warden is next on the list, as he is most likely involved.'

'You sure?'

'Positive.'

'Major, finish your investigation ASAP. I need you here. We have far more important matters to deal with. The Sukhoi is ready when you are.'

'Yes Sir. One more thing. Are any of our assets in Cuba? I need someone to watch my back. I don't want to be "accidentally" buried next to Niall.'

'Right. I'll do one better. Presently, there are two of our subs in Havana's naval base. Within the hour, a unit will fetch you. You'll overnight on one of the subs as their guest, and they'll be your detail until you board the jet. In the meantime, you don't leave the commissioner's office, not even for the bathroom.'

'Yes Sir.'

'Please put the commissioner on. Believe me, by the time I'm finished with him, he'll be very obliging,' Maj Gen Lukyanov assured her.

Chapter 18

Turkey

The wooden planks creaked noisily under Danylo's feet as he climbed the stairs. He did not care. Draped in his arms, Klaara's disease-ridden body felt weightless. Her head lolled against his chest, her tears staining his shirt.

Consumed by hatred, he stepped over the corpses, avoiding the pool of blood. He felt no guilt for killing the pigs.

He had found her two hours ago. But having no choice, he had returned to Chusovoy with the other men. It did not take long to steal a car and race back to Verchnee Kalino, to where she lay dying. Entering the house, the two bastards had thought he had returned for another round of sex with the woman in the basement. The gun had appeared in his hand. The bullets fired at point-blank range had felled them instantly. Furious, he had fired two more rounds into their lifeless bodies.

With the utmost care he laid her down on the front seat of the car. He looked at her and smiled feebly; the set of clean clothes looked far too big on her. It would have to do.

He glimpsed at his watch. It was 2:20 AM.

The city of Perm was more than eighty kilometres away. If he wanted to catch the first train to Moscow departing at 6:00 AM, he had to hurry. Hopefully, by the time someone discovers the bodies and Klaara missing, they would be long gone. It was Saturday. There would be no great urgency for anyone to get up early…

116

Focussing on the yellow glow cast on the road by the Lada's feeble headlights, he prayed he had not been too late to save her. Would she survive the arduous journey ahead? He was not so sure. She was too weak. But he would not leave her behind. He would rather die by her side.

The fact that he would never find their child alive somewhere in the USSR, was killing him. All he could do was hope that wherever she was, she would be safe and happy.

At last the lights of Perm appeared on the horizon. Fast asleep, Klaara's head rested in his lap. She had hardly stirred since leaving the house in the woods.

'No, no. It's not possible,' he moaned, seeing the row of approaching flashing blue lights...

'Colonel, time to go,' Cpl Müller whispered, shaking Thomas by the shoulder.

'Right...yes. Thanks, Corporal,' Thomas stammered, waking up from his dream, slightly disorientated by the cave's semi-dark interior. 'Are the men ready?' he asked, taking command.

'Yes Sir. We're set to go as soon as you've finished your seven-course meal,' Cpl Müller joked, handing him his survival-pack rations.

Ready to move out, Thomas pointed at the two trussed figures on the floor of the cave and ordered, 'Jab them.'

Two syringes plunged into the Kurds' exposed arms, rendering them unconscious in a matter of seconds.

'We have a two-hour head start. Plus, another eight to ten before they'll be reunited with their unit. That's if the Turks or wolves don't kill them first,' Thomas said, exiting the cave.

Immediately he cut a path down the steep slope. With no moonlight he risked nothing more than a brisk walk. The clouds accumulating against the higher peaks would soon drop to their level. Rain or snow were on the way. But the weather was the least of Thomas's concerns. The information extracted from the Kurds was far more disconcerting.

Was the gas-line attack carried out by a radical faction in the military or was it a false-flag operation ordered by Russian

High Command? Too soon to tell. Col Polyakov, if that was his real name, could be the first step in uncovering the truth. No one in NATO would believe any theories without irrefutable proof.

Deep in thought, Thomas's ears picked up the chopping sound of an approaching helicopter. He snapped to it and indicated for his men to take cover. Hiding in the dense foliage, four gun-ships shot over their heads, climbed up the steep mountainside and vanished over the ridge.

Ten minutes they waited before moving out, confident the threat had passed.

The hike down the valley took over two hours. Another three hours march brought them to the outskirts of a small town inside Turkish-controlled territory. They gave the sleepy town a wide berth and took shelter on the far side.

Dressed in civilian clothes, two men disappeared in amongst the dark buildings. They were not hopeful. The chances of finding a car were slim. Let alone finding two...

Waiting for his men's return, Thomas considered plausible scenarios which could unfold.

If Col Polyakov and his unit sneak across the northern border, it would be impossible to find them. Not with such limited intel. And with a minimum of seven hours' drive separating them, the odds of reaching the Russians in time were not in their favour.

Trekking after the colonel into Georgia would be an exercise Thomas did not want to entertain. Armed to the teeth, entering the country by road would be out of the question. And hiking across the mountains could take days. They would have no alternative but to return to Germany, prepare for a sortie into Georgia, and start the hunt fresh.

The chugging noise of an old Renault panel van broke the stillness of the night.

Our ride? They must be joking. Forget seven hours' drive... Make that fourteen.

Three minutes later the van's doors shut.

'Hit it! Let's see what this Lamborghini can do,' Thomas mocked.

The vehicle coughed a few times, belched out a cloud of smoke, and continued to choke contently along the deserted road.

'And this is the best they had in that *metropolis*? Well, we better get to Elazig before the Turks issue an APB (all-points bulletin) on this treasure,' Thomas laughed.

Crawling at a snail's pace they followed the winding road through the mountains. The sky was heavy, threatening to release its burden on the dry land. And as the first drops of rain splattered the windscreen, the driver set the old wiper blades in motion. It had no impact on the downpour. With their vision limited to only twenty metres, it did not matter at the speed they were going.

Turning on to the D300 national road they picked up speed. At Elazig they abandoned the van in a supermarket parking lot. Having hot-wired two vehicles, they aimed to regroup north of Tortum – twenty minutes separated the two units. Back on the D300 the first hint of daybreak appeared on the horizon.

Surrounded by mountains, a blanket of fog obscured the town of Tortum. Fortunately, the long drive had delivered no surprises. Thomas pulled his shoulders back and massaged his aching muscles. He looked at his watch: 11h00. Thirty minutes earlier than his ETA.

Eleven kilometres north of the village they exchanged the relatively busy D950 national road for the deserted DA2 regional road. Another three kilometres and they swung on to a dirt road. Seven minutes later, Thomas spotted Lt Schmidt in the shade of a tree.

'Glad you could join us, Colonel,' the lieutenant greeted. 'First track on your right. Aim for the derelict barn. Can't miss it.'

The car hobbled over the dirt road, its low chassis scraping the ground. Reaching the barn, Cpl Müller opened its door, or what was left of it – a few pieces of vertical planks held together by rusty nails. They parked inside, not wanting to attract attention.

119

The men gathered around Thomas for a final briefing as he placed the monitor – hooked up to a live feed from Germany – on top of the car's bonnet. Seven kilometres of mountainous terrain separated them from the rebel base with its unknown number of troops. Above in space the powerful camera continued its trajectory and zoomed in on the target. Its lenses reacting to the signals beamed up from Germany.

The exact location of the base had been pinpointed by HQ a few hours earlier. It had not been easy. Was it not for the compacted clearing marking the parade ground, the technicians would not have found the base. Sheltered by a large overhanging rock and shielded by cliffs, nothing else was visible. Presumably, the cave's entrance was somewhere below the rock canopy.

Traversing the terrain, the camera identified several fortifications.

'I guess there would be more hidden inside tunnels,' Thomas said, his eyes not straying from the monitor.

The camp seemed impenetrable. Overlooking the valley were five batteries armed with large quantities of ground-to-air missiles. Six defensive positions on the lower slopes were equipped to stop a ground assault.

'There must be an escape route on the other side. They would not corner themselves in,' Lt Schmidt said.

'I concur. Could be a few,' Lt Gen Beck's voice echoed over the speaker. 'We'll soon find out where.'

Next, the lens shifted over the ridge and started a search pattern looking for disturbed vegetation and any rigid straight lines which would indicate a man-made object.

'Thomas, you proceed while we continue the search. Best to enter by one of their escape routes,' Lt Gen Beck advised.

'Roger, Sir. We'll do a snatch and grab from the rear. When we're in position, we'll contact you. ETA two hours,' Thomas confirmed.

'Roger and out,' Lt Gen Beck said, signing off.

Lt Schmidt removed his headscarf and scratched his blond brush cut. 'Colonel, you can't be serious? You want to sneak in the back just like that?' he asked, somewhat bemused.

'Watch me,' Thomas said. 'If no alternative presents itself, then that's our way in. Won't be easy. I need two volunteers. The rest will provide covering fire.'

'Colonel, count me in,' Corporal Johann Müller said.

'Me also,' Corporal Hermann Schneider echoed.

'Best I go instead of you, Colonel. You are too valuable,' Lt Schmidt said.

'Thanks Lieutenant. Can't do. We'll manage,' he replied and regarded the two volunteers in front of him, riddled with youthful energy. 'Any more questions?'

No one responded.

'Good. Move out in five minutes,' Thomas said, checking his weapons.

Accompanied by corporal Müller and Schneider, he stepped into the hazy sunshine and frowned. 'We better hurry. Seems like a wet day ahead. Our eye in the sky won't be worth much if the weather has its way.'

Inside the rebel base in the northern mountains, a radio buzzed alive. The operator manning his post jotted down the message received from the rebel stronghold outside the village of Malkaya in the south. He ripped the note out of the pad and gave it to his comrade. 'For Col Hakim. Move it!'

Summoned by the CO of the rebel base, Boris entered the commander's office five minutes later. Struck by the anxious expression on Col Hakim's face, he asked, 'Something wrong?'

'We've received intel of a NATO unit having discovered your involvement and our general location. We expect they're on their way here.'

Boris swore and rubbed his chin. 'Right, we'll move out ASAP. No point getting your unit involved in a senseless battle and signal your location to the Turks.'

'Maybe too late. But thanks for your concern,' the colonel said pensively. 'Anything you need?'

'No, we're fine. Comrade, next time we meet the world will be a very different place. And we'll help rid you of the Turks for good,' Boris replied.

Chapter 19

Turkey

Hidden behind a cluster of boulders three kilometres south of the rebel base, Thomas contacted HQ. Overhead the heavy cumulus clouds blocked the sun. There would be no more clear imagery transmitted by the spy satellites. They would go in blind.

Lt Gen Beck's words did not lift his mood either. 'Colonel, it seems the Bear is stirring. Our assets in Russia confirmed Col Polyakov is very much alive, and a decorated war hero.'

Thomas considered the news in silence. If that were true, and the colonel carried out orders, then he might just as well return to Germany. His operation would serve no further purpose.

'Colonel, are you there?'

'Yes Sir. Doesn't sound good.'

'Let's not lose heart. Still not irrefutable proof that Russian High Command is behind the attack. The colonel and his men are supposedly on a few weeks' *holiday*. In other words, on a black-ops mission. But we must ask ourselves: is this government backed or not?'

'One cannot ignore the president's ambition of a new USSR. I just hope it's only a faction inside the military who is involved,' Thomas said.

'We'll keep digging, see what turns up.'

'Copy, Sir. Any luck with the escape tunnels?'

'Yes, we've found two potential access points. When you're in position, I'll guide you in.'

'Roger and out, Sir,' Thomas said, signing off. Filled with a sense of foreboding, he ordered the two men by his side to fall in.

This will not end well…

The winding goats' trail led them across barren terrain deeper into the mountains. At the fork up ahead they veered left towards the escape tunnels in the next valley and picked up the pace. They wanted to be in position before the rain would start.

The quiet desolation so close to the rebel base did not fool them. The rebels would be watching all access routes. From a distance the traditional Kurdish herders' clothes might conceal their true identities, but whether they would pass closer scrutiny remained to be seen. They reduced their pace to a lazy stroll and huddled together as if in idle conversation.

Four gunshots echoed off the granite boulders lining the deep valley, shattering the silence.

'Follow me,' Lt Schmidt whispered into his mic and scrambled up the steep incline.

Using what cover there was, the nine-man unit paused at an altitude of 2 133 metres. Far below, seven rebel soldiers stooped over three bodies stretched out on the ground. Their CO had walked into an ambush. Lt Schmidt scrutinised the area and counted three snipers on the opposite slope, bringing the total enemy number to ten.

Sgt Maj Koch broke the silence. 'The colonel and Müller are still alive.'

'Acquire targets, confirm, and neutralise,' Lt Schmidt replied. They had to take out the Kurds before they executed the fallen men.

Eight affirmatives…

'At three,' Lt Schmidt instructed.

The heavy clouds rolling down the mountainside swallowed the popping sounds of the muffled shots. Six Kurdish rebels fell to the ground. Higher up, the snipers' heads exploded. A second volley followed, eliminating the last rebel.

Six German soldiers broke cover and scrambled down the slope. Three held their positions, their rifles trained on the Kurds sprawled out on the ground.

'Colonel, can you hear me?' Sgt Maj Koch asked, reaching the fallen men. His CO's face was covered in blood.

'Yes, Chris… I'm okay.'

'Don't move,' Sgt Maj Koch warned. He unwrapped the stained headscarf, wiped the blood clean and inspected Thomas's wound. 'Sir, you'll live. The bullet grazed you… Knocked you flat. You're a very lucky man.'

'How're the others?' Thomas asked, getting to his feet.

'Cpl Schneider didn't make it,' Lt Schmidt replied, attending to Cpl Müller's wound. 'Johann is fine. Clean flesh wound through the shoulder. Missed vitals and bones. We'll have him patched up and ready to move out in a sec.'

'Damn! Sure about Hermann?' Thomas asked, infuriated by the loss of the young corporal.

'Affirmative, Sir. Got it in the neck.'

'Understood,' Thomas said. Feeling somewhat groggy, he brushed himself off. 'Any rebels alive?'

'Two. The rest are going nowhere.'

'Chris, ask them where the Russian colonel is.'

'Copy, Sir,' Sgt Maj Koch said and fixed his eyes on the two wounded Kurds. Removing his pistol from its holster, he fitted a suppressor while addressing them in a cold monotone. With each word spoken their eyes grew larger.

Preparing a collapsible stretcher for Cpl Schneider, Lt Schmidt suggested, 'Sir, we'll need air support if we're to make it out of here alive.'

'Yes, we do. But I reckon the soonest a gunship will reach us is in an hour or two. That's if the Turks agree to help. Imagine how—'

A terrifying scream cut Thomas off in mid-sentence as the one Kurd's kneecap disintegrated. At the sight of the blood and splintered bones sticking out through mangled flesh, the other rebel retched violently.

Sgt Maj Koch said nothing. Staring without care at the vomit-covered face, he aimed the pistol at the distraught man's healthy knees. The man wiped his mouth, and realising he would be next, started to talk. The smouldering eyes above the gun stopped his babbling. Again, the same question. The tip of the pistol inched closer.

With no will to resist, the Kurds shared what they knew about the Russians.

'It never fails. Nobody wants to live a cripple,' the sergeant major said. 'Colonel, according to them, someone tipped them off. They were expecting us. The colonel fled to the border an hour ago. And yes, they were all Russian. Anything else?'

'How many were there? Means of transport?'

Three minutes later, the sergeant major updated Thomas. 'Total number, ten. They're travelling in three white 4x4s; makes unknown. The Russians helped train the Kurds for another attack on some unknown installation – they don't know the specifics. That, I believe as it will be classified.'

'Thanks, Chris,' Thomas said. 'Lieutenant, ready to move out?'

With the two survivors tied up and the area cleared of evidence, Thomas led his men down the gorge. Contacting his commander, he gave a SITREP (situation report). His request for air support and extraction received a firm. 'Yes, will do. And if the Turks don't help, then I'll personally fly there and get you and the boys out.'

Thomas wanted to smile, but with the failure of their mission eating him like acid on a raw nerve, he banished all frivolity. One dead, one wounded, and their prey having escaped to Georgia. The mission was an unmitigated disaster. Even worse, the evidence so far pointed to the Russians spoiling for war.

Or was it only a faction inside Russia's military wanting to grab power and turn back the clock?

It was common knowledge that many old-school Russians in the military were fed-up with the immoral West's doctrine of freedom of speech, capitalism, democracy, and decadence while blind to their own leaders' sins, being amongst the most immoral and corrupt in the world. Years of state propaganda had failed to stop the rot from spreading. Many young had become like those in the West, spineless, shunning their values and culture. This, they felt, had to be corrected.

Or did the orders come from the president? Only time would tell.

Within Thomas burned a pure spirit, strong and resilient. He refused to give up, vowing to hunt down Col Polyakov, whether in Georgia or Russia.

The first drops of rain pelted down, turning the animal track into a muddy stream. Not breaking their stride, the men pushed ahead, taking turns in carrying Cpl Schneider's body. Cpl Müller refused help, bravely traversing the treacherous terrain as some rotated at regular intervals, providing cover-fire.

There was still an hour's hike to the barn. Thomas glanced over his shoulder; no sign of the rebel force. He suffered a slight headache – hopefully, the wound to his forehead was only superficial and nothing more sinister.

'Sir, any word on the choppers?' Lt Schmidt asked, popping up by Thomas's side.

'Nothing yet.'

It was not the news the lieutenant had hoped for. But a deal had been struck by the Turks. Pinpointing the rebel base had secured their full cooperation.

But where were they?

Thomas's phone beeped.

'Are you clear of the base?' Lt Gen Beck's voice piped in his ear.

'Affirmative.'

'Take immediate cover. I repeat, take immediate cover! They're to strike the base any second now, over.'

'Copy, Sir.' With his words hanging in the air, four F-35A Lightning II jet fighters screamed low over his head.

'They're here, Sir!' Thomas said and ducked down in behind a large boulder. Shielded by the wall of granite, he watched the sky lit up as eight air-to-surface missiles slammed into the Kurd's stronghold.

'Hold your positions. They're turning for a second sortie!' Thomas warned.

The roar grew louder.

Four jets appeared below the bank of clouds.

Suddenly, a barrage of surface-to-air missiles exploded directly in their path, creating a wall of fire. The two leading fighter jets burst into flames. The others swerved upwards, their metal bodies screaming, pushed to the limit by the thrust of the afterburners. They vanished into the dark clouds.

As the last pieces of debris clattered to the ground, four vertical streaks of light raced towards the rebel base. With their missiles released the pilots pulled up and headed for safety, not interested in the mayhem the missiles would cause.

A second later, two heat-seeking missiles ruptured from the mountainside, fired moments before the batteries exploded.

The jets swerved, trying to evade the locked-on projectiles. The pilots reduced their engine throttles, and as the fighters' IR signatures dropped they deployed their decoy flares. *Confused*, the surface-to-air rockets exploded harmlessly over the mountains.

The valley fell silent.

'Sir, you're still holding?' Thomas asked into his phone.

'Yes. Sounds like you have a war on your hands. Get moving. Head south. The choppers will be with you in ten minutes.'

'Wilco, Sir. Signing off.'

Three men hung back to cover their retreat. The rebels would be out for blood after the airstrike and the slaughter of their men.

A few minutes later, two camouflaged Cougar search-and-rescue helicopters popped up over the small rise. Alerted by the German's flare, the machines swooped towards them and touched down. With Thomas and the sergeant major providing covering fire, the men boarded.

Thomas, last to join them, placed his foot on the first rung. Next to his head a bullet ricochet off the armoured-plated panel of the helicopter. The enormous machine jerked upwards; the pilot hurrying to get them to safety. Thomas slipped and hit his chin on the metal floor. His teeth cut into his tongue. As the chopper rose, he grabbed the vertical handlebar inside the door, leaving him dangling in mid-air by one arm.

Hands reached out and propelled him inside.

The second helicopter, already airborne, released two missiles towards the attackers and veered right to evade enemy fire. Fleeing the scene, the pilots hugged the ground and dived over the rise before climbing to a safe cruising altitude.

'Well, tonight we'll be home,' Thomas said, in no mood to celebrate their narrow escape. That they have lost one man was bad enough, but it paled into insignificance compared to the untold number of men, women, and children who would die if they failed to find proof which could avert the war.

Although a setback, the mission was far from over.

The same force which had steeled him so many years ago in finding Klaara drove him on. He sat back and allowed the medic to attend to his wounds.

Chapter 20

Cuba

The mid-morning sun scorched Svetlana's neck. Another sweltering day, she thought, feeling relaxed after eight hours of sleep in the safety and relative comfort of the submarine.

As the pine coffin rose, gravel and dirt cascaded into the grave. Alongside her, the submarine's doctor and sixteen armed marines observed the proceedings. Their presence was reassuring; she could now complete her assignment without constantly looking over her shoulder.

Maj Gen Lukyanov's telephone conversation with the Cuban commissioner of police had resulted in a *keen willingness* by the Cuban men in uniform to assist her in any way possible. Their grumbling protest did not bother her.

A crowbar wedged in under the lid and popped out the rusty nails. The lid slid to the ground. Svetlana moved closer. A blackened torso! 'Unbelievable! This could be anybody!' she seethed. 'Doctor, we need DNA samples. Please.'

She inspected the body. Something was not right. She had known him intimately. 'Measuring tape,' she asked.

Reading the digits on the tape, she said, 'Just as I thought. This corpse is at least twenty centimetres shorter than Niall.'

'Doesn't mean much. It's badly disfigured,' Dr Lopatin cautioned. 'Only way to tell is the DNA.'

Svetlana shrugged her shoulders, frustrated, having to wait a few days for confirmation whether it was Niall. The prospect of him being alive was awful. If true, he would be out for revenge and he would have had far too much time to plan and execute whatever he had in mind.

'I've seen enough. Whenever you're ready, we can go,' she said, itching to get off the island.

If the corpse in front of her was not Niall, then the murders of the four Cubans could all be ascribed to him. Of that she was certain. She was also certain that serious repercussions would follow, executed by a lethal psychopath thirsting for blood.

Chapter 21

Dublin
Ireland

'You're too kind,' Sinead said, giving Brendan one of her enigmatic smiles, grateful for his show of chivalry. A simple gesture pulling the chair out for her, but one nonetheless. He reminded her of a forgotten era of courteous men she read of in old-fashioned romantic novels.

At last, life was changing for the better, filling her with creeping optimism. And about time too, she thought. Especially after the accident, one she would never forget. Breaking out in a cold sweat at the most unholy hour continued. Something the doctors had said would pass.

Easy for ye lot to say, but when?

'You're welcome,' Brendan beamed. 'Yikes, I'm starving. I overdid the work-out in the gym a bit…'

'And I suppose the antics in bed for afters have nothing to do with it,' Sinead joked, raising an eyebrow, warming to the passionate hour spent.

'Are you complaining?' Brendan's dark eyes glistened with pleasure, feigning disappointment. He must admit she was good – she would keep any man happy. 'I think it is the other way round… You seem insatiable.'

'Grand. Then after dinner, I'll love and leave you so you can get an early night and recover your energies. You're okay with that, Mr Walsh?'

'I respectfully decline your offer of rest, as I must attend to some rather pressing matter.'

Up to recently she had believed she would never love nor tolerate the touch of another man. A dour perception which had unexpectedly changed.

Standing in front of her at the checkout in Dunnes Supermarket, the belt laden with groceries; he had noticed her frustration. The man ahead of him was taking forever in counting out his money to pay for his purchase. Like the gentleman Brendan was, he had offered for her to jump the queue.

Slightly embarrassed, clutching a pre-cooked meal and bottle of red wine, she had declined his offer. With the last Burgundy finished, she had needed a replacement. And being single and living on her own, she did not see the point in cooking for herself. Dunnes down the road was handy enough with its ready-made meals.

But he had insisted. And that was how it had started.

Wow, that was four weeks ago! So much has happened since then, she thought. Not that she was complaining. But she found herself hurtling headlong into the unknown. Of caring about someone other than herself.

For the umpteenth time she studied his features. He was forty-five; fifteen years her senior. Perfect. Though he looked his age, his eyes told a different story. An immense sadness lay hidden behind the smiling veneer. He was obviously hurting. For a fleeting second his eyes lost their focus.

Like her, he had had his share of misfortune. Both his six-months pregnant wife and three-year-old son were killed in a car accident seventeen months ago. Having misjudged the speed of the approaching lorry, he had swung on to the national road. By some miracle he had survived having spent twelve weeks in intensive care – much to his regret. Only once had he spoken of this terrible loss.

133

With the death of her brother in a horrific car accident years ago, and soon after the passing of her parents, she understood what it meant to lose someone you love. The interminable emptiness. Never to see or hold them, or hear their laughter again. But losing a child. No.

Life can be so bitterly unfair…

Snapping out of her melancholic mood, she asked, 'And who did you rescue from the gallows today? Or, is it rather a case of: which old lady did you rob of her pension? Come on… I won't tell.'

'No, nothing that exciting.' He laughed, his eyes bright, alert again. 'Won't be a bad idea to bring back the guillotine. Then watch murders and crime disappear overnight. Fact is, today was rather miserable. Liquidation after liquidation. Most depressing to fight the system when someone is about to lose everything, knowing there is nothing to be done to salvage the situation. Okay, enough shop talk. You ready to order? By the way, the fish is supposed to be exceptional. I think I'll go for the Turbo and…'

Brendan's recommendation had been spot on. The Turbo was exquisite – she ate far too much. Well, he did say he likes a woman with a healthy appetite. A woman with curves in all the "right places", like her. Said he detested women who diet themselves until their eyes popped out of their skulls like chameleons. She must agree. Why they did was beyond her?

About to take another bite of the fruit parfait, her dessert spoon clattered to the table. She grabbed the back of her head to stop the sharp pain. Gently, her fingers massaged the scar, wary not to do any damage. They had warned her that this might happen for a while, but was nothing to worry about.

'Another headache?' Brendan asked, concerned. He reached forward and stroked her hand.

'I drank too much. An aspirin and I'll be right as rain. Ever since the accident—' too late she stopped herself.

'What accident?' Brendan asked, surprised.

'Oh, it was nothing… I'd rather not talk about it.'

'Understood. Although, sharing does help.'

134

'I know.'

'Okay. Whenever you feel like telling I'll be here… That's if you permit me?'

'My dear, careful what you wish for!' she said and smiled disarmingly. 'Say I tell and you don't like what you hear. What then? Will you disappear, as I'm sure most men would? And how will I ever survive that? Heartbroken because someone I liked dumped me.'

'Only, "I liked", not even a teeny weenie, "I loved"?' he said, putting on a sulky face.

She remained quiet. An uncomfortable silence settled between them. The restaurant was nearly empty. Only three other couples shared the subdued ambience. Embarrassed, he squirmed in his chair. He had miscalculated.

Taking a deep breath, she opened the window to her past ever so slightly. If he discovered she used to work as a sex escort and not a jeweller, he would most likely die of shock or kill her.

'Okay, here goes. Stop me if I bore you.'

Oh boy, this is going to be tricky.

'Two and a half years ago, I went on a business trip to Greece. A friend had arranged for me to buy a few diamonds at rock-bottom price. My business was floundering, so I needed a break. And I had no reason to question her judgement. So, to Mykonos I went. Everything had gone according to plan. The dealer had delivered, I had paid, and that was it. That was till we stepped outside the apartment. There they were. Six of them.

'They wouldn't let us pass, claiming the dealer had stolen the diamonds. Of course, he had denied it, calling them everything under the sun. Before I knew what was happening, he had pulled out a gun and started shooting. When they retaliated, a stray bullet had hit me, sending me reeling backwards and trip over a low wall. Someone had grabbed my ankles, breaking my fall. But in doing so, I had slammed my head into the wall. Eighteen months later, I had woken up. For a long time, I could not remember the incident, suffering partial amnesia.'

135

'Incredible,' Brendan whistled, brushing his hair back. 'That explains the scar. And your friend, did she survive this…um, skirmish?'

'Yes, she did.'

'And where did the diamonds end up?'

'She took them.'

'And they did not stop her?'

'They tried, but someone helped her get away.'

'Who? A bystander?'

'No. It was the guy in charge of these men sent to retrieve the diamonds. Imagine my shock when I recovered and learned that my best friend had married him! During the shoot-out, he had stopped a bullet meant for her. So, they fell head over heels in love. Quite romantic, don't you think? I wonder, would you do the same for me, Mr Walsh?'

'For you, I'll swim the widest ocean, climbed the highest mountain, steal the moon and cross the—'

She smiled. 'Yes, of course you would… And take a bullet?'

'To be honest, I'll do anything… Whenever, wherever,' Brendan said thoughtfully. 'Now that you know I'll die for you, back to your story. Who was this man claiming to be the rightful owner of the stones? Surely, he did not just walk away from the diamonds. Because if it were me, I would not have.'

'He was a real crook. You might have heard of him. Niall McGuire?'

'You're kidding! Not Mr McGuire, the tycoon? Yes, I remember him. Didn't he die somewhere in the Caribbean? The revelation of his business affairs and death was a big sensation. Many were glad to be rid of him, especially the politicians, as he had one of them killed. Pity he didn't knock off a few more; would have done us all a big favour.'

'Mr Walsh, you did not say that! If they know your sentiments, you'll be struck off. And then, what will we do with you?'

'Please, don't tell,' Brendan grinned.

'That depends on how you behave yourself…hmm? Anyway, I had met this Niall through work. And believe me, if I had known we were about to cross swords, I would never have gone to Mykonos. He was an evil man. Thankfully, that is in the past, and I, or rather we, can live without looking over our shoulders.'

'As I've said; you have me to protect you. And, I will let no one hurt you… Ever.'

'Thank you.' Sinead wanted to believe his words. She sat back and dabbed at the corners of her mouth with the serviette.

Beneath Brendan's relaxed demeanour was a strength which, if put to the test, would fend off most. But fiends like Niall McGuire, she doubted. Her eyes held his, wanting so much to trust him, confide in him. But she could not, not yet. It was too soon. Despite his age, he was quite naïve, Sinead thought as he continued jabbering like a boy scout, sounding rather pitiful.

'Sinead, these are not idle words. Now that I've found you, I will not let you go – unless, of course, you choose to leave,' Brendan said with a hint of remorse, dreading even an inkling of such a notion.

'Well, I have to "disappear" for a while.'

'Why?' he asked, surprised, and straightened up.

'Nothing sinister,' she added hastily. 'I promised my friend Vera, the one who went to Greece with me, to be by her side when she gives birth. I'm leaving in three days.'

'Phew, that's a relief. Thought for a second I might have scared you off.'

'Not that easily…'

'Is your friend Vera not in Ireland?'

'No, she's in Europe.'

'How about I join you? I would love to meet her,' he suggested, his eyes twinkling at the prospect.

'Sorry. Maybe next time. I want to spend some time alone with her. To catch up on girlie talk. You know.' He sagged. 'Come on, don't sulk. I'll be back before you know it.'

'Forgive me for being so presumptuous. Of course, I understand. As long as you return and not swap our lovely weather for the dreadful European sunshine.'

'Hmm, now that's a thought. Don't know how I'll survive those dreadfully warm summers?' she said and smiled. 'If you're free, would you mind dropping me off at the airport?'

'Of course. Coffee?'

'Not for me. You go ahead.'

'Right, I don't mind if I do while you tell me all about your friend. She must be quite a character to have escaped with a bag full of diamonds? Which county does she hail from?'

'Kerry,' Sinead lied, not daring to reveal more. 'Real country girl, and as tough as they come. A few years older than me, and stunning. I pale in comparison.'

'Now that, I don't believe. I can't imagine anyone more beautiful than you,' Brendan said, whistling softly. 'If she is that "stunning", the two of you must have made quite a pair.'

'I tell you; the Swiss men can count themselves lucky,' Sinead said. As the words slipped out she clasped her hand over her mouth, realising she had said too much. Nobody was supposed to know. *Vera, I'm sorry.*

Chapter 22

Dublin

Sean stood his ground, sick and tired of the same answer. 'We can't help you. Our files show no record of an Irina Mironova from Kursk. She does not exist.'

'You're wrong. See this photograph? Well, she's real. Please check again. She must be somewhere on file. She had to have had a visa to enter Ireland. And I'm sure you keep track of all your citizens visiting other countries. Maybe your records are better than my country's?'

Sean's enquiries with the home office had been a dead-end. They had no record of a visa for Irina.

'Mr O'Donovan, your *girlfriend*, Irina Mironova, lied to you. She used you and ran off with another boyfriend. Don't you think? You're not the first and won't be the last to suffer this indignity. And as for her real name, who can tell? My advice to you, my friend, forget her. I'm sure she's fine. No one else has reported her missing. Neither has a body been discovered remotely like her.'

'What about her involvement with Niall McGuire? Do you think she just made that up?'

'No, that checked out. However, as he's dead, there's no telling where she has disappeared to. Most likely swindled a bag of money out of the crook and vanished. Whoosh, gone,' the Russian Embassy official said, feigning sympathy, not in the least bit interested to assist Sean any further. He had his orders. Get rid of Sean O'Donovan in the nicest way possible and close the file.

Irina Mironova was off limits.

'You're wrong. How many times do I have to tell you she was not my girlfriend? She helped us at great personal risk, knowing that if caught, this Niall character would kill her. And I'm convinced he did just that. Therefore, I won't let it go. If you will not help, I will go to the papers. Someone may know something and might come forward,' Sean exclaimed, exasperated.

Sean firmly believed that if she were alive, she would have contacted him, or contacted his sister Sinead. But not a word. He liked her; in fact, he was crazy over her.

'Right, Mr O'Donovan, you do that. But be warned, it will serve no purpose. To be honest, you seem obsessed. And that's no way to live. It's been more than two years. Forget her. Now you must excuse me. Good day.'

'Good day to you too, and thanks for nothing,' Sean huffed and stormed out of the Russian Embassy in Dublin.

Chapter 23

FSB HQ
Moscow

The austere Neo-Baroque edifice with its yellow facade overshadowed Lubyanka Square. Because of the endless arrests during the Great Purge of the 1930s, the building had doubled in size with the addition of another floor and an extension to the rear.

Built in 1898 as the headquarters of the All-Russia Insurance Company, its basic function had never changed. It continued to serve as the home of insurance, albeit of a very different nature.

Seized by the government after the Bolshevik Revolution, it had served as the HQ of the secret police, the Cheka – subsequently renamed several times till the now-defunct KGB. It became the new institution to ensure the security of the USSR.

During those years, amidst the torture of political prisoners inside its walls, people in jest had referred to the building as the tallest in Moscow as one could "see" Siberia from its basement. And now, under the current president, a new power was in control. It was one which had developed from the ashes of the old USSR, and was no less lethal or revered than its KGB forerunner. The FSB – *Federal'naya Sluzhba Bezopasnosti* – the Federal Security Service of Russia.

Its aim was the same: to ensure the survival and safety of Russia and its people by whatever means necessary. Be it mind-control, counter-intelligence, internal and border security, counter-terrorism, or surveillance.

During any crisis, all law enforcement and counter-intelligence agencies in Russia fell under the control of the FSB, the Spetsnaz, and Internal Troops – a brutal force in fighting organised crime, terrorism, drug smuggling and neutralising foreign espionage. Thereby safeguarding the economic and financial security of the country.

Russia was the last country in the world a terrorist organisation or spy network would want to operate in. National security overruled all civil rights if and when required.

And twenty stories beneath this old structure, a new three-storey network of offices and general staff quarters existed; an impregnable, self-sustainable fortress equipped to survive any nuclear attack. It was a stronghold to conduct a war in safety. Impenetrable to eavesdropping, it was ideal to facilitate the most secretive meetings.

This fully operational underground nerve centre covered an area of three-square kilometres and linked the Kremlin with the FSB HQ on Lubyanka Square, the only access points inside Moscow. Where exactly the two 195-kilometre tunnels with their eight-coach electric trains began and ended, only a handful of high-ranking government officials shared.

In the southwest corner office on the seventh floor of the FSB Headquarters, Svetlana faced her superior. Shielded from the outside world by the armoured-plated glass windows, the flapping of a fly's wings could be heard as Maj Gen Lukyanov regarded Svetlana's bruised face.

His expression contorted into an angry scowl, as if bracing a howling winter storm. 'Next time that warden touches one of my staff, I'll wring his bloody neck! And Major, you should have told me.'

142

If my men get roughed up, it's one thing, but her, no. That is quite a different matter altogether, he scowled silently.

'Yes Sir,' she agreed, failing to see how that would have helped the investigation. She knew his temper, having witnessed it frequently enough. Luckily never directed at her. She smiled to herself at his manly bravado, coming to her rescue on a white horse. Despite his bark, he had a good heart. Since he had slipped in behind the desk of the corner office on the seventh floor a year ago, she had seen enough to know him.

'Well, just be glad nothing worse happened,' he said acquiescently. 'Right, let's get back to Niall McGuire. You think he's still alive?'

'Yes… But I have some reservations. On the one hand, everything points to him being responsible for the four murders in Cuba, and the cover-up by prison staff. Trying to kill me. The scorched body of which size and build is nothing like Niall's. The worrying thing is, if he had escaped, he would have had nearly two years to seek revenge—'

'And who would the targets be?'

'Without doubt, Sinead, Vera, Michael – Vera's husband – and of course me. The fact that we are fine casts some doubt on that theory. The DNA results should clear up any uncertainties.'

'Then let's wait for that,' Maj Gen Lukyanov said before asking, his eyebrows raised, 'Are you worried?'

'For myself, no. Getting to me won't be easy. However, I am concerned for the others.'

'You're convinced he'll come after you?'

'Yes. He doesn't enjoy losing. Most of his money was never found, so he has the means.'

'In that case, if the DNA results are negative, we'll take it that he's alive. And when we catch him, we'll shut his file for good. In the meantime, I'll arrange for some men to watch over your family.'

'Thank you, Sir.'

'Major, dot down your report and have it on my desk by the end of the day. I'll take it from there.'

'Will that be all, Sir?' She got up, ready to leave.

'Not so fast. We have a far more pressing matter. This stand-off with the Americans is getting out of hand. They're adamant in pushing ahead with the installation of their surface-to-air missiles in Poland and Ukraine. An act of aggression we cannot allow. Unless we can change the world and NATO's opinion on our alleged involvement in Turkey – NATO's excuse for the immediate deployment of the missiles – war will be inevitable. But we might have a break.'

'What may that be, Sir?'

'A cell of our field-operatives investigating the explosion in Turkey reported an attack two days ago on a rebel base near the Georgian border. Some intercepted messages lead me to believe this group may know who carried out the attack on the gas pipeline.'

'You think this might not be our doing?'

'I would like to think so,' Maj Gen Lukyanov said. His gut told him something was going on. For the past two months he had been excluded from his superior's meetings with High Command. 'As we speak, my men are on their way to this base. Therefore, you'll be joining them on Wednesday. Major Vadim Denisov and Lieutenant Pavel Prokhorov will support you on this mission. Your flight departs at 22h00 from Kubinka Air Force Base. You'll parachute in and gather whatever intel you can. Major, find out what the hell is going on.'

'I'll do my best, Sir.'

'I'm counting on that.'

'Any theories, Sir?'

'Yes, but I rather not speculate. And a word of warning. Keep your thoughts to yourself, don't discuss them with the major and lieutenant.' He hated sending her into the field; it was far too dangerous, but he trusted few other than her. 'Report in tomorrow for your briefing and kit-out, 08h00 sharp. That is all Major.'

'Sir, I have a request. I want to visit my daughter before I leave for Turkey.'

'Of course. You have till Wednesday evening.'

'The problem is, she's staying for a few weeks with my parents in Kursk. I was planning to—'

'Major, are you suggesting I put the war on hold while you attend to your private affairs?' Maj Gen Lukyanov interrupted with a twinkle in his dark eyes. Where she was concerned, he was like an old dog: all bark and no bite. After all, he was not carved out of stone.

'No, of course not. I would never be so presumptuous as to even think that. I was wondering whether I may leave after the briefing and report back on Wednesday,' Svetlana said, not having missed the expression in the deputy director's eyes.

'Granted. As long as you're here for your flight.'

Emphatically married to his desk, loving the daily excitement and intrigue of the world of espionage and counter-espionage, he found himself single and alone. There was no point in being with a woman who did not share in his dreams. So, for now, personal ambitions and needs could wait. Regarded in today's world as still in the prime at forty-eight, there was enough time to find someone new.

Highly intelligent and well-educated, he was one of the chosen few *young* nationalists whose first task was to reverse the effects of the silent war waged against Russia.

One casualty of this war he regretted was his marriage. Two years ago his wife had left, unable to live with a man she never saw – someone committed to saving his country. Taking their two teenage daughters with her, she had found a more placid existence in the arms of someone else.

Back behind her desk, Svetlana checked the availability of flights to Kursk. She was in luck and re-booked her flight, departing noon the following day, and returning at 18h00 on Wednesday. The extra charge levied for the change was extortionate. But she did not care, willing to pay anything to see her child, for however short a time.

On impulse she picked up the framed photo on her desk. Dasha, barely four years old, was the closest to a living doll she had ever seen. She was a miniature replica of her and the father: dark eyes like his, porcelain skin like hers, and a full lock of light auburn hair.

Yes, missy, you'll be trouble one day – the boys better watch out. Svetlana smiled, her heart becoming all mushy.

Like her, her parents also doted over Dasha; their only grandchild. For them she had been a gift from heaven. Although she could never replace their eldest daughter.

The terrible circumstances her sister had endured during her last few years had made her passing so much more painful. Her parents had never come to terms with her death.

Filled with great hopes and with her work permit in hand, to be employed as a translator in Niall McGuire's company, her sister had left Russia. But on arrival in Dublin, she had been drugged and thrown into a brothel. After two years of suffering, she had escaped. And as she was about to enter the Russian embassy in London, they had snatched her off the pavement. A few days later, her mutilated body had been discovered in a skip in London's East End.

Svetlana replaced the photograph and turned her attention to the post and memos on her desk. Nothing urgent; it could wait till she got back. She still had to compile the report as ordered.

But first things first.

She rang her parents with the new itinerary.

At 16h00, she dropped the file documenting events in Cuba on the deputy director's desk. Not having fully recovered from her trip, she focused on a quick exit. She needed a good night's sleep. But her plan evaporated as Maj Gen Lukyanov indicated for her to sit down.

'Irina Mironova, we have unfinished business in Ireland,' he said in a measured voice.

Surprised hearing her alias Irina and Ireland, her smile disappeared. 'Is it him?' she asked.

'No, no, calm yourself, *Irina*. This has nothing to do with Niall,' he reassured her. 'It appears you made quite an impression on a certain young man – someone extremely concerned about your well-being.'

146

'Sean…? Still on his crusade to rescue me?'

'Seems so, Major. Dublin informed me he wants to go to the press. It is time we put him out of his misery, don't you think? He won't feel a thing.'

'Better not,' she laughed. 'I just can't understand why he's so persistent? We met twice, briefly. And exchanged a few messages while he tried to locate his sister in Greece.'

'You mean to say you don't know why he hasn't given up on you?'

'No Sir.'

'Do yourself a favour, Major. Next time you look in the mirror, try to imagine how men might perceive you.'

'Oh…' she mustered.

'Right then. Any suggestions what we'll do about Sean O'Donovan? We can't let him go to the press.'

'Not quite sure. I haven't given it much thought.'

'In that case, I'll inform the Embassy you died seven months ago during a nightclub shoot-out amongst two rival gangs. One of three innocent bystanders, killed in the crossfire. And why your name does not appear on any records is because you used an alias, as many girls do. Your real name was, um…Oksana Semyonova. Yes, that's got a nice ring to it.

'And thanks to his insistence and the photograph he had left at the embassy, some agent had tracked you down… What are you grinning about? I said something funny? You're not happy with Oksana Semyonova? Or is it something else you would like to share?'

'No, nothing, Sir. Please continue,' Svetlana replied.

'Right, where was I? Oh yes. "We are sorry for your loss, etc, etc. Therefore, it would be best you forget Irina ever existed." Major, if you're happy with that, I'll forward the details before he shoots his mouth off.'

'That's fine, Sir. By the way, I had no intention of contacting him,' she admitted, regretting not having dealt with him sooner. But who was to know he would be so persistent? 'He's nice. And I'm sure he'll make someone very happy one day. But that was never going to be me.'

147

Chapter 24

Turkish Airspace

The blue glow radiating from the bulkhead's nightlights bathed the plane in an eerie air of anticipation. In the near dark, the twelve Special Forces Commandos, members of the KSK (*Kommando Spezialkrafte*) of the German Armed Forces, and their commander, Colonel Thomas Bauer, sat in silence. Unrecognisable in their Ops-Core helmets – an all-in-one-unit fitted with oxygen masks – they waited for the signal to execute a High-Altitude High Opening (HAHO) jump.

Free-falling six hundred metres, they would rely on their wrist-mounted altimeters to end a three-second dive, and regroup in loose formation at nine thousand metres altitude. The cloud cover, mountainous and unfamiliar terrain ruled out a High-Altitude Low Opening (HALO) jump. They had no choice but to drift in from a much greater height and brave over minus twenty-five degrees Celsius temperatures.

Despite each man having completed over a hundred jumps, the ever-present dangers of combustion, hypoxia, canopies tangling or failing to open, and detection from the ground could not be ignored. Even in the event of them landing unhurt, the possibility of someone getting the bends existed because of gaseous nitrogen: the formation of gas bubbles on the nerves, resulting in possible neurological damage or death.

By now the hour of pre-breathing hundred per cent aviation oxygen had flushed out most of the nitrogen from their bloodstreams. They were ready.

Debriefed on their return from Turkey, and declared medically fit, they had embarked upon their next mission: enter Georgia by stealth and catch the Russian colonel.

After a good night's sleep, avoiding alcohol and gas-forming foods, they had spent the day formulating a reasonable plan of action.

Fortunately, their sortie into Turkey had delivered far better results than a disheartened Thomas and his men first believed. The Intel extracted from the Kurdish rebels – the colonel's escape route and means of transport – had resulted in satellite surveillance picking up Col Polyakov's convoy along the road from Tortum to Artvin, racing towards the Georgian border.

When German Intelligence at NATO HQ, Allied Force Command Heidelberg had first spotted the three white 4x4s, they had not been too sure it was their target. But once the convoy had transited Hopa, their confidence had grown tenfold. Fifteen kilometres south of the border town of Sarpi, the convoy had turned on to a minor road, travelled one-hour east, cut across the open countryside and slipped undetected into Georgia.

Tracking them, the eye in the sky had monitored their arrival at a remote monastery in the mountains east of Batumi. There, a unit of soldiers had welcomed the ten passengers. The illusive colonel was amongst them.

Thomas's squad, briefed and armed with digital-images detailing their target, intended to pick up the Russian as soon as he would venture outside the monastery. Failing that, they would penetrate the building the following evening and abduct him from his bed.

Since establishing the location of the Russians, a team of intelligence personnel had worked around the clock to gather and analyse as much intel as possible. Up to that point, no one had known of the base's existence. Therefore, they desperately needed the compound's strength, defences, and rotas.

Time was critical. They could not allow the colonel and his men to slip into Russia. The race would be lost if that happened.

Above the men's heads, an orange light blinked three times. Ten minutes remained. The Jump Master gave his first order over the intercom system installed inside the men's helmets. 'Pre-jump checks, now!'

With all straps and weapons tested, the Ops-Core helmet visors shut.

Thomas's mask fitted securely, allowing no movement, permitting the safe feed of pure oxygen.

Before dressing in their flight-suits, he, like the others, had a close-shave. Oxygen, classified as a non-flammable gas, worked like an oxidiser in rocket fuel if mixed with organic materials, speeding up combustion. Therefore, friction inside the mask could not be risked; beard stubble and moustaches were forbidden. Greasy foods which might leave a layer of oil in the mouth, had been avoided.

Ready, the men lined up in pairs.

Next, an instruction to activate their bailout bottles sounded – a process whereby oxygen was forced into their lungs to counteract the lower air pressure encountered at such extreme altitudes. A quick check by the Jump Master confirmed enlargement of the men's eyes. The bailouts were functioning correctly.

The dead of the night concealed the Luftwaffe insignia of the converted commercial Airbus A310MRT (multi-role transporter) as it continued its cleared flight-path: chartered commercial flight UTH 415. Destination, Yerevan, Armenia.

Like a deep roll of thunder the plane cut through the freezing air at an altitude of 9 200 metres above the Black Sea. On schedule they entered Turkish airspace thirty kilometres south of the Georgian border. The pilot eased back on the controls, dropped the speed to 280 knots, and opened the rear door.

Two minutes till the men would dive out and glide sixty kilometres through the night sky. The intended landing zone was a riverbank outside Keda, a settlement forty-one kilometres east of the coastal regional town of Batumi.

For seven of the team this would be their second HAHO jump in a fortnight. And the first for the six men who had joined them in the Bavarian village of Calw in the Baden-Wurttemberg district, home of the KSK.

'Disconnect hoses, now!' the Jump Master ordered.

'Checked, checked, checked,' echoed the men's voices on the speaker, confirming release from the plane's oxygen supply – tubes attached to their chest-mounted receptacles.

'Clear to go. Go, go, go!' the Jump Master bellowed.

Thomas and Lieutenant Bernd Schmidt raced through the open door. Followed by the rest of the unit, the bundle of men disappeared into the dark, whisked away at 280 knots per hour.

Falling at 300 kilometres per hour, Thomas, assisted by the drogue canopy, controlled his turns, and navigated towards the landing zone. Fifteen seconds into the fall his main canopy opened with a jerk, ending the free-fall. There would be no communications amongst the jumpers till they would be safely on the ground.

For Thomas, it was a jump a world apart from the first paraglider sortie he did thirty-four years ago, entering the USSR on his own. Now he was armed, well trained, and not alone.

At three-minute intervals the men touched down on the wide sandy riverbank. Gathering their paragliders they vanished into the undergrowth. As soon as the sixth commando's feet hit the ground, three men sauntered toward the sleeping town of Keda.

With the last team-member accounted for they scrambled up the embankment. Hiding in the shadows next to the road, they waited for their transport. But luck was not on their side.

By the time the last of the three "borrowed" cars pulled up, they were fifty minutes behind schedule.

Leaving the Batumi main road, they followed the winding mountain path past the settlement of Chinkadzeebi. The road was quiet. Three kilometres south of the monastery they turned into the snow-covered woods and concealed the cars. Batumi and the Black Sea were eleven kilometres to the west.

On foot they continued deeper into the woods and set up a Temporary Patrol Base (TPB), confident no one would stumble into them. Not many would venture into the woods at night with brown bears, wolves, and wild boars in the area. But they could not rule out hunters or a patrol from the compound prowling around in the dark.

The latest update from HQ confirmed the situation unchanged at the monastery. No-one had left in the past hour. The six Mi-35M attack helicopters sitting in the levelled field north of the compound had not moved. Neither did the twelve Didgori-II armoured multi-role and special operations vehicles. Nor the Russian's three white 4x4s parked inside the compound. Only one of the six camouflaged Toyota Land Cruisers had departed forty minutes ago with two Georgian occupants. Therefore, Col Polyakov and his men must still be present.

Making swift progress inside the treeline, Thomas and nine men approached the monastery. As the building came into view, two men peeled off and took up a position next to the road, monitoring all movement. The rest of the men split up and covered the sides and rear of the compound, and the airfield.

Hidden in the trees near the T-junction leading to the east-facing main entrance, Thomas and Corporal Hans Krüger kept their eyes peeled. The lane was two hundred metres long with all vegetation cleared sixty metres on either side. The manned roadblock approximately two-thirds of the way down prevented them from moving closer.

Thomas hated killing time, wanting to complete the mission. He took a deep breath and sat back. They could be stuck there for days, not knowing when the Russians would venture outside the monastery.

Through his night-vision binoculars he scrutinised the three-storey structure, searching for a way in. The satellite images had given them a detailed layout of the complex and visible defences. But it was not enough.

The new roof to the north and west was proof that the monastery had recently doubled in size. The original building used to be a simple L-shape before it was converted into an eighty-metre square structure. Based on the movement of men recorded during the day, they had been able to determine the usage of sections of the compound. But assumptions like these were inherently flawed, and therefore could not to be relied on.

Studying the structure in real-time, Thomas was certain of one thing: the modified monastery was an impenetrable military fortress.

The satellite images had revealed the periphery of the compound consisting of four, twelve-metre-wide structures with tiled pitched roofs – the innocuous dormer windows were most likely reinforced defensive positions. These wings probably accommodated the staff's quarters, offices, training rooms, and stores.

A twenty-metre long, two-storey structure jutted into the larger courtyard, creating two minor enclosures where a few military vehicles were parked. Inside the entrance – a set of four-metre-high solid gates – was a six-storey tower. Small, high-level windows broke the top of the otherwise blank external walls.

Thomas fully appreciated what they faced, although still puzzled why they had no record of this base. Or any intel on which unit was stationed there.

The reports from his men confirmed only two visible access points: the main entrance plus the six-metre-wide gate leading to the helicopter landing pads and three hangars. It was an area guarded by eight sentries and two guard towers at the far end of the fenced-off field.

*

With no easy way in, their plan to extract the Russian under cover of darkness was madness.

Chapter 25

Monday
Kursk, Russia

On the outskirts of Kursk, a provincial city of 426 000 inhabitants located 450km south of Moscow, the single-storey house at 28 Zarechnaya Street was dark. The curtains were firmly shut. There was no car in the driveway. The place felt deserted. Not a good sign, Sergeant Vladimir Alexeev thought.

Why was the driveway empty? the two Kursk Special Task Force officers in the unmarked car wondered. Were the occupants asleep and had no car? Or was the car useless and in for a service? Or were they away for a few days?

Most likely the latter, they decided. But it would be wise to check.

Twenty-five minutes earlier, Sgt Alexeev and Private Anatoly Ozerov had received instruction to carry out a low-key surveillance on this property. An order shouted at them by an extremely irate commander, hoping the Nikolaevi couple and their granddaughter were safely in bed. The man had been deeply troubled. He had reason to be.

Maj Gen Lukyanov, Deputy Director Counter-Intelligence FSB HQ Moscow, had to wait four hours for his urgent call requesting immediate assistance to be complied with.

Understandably, the deputy director had not been pleased, threatening unimaginable consequences if anything untoward would befall this family.

The phone of the commander of the Special Task Force Unit stationed in Kursk had been switched off while spending four hours with his mistress. A slip of duty he might live to regret.

Under Government Security Regulation CV0361/92, all commanders must always be contactable. If one transgressed, the penalty could have disastrous consequences. In a time of national crisis, deserting one's post was an act equal to treason. But a glimmer of hope shone for the commander. That this was a personal favour by the deputy director for a member of staff and not one of a national crisis, some might perceive as an abuse of office.

Unaware of the possible ramifications of the recon, Sgt Alexeev and Pte Ozerov exited the car at exactly 23h35. They approached the front door. It was locked. They circled the house, inspecting the windows and rear door. They found no signs which could be construed as suspicious. No evidence of a crime committed.

Sgt Alexeev jerked his head in the direction of the car to report their findings. Crossing the vacant parking space, Pte Ozerov grabbed the sergeant's arm and shone the light on the cobblestone driveway. On the fresh oil stain.

'They could be out visiting. Come to think of it, it's Monday and with work tomorrow, it's unlikely,' Sgt Alexeev said. 'Nor could they be on a trip as the child's mother is due to arrive tomorrow midday. That leaves one possibility: the old car is in the garage with an oil leak, and they're at home fast asleep. Figures.'

'Yeah…' Pte Ozerov agreed half-heartedly. Something didn't feel right.

Relieved by the news, their commander sighed. 'Thank you, men. Good work,' he said. Deep down he did not care about this babysitting request from Moscow. It had spoiled his evening. 'You know the routine. Keep a safe distance. No need to announce your presence to anyone, and don't disturb this family.'

'Sir, I suggest we put out an APB on their car. If they're out, someone may spot them. In the meantime, it would be wise to check if they're in: wrong address scenario, etc.,' Sgt Alexeev said.

'Roger. Go ahead, but be quick. I'm not sitting around here all night. I have better things to do.'

Twenty minutes later, Sgt Alexeev radioed HQ. 'Sir, we've been inside. They're not there.'

'Any sign of foul play?' their commander asked, unable to hide his anxiety.

'No, not that we can tell. We'll give it one hour and if they're not back by then, we'll turn the place upside down.'

'If you find anything you think I need to know, call me on my mobile.'

'Copy, Sir,' Sgt Alexeev said and looked at his watch: 00h30hrs.

The two agents waited in the car, the front windows slightly down to stop the windscreen from misting over. They needed an unimpeded view of the house in case someone turned-up.

An hour's drive east of Kursk, the snow-covered winding road was deserted. Suddenly, the car swerved violently, barely avoiding the large wild boar in the middle of the road. The driver lost control. The next instant the car disappeared into the ravine. Colliding with the smooth round boulders lining the river below, it burst into flames and exploded, blowing its passengers into a thousand pieces. Amidst the crackling sound of fire, their smouldering remains lay scattered along the riverbank.

It was thirty-five minutes past midnight.

Chapter 26

Monday, Midnight
Dublin

Sinead released the clip and let her hair fall free. She pushed him towards the bed. Their lips touched as her leg slipped through the slit of the black silk dress. He fell back and pulled her on top of him. Hungrily his hands caressed her thighs. He wanted her.

She pulled free, teasing him. She was in no hurry; they had all night. Light as a butterfly her lips flitted over his chin. She removed his tie and unbuttoned his shirt. With her warm breath on his skin, her mouth slowly moved down over his chest. Her hands moved expertly, touching him, stirring his desires...

As a prelude to this erotic encounter, they had spent the evening wining and dining; an unforgettable experience once more. One far greater than she could ever have hoped for.

During the four hours he had danced to her every whim, desperate to please. Together they had leisurely dwelt in each other's pasts, shared in their dreams of a future together, and exulted in the present as the two-carat brilliant-cut round diamond had sparkled on her left hand.

The ring had been a huge surprise; the last thing she had expected was to be proposed to. They hardly knew each other. But she did not hesitate and had accepted with tears in her eyes. At last, a future… A new life awaited her. She would be a mother with her own family. Her days as escort would soon be a distant memory. A secret she would take to her grave. Brendan must never know.

Swept along by the occasion, they both had drunk far too much. Neither cared. They were happy. By the time they had climbed into the taxi, they could not wait to reach her apartment and spend the night in each other's arms.

The thought of having to get up early in the morning had niggled as she did not dare oversleep; Aer Lingus flight AE 072 for Geneva, Switzerland departed at 08h15. Therefore, she must check-in before 07h00. She would barely manage a few hours of sleep.

Having to leave him behind had tempted her to phone Vera and postpone her visit. But being the sister Vera had never had, she had vowed to be there when the baby would arrive. Not being present would be unforgivable. But what if she took Brendan with her?

No, can't do. Next time.

The Irish weather was as expected on a winter's morning: grey with a sharp bite in the northerly wind. Sinead wrapped her coat tight around her shoulders. Tucked in under Brendan's arm, they hurried towards the entrance below the pedestrian bridge.

'I'll be lucky if I make it!' she gasped, annoyed.

'Don't worry, you'll make it. Again, I'm sorry. Am I forgiven?'

'Well… Okay. You just better hope I board this flight.'

'This way, quick,' Brendan said, looking up at the display board. 'Well, no need to. The flight's delayed. We could have stayed in bed longer.'

'Now you're pushing your luck, Mr Walsh.'

Ten minutes later, Sinead was ready to board.

'How about a coffee while you wait?' Brendan suggested.

'I'd rather not, in case the plane leaves earlier.'

'Yes, you're right,' Brendan agreed, adding, 'I'll miss you.'

159

'And me, you too,' Sinead confessed with a tinge of sadness. 'I'll be back on Sunday…'

'Please call when you get there. And remember, if you need me, call and I'll be on the first available flight.'

'Don't worry, I'll call as soon as I'm in Lauenen,' Sinead said, and gave him a sensual kiss, ignoring the queue of travellers gawking at them.

She tore herself away and proceeded through security. Placing her handbag on the plastic tray she looked at him. He seemed so alone. She could not recall the last time she had felt so miserable leaving someone behind.

Chapter 27

10h35, Tuesday
Moscow

Svetlana's fingers drummed on her desk; she wanted confirmation before leaving for Kursk. The briefing and kit-out for her mission to north-east Turkey had ended five minutes ago. There was still time to make the call before grabbing a taxi to the airport.

'Dimitri Danilovich, when will the DNA results be available?' she asked.

Patiently, the head of the Genetic Science Department of the FSB replied, 'Svetlana, it will be at least another thirty hours. Working with bone and teeth samples to establish DNA is a lot more complicated than an oral swab sample.'

'Is there no way to get it sooner?'

'Not if you want to be a hundred per cent certain.'

Disappointed, she ended the call. An answer before going to Turkey would have eased her mind considerably. Was Niall McGuire dead or alive? She needed her head cleared of unnecessary worries when going on a mission, especially one so important.

14h20, Kursk Airport

Are they stuck in traffic…? Svetlana wondered. Her calls and messages remained unanswered. She paced up and down the

161

pavement in front of the main terminal building. It was not like her dad to be late.

After forty minutes she hailed a taxi. Armed with her overnight bag and some gifts bought at Moscow Airport, she gave the driver her parent's address.

For Dasha, there was a cute white cuddly rabbit. For her father, Konstantin, a new tie. And for her mother, Marina, some Russian Bird Milk cake. She would most likely scowl, claiming it would ruin her figure, then on her own enjoy every morsel of the sponge base souffle with white mousse and chocolate glazing.

Turning on to Zarechnaya Street the house where she had spent her childhood came into view. No car? Don't tell me I've missed them, she fretted. Mobile phones can be such a let-down.

The spare key was in its usual place underneath the metre-high stone-carved African statue on the porch – the sculpture, a gift by some colleagues bought in Kenya. Considering the icy winters in Kursk, she always thought the near-naked old man was somewhat out of place. But her parents liked it standing boldly on the front porch, weathering the storms.

She entered the hallway, dropped her bag on the floor and glanced at the sideboard, expecting to find a note explaining the confusion. Where they could be.

Strange, she thought. Searching the house she drifted from one room to the next. The beds were perfectly made. The kitchen was tidy; the fridge filled with food. But no simmering pots on the stove and nothing in the oven? Did they plan to take her to a restaurant? Highly unlikely. She told her mother she wanted to spend every hour at home. She did not want to eat out. Her mother would do nothing to displease her. She never did.

No note to be found anywhere…

What's going on? She felt uneasy.

By now, they would have been to the airport or called. She checked her phone. It was still on. No messages or missed calls.

162

In Dasha's room she placed the soft toy on her bed next to the row of smiling animals and sleeping dolls. A deep sense of loneliness filled her. There must be a simple explanation. Maybe the neighbours knew something; they usually did.

The doorbell's gentle chime floating through the empty rooms of the house interrupted her thoughts. She hurried to open the front door. Two grim-faced men in civilian clothes looked at her.

'Good afternoon, Major Svetlana Nikolaeva,' the one greeted.

'Yes…'

'I am Sgt Alexeev. My colleague, Pte Ozerov. We're from the FSB Special Task Force, Kursk.'

'Of course,' she said, easing her tone. They must be the protection the general had promised. 'May I see some IDs, please?' she asked, not liking the sombre faces.

Obligingly, they produced their identity cards as Sgt Alexeev asked, 'May we come in?'

She stood aside.

Sgt Alexeev closed the door behind him. He shuffled his feet uncomfortably and cleared his throat. 'I don't quite know how to say this…' He paused and cleared his throat again. 'There has been an accident, and based on the evidence collected at the scene, it involves your parents—'

'What do you mean?' Svetlana interrupted. 'Are they hurt? Where are they?'

'No, Major—'

'So, where are they?' she repeated.

'They were killed. The car had exploded on…'

Svetlana did not hear the rest of the sentence. She turned away, entered the lounge, and sat down on the couch.

'And Dasha? Where is my child?' she asked, already knowing the answer.

'Unfortunately, no one survived,' Sgt Alexeev said.

At the morgue the sight of her parents' and Dasha's charcoaled remains had wrenched her soul from her chest.

163

And the crushed toddler's skull had sent a dagger pierce her heart.

Sgt Alexeev and Pte Ozerov flanked her sides as she got out of the car. Her eyes were red and puffy. She did not care what they thought. Stubbornly, she put one foot in front of the other, not feeling the ground beneath her feet. She had shunned the general's words, suggesting she should stay at home and rest. No, she had to see the place which took them from her.

Feeling somewhat guilty, the men next to her did not say a word. Could they have prevented this tragedy? No, they were not to be blamed. It was fate and nothing else. The wild boar's mutilated carcass flung into the shrubs next to the road was enough proof of what had transpired. Her father must have over-reacted by trying to avoid the animal, swerved too wildly on the icy road, and crashed into the ravine.

Minding the tracks, Svetlana stopped short of the long skid marks, cutting through the snow like striking serpents. Her eyes followed the lines. It ended abruptly at a metre-high lump of snow and clay. Acting like a launching pad, the car had been catapulted through the air and crashed into the bottom of the ravine.

She rubbed her eyes and wiped away her tears as she walked to the edge of the road. Staring into the abyss where the smashed and burnt pieces of her parents' car lay, she sank to her knees. Refusing to tear herself away, she cried, 'My baby, Mama, Papa… Why?'

And so she remained. Alone, lost in a world which had shown her no gratitude.

Behind her the two agents kept their distance and concentrated on fending off nosey passers-by. A BMW 4x4 slowed down and pulled off the road. They approached the driver, ready to send him on his way. A man in his late forties climbed out, exchanged a subdued greeting, and introduced himself. They allowed him to pass.

A hand touched Svetlana's shoulder. 'Don't be alarmed, it's me,' the man said, and fell silent. She did not move away and placed her hand on top of his.

The news of the tragedy had shocked Major General Ivan Lukyanov. Why Svetlana was being punished like this was beyond him. He knew she had no-one left, therefore he had hurried to her side.

Svetlana turned her head and looked at him, searchingly…

He lifted her up and embraced her. She buried her face in his chest. Her shoulders heaved uncontrollably as she let her grief run its course.

Across the kitchen table, Svetlana gazed despondently at the silence which draped itself like a cloak of lead over her hunched shoulders, weighing her down. She did not touch the glass of vodka. For an instant her eyes held his.

Ivan's rugged face showed no emotion as he maintained his composure. For two hours he had shared in her sorrow, kept his distance.

By nature, not a man glib of tongue, least of all one to utter false, meaningless gibberish, he refrained from speaking. In the days to come she would undoubtedly receive her fair share of empty words by well-meaning sympathisers. What words of condolence could he pose?

Don't worry, it was just a huge mistake. They're fine and will be home soon. Or, let's get you back to work and you'll soon be your jolly old self. No point in mourning. What's done is done, etc., etc.

No. Frivolous words, however well-intended, would not ease her pain. Of one thing he was certain, she would not be going anywhere soon. The two agents would have to do without her in Turkey.

There were the funeral arrangements to take care of and to cater for her family's arrival. Two aunts and a few cousins were expected in the morning to help.

The front door opened. Two pairs of footsteps. Sgt Alexeev and Pte Ozerov entered the lounge. Ivan got up and asked, 'And?'

'One neighbour mentioned the arrival of four visitors late last night. We have nothing else,' Sgt Alexeev said.

'Continue,' Ivan snapped, not impressed. He wanted to get to the bottom of what had happened.

165

'They did not stay long. About fifteen minutes, Sir.'

'Wonder why? Any idea who they were?'

'No Sir. They couldn't ID anyone. It was too dark. When they left, the Nikolaevis had followed them in their car.'

'Did any of the visitors join the Nikolaevis?'

'No Sir, not that they could recall.'

'Would receiving late visitors and them leaving at such an odd hour be unusual?'

'Yes Sir. They thought it strange. Her parents kept to themselves most of the time. Not many visitors.'

Ivan's frown deepened. Something was wrong. 'Get your commander on the phone.'

Two minutes later, he issued his orders to the perplexed local commander. 'It's time to start over. I suspect your men missed some crucial evidence. Cordon the accident-site off, and fine-comb every square millimetre again.'

'Again?'

'Yes, again. Are you deaf or just playing dumb? Your men shall check under every shrub, rock, stone, and what's left of the car. This they'll do for an area of no less than five hundred metres of the road either side of the accident. Even the damned wild boar – hopefully, some animals haven't devoured it by now. Get to it and let the lab analyse each item found. Do I make myself clear?'

'Yes, Major General.'

'Also, I need a team of your best men over here. I expect them within fifteen minutes. This house needs to be turned upside down.'

'Why the change of heart?' the commander asked.

'No, there is no change of heart on my side. Merely a case of murder. Maybe it is your heart which is in the wrong place? Your men arrived too late last night. Until I learn otherwise, that is what the record will show. Commander, you have failed me,' Ivan growled. 'Report your findings directly to me and to no one else. Understood?' he added, trying to fathom the consequences of his words if proven correct. He had issued his instructions early enough.

'Svetlana, it is imperative we talk,' Ivan whispered.

His tone was most unnerving. 'Is something wrong?' she asked, fearing more bad news.

'Maybe nothing, but we have to make sure.'

Her eyes opened wide as she listened to him. She jolted upright. 'That never occurred to me. I better check.'

His large hand stopped her. 'Are you sure you're up for this?'

'I am,' Svetlana replied. 'Old friends visiting late at night? No.'

Chapter 28

Tuesday
Lauenen, Switzerland

Like a conveyor belt transporting a never-ending supply of coloured gemstones on to a brilliant-white spoil heap, the ski lifts carried passengers up the piste outside Gstaad. The thirty centimetres of fresh snow had attracted ski-enthusiast to revel in the scenic setting in the Swiss mountains.

Sinead was remarkably cheerful. And why not? Engaged, and now on her way to see her best friend give birth. The sun shone. People were enjoying themselves once more after the lockdowns. And no boss to report to – master of her own destiny. It felt good to be free, to be alive, and deeply in love.

Lazily, the taxi climbed the narrow lane to Vera and Michael's modest chalet above Lauenen, five kilometres south of Gstaad. Situated on the Southwest slopes of the Giferspitz, it had breath-taking views of the 3100metres tall Wildhorn and lower Gelternhorn mountains.

Deep in conversation with Vera, Sinead asked excitedly, 'Any sign of the little darling?'

'No, she's too comfortable. Maybe she'll decide to say hello in the next few hours. Hope so, I can't wait!'

'Poor you. It's not going to be an easy birth by the sounds of it. Blame that big oaf next to you,' Sinead said laughingly. 'Shall I come straight over?'

'No. Make yourself at home first and when you're ready, we'll send the car to collect you. Just don't take too long, one can never tell. Our housekeeper, Sarah, will let you in and show you to your room.'

'So sorry for being late. My flight was delayed. Anyway, I have some wonderful news.'

'What?'

'No, guess.'

'I'll be giving birth any second now and you're playing silly games.'

'I'm engaged!'

'I don't believe you! Really?'

'I swear. Last night Brendan proposed out of the blue. I'm soooo…happy!' Sinead shrieked with excitement, ignoring the dour looks of the Swiss taxi driver.

'Congratulations, that's wonderful! When will we meet him?'

'Next visit. He wanted to come, but I thought better not.'

'Pity. We could have had a double celebration.'

'Give me half an hour and I'll be ready. You hang in there. Bye,' Sinead replied.

Yes, Vera was right. Her words added to Sinead's jubilant mood. No reason not to enjoy life again, to be happy. Nothing and no-one would take that away from her.

The taxi slowed, turned into the private driveway, and stopped in front of the security gate. The driver rolled his window down and buzzed the house. As the gate swung open, neither of them noticed the 4x4 sneak up and slip through the gate before it could shut.

It took another thirty metres before the driver commented on the silver vehicle closing in on them. 'You're not the only visitor by the look of things.'

Surprised, Sinead turned around. Seeing the 4x4 careen towards them, she rang Vera. 'Are you expecting any other visitors? Someone owning a silver Lexus 4x4.'

'No, not that I know of. Why?'

'Because one followed us into your driveway.'

'Hang on, I'll ask Michael.'

In the background, Sinead heard Michael's response, clear and decisive. 'No. Tell Sinead to make a U-turn and head for the police station in town. And to stop for no one. I'll meet her there!'

'You got that, Sinead?'

'Yes, I did. I will see—'

She did not finish her sentence as a bullet sliced through the rear window, exploding the driver's head, splattering her with blood and brain tissue. Sinead screamed. The car lurched forward. As the driver's body slumped over the steering wheel his foot pressed down on the accelerator. It swerved off the road and crashed into the embankment.

Stuck in the ditch, the rear-door window disintegrated, covering Sinead with glass. An arm reached inside, unlocked the door, swung it open, and pulled her out. There were three of them, their heads covered. Forced towards the Lexus, she did not resist; it was pointless. Meekly, she climbed inside, her shoulders drooping.

'Give me your fucking phone!' a voice demanded.

Sinead did not respond and clung to her phone. She could not recall the Irish voice.

Someone wrenched it from her hand.

'They've got my phone!' she shouted, hoping Vera could hear her.

Seated behind the steering wheel, Larry spoke into the phone. The line was dead. He redialled the last number: Vera's. The answering service stated, "The number you have dialled is currently unavailable". 'The bitch's phone is off. Most likely ripped out the batteries.'

He swung the 4x4 around and raced back to the shut gate. Slamming the brakes, Seamus jumped out in search of the override switch next to the gate's motor. As the gate rolled open, Larry drummed his fingers on the steering wheel, urging it to roll faster on its track. 'Come on, come on!'

If they were to complete the first phase of their plan, they must reach Gstaad before the roads would be sealed off. If not, they'd be trapped and the second part of their plan would not happen. The diamonds would stay with Vera and the rat Michael; the man targeted to die next.

Larry knew there won't be sixty-five million euros left. Not with the chalet and everything else they had bought. But there should still be enough. Their payday had been a long time coming. Watching Sinead had paid off. And now they had Vera in their sight as well.

And the third and final part of the plan would be carried out immaterial whether the second one would succeed.

Turning on to the public road, Larry removed his hood and powered towards Gstaad. Focussing on the road, he asked, 'Sinead, where are Vera and Michael?'

With the mention of her friends' names, the voice and face returned. Larry, Niall's stooge. How could I have been so stupid, having led him to Vera? What was I thinking, believing they'd all disappeared? 'I don't know, you pig.'

'Aha, you're back. Welcome princess, it's been a long time. You must have thought we crawled into a hole and died? Big mistake,' Larry said, ignoring her show of defiance. 'You and your friends' days of drinking champagne in the Alps are over. We'll teach you to be a good old-fashioned whore again. We can all do with some fun, not only that jerk, Brendan.'

'I'm so scared, boohoo. If anything happens to me, believe me, Michael and Brendan will kill you.'

'Brave words, princess. Jeezus, you are thick, ain't ya! We're not playing games,' he said, fed up, not interested in continuing the bickering. He must stick to the plan. At Saanen airport a private jet sat ready for take-off.

Regarding Sinead's future; she would soon find out how much Vera and Michael valued her friendship. Larry had no doubts they would exchange the stones in a flash for her safe return.

Vera and Michael immediately knew someone from the past had resurfaced. Having followed Sinead to Gstaad, they were hoping to get their hands on the diamonds. Must be the late Niall McGuire's men.

Michael ordered an ambulance-helicopter to airlift Vera to a private clinic in Bern within the hour; nothing would interfere with the birth of their child. And after the birth, Michael would help find Sinead. In the meantime, he left the hunt for his colleagues at Interpol and the Swiss Police to pursue.

Using the influence of Interpol's office in Bern, it took two phone calls to recruit all available patrols in the area to track down the silver 4x4. While the police coordinated the operation with Sinead's photo posted on their network, the local police superintendent met Michael.

The footage recorded by the security cameras covering the driveway and entrance detailed the abduction. The Lexus's registration plates were clearly visible. But with their heads covered, the abductors had remained incognito.

Regardless of these actions, they were too late. The jet parked at Gstaad airport was already flitting through the sky over France.

Bern, Switzerland

Vera's transfer under heavy security from the clinic in Gstaad to the Klinik Beau-Site outside Bern had sprung no surprises. And two hours after their arrival, Vera had given birth to a healthy 3,4 kg baby-girl.

In the meantime, they put arrangements in place to move Vera and the baby to a sister-clinic of the Klinik Beau-Site in Bern as soon as they would be fit to travel. There they would stay under twenty-four-hour police guard.

Michael had his reasons. He knew Sinead's abductors were after the diamonds and would not stop till they found Vera. And by now they must know she was in hospital giving birth – information Sinead would not have been able to deny them.

And if she was not at the clinic in Gstaad or at home, the abductors would bribe some clinic staff in locating her. It would not be long before they'd show up in Bern.

Therefore, to keep his small family out of harm's way, he would return to Lauenen. But for now, he would like to see his wife smile.

'Thank God she looks like you: perfect eyes, mouth, ears. Except for the cute button nose! If she had looked anything like me, poor missy would have ended up a spinster for sure. Instead, I'm going to have my hands full fighting off testosterone, pimply teenagers vying for her hand in marriage,' Michael quipped.

His attempt to lighten the mood in the gloom-filled room failed.

Vera fretted over Sinead, unable to appreciate his dry sense of humour. She gave a wry smile. 'Please, not now, Michael. I'm sorry,' she complained. Forlornly, her slender fingers stroked her baby's mop of black hair as her little mouth latched on to a nipple and sucked eagerly. What did we bring you into, my baby? Vera thought. The ever-present threat of them finding her had become a reality. Whoever took Sinead was after her as well.

'I understand. I just hate seeing you so sad when you should be happy. Especially now.'

'I know. I just can't help worrying about Sinead. Where is she?' she asked. Looking out of the window, her eyes drifted across the river below, the dark rooftops of the old town, and towards the snow-covered mountains.

'We'll find her, don't worry. We've narrowed things down. Twenty-five minutes after they took her, a private jet had left Saanen airport. They found the Lexus there. Hopefully, someone can verify whether she was forced on to the plane.'

'That's not very encouraging.'

'I know, I know,' Michael replied, somewhat annoyed, not wanting to become negative. 'Since her abduction, the searches carried out of all cars, trucks, and trains at every Swiss border crossing show that she's still in the country—'

'Except for the plane,' Vera finished the sentence for him.

'Yes, except for the plane,' Michael acknowledged. His wife would not be placated easily. 'Okay. Fact is, all other airports, doesn't matter how insignificant, are out of bounds for the abductors. So, we must assume she's in Switzerland or onboard that jet, which seems to be heading to Morocco. As a precaution, we've activated our agents there. You and I know, whoever they are, they will contact us soon enough to demand the diamonds.'

'*Da*, the damned diamonds. What I don't understand is why take her abroad if they wanted to trade?' Vera asked. Uttering the words, another awful prospect dawned on her. 'Or they'd kill her.' As dreadful a thought of Sinead's limbs turning up at her door was, it would also be a clear warning to her. To hand over the diamonds or she would be next.

'Slow down, Sweetie. Let's not get ahead of ourselves,' Michael cautioned. 'Yes, if they took her abroad, you may have a point. But if it is who we think, then I don't believe they'll harm her. They saw what happened to their boss, who thought he was invincible. No, I doubt they'll go that far.'

'My love, always the eternal optimist,' Vera sighed. 'What if you're wrong?'

'Let's hope I'm not. My office is trying to locate Niall's men, those who had survived Mykonos. It must be one of them or someone somehow connected to him. Damn, I should have killed them when I had the chance.'

'No, Michael, I should have killed them. You're lucky to be alive and don't you dare forget that. I know I never will,' she said, remembering only too well how she had nearly lost him to a bullet meant for her.

'Still, I should have… Anyway, we'll offer them the stones before they do anything stupid,' he said, having no intention of complying with any of their demands. It was time for him to do what he was best at: to go hunting.

Michael had one big advantage. At the time of the incident in Mykonos, and employed as the head of Niall's security network, none had been aware that he was an Interpol undercover agent. A fact which had not changed. And having worked for the agency for fourteen years, and as the newly appointed Senior Intel Officer (Swiss Divisional Manager), he had the organisation's apparatus at his disposal.

'Michael, I know you'll find her. Just please be careful. You're not alone anymore. We need you,' Vera implored.

Chapter 29

Tuesday
Batumi, Georgia

'Yes Sir. Affirmative. No one has left the base. If the status remains unchanged, we'll move in at 02h00. Over,' Thomas informed his commander.

'Roger. The extraction team will be in position tomorrow at 22h00,' Lt Gen Beck replied.

At that very moment, a thirty-eight metre, triple deck civilian super yacht sped across the Black Sea at forty-five knots per hour to a levy fifteen kilometres north of Batumi. Three SWCC (Special Warfare Combatant Craft) would wait for Thomas, his men, and their prisoner.

'Next contact, 0h30. Confirm, over,' the general said, knowing the odds of success were heavily stacked against his men. How many good men would be sacrificed tonight? he wondered. But they had no choice, as the alternative would be far worse.

'Roger and out,' Thomas signed off and leaned against the tree trunk at the TPB. He had three hours to catch some sleep before trekking up the road and relieve Corporal Hans Krüger who was watching the compound's entrance.

He hated the empty hours during operations, having to keep his mind occupied, aware that plans could go very wrong during these hours of relative idleness. But there was not much more to do other than to stay alert, rest, and reserve one's energy.

Next to him, four of his men had already nodded off. Corporal Wilhelm Dietrich held the first watch.

The rest of the men were in position, ready to execute Plan A the moment the Russian colonel would leave the monastery. At that instant, a "fallen" fir would be dragged across the road four kilometres south of the compound. Forced to stop, his men would grab Col Polyakov. It was a simple plan, one filled with ifs and buts.

Making a positive ID of passengers in the dark would be difficult even with a night-sight. But if they use the same three 4x4s, it should make recognition easier.

And how many will we face at the ambush? Who knows? Well, we'll deal with that when the time comes, Thomas thought.

The second option was to be executed in case the colonel was still on the base by 02h00.

Plan B.

Four men would wait at the fallen tree to stop anyone from making a quick getaway by road. Three men would take up a position in the treeline south of the monastery and provide cover fire for the advancing team of five. His team. They would have to cross the fifty metres of open field, scale the monastery wall with grapples, slip inside, locate the colonel, and snatch him from his bed.

This plan Thomas would prefer to avoid at all cost. There were far too many unanswered questions.

The last satellite images received showed no guards on patrol in the monastery's courtyard. So, he had to assume that whatever defences there were, were hidden behind the dormer windows or inside the turrets.

Having triangulated the sightlines from these vantage points, he had found a blind spot: a two-metre-wide, sixty centimetres deep recess. Their way in.

However, the first obstacle was to reach the wall undetected. And to do so, required cutting an opening in the three-metre-high perimeter fence, sneak across the cleared field by hiding behind every non-existent shrub, rock, and blade of grass. And if by some miracle they managed to avoid physical detection, then to avoid triggering possible booby-traps, landmines, and the movement- and body-heat sensors along the way.

The only element in their favour was the blanket of low cloud blocking the full moon.

Plan B was a risky venture they either pulled off or not.

Would most of them end their lives tonight on this desolate mountain, making the ultimate sacrifice in vain? Thomas wondered as he zipped up his sleeping bag.

And what if the colonel left in a chopper?

Then the race would start all over, yet again.

Thomas closed his eyes.

'Colonel, Sir, wake up, they're on the move,' Cpl Dietrich whispered in his ear, shaking Thomas by the shoulder. As Thomas blinked, registering the urgency, Cpl Dietrich moved towards the other four men. Nudging them awake with his foot, they were ready to move out within seconds.

'Corporal, a SITREP, quick,' Thomas said and checked the time: 20h00. He had hardly slept.

'Three white 4x4s plus another making up the rear. Total number of passengers, eighteen.'

'Damn, too many. Which vehicle is he in?'

'Second.'

With the element of surprise on their side, they may eliminate two vehicles if they executed Plan A. But they needed the colonel alive, not riddled with bullet holes.

And outgunned, his men could be pinned down by rifle fire with Georgian re-enforcements on the way, giving the colonel an opportunity to slip away. If the rest of his unit were present, they could have selected targets and eliminated twelve men within seconds, leaving the colonel and a few others isolated.

Well, we're not. So, change of plan...

'Get to the cars. Go! We'll ambush them en route once the others have joined us,' Thomas ordered, grabbing his kit and rifle.

With all the backpacks dumped into the boots of the three vehicles, they cleared the branches. Five men piled into one car. The sixth man guarded the other two vehicles.

Slowly the car rolled to the edge of the wood and stopped twenty metres inside the treeline.

Ten seconds later, four 4x4s shot past.

'Let's go, and keep your distance,' Thomas cautioned Corporal Werner Krause behind the wheel.

With the car's lights off, the corporal eased on to the road.

'Dietrich, radio the lieutenant and inform him of the situation.'

Twenty-eight minutes later, traversing Batumi, the convoy's destination became obvious. 'They're flying out of here,' Thomas growled and grabbed the mic. 'Come in, Lieutenant. Over.'

'Receiving you, Sir. Over,' Lt Schmidt responded.

'What's your position? Over.'

'Picked up the trail a minute ago. All present. Over.'

'Head for Batumi Airport. We'll be inside the terminal. Once we know their destination, two men will join their flight. On your arrival, secure the carpark. Werner will be there. Expect some hostiles guarding their vehicles. Copy that, over.'

As they slipped into a parking space, the poorly lit carpark was seventy per cent full. The doors flung open. Men scrambled out and retrieved their packs. Quickly, they donned civilian anoraks over their black combat fatigues.

Thomas, Corporals Wilhelm Dietrich and Albrecht Fuchs raced after the Russians inside the terminal building.

A minute later, Corporal Reinhard Baum followed them. Cpl Fuchs waited outside the large plate-glass window of the main hall, his eyes on the three Georgians guarding the parked 4x4s.

The overhead monitors displayed four flights departing within the hour. Amongst the crowd of travellers milling around the main hall, the group of Russian soldiers strolled towards the stairs and escalator. Col Polyakov, looking older than his picture, was amongst them.

Thomas's mood lifted. Finally he had eyes on the target. Maintaining a discreet distance he followed them up the escalator. But on the mezzanine level there was no sign of the Russians. He did not break his stride. With his eyes fixed on the doors up ahead, he hurried past the VIP Lounge on his left.

He opened the double doors a fraction.

Thirteen men crowded the reception area of the private jet terminal. Col Polyakov was well over 1.9metres tall and carried with pride the scars of war on his face. He was in deep conversation with a burly Georgian in military fatigues. A general.

Smiling broadly, the colonel gave the Georgian a sharp salute and led his men past three airport attendants towards the boarding gate. Despite their bulging holdalls, no one dared question them.

Thomas had seen enough and rushed downstairs. The Russians were leaving by private plane! He could not believe his luck, or rather lack of it. But one hope remained. The Georgian. He had to know something?

Spotting Cpl Fuchs near the entrance, he signalled him over. Having regrouped at the small café, Thomas asked, his voice low, 'Albrecht, is Schmidt in position?'

'Affirmative.'

'Good. Advise him to neutralise the three hostiles outside and prepare a reception for two more. That officer coming down the stairs: mid-sixties, white hair, and his sidekick. He could be the local commander. Next, get HQ to ID all private jets on the runway and track any leaving within the next two hours. We may be lucky with one of our satellites floating overhead.'

'Wilco, Sir.'

'Go. We'll stall him,' Thomas instructed.

The Georgians reached the bottom of the stairs and turned towards them. Thomas's hand moved inside his anorak and gripped the butt of the Heckler Koch USP, Compact Tactical .45 ACP. The Georgians brushed past. At the kiosk they ordered drinks and, with tumblers of clear liquid in hand, sat down at a vacant table.

Not to be conspicuous, Thomas walked to the counter and bought two coffees. Keeping the Georgians in his periphery, he sipped the thick, hot drink. His tongue hurt with the two-day-old wound still raw.

After another round of vodka, the Georgians got up and left the building. The carpark was quiet. Three men, impossible to identify in the soft light, huddled together next to the 4x4s.

At ten metres, the Georgians slowed. With their attention focused on the three drivers, they were unaware of the four shadows stalking them. Quick blows to their necks collapsed them into the arms of Schmidt and Koch. Seconds later they were bundled into the nearest 4x4.

The vehicle swung out of the carpark. Time: 20h40. Eighty minutes till the rendezvous with the rubber ducks on the beach north of Batumi. Soon, someone would come looking for the missing men – a commander and four men of a secret base would not go unnoticed for long.

And who that someone would be would be none other than the Georgian army, Thomas thought, glancing at the ID card in his hand. They had unknowingly opened a can of worms. Their captive was Brigadier General Katsia Bolkvadze, Commander of the Georgian Special Forces Division based at the monastery.

For a moment he said nothing, simmering, relieved, and troubled at the same time.

Relieved, because if they had stormed the compound, they all would have been slaughtered – that they had no intel on this Special-Forces base was unforgivable.

And troubled, because the Georgian Special Forces were undoubtedly in cahoots with the Russians. It made no sense.

181

Georgians disliked Russians. But for some obscure reason they were working together. Why?

'Werner, the beach, quick. As soon as they review the airport's security footage, they'll be after us,' Thomas said.

'Roger, Sir,' Werner replied, and accelerated, pushing the speed limit.

Turning to his second-in-command, Thomas asked, 'Lieutenant, any luck with HQ?'

'I informed them. They're not impressed.'

'Private jet. Who would have guessed! Upside, at least we have this man. The commander of the special-forces base we nearly waltzed into.'

Lt Schmidt gave an almighty whistle. 'Thank God we did not scale that wall. And that explains why the three guards in the carpark had reacted so quickly, forcing us to eliminate them.'

'Amen to that,' Thomas reiterated. 'Well, at least we have the general – will be hell to pay for kidnapping him, but the politicians can deal with that. I believe he may know what is going on. And where our Russian friend is heading.'

He was fast losing faith in his mission, as the colonel had slipped through his fingers again. Patience, patience, he cautioned himself.

But what if the Russians were to land in Moscow? What then? Do we send a raiding party after them? With the Russians on high alert and the country locked down, ready for war, it would be an extremely dangerous exercise.

Hopefully, Brig Gen Bolkvadze would he be able to shed some light on the events in Turkey and Russia's involvement, sparing him and his men such an endeavour.

At 20h30, Col Polyakov and his unit boarded the private jet. On schedule, at 20h45, the wheels of the plane cleared the runway and veered north towards Russia. The passengers, a unit of black ops soldiers, were resting, preparing themselves for the risky mission ahead.

Boris closed his eyes and dreamt of the rewards awaiting him when this would be over.

Chapter 30

22h30, Tuesday
Kursk, Russia

Svetlana peered in behind the heavy chest of drawers, searching for clues. A small crystal vase lay shattered on the polished wooden floor of her parents' bedroom. Three snapped stems of orange-white chrysanthemums protruded out of the spherical base. The vase was a birthday gift to her mother two years ago.

Bending down, she touched the dark stain on the floor. It was still damp. Tempted to pick up the flowers and pieces of glass, she paused, frowned, and called Maj Gen Lukyanov.

'Sir, look at this,' she said, and pointed at the broken vase. 'It may be nothing, although—'

She stopped and pulled a strand of grey hair from the thin crack in the dresser's side panel. Next to it, a few tiny red specks stained the wood. She gasped, took a breath, and with her nail scraped one speck off the wood. The dark red was unmistakable. She applied some spit. Blood.

'This was not an accident. Someone attacked her. Banged her head against the dresser,' she said, her lips tight as her body filled with anger.

'Svetlana, you have helped enough,' Ivan said, taking her by the elbow. 'I'll deal with this.'

'No, I'm fine,' she resisted. 'If they were murdered, I want their killers. I will not rest till they are caught.'

'Let's not be too hasty. Best we wait for the men to finish, see what they uncover. This may be totally unrelated to the accident,' Ivan said. 'Maybe your mother tripped and banged her head, and nothing more.'

'Yes, possibly. But not cleaning up the mess? No. It's not like her.'

'Maybe she did not feel well and your dad rushed her to the hospital. Head injuries can be quite dangerous.'

'Yes, you're right…'

'Mind if I ask you something personal?'

'Of course.'

'Your parents, did they get on well? Any problems between them you knew of?' Ivan asked, treading on dangerous ground, inferring her father might have lost his temper and shoved or hit her mother.

'Yes, they got on very well. And no problems I'm aware of. They loved each other dearly. Never fought.'

'Good. Then, before we can be certain this was foul play, we need more proof.'

'Yes. But I'm sure someone attacked them. And, as soon as the assailants had left, my parents had fled and crashed,' Svetlana said.

Ivan nodded his head. It made sense, however speculative. To uncover events leading up to the accident, they needed to track down the alleged visitors. Discover a message. A clue left by her parents. Or a motive.

'If my assumption is correct, then it puzzles me, who…or rather, why, would someone threaten them?' Svetlana said. 'As far as I know, they had no enemies.' But as she spoke, the obvious dawned on her. 'These so-called "visitors" were after me! And the only person I know of who could be so desperate for revenge is Niall McGuire. Remember, he knew my real identity. Then again, it can't be as he's dead. It must be someone else. But who?'

'You're sure he is?' Ivan asked. 'When did they say the DNA results will be available?'

184

'Tomorrow afternoon, the earliest. But even if he is alive, how did he find my family? Their details are classified.'

'Easily done with some help. I'm sure his mafia friends have ties within the heart of our organisation. So, for now, let's take it he's alive. And if any fresh evidence indicates a crime, then yes, he will become our prime suspect. Agreed?'

'Yes.'

'Let's put this possibility on ice for now. Say it's not Niall, but someone else you have crossed swords with, or—'

'No one I'm aware of,' Svetlana interrupted.

'Understood. As I was about to say, your father might have been involved in research which could have put him in danger. Big money in industrial espionage... And some people will stop at nothing to get what they want.'

'Yes, that could be.'

'I'll instruct a search of your father's office. Maybe he discovered something of great value, and—' abruptly Ivan stopped. He had better do that on his own. She needed rest. She had suffered enough. 'Come, I'll take you to the safehouse.'

He could not rule out the likelihood of someone watching the house, wanting to finish what they had started.

Chapter 31

Tuesday Night
Batumi, Georgia

The SWCC (Special Warfare Combatant Craft) ploughed through the fluorescent waves. Beaching to a halt, eight commandos jumped out. Six grabbed the guide ropes, heaved the boat out of the water, and ran for cover. Two men squatted in the surf and combed the beach with their night-sights, their rifles following the arcs of their heads. In their black neoprene suits, the men scurried like roaches into the shadows of the levy, melting into the night.

Blue lights flashed and sirens wailed in the distance. The disappearance of Brig Gen Bolkvadze and the discovery of the bodies at the airport had initiated a full-scale search and rescue operation in and around Batumi.

A minute later, Thomas's unit joined the commandos. Amongst the group of German Special Forces was the drugged and disorientated Brig Gen Bolkvadze. No one took any notice of the muffled complaints coming from behind the tape covering his mouth with his eyes swimming in their sockets.

'We're set,' Thomas whispered to the lieutenant next to him.

The young officer blipped a signal across the water, giving the all-clear to the two SWCC bobbing in the surf.

Thirty-two minutes later, the men on the three SWCCs boarded the powerboat ten kilometres offshore. With the rubber ducks stowed away, the boat's diesel engines roared and powered back to international waters.

On the lower deck, they strapped the Georgian Special Forces commander to a bunk bed and attached a drip to his arm. Hopefully, he could shed some light on the elusive Russian colonel's destination. And why the Georgians were working with the Russians. What they were up to?

Having serious reservations about how much the Georgian knew, Thomas began his questioning. This was the first opportunity to ascertain the colonel's agenda and destination.

At least NATO's ever-present eye in the sky had ID'd the private jet which had departed Batumi at 21h45 – assumed to be carrying the Russian unit. Only two other flights had left between 19h30 and 21h30; both commercial. Establishing the jet's flight-plan had confirmed Russia as its destination. If correct, the colonel was out of reach by now.

Not deterred by this, Thomas continued to extract what information he could from the Georgian.

The confirmation of Russia's direct involvement in the gas installation explosion in Turkey was not encouraging. But then a second picture materialised, one far more disturbing than the sabotage of the gas pipeline in Turkey: the imminent attack on five nuclear power plants in Europe!

Stunned by this revelation, Thomas asked, 'You said five nuclear power plants are to be destroyed. Is that correct?'

'Yes…'

'Where? When?' Thomas demanded as the Chernobyl disaster flashed through his mind's eye. It did not bear thinking about just how many people would die, and what the long-term consequences would be.

'Where and when?' he repeated.

'England… France… Germany.'

Thomas looked at Lt Schmidt. 'Compile a list of all nuclear plants in Europe.' Once more, his blue eyes glared at the Georgian. 'Which ones?' he demanded.

'Don't know…'

'Try to remember. You do not want the blood of millions on your hands. Do you?'

'No. I told them… Too many will die.'

'Then help us stop them,' Thomas coaxed. As the Georgian spoke, they dotted down any information of value.

'How do they intend to carry out these attacks?'

'Sleeper cells… Already activated… No one can stop them.'

We'll see about that, Thomas thought.

'And Col Polyakov, what's his involvement?'

'Co-ordinates attacks.'

'Sir, the list,' Lt Schmidt interrupted, presenting a detailed map showing all locations and names of operational plants in Europe.

'Right, General, let's start with England. Jog your memory,' Thomas said.

Methodically, he worked his way through the list, starting with Scotland and moving south. At the mention of Suffolk County and the Sizewell Plants, the Georgian interrupted him. Targets: both plants B and C.

Sharing his findings with his commander, Lt Gen Beck asked, 'Are you sure those are the names, and the attacks are imminent?'

The alleged attacks involved five nuclear power plants: two at Sizewell in England; two in France at the Nogent plant 120km south-east of Paris, and another at Saint-Laurent 30km east of Orleans. The fifth in Germany, the Emsland plant in Lower Saxony.

As the two intelligence officers debated the intel, uncertainty crept into its validity; the serum may cause non-fictional as well as fictional facts to be revealed. They had to be careful not to jump to conclusions. These attacks sounded unrealistic. Neither of them believed that Russia, despite its leader's aggressive rhetoric, would ever go to such extremes.

But one could never tell considering current events. If they do, it would unleash a nuclear response by NATO they'd regret. The picture looked grim.

'Doubts I have. The general may believe his knowledge to be fact, but it might be nothing more than a deception. Why would the Russians share such sensitive information with him? Unless, of course, Col Polyakov had a few vodkas too many and shot his mouth off? But as he's clearly not a fool, it's doubtful. Therefore, was he acting on orders? Possibly. But with so much at stake, there won't be any loose tongues. Every action would be well orchestrated. Or are the Georgians part of this?' Thomas concluded.

'I agree. There are too many anomalies to be certain. Find out how he came about this intel. I'll hold off alerting the relevant authorities. We need confirmation before pressing panic buttons. Governments are nervous enough as it is, and they may do rash things under the circumstances. This war can wait. Our assets in Russia can confirm whether this is fact.'

'Roger, Sir.'

The Georgian general tried to blink under the bright lights, but could not. With his bloodshot eyes taped open and head strapped back he was powerless to do anything. Underfoot, Thomas felt the vibration of the powerful engines as they raced across the Black Sea towards the next rendezvous.

'We're nearly finished. Then you can sleep as much as you want. But first you tell us who is behind this.'

'Russian… Georgian military…'

'You think I buy that? You lot hate each other's guts,' Thomas retorted. 'Try again.'

'What do you know? Nothing. We help them, they help us.'

'General, you're wasting time. You either come clean or we drag you behind the boat and you can swim the drug off. It's your call.'

'We'd rather be part of Russia than of the pathetic West,' the general said, tauntingly. 'Not all of us want your D-E-M-

O-C-R-A-C-Y. You are fools. America and London control you. You are weak… No backbone. I am not like you. Drag me behind this fucking boat and see if I care!'

'Really. Any more wisecracks you would like to share before we dump you overboard?'

'Europeans are the laughingstock of the world… In the world of real men. Every day, scum invade you on tiny boats. They rape your women… Stab, murder, blow you up, and mow you down with trucks. Your leaders cry on TV like babies. And your men, what do they do? They weep and wear miniskirts…burn candles. Why don't you fight back, for God's sake! You disgust me. And you tried to destroy us as well. That will never happen.'

Thomas ignored the man's ranting and continued, 'And you think your attack will succeed? Why? Because the Chinese told you so?'

'Yes… No. Not Chinese. Russia… We planned this. We'll show you. Next week, we shall be victorious!'

Thomas had heard enough. Either it was the truth, or a clever manipulation by the Russians. 'Doc, excuse me while I report this in. Please continue. You know what's required.'

Flying over Russian territory, Boris received word of the general's abduction. His location was unknown. Therefore, he must be regarded as compromised.

Ignoring this setback, Boris smiled to himself, confident to complete his mission. But to be safe in case NATO was tracking them, he instructed the pilot to detour to Moscow.

'Thomas, we've lost them,' Lt Gen Beck said over the phone. 'Col Polyakov did land at a military base on the outskirts of Moscow. This could mean he is active and has not gone rogue as we've thought. It looks like the Russian military is involved.'

'Is he still there?'

'Could be. Fact is, we don't know. The plane has not budged since it landed. Activity on the ground is high. No way of knowing whether they're on the base. However, it supports the Georgian's claim. The colonel is back on Russian soil. Therefore, we must assume he is helping to expedite the strike on the nuclear plants. All signs indicate Russia is set on war.'

'Any word from NATO assets in Moscow?' Thomas asked. The Russian leaders' willingness to drag the world into chaos infuriated him. Their resistance to America having a first-strike opportunity with missiles stationed near their borders was understandable. But it did not justify a war.

'Other than intel about troop movements towards their western and Ukrainian fronts, no. And nothing on Russia's involvement in Turkey, or the nuclear plants' attacks. Did you squeeze any more out of the general?'

'Nothing of value, Sir. I suggest we alert our colleagues of the planned strike without further delay.'

'I concur,' Lt Gen Beck said. 'We'll work on the Georgian when you're back. He might know more. You get some rest and report for a debriefing at 11h00. Our task is far from over.'

Chapter 32

Lauenen, Switzerland

Twelve hours had elapsed since Sinead's abduction. The time and date on the screen: 23h30, Tuesday, 16/02/2022.

Michael's home office, a secured bunker concealed beneath the modest chalet, was a fully equipped Interpol satellite-office. It placed him in the fortunate position to carry out most of his surveillance, daily administrative functions, planning of operations, and managing his cells and agents from the comfort of his home.

He hardly left his wife's side except for the weekly briefings he attended in Lyon and Bern. Or when a mission required his presence in the field.

'You're telling me the plane just vanished?' Michael asked, unimpressed. Finding the jet which departure tied in perfectly with events around the time of Sinead's abduction was their only tangible link in locating her. Angrily, his large hand pushed the mouse across the pad as he viewed the plane's route: a red line drawn across the world map displayed on the 2,4-metre wall-mounted monitor.

'Nothing we could do about that. It was on-course for Morocco when it had suddenly dropped below radar. We also lost satellite coverage before then. This means they knew the exact times and locations of our satellites' orbits. This is worrying. Few abductors will have access to such intel. Who are we dealing with, Michael?' Robert Guigues asked from his office in Morocco.

'No idea.'

'Why would these powerful and well-connected people be interested in your friend?'

'Maybe she got involved with a high-ranking EU official and one of his friends wants her for himself. She is quite a looker.'

'Hmm... No, my friend, sounds like you're composing a fairy tale.'

'Robert, the fact is, I don't know who's behind this. There was a chap...'

'Who?'

'Niall McGuire, a billionaire. The Russians killed him a few years ago. Thing is, the location of his fortune died with him. Considering Sinead's role as one of his mules, it is possible that his friends think she might know where it is. And they will be the Russian mafia.'

'I see. Are you sure there is no other reason you can think of why she was abducted?'

'None.'

'Why do I get this feeling you're not telling me everything?'

'You're wrong, Robert. Everything I know, you know.'

'Okay, so you won't tell me what's really going on. But I hope someday you will. Now, we concentrate on finding her.'

'Of course,' Michael said. 'So, any idea where she could be?'

'We believe they landed in Morocco. The police are searching all private airfields in the northern territories. But as yet, they have found nothing,' Robert said. 'Unfortunately, we can forget a quick result. Just hope she doesn't end up in a brothel in the desert.'

'Damn,' Michael huffed, knowing full well Sinead's abduction had nothing to do with sex-trafficking... For the moment.

Niall's men, who had survived the skirmish in Mykonos, must have seen Vera escape with the bag of diamonds. Therefore, they had no interest in Sinead as such. However, if they did not get the diamonds, they might just sell her to traffickers.

'I'm sure they will contact us soon, demanding a ransom. Best we prepare for such an eventuality,' Michael said.

He did not want to disturb Vera; she needed rest. But she had insisted, wanting to be kept informed of developments, whether good or bad. The fact was, she could do nothing to help matters. And the less contact between them by phone, the better; they might trace the calls.

As expected, Vera bemoaned Michael's plan. 'I know you want them dead. But the only way we'll get her back alive is to give them what they want. So please, don't play games with them.'

'I won't. And we'll do so,' Michael lied; the diamonds would not be going anywhere. He knew of no one other than Vera and Sinead who would put this fortune to good use and rescue women trapped in the sex industry. Definitely not some government agency or NGO who would pocket it themselves.

'Somehow, I don't believe you. Please, Michael, don't play games. Swear you'll do the right thing,' Vera pleaded, knowing her words were in vain.

'Scout's honour,' he replied meekly.

His response confirmed her suspicion. 'You're a terrible liar,' she said despondently. 'And please tell Sean and Brendan what happened. Brendan must be beside himself by now, not having heard from her.'

'Of course. Now get some rest. If I have any news, I'll phone right away. Kiss the little monkey for me. By the way, I love you more than you'll ever know. Bye, bye, bye, bye…' Michael said, his voice fading away, saying goodnight. Why this was happening now, at such an important time, irked him immensely.

Sean did not take kindly to the news of Sinead's abduction and shouting obscenities, did not allow Michael to get a word in. But as he calmed down, he agreed to disappear for a few weeks along with his siblings; he knew the dangers.

Next, Michael phoned Brendan. He went dead quiet. But as soon as he recovered his poise, he lashed out, wanting to rush to Sinead's side and rescue her. Michael remained firm, stating that such an action would serve no purpose. The best was for him to stay in Dublin, out of harm's way. Brendan reluctantly agreed, but only if kept informed of developments at all times.

Alone in his office, Michael tried to form a clear picture of what had happened. Who was involved?

Sinead's siblings, all surprised by the news of her visit to Switzerland, were all unscathed. Therefore, none of them could have revealed her plans.

Perhaps it was a confidante she had shared the secret of the diamonds with? Someone who had seen an opportunity to get rich quickly…

Or this confidante could be lying in a ditch somewhere in Dublin with her neck broken.

Or did the abductors garner her itinerary details at the last moment and track her to Switzerland? No, that would have cut it too close to arrange a plane and getaway car in the time Sinead had travelled from Geneva to Gstaad. The fact was, the private jet had been parked at Geneva airport since late the previous evening. So, no. They knew well in advance where she was heading.

Sinead, you were compromised before you left Ireland. And we know why. So, it's either Niall's stooges or your confidante, if she exists, Michael decided.

Or am I so blinded by the diamonds that I don't see it for what it is? What if this is a case of revenge, Sinead to be punished, destined to become a sex slave? If so, then they will also come for Vera. She will be next.

He phoned Vera. 'Did I wake you?' he whispered, feeling bad calling so late.

'No, I'm up. Feeding time. What's wrong?'

'Nothing. Just wanted to hear your voice.'

'I miss you too. I'm so angry about all this. Why now?' she asked, frustrated.

'I don't know,' Michael sighed. 'Sweetie, I won't keep you long. I'm just checking Sinead's last movements, friends, etc., etc. I was wondering, do you know of anyone in Ireland she would have confided in about the stones?'

'No. Why?'

'I'm trying to find out if anyone other than Niall's stooges could be behind this.'

'It can only be them. I'm sure.'

'That's what I thought. So, the only one who might know anything about her movements is Brendan.'

'You don't think he could be involved?' Vera asked, surprised.

'No, not directly. When I spoke to him, he sounded genuinely shocked. But no harm in doing a background check on him. Find out who his friends are. He could have shared, in confidence, Sinead's story with a friend who sniffed an opportunity. Do you have a photo of him? I need to run it through our computers.'

'Yes. Sinead sent me a few. They're on the way.'

Michael looked at the pictures on his phone and downloaded them for editing. He ignored the settings of restaurants, backdrops of the Irish coastline, and zoomed in on Sinead's fiancé, preparing a portrait for processing by the CIA, Euro- and Interpol's technicians. Once loaded into their systems, it could take hours for the computers to search the databanks. No doubt there was more than one Brendan Walsh on file.

Right, Mr Walsh, who are you and who are your friends? Michael thought, studying the smiling face on the monitor.

Thirty minutes later he went to bed, knowing the abductors would contact him soon. He had done as much as he could.

Five thousand kilometres south of Lauenen, the powerful jet engines droned monotonously at ten thousand metres above the African desert.

The ploy of flying in under the radar and landing on a private airstrip north of Marrakesh had worked. Having refuelled and changed its signature, the jet had left. Skimming over the Atlas Mountains, the pilot was confident no one had picked up their trail.

Back at cruising altitude he cleared a flight-plan. No-one would link their entry and exit of Moroccan airspace as the same plane. They were untraceable unless there was a tracking device fitted to the undercarriage, which there was not.

The success of the plan and what would happen next was up to Larry and his men casing Michael's house in Lauenen.

Sinead stirred in her bed. She had no idea where she was. The last she remembered was racing down the narrow lane in Lauenen. Stopping somewhere and Larry jabbing a needle into her neck. And then nothing.

Groggy after the strong sedative, she stared forlornly through the large feature window at the bright star-filled sky. Nervously, she fiddled with the new engagement ring on her left finger.

How did they find me? Were they watching me all this time? How stupid of me returning to Dublin thinking I could live as if the past never happened. Why did I not disappear like Vera? Sinead thought, furious with herself.

The image of Brendan tortured to reveal her destination was most upsetting, convinced that was how Larry had found her in Switzerland.

But why did you not take me in Dublin? Why this? Or am I being punished for having robbed Niall?

As the reality of her situation dawned on her, she realised she would never see Brendan, Vera, or her siblings again. She would spend the rest of her days in some far-flung corner of the world as a sex slave.

Chapter 33

Kursk, Russia

'Run that by me again!' Ivan ordered.

'Tied up in the middle of the road, the wild boar had no chance of avoiding the approaching car,' Sgt Alexeev repeated. 'His neck was badly chafed. Two trees on opposite sides of the road also showed signs of rope damage.'

Ivan's frowned deepened. 'You're telling me someone secured it there?'

'Yes Sir. Also, we've picked up many footprints near the car wreck which do not match ours.'

'Could be a nosy passer-by?'

'Might be. We thought that…'

'Sounds like you're holding something back. Continue Sergeant?'

'We also found traces of explosives in the wreckage. The accident was staged. They died before the car had exploded,' Sgt Alexeev said hesitantly, unsure how his superior would respond. He lowered his head, avoiding eye contact.

Furious, Ivan stood up, towering over the two men. 'Why were you not there? What took you so long?' His words were bitter, measured. He felt like strangling them.

Sgt Alexeev did not hesitate and replied defensively. 'We received our instructions at 23h05 and were in position by 23h30, Sir.'

His response missed the point of the rhetorical question; the time did not matter. Their entire unit had failed because of their commander. Ivan knew the facts but for now needed their co-operation and trust if he were to succeed. Once the killers were apprehended, he would lock this commander up for having failed in his duties.

Damn him! It won't bring her family back, but it might save someone else's.

'And you can swear by those hours?' he asked, seeing they had jumped to their own defence.

'Yes Sir. It's on record,' Sgt Alexeev added hastily.

'You sure? Because if I were you, I'll make a few copies. Believe me, soon, someone will want to pass the blame. You know who I'm referring to.'

'Yes Sir, we thought the same. We've made some copies if you care to look,' the sergeant said, proffering a piece of paper for Ivan to study. The agents firmly believed they did nothing wrong – a sentiment shared by Ivan. They had come prepared.

Ivan took the damning evidence and glanced at it. 'Some advice. Not a word to anyone. For now, this conversation stays in this room. That's an order,' Ivan cautioned. 'Best we sign and date a copy for each of you.'

With three copies signed, he said, 'Let's leave this for now and concentrate on finding a motive. Therefore, I'll need everything you've discovered so far. Let's start with her father. Any more from the men searching his office? Any theories?'

'No Sir, nothing. His colleagues confirmed he was not currently involved in any research which might warrant him being murdered. We're afraid he might not have been the target, purely someone they wanted to get rid of for some unknown reason. Did he owe someone money, had an affair? It seems there is a lot more to this incident than first thought,' the sergeant said, unable to offer a motive.

'Yes, that's if they died in the house. Something an amateur would have done. But we're dealing with professional killers who had planned it to the last detail.

Other than the obvious, why go to such lengths? The ruse with the wild boar might have worked if someone else had been the victim. But they knew who they were dealing with. So, why?'

'To get away as far as possible before we would discover what happened.'

'Hmm… Let's try another approach. Say they were after Maj Nikolaeva. They kill her family and then, when she least expects it, eliminate her as well. For instance, at the funeral. Or, they do nothing for now. Let her live in fear, aware they could strike at any moment; the Sword of Damocles hanging over her head,' Ivan said.

Every word he uttered reinforced his and Svetlana's fears. He did not want to delve any deeper into the matter without proof. Nor did he want to share his views with his men. He had said too much already. 'Or, as you've mentioned, they were buying time to cross the border,' he added, as if it were the more plausible scenario.

'That's close to here. They could have slipped into Ukraine long before the accident would have been reported. Does not add up, Sir,' Pte Ozerov stated the obvious.

'Yes, it's not that simple. Now, you're excused to carry on. We'll reconvene at 14h00 sharp,' Ivan said, dismissing the men. He had the unenviable task of sharing the news with Svetlana.

His knuckles rapped lightly on the closed bedroom door. 'Svetlana, we need to talk.'

There was a faint shuffling sound from inside the room.

'Yes Sir. Give me a second.'

'I'll be in the lounge,' Ivan replied and returned to the spacious room of the sixth-floor corner apartment rented the night before. Their temporary safehouse represented a military base on high alert. Only a fool would dare to attack them.

Ivan stared at the sprawl of snow-covered roofs below, dialled his office, and asked to be connected to the bureau's laboratory.

Outside, a stiff wind whistled through the bare trees. The area looked dull.

Most likely, nothing ever happens around here. No, I cannot imagine living in this monotonous jungle. A small village any day. Not this.

Although, being able to live anywhere remained to be seen. The sound of war drums threatened any peaceful existence on the planet. He had no illusions what the outcome would be if the Americans proceeded with their threats, installing missile bases in Poland and Ukraine. Ukraine would fall first. A prospect he personally would try to stop at all costs.

'Maj Gen Lukyanov, this is Professor Dimitri Danilovich, head of the Genetic Science Department, the criminology laboratory,' a deep baritone voice said, shaking Ivan out of his reverie.

'Ah yes, Professor. Any sign of those DNA results Maj Nikolaeva requested?'

'No. We need another ten hours for a conclusive result.'

'Understood. Contact me when you do.'

'Will do, Sir,' the professor said. 'Anything else?'

'No, that will do for now. Goodbye Professor.'

'What's wrong?' Svetlana asked behind him as she sat down on the empty couch.

'Some disturbing news.'

'Yes...?'

Ivan did not know how to say this other than call it for what it was. 'Someone murdered your family. It was no accident. The incident was staged. And the bastard is most likely behind it.'

'Niall McGuire...?'

'Yes. Although we still have no result from the lab. They need another ten hours.'

Consumed by guilt, Svetlana felt responsible for the murders. Having avenged her sister's death, she had inadvertently subjected her parents and child to this psychopath. She did not make a sound as her eyes clouded over.

Unable to stand by and watch her suffer, Ivan lifted her into his arms. She did not resist and looked up into his eyes. Gently, he smoothed away her tears.

Ivan slipped out of bed, showered, and dressed. He would give anything to remain by her side. But as deputy director of FSB Counter-Intelligence, he had to fulfil his role in averting the impending war. Also, he had to bring her family's murderers to book. And, even if prematurely, warn people close to her that the psychopath may be alive and out for revenge.

If he were, her family had been one of the first victims, and most probably not the last. The murdered guards in Cuba were witnesses, a threat, and therefore erased by Niall.

At last, Svetlana reached Michael. Using her alias Irina, she enquired how they were. Whether they were parents yet.

To Michael and Vera, Irina was a trustworthy friend rescued by the Russians during Niall's arrest. Sworn to secrecy, enquiries regarding her were always met with silence. They had "no idea" where she was. They knew nothing. Period.

Svetlana did not tell Michael anything more. Not about her family, and neither of the possibility that Niall could still be alive, even when told of Sinead's abduction.

Ending the call, Svetlana lowered her head, realising they had been too late. If it were Niall, then he had struck twice.

'If Niall did this, there will be no court this time. I shall do what should have been done back then,' Ivan said.

With her eyes fixed on him, she said, 'You won't be alone. But where do we start?'

'If we find the killers, we'll find him. Though, it may take too long…'

'As he is so set on killing me, I'll make it easy for him. I won't hide. There's the funeral…'

'What are you saying?'

'I'll be bait. Lure them out in the open. And—'

'No. I will not expose you to a sniper,' Ivan cut her off.

'Ivan, please. I have to,' she insisted, not to be swayed.

'Say, I agree, then we'll employ another agent. A wig, headscarf, and sunglasses would fool anyone. No one will know it's not you.'

'No. I'll do this myself.'

'Svetlana, please.'

'Sorry, but, no.'

Chapter 34

Lauenen, Switzerland

'Vera's at the Klinik Beau-Site outside Bern. The lads traced the eejit's calls,' Brian Murphy said.

'Grand job,' Larry replied, quite pleased with the news. Bern was a thirty-minute drive from their base – a fortified chalet a few kilometres south of Schwarzenberg. The change of clinic made things a lot easier for him and his men. 'When Michael leaves, don't lose him. Ya got that?'

'No worries, we'll stick to him like a tick to a bitch.'

'Has he got the letter yet?'

'Just delivered,' Brian confirmed, his binoculars fixed on Michael's chalet across the valley.

'Good. See you back at base.' Larry ended the call.

Inside the confines of his chalet, Michael opened the plain white envelope addressed to him. With the Cantonal Police Superintendent, Werner Schaffhausen, peering over his shoulder he could not hide its contents.

The first part of the letter did not surprise Michael, stating, "Sixty-five million Swiss Francs for Sinead, hard currency" – the estimated current black-market value of the diamonds in Vera's possession. Thankfully, they did not mention the diamonds, sparing him the trouble of explaining their origin. The cryptic reference to the diamonds as "hard currency", only Vera and he could appreciate.

His relief was short-lived. The second part of the letter would be impossible to comply with. In three days' time, the payment must be delivered by his wife in a country of their choosing.

Forget it. If you want the stones, you deal with me and me alone, Michael simmered.

And as he read the last sentence, "Michael, we have your number and will call with further instructions," he grabbed his phone, alarmed.

Hearing her sleepy voice, he asked after her and Natalya, hoping she did not detect his anxiety. The abductors had his number. Therefore, they would have traced his calls and pinpointed Vera's location.

Vera and Natalya had to be relocated immediately.

'Quite a large sum of money they want,' Superintendent Schaffhausen said, surprised by the amount. 'Forgive me for asking. Do you have access to such funds, Herr Mahoney?'

'No, I don't. They're mad. Wonder what they're after? They must know I have nothing close to that. Best I can do is raise a million against the chalet. Plus, another couple of hundred thousand in stocks and bonds. Anyway, it doesn't matter. I will not give them a bloody cent.'

'You're right not to. They're testing your resolve. See how much you can come up with.'

'This may be more personal.'

'What do you mean, "more personal"?'

'Sinead and my wife made a powerful enemy in Ireland two years ago. Seeing he's dead, I suspect the abductors could be business associates eager to settle the score. Therefore, I doubt it's money they're after. I think they plan to kill them. It's a trap.'

Furious, Michael waited for the security gates to shut behind him. Clutching the steering wheel with brute force, eager to see Vera and his newborn child, his foot hit the accelerator.

The 4x4's wheels screeched and careened down the lane towards Gstaad, slipping and sliding on the icy road.

First, he had to make a detour via the bank in Geneva – an annoying delay. He had very little to feel pleased about, except for Vera and Natalya still being unharmed. There had been no suspicious activity near the clinic. But the gloves were off. This would be a fight to the end for all concerned. He was as much a target as Vera and Sinead.

Pre-occupied, Michael did not notice the marine-blue Volvo 4x4 shadow him in the lane below, running parallel to the main road.

As far as Brendan was concerned, he was an enigma. The searches of the three agencies' databanks had triggered no alarm bells. With luck, this would not change.

Then again, no one is that clean. We all carry baggage, secrets. Just to be sure to be sure, best I access the Board of Solicitors' records in Dublin. Brendan, you better be who you claim you are. If they tortured you to reveal Sinead's itinerary, I may forgive you. Then again, maybe I won't. But if you are part of this abduction for a cut, you are as good as dead my friend, Michael vowed.

But that they had made no progress in locating Sinead was of more concern. Her plane had vanished. She could be anywhere by now. It was unlikely the kidnappers would do anything to her till they had the stones.

Michael checked his watch, 9:50 AM. Notwithstanding the treacherous road, he was confident to reach the Credit Suisse in Geneva by midday. He needed a few diamonds to show intent and convince the kidnappers to meet for a second time to complete the exchange. It would be a rendezvous which would mark the end for these criminals. A team of Interpol agents would be ready to pounce.

The 4x4 Mercedes's turbo kicked in and catapulted him through the snow-covered valley. Behind him, the Volvo kept its distance, the driver content in Michael leading the way to the diamonds and Vera.

As Michael dropped towards Aigle on the shore of Lake Geneva, he rang Vera a fourth time. He hated not being by her side, having to rely on others to protect her and their newborn child. Across the valley, the snow-covered peaks glistened in the midday sun. He ignored the splendid scenery, determined to get the diamonds and return to Bern.

The news Vera shared did not impress him. They were still stuck in the same clinic. They should have been relocated half an hour ago.

'I don't know what the delay is. No one can give me an answer, except for reassuring me that I don't have to worry. Michael, what if something is wrong?'

'I'm sure everything is fine. But I'll speak to the superintendent and tell them to get a move on. Are the guards still there?'

'Yes.'

'Good. I'm approaching Geneva. Shouldn't take too long. I'll ditch the car at the airport and charter a jet; cut the trip by an hour.'

'Don't waste money, I'll be—'

'Your safety is far more important than a few franks,' Michael interrupted. 'Oh yes, we still have no news on Sinead. I—'

'Michael, I think they're ready to move us… Yes, I must go. My goodness, they meant what they had said. All the Bern Police force is here. Maybe that's what caused the delay.'

'Most likely. Call me if you notice anything strange.'

'Of course. Love you, bye,' Vera said, sounding upbeat.

Leaving the Crédit Suisse AG, Place de Bel-Air in Geneva, Michael hurried to his car. From behind his sunglasses, he caught sight of the marine-blue Volvo 4x4 parked two hundred metres up the road. This was the fourth time in the last hour he had spotted the same vehicle. As he continued his stride he recalled each sighting.

The first time was near Lausanne. Something had triggered him to note the Volvo. It was one of those inexplicable things registering an event at a specific time. Could have been just another traveller heading the same way. The second time was when he had crossed the Pont du

Mont-Blanc. Still, it could have been no one in particular, en route to France. The third time, circling the Credit Suisse building looking for parking, had been a dead giveaway.

'Yes boss, the Crédit Suisse AG, Place de Bel-Air branch. Eamonn had followed him inside, but by the time he got there, Michael was already gone. Twenty-five minutes later he had re-appeared from the lower level,' Brian Murphy said into his phone.

'Good. And ya sure he didn't see Eamonn?' Larry asked.
'Positive.'
'Where's he now?'
'In a coffee shop. Most probably grabbing a bite to eat. The lads and I can do with some food ourselves. Okay if we do?'
'Yeah. But as soon as he leaves, you go. You wait for no one. Got it?'
'Got it, boss.'
'Did you attach the tracker to his car?'
'Yes. He won't go anywhere without us.'
'Good. Stay with him till he heads for Bern, then fall back,' Larry ordered.

Michael swung into the traffic and crawled along the Rue du Rhone, making his way back to the Pont du Mont-Blanc. In his rear-view mirror was the Volvo. At the Basilique Notre Dame he turned right into Rue de Lausanne, drove past the main train station on his left, and continued at a leisurely pace north-easterly. A few minutes later, the Palais des Nations slipped by on his left. Two hundred metres back the Volvo weaved its way through the traffic.

He passed the airport turnoff and followed the E62 motorway. The chartered jet could wait. He looked in his rear-view mirror. Three hundred metres separated him from the Volvo tailing him.

Keep going, lads, Michael encouraged them as he motored through the gentle curve of the motorway. Surrounded by forests, only a few hundred metres of the deserted road was visible ahead.

'What's the matter with the fecking eejit? Drives like a woman. Slow, fast, slow, fast,' Brian cursed and accelerated. The speedometer's needle climbed to 150km/h. With no other cars on the motorway – surprisingly empty for this time of the day – he sat back and relaxed.

'Jeezus, I think he spotted us!' Eamonn shouted next to Brian.

As the men in the Volvo focused their attention on Michael, none of them noticed the convoy of six cars race after them with blue lights flashing.

The next instant, Brian slammed the brakes and blurted out, 'Fecking hell!'

Three armoured personnel carriers blocked the motorway up ahead.

Slowing down his eyes caught sight of the police bringing up the rear, fanning out and blocking the road. 'Lads, we're fucked,' he said. Frantically, he searched for a gap in the fence and woods lining the motorway. Spotting a gate he swung right. 'Eamonn, check the GPS. See what's on the other side of this!'

Ramming the gates open, he left the maintenance track and forced his way through the trees, bumping over the rough terrain with branches snapping, wrecking the 4x4's bodywork.

He phoned Larry. After two rings he answered. 'What's up?'

'We're fucked! He led us into a trap! The Swiss pigs are chasing us. We're ahead of them, but won't be for much longer. What do you want us to do?' Brian asked in a panic.

'First, you calm yourself the fuck down. Then try to get away. And no worries if you don't. You'll be fine. Dump your phones and weapons. They have nothing on you, except for suspecting you were following him. Nothing wrong in that, so if they catch you, deny everything.'

'Got ya, boss.'

'Did you get the bottles of Jameson?'

'Yeah.'

'Well, now's the time to drink them. And no, it wasn't for a big piss-up once the job was over, in case you were wondering. It was for an incident like this. Your excuse for fleeing: you're drunk and do not want to get caught. None of you know him and neither does he know you. All you'll get is a warning and a heavy fine. When you're free, contact me. Cheers.' The phone went dead.

'Right, lads. Time to get drunk and lose the phones and hardware. Boss's orders,' Brian joked. 'Any luck with the GPS?'

'Sports complex on the other side. Also, a few roads leading back towards the town and the lake. We can dump the car in the city, split up and make our way back to Bern by train.'

'Agreed. The fake papers will get us out of here,' Brian said as he took another gulp of whiskey. He had no idea where the police were. No one had followed them into the trees.

Yeah, your fancy Porsche ain't made for off-road fun and games. Eejits, Brian thought, as the 4x4 broke free of the woods. The sports complex was sixty metres to his right. Back on the tarmac he sped towards the houses, hoping to reach them before the police would show up. With most of the trees in the area still bare, cover was sparse. They had nowhere to hide if the Swiss were to pursue them by helicopter.

'There's a train station and carpark five hundred metres from here. Take a right!' Eamonn shouted. 'Go, go, go!'

Brian floored the 4x4, ignoring the attention they attracted. Turning into the parking garage he checked the rear-view mirror. They had lost the police.

'Right, lads, split up and try to make it back to town. Then head to Bern airport. We'll rendezvous there and not at the base. And ye know nothing if picked up, understood,' Brian warned the four men. With the interior wiped clean and all evidence removed he stumbled out of the 4x4, having drunk too much whiskey.

Down the road from the parking garage the three APCs pulled up. Directed by the drones, they had shadowed the marine-blue Volvo the instant it had broken free from the trees. In the opposite direction, six Porsche also swung into parking bays. And behind them, Michael's 4x4.

'Thank you for your quick response, Herr Kaufmann,' Michael said, facing Geneva's cantonal police commander dressed in a stylish Armani suit.

'You're welcome, Michael. Superintendent Schaffhausen in Gstaad has informed me of the situation. Shall we pick these men up for interrogation? Or do you want to play this another way? They have split up. Our drones are monitoring five males.'

'No point. It will take days to get anything out of them. If you don't mind, best we keep our distance. With luck, they'll lead us to whoever's responsible for Sinead's abduction.'

'*Ja*, I was hoping you'd say that.'

'Shall I tag along?'

'Best you leave it to us. They may spot you.'

'Yes, you're right. In that case, I'll head over to Bern to take care of my wife and child and deal with the abductor's demands.'

Chapter 35

Russia

Dark clouds rolled in across the bleak Russian winter landscape southwest of Moscow. A line of Bumerang APCs (Armoured Personnel Carriers) emerged from the forty-hectare underground bunker – a warehouse filled with military hardware and planes, forty-five metres beneath the surface. The old disused quarry had been converted into an impregnable underground fortress and covered by a forest.

Filled with armed men, the twenty-eight-ton armoured vehicles joined the convoy parked at the edge of the woods, ready to proceed to their designated targets. The camouflaged, rotating-ground-to-air missile installations safeguarded their advance, adding to the atmosphere of impending doom.

Boris braced himself against the freezing wind buffeting his combat jacket and glanced at the procession of vehicles, his mind fixed on the debriefing. Despite the slip-up in security, he was positive to survive the encounter with his superiors, however bruising it might be. They needed him. To replace someone with his experience at this stage was inconceivable. It would delay the operation by months and risk failure.

With the crunching of boots he marched across the gravel driveway towards the imposing set of double oak doors. A four-colonnade portico sheltered the three-storey mansion's entrance from the elements. The explosive-proof metal shutters were neatly stacked against the tall windows' sandstone mouldings. The sombre building looked as formidable as its occupants.

Two paces ahead his commanding officer, Colonel General Vladimir Coshenko and three senior officers did not utter a word; their stern faces lost in thought. Swiftly, they ascended the six steps. The general snapped a sharp salute in response to the two men on guard at the front door. Notwithstanding the general's seniority, there was a camaraderie amongst the men of Unit 14-BOPS Corps, nurtured by years of serving their motherland on the battlefield.

Twelve storeys below the old mansion, the five men joined their comrades in the underground bunker, impregnable to nuclear attack and outside surveillance.

Seated around the eight-metres-circular table with its holographic-monitor, the faces of the twenty-three senior officers glowed in the dark room, fascinated by the holographic-display projecting possible hostilities. Events which should play itself out on the battlefields of Europe. Above the table's surface the holographic northern hemisphere hovered. The terrain where the short and destructive war would be fought and won.

The display was the culmination of four years of round-the-clock commitment by teams of men and women perfecting their plan. Incorporating minute by minute intelligence reports of manpower, military and economic capabilities, natural resources, weather patterns, psychological profiles of leaders, decision-makers, and citizens of countries to be targeted. It was a computerised war-game, which they believed would have only one result. A quick and decisive victory for Russia.

They were ready.

And so were their powerful friends across the Atlantic.

Only five days remained until the world would wake up to a new era, and the borders of Russia shut to the putrid West.

213

Boris re-emerged from the bunker, invigorated by the display, determined to fulfil his role in this historic occasion. His spirits were high, regardless of the accusations levelled at him for failing in his duty – allowing foreign spies to track him to Batumi. With a slap on the wrist, these had been brushed aside.

In all probability, the spies would by now have discovered the planned attack on the nuclear plants in Europe. As unfortunate as this leak of information was, it was part of war, and therefore one they had prepared for.

The cells in Europe would go ahead with the strikes. NATO could do nothing to stop what was about to unfold.

The last phase of Boris's mission, if successful, would guarantee emotions reaching fever pitch throughout America and Europe. Its leaders and citizens, as pathetic as they were, would demand a military response. NATO would enter the war unprepared.

Deploying Russia's best-kept secret – the world's most advanced weapon system – NATO's nuclear capability would be obliterated. Their leaders would have no alternative but to capitulate, allowing those waiting in the wings to step in, take control, and *negotiate* peace.

Hurrying to join his men, a suffocating tension gripped Boris's chest. The thought of Maxim, their only child, sucked into a world of drugs and crime in the West, filled his heart with bitter hatred.

Craving revenge, nothing would give him and his wife Ludmilla more pleasure than witnessing the destruction of the West. A society responsible for their son turning his back on his values, his family, and his country. This behaviour might be fine in the immoral West, but not to him, and neither his wife.

After eight months at Cambridge University in England, Maxim had become a drug addict and dealer. Dropping out of university, he had traded his future as a lawyer for that of a street criminal. The last they had heard from him was three years ago. Their many attempts to bridge the divide had

214

failed. Their only child wanted nothing to do with them or his country of birth.

Boris would never forgive the West for the ruination of Maxim. Gladly, he would help decapitate the head of the demon.

Chapter 36

Hunched forward, her body tense, Sinead scraped the snow off the balcony's stone coping. The air was freezing, the gentle winter sun too weak to thaw the snow. Searchingly, her eyes drifted across the winter landscape. No longer was the scenery blurred. She had cried enough.

Grand! So, what did I do to deserve this? Because I made *easy* money? Jeezus, give me a break. I've paid my dues, she fumed.

Or was it because she took what did not belong to her?

Or not having given it a second thought about where the diamonds had come from...? How many people had suffered?

But she had always intended to put the money to good use and help girls trapped as sex-slaves.

And did she?

No.

She had been too busy enjoying herself, indulging in the pleasures of love. Not giving it a second thought of how she was going to carry out her noble quest.

As the guilt gnawed inside her, she hanged her head in shame. Yes, maybe I deserve this? Whatever it is they intend to do with me, she thought.

The next instant she shook her head defiantly.

No. I won't stand for it. Not again. This time I won't give them that pleasure. Michael and Vera will not let them get away with this. And Brendan will find me. But how? None of them know where I am, she argued, trying to convince herself that she would be saved.

Her world consisted of the tower she was in. A castle surrounded by forests and mountains. She felt like a real-life Rapunzel. Except there would be no prince charming on the horizon riding to her rescue.

The cold, Eastern-European guards had been tight-lipped when asked where she was. So, if she had to guess, she could be somewhere in Europe, most likely the Alps. Then again, her geography was never very good. For all she knew she could be in Eastern Europe, Canada, America…

And regarding her grand lodgings, she took no pleasure in it.

Deep-red Persian rugs covered the warm-coloured sandstone floor slabs in the bedroom; a room the size of a small apartment. Heavy gold-red curtains adorned the tall French doors which led on to the balcony. Two aged-brown leather chairs and a comfortable upholstered couch were arranged around a large solid wood coffee table with an exquisite arrangement of fresh flowers.

Two wall-tapestries, four antique lamps, a desk with twelve classic novels held upright by sterling silver dragon bookends, a wardrobe, and a large four-poster bed completed the room's furnishings. The dark wood, polished to a silky sheen, looked plush and very expensive. But used to her apartment in Dublin, alive with light and vibrant colours, she found the suite stifling.

Since her arrival she had spoken to no one other than the two guards. Isolated in the tower with a view of the wilderness, she did not know who else lived or was being held captive there.

And the owners, where were they? Were they hiding in some dark corner? Or gallivanting somewhere exotic, shopping for more junk to fill the place?

Trafficking girls like me pay well, ain't it? Ye make me sick, Sinead huffed.

As more questions mulled through her head, trying to understand why she was in this plush room instead of some dark dungeon, she lowered her gaze. Eight storeys below, in a clearing in the woods, stood four black-clad men with rifles slung over their shoulders. Woollen hats protected their heads from the cold. Their laughter drifted up to her.

The thought of escaping now seemed childish. Armed men would be everywhere. Even if she sneaked out of the room, or somehow into the garden below, where then? How far to the nearest neighbours? And what about wolves or bears prowling in the woods, ready to tear her apart?

Still slightly dizzy after the drug, Sinead rubbed her eyes. She was tired, cold, fed-up. And not having eaten anything since her breakfast in Ireland, her body craved sustenance.

Time to fix that, she thought. And as soon as I have, I'll curl up on the bed and sleep. But will I...? Most likely not.

The guards had told her not to worry. To enjoy her stay as she would be back in Ireland soon. And if she needed anything, to buzz the kitchen.

She did not believe them, thinking they were only trying to keep her relaxed before selling her off to some rich schmuck. And the possibility of them killing her, she had banished. If they wanted her dead, they would have done so in Lauenen, saving themselves a huge amount of trouble.

The cold cut into her bones. She rubbed her shoulders vigorously and hurried back inside. She picked up the old-fashioned phone and rang the kitchen.

Having ordered some food, she opened the wardrobe and rummaged through the clothes. She took out a low-cut, black-lace evening dress. The long splits on the sides left very little to the imagination. The next dress was even more revealing, and so was the next, and the next. Her hand froze, touching the fifth hangar.

She looked no further. Vivid memories of her life as an escort returned. A nauseating pain gripped her stomach, realising she would not leave there. The diamonds would not save her. This was her new home.

Chapter 37

NATO HQ, Belgium

'Gentlemen, does anyone have something of value to add?' the Supreme Allied Commander of Europe (SACEUR), Gen William Oswald, asked, winding up the NATO Military Committee meeting.

Across the table, Lt Gen Beck sat disillusioned, his hopes dashed. No one had presented any credible evidence, or intel, by deep-cover agents inside Russia which might have given them the upper hand for once. The result. A unanimous vote in favour of the motion tabled.

All speakers who contributed to the lengthy debate had agreed that, primed for war, Russia could launch an assault on Ukraine and Europe at any moment. They had already annexed the self-proclaimed independent states of Donetsk and Luhansk in Ukraine. Therefore, they, as members of NATO's Defence Planning Committee, must advise NATO's North Atlantic Council (NAC) that war was imminent. The current economic sanctions had failed to deter Russia. The consequences, if delayed, would be disastrous.

SACEUR studied the members' faces, each deep in thought, preparing to leave. The nervous rustle of papers filed, ledgers and laptops shut, was the only sound disturbing the air of gloom. The time for theorising and talking was over. It was time to act. With all diplomats pulled out of Russia, communications had ceased. Diplomacy had failed.

'Thank you, Ladies and Gentlemen. This meeting is now closed,' Gen Oswald said. Lifting his dossier off the table he left to report the committees' recommendation to the next tier in the hierarchy of NATO. As well as the British prime minister.

The intel tabled during the meeting was condemning enough. The twenty-nine representatives of NATO had decided the Russians were lying, being actively involved in sabotage to justify a major offensive. The confession of the Georgian general reinforced this conviction.

This belief was further enhanced by the scale of deployment of Russian and Belarusian forces on the Ukrainian, Polish, and Baltic States borders. The warning by the Russian president for America to withdraw its forces from these countries underlined this threat. This warning America had ignored. Instead, they were sending more troops and weapons to bolster NATO defences.

Russia demanded Ukraine to remain neutral. They would not allow any further expansion of NATO to the east. With the Minsk agreement dead, they had already moved troops into Donbas and were fighting alongside the separatist to reclaim *lost territory*. If Ukraine did not comply, this conflict would spread across the country with the second largest city, Kharkiv, within easy reach.

Off the coast of Odessa the Russian naval force waited to discharge its arsenal. On the Belarus-Ukrainian border in the north, the military exercises could turn south at any moment and head towards Kyiv.

Of the six "W's" relating to the attack on the gas pipeline installation, NATO Intelligence could answer all with certainty; a false-flag by Russia. But concerning the alleged new targets mentioned during the meeting, all six W's – Who, What, When, Where, Why, and How – they did not know.

At least if they knew the "Why", they might avert a major conflict through negotiations. Appeasing Russia might succeed – up to now a futile exercise. NATO no longer believed a word Russia said.

Was this merely a show of strength to ward off the Americans' threat of installing missiles on their doorstep? Or was there more?

Did they want to retake the Eastern Bloc countries and reinstate the old USSR – a well-known ambition of their president? Or, Europe to be held at their mercy with all energy supplies originating in Russia and the Middle East under their control? Boost energy prices. Boost weapon manufacturing?

None of these objectives had been ruled out during the discussion in the boardroom of NATO's futuristic new headquarters in Mons, Belgium. A building which might be one of the first targets to be destroyed if war were to ensue.

The proposed sabotage of the nuclear plants would render large parts of Western Europe uninhabitable. Crippled. It would be a perfect target. One which would struggle to survive a conventional war.

The US Ambassador to NATO, Margaret Jean Hopkins's words of encouragement, did not fool anyone.

They knew that if Europe were to be attacked, America would not come to their aid. Having to defend their own territory against an invasion by Russia and China, they lack the resources.

As the earnest faces around the table rose, one person did not move. It was a tall colonel from the German Armed Forces, Colonel Thomas Bauer. Next to him, Lt Gen Beck paced angrily.

That the leader of Russia had instigated the invasion of Ukraine eight years ago was a fact. And with no significant response from the West, he could now be emboldened to invade the rest of Ukraine.

But Thomas remained dubious about whether a full-scale war with NATO was on the cards. Were the Russians really that ignorant? They might think themselves invincible, believing their own propaganda, but with its forces never tested since WW2 there would be no guarantees. Over-confidence was never a good thing.

The bulk of Russia's military consisted of young conscripts with no battle experience. And that applied to their officers as well. Therefore, they might find themselves bogged down and driven back with their supply lines and convoys destroyed; a situation they did not expect.

And even if Russia wins a conventional war against Europe, why would they want to rule over a massive devastated landmass? Where's the logic in that? But then again, Russians did not reason like those in the West.

Or was it someone else, a sector within the armed forces, spoiling for war? Possibly, but he had no proof.

The deciding factor during the meeting had been his first-hand account of the Georgian's report on those responsible for the gas installation's destruction and the planned attacks on the nuclear power plants. Having cross-examined him, the committee members had ended the debate with the room erupting in protest, demanding action.

The fact of the matter was, he had failed in providing Lt Gen Beck with intel, which could have swayed the committee. All he had was his opinion. And an opinion was a luxury no one could afford. Too much was at stake.

Finding irrefutable proof that the leaders of Russia were not responsible – which now seemed unlikely – was the only way to stop NATO from escalating tensions.

Agitated, Thomas got up. His mission had failed.

Thomas dialled the number he knew off by heart. After a few rings, someone answered. 'May I please speak to Major General Jakob Luik?' Thomas asked in fluent Russian.

'Who may I say is calling?'

'Vladimir Pavlov,' Thomas replied, prepared to answer the next question of verifying his identity.

Having answered the list of pre-arranged security questions, his call was transferred to his friend.

For eighteen years Jakob Luik had toed the line as a colonel. The events surrounding his daughter in the mid-eighties had put him in disfavour with the Party. Therefore, he had been overlooked for promotion for all that time. But he had persevered, finally retiring a general fourteen years ago. Despite no longer active, he was still regarded a risk to the security of Russia. As the FSB was most certainly monitoring his calls, extreme caution was required.

'Hello, Vladimir, how is Vienna?' Jakob asked, ending the silence.

'Same as always.'

'And the ladies?' he added, and laughed good-humouredly.

'Beautiful. But nothing compared to ours. No wonder the West wants to invade our country,' Thomas replied and gave a loud guffaw. 'How are you and Mrs Luik?'

'We're fine. Although, she still suffers from a nasty cough.'

'Has she been to the doctor? She doesn't want it to get worse. Just hope it's not some nasty flu?'

'Vladimir, you know her, stubborn as ever. It took quite some persuasion, but she finally went. I only trust the doctor's prescription will help. Anyway, that is the least of her worries. This talk of war keeps her up more than anything else, wondering why bother to overcome an acute infection when we all face certain doom. As much as I dislike her pessimism, she has a point.'

'Yes, these rumours are most distressing. Here, people are also extremely nervous. Well, let's hope it won't come to that.'

'Wish I knew who is behind this. Might not be the government. But one can never tell,' said the Gen Luik. 'I have spent my whole life in the service of my country and just as I've hung up my rifle, this happens. Nevertheless, I intend to enjoy my old age, war, or no war. At my age the only shooting I want to do is hunting, as I plan to do this weekend. Will you be back by then?'

'Yes, why?' Thomas asked, curious, grasping the meaning of the general's words, "doctor's prescription" – he did get some information and confirmed that the troubles might not be solely the government's doing. And what about the hunt?

'Good. How about joining me?'

'Of course. Where are you going?'

'The woods south-west of Moscow are currently teeming with Teterev. They're canny buggers; not the run-of-the-mill birds. So, will be difficult to catch.'

'Nothing like a good challenge – sounds fun. I'm in,' Thomas said, pretending excitement.

The last thing he was, was excited by the intel the general shared. "Canny... Not the run-of-the-mill birds". Must be special forces. And Teterev equals black; black-ops unit, based south-west of Moscow.

And the location? Thomas thought as he posed a last question, aware someone might be listening to their conversation. 'Where shall we meet?'

'My place. I'm meeting my friends at Yukhnov on the A101. It's half an hour's drive from there. Try to be here by one. How does that sound?'

'Perfect.'

'Good. Sorry for digressing. So, what can I do for you?' the general asked.

'I need a favour and wondered if you could help?'

'Sure.'

'I want to get a specific gift for my Austrian host. I tried on-line, but no luck. However, as I recall, there's a store near you which...' Thomas said, hoping his cover story would suffice.

Ending the call, he rushed back to the operations room. The area located 200 to 250km south-west of Moscow along the A101 needed immediate scrutiny. If some black-ops units were involved, then how far up the food chain did this rot reach?

Thirty minutes later Thomas sat back and watched the live images transmitted by satellite of men and machines moving about on the two runways. Its lenses focused on Unit 14-BOPS Corps, 30km north of the A101 south-west of Yukhnov, Russia.

On the shorter runway, two civilian jets were preparing for take-off. Thomas zoomed in on the group surrounding these planes and examined their features. Close by, more troops piled into twenty-four helicopters.

At the start of the second runway, twelve Iluyushin-II-476-paratrooper-planes taxied forward. Next to these the engines of twelve MiG fighters ran hot, ready to scramble at a moment's notice.

Where are you heading? Thomas wondered.

Eight hundred metres from the runway stood a formidable building. The HQ. And in the surrounding forests, he counted four hundred-and-fifty barracks. Several surface-to-air missile batteries were active. At the edge of the treeline near the runway, armoured vehicles disgorged from an underground bunker.

Besides being home to the black-ops unit, the base also served as headquarters of the Rapid Deployment Unit of the 21st Airborne Division.

'They're active!' Cpt De Clerq from the Belgium Intelligence Corps announced and brushed his hair back. 'What are they up to?'

'Trouble. Maybe only an exercise and nothing more. But for now, I need to know who are on those two planes and where they're heading. The subject we want may be amongst the passengers,' Thomas said, convinced his information was correct. He was like a bloodhound which had picked up on its quarry. 'Can you ID the men on the runway?' he asked one technician operating the spy satellite.

'*Bien sûr,* Colonel. If they're on file with a criminal record, then we can ask Interpol for their names,' the young French lieutenant sneered cynically, thinking the German colonel's request was ridiculous.

'Here, see if any of their features match this,' Thomas snapped and shoved a photograph of Col Polyakov under the young officer's nose. 'And I need to know now. If this colonel's presence cannot be confirmed, there would be no harm in tracking these planes.'

Five minutes later the planes' doors shut. To Thomas's disappointment the colonel was not amongst the passengers.

Discouraged, he watched the planes lift into the air and turn west.

Next to him, all eyes were focused on one monitor, relaying proceedings on the ground in Russia. Armoured vehicles and men still poured from the bowels of the earth. A chill filled the room as they watched Unit 14-BOPS Corps and the 21st Airborne Division's Rapid Deployment Unit carry out their orders. Whatever hideous consequences it might hold was a frightful prospect.

How many innocent women and children would die at their hands?

Chapter 38

Kursk, Russia

'It is a negative, General. Whoever this is, is not the subject in question,' Professor Dimitri Danilovich, head of the Genetic Science Department of the FSB, said.

'You're certain? No doubts?'

'Yes, hundred per cent.'

'Could someone have switched records, samples?'

'No-one has tampered with the records. The DNA samples of all criminals are as safe as the English would say, the Crown Jewels,' he said with a hint of humour in his voice.

'Therefore, the DNA is not that of the individual Niall McGuire?' Ivan repeated, hoping for an alternative response. Hoping that by some miracle the man was dead and buried.

'Yes Sir. They're not.'

'Please forward the report to my office. Not a word of this to anyone,' Ivan said, realising Svetlana had been right all along.

'I knew it. I better phone Vera,' Svetlana fumed, seated on the edge of the couch next to Ivan.

She felt betrayed, having given herself to what she had believed to be a worthy cause. To fight for what was right.

For justice. She deserved at least something in return. But, except for Ivan, all she had received was misery.

Thirty-five minutes she tried in vain. She gave up and raised her shoulders in defeat. Vera's and Michael's phones remained switched off. She could not leave a message.

Ivan took her hands in his. 'Svetlana, I think you've done enough. Best to get you out of harm's way so we can set our plan in motion. Niall may think he is holding all the cards. Let him. We'll play it his way. He's a fool if he thinks he will get away with this. He's bound to make a mistake.'

Svetlana rested her head on Ivan's shoulder, glad to have him by her side.

Klinik Beau-Site, Bern Centre

'Goodbye, Herr Wyss,' Michael said, and switched his phone on in case the commander needed to contact him.

Outside Vera's room, two Bern Schutzpolize stood guard. In the adjoining rooms, six armed police officers – sneaked in during the afternoon while patients had been relocated to other suites – monitored the corridors covered by security cameras. In addition, ten men of the Swiss special-forces watched all movement in and out of the clinic.

Other than the manager, the clinic's head of security was the sole person privy to the contingent of armed men. The official story told to the rest of the staff was that a wealthy socialite had undergone plastic surgery and was taking refuge from the press.

'Any word?' Vera asked, more relaxed with Michael by her side.

'Nothing yet. I expect we'll hear from them soon. They are aware the police are involved. So, they'll want to get this dealt with ASAP. When they do contact us, we'll trace the call. In the meantime, the police will pick up two of the guys who followed me earlier today in Geneva.'

'I know you'll find her,' Vera sighed and kissed Natalya's perfect nose. 'Did Brendan call again?'

229

'At least five times. I told him not to worry; everything's under control. I think the abductors must have watched Sinead for a while, ready to strike at the first opportunity. Therefore, Brendan could also be targeted to gain extra leverage. It will be a disaster if they grab him and we don't play ball. They will not hesitate to kill him…'

Michael was the only person Vera trusted. As an ex-mercenary having survived many skirmishes, who better to watch over them? His sheer size was enough to scare anyone off; 1,98 m tall and 125 kg of muscle. And the long scar to his temple added to his overawing presence – he did not even have to try to look mean or intimidating. Those too scared to peek past his raw, masculine exterior would never see the real him. Warm and kind.

Watching him speak she fell in love all over again. She had been lucky to have found him after all those horrible years. And not once had he referred to her past as an escort. Nor the killing of her husband in self-defence back in Russia. No, he had never judged her. Instead, he had asked her not to judge him for having killed many for money as a mercenary.

The ring of Michael's phone snapped her out of her daydreaming.

'Michael speaking. Who is this? Irina, two calls in one day. I'm honoured. Hang on, I'll put you on speaker. Okay, all set.'

'Hi, Vera. Congratulations! Wonderful news. Michael told me she's adorable and takes after her mummy,' Svetlana's voice cooed.

'Hello, Irina. Thanks, and just as well, or else she would never have found a husband,' Vera giggled.

'Michael, ignore her.'

'Don't worry, I'm used to it,' Michael's deep voice rumbled, filling the room with laughter.

'Are you alone?' Svetlana's voice cut through the banter; her voice sombre.

'Yes, we are,' Vera said, sitting up.

'I have something to tell you. But before I do, you must swear never to repeat a word I'm about to say.'

'Yes, of course,' Vera replied without hesitating.

'That goes for me too,' Michael added.

'Okay… Well… I'm afraid I haven't been quite honest with you. I had my orders. But it no longer matters. Firstly, my name is Svetlana, not Irina. Also, I am an FSB agent, and—'

'You're kidding!' Vera exclaimed.

'No, I'm not.'

'That explains a lot,' Vera said. She finally understood why Svetlana had been Niall's lover. And why she had helped them to escape.

'Sorry about the deception. There's more.'

'Yes…?'

'We have just received evidence which leads us to believe that Niall McGuire is alive. We also think he—'

'Bloody hell! What are you talking about? He's supposed to be dead,' Michael interrupted.

'Hello, Michael, Vera. Excuse me for cutting in. I'm Major General Ivan Lukyanov, Deputy Director of FSB Counter-Intelligence. Sorry, the Major… Svetlana, is too upset to continue. If you please give me a moment, I'll explain,' Ivan interjected protectively.

'Hello, General,' Michael greeted.

'Call me Ivan. As colleagues, we can lose the formalities.'

'So, you know my occupation,' Michael replied, intrigued. 'It's supposed to be a secret.'

'Sorry, comes with the territory.'

'Of course. Please proceed,' Michael said.

'Our government made an unforgivable mistake two years ago. One which has now come back to haunt those who had stood up to Niall. Just so you know, I was not involved with this case. Had I been, he would not have escaped execution. But here we are.'

'Yeah, you can say that again,' Michael re-emphasised, withholding judgement.

'And the danger of him being alive and seeking revenge applies to no one more than Svetlana. Why her? Because, having found the proof needed to incarcerate him, she had

231

brought an end to his vast network of illegal arms dealings, as well as exposing those involved in the theft of top military secrets. Her mission to Ireland had been a brilliant success.'

'Svetlana, you may not know this. I was also working undercover to get him locked up. But you beat me to it. Great job,' Michael congratulated her.

'Yes, she did extremely well, but at an unacceptably high price.'

'What do you mean?'

'Just a quick recap of events leading up to Niall's supposed end. About to be arrested in Ireland, Niall had fled to his island in the Caribbean with Svetlana. Stopping over in Morocco, someone had kidnapped her. But she had escaped. And while fleeing through the mountains, two men had attacked her. She had killed both and, in the process, had suffered a near-fatal stab wound. A few days later, as a parting gift, Niall had added two gunshot wounds to her injury.

'On her return to Russia, she had shut down Niall's brothels and human-trafficking network, reuniting more than a thousand young women with their families. What she had achieved was at great personal risk. And now it seems she has paid the ultimate price. Not only did Niall kill her sister years ago, but have now also murdered her parents and three-year-old daughter.'

'My God, Svetlana…' Vera whispered. 'I'm so, so sorry…' Having lost her parents when still very young, and the child she was carrying kicked to death by the father-to-be, Vera knew what pain was. But to suffer such a loss as Svetlana, she could not begin to contemplate.

'Thank you, Vera…' Svetlana managed to say.

Ivan cleared his throat and continued. 'Instead of executing Niall, he was sent to a Cuban prison to rot. But he had bought his way out. Something we have only discovered this week.'

No one said a word.

Michael was the first to break the uncomfortable silence. 'Right, so now that we know who we're dealing with, I

232

suggest we join our resources and hunt him down. And when we… I better refrain from saying anything else.'

'Yes, I agree. And I'll make sure he won't be able to kill anyone again,' Ivan reiterated.

Wednesday, 20h30, Klinik Beau-Site, Bern Centre

'No, Michael, please don't. I have a terrible feeling about this,' Vera implored. Her gentle, deep blue eyes brimmed with tears. 'Can't someone else go?'

'They know me too well. So, no. Even in the dark they'll spot the difference. Remember, I won't be alone, and this body armour should give me ample protection,' Michael reassured Vera. If they wanted him in the open to take him out, then a head-shot would do nicely. No armour there. He grimaced.

As if reading his mind, Vera said, 'That's fine. And what about your head?'

'Sweetie, the area will be swarming with agents. Neither will I stay put long enough for someone to take a shot. Don't worry, we'll have eyes on them before they know it. I suspect the Clock tower is only the start. The men we tracked from Geneva are in Kehrzatz close to the airport. I reckon we'll be meeting somewhere near there; it allows for a quick getaway.'

'What if you're wrong?'

'We're allowing for that possibility. Two drones will cover my progress with backup cars not far behind. And the tracker, I'll activate during the meeting. Sweetie, I'll be fine. I can take care of myself.'

'Yes, I know,' Vera said, unconvinced. She knew Niall too well. The last thing he was, was stupid. 'Please, don't underestimate him.'

'Of course not,' Michael replied, unconcerned. 'I'll be back in a few hours. Just please don't leave this room; plenty of men are watching over you,' Michael said as he kissed Natalya on her head, hugged his wife one last time, and got up. 'Love you.'

233

'Love you too. Please be careful,' Vera said as Michael retreated out of the room, leaving her with a gnawing unease. Would she see him again?

Vera looked at the peaceful eyes of her baby and sighed. She feared that her innocent child might never know her father, the man who had rescued her from hell. The awful memories of the years of suffering as a trafficked sex-slave under Niall's control were still too fresh to be forgotten. With Michael by her side, everything had become easy, safe, comfortable. Now that they had a child, she couldn't imagine a life without him.

She despised Niall and what he represented. She flicked on the TV, hoping to find something to distract her. At least she and Natalya were safe, guarded by the best the Swiss Police had to offer. But the worry that her husband was heading into a trap did not subside.

Chapter 39

Bern Centre

The sniper's rifle rested on the third-floor window sill with Michael's head squarely in its crosshairs next to Bern's Zytglogge solid cornerstone. A second sniper covered the only other vulnerable angle.

Pre-empting a drive-by shooting, four plainclothes police lingered in the vicinity, ready to raise the alarm if a car entered the pedestrianised zone. Six uniformed officers scrutinised those braving the frosty night. None raised any concerns.

Impatiently, Michael shuffled his feet, wanting to finish the meeting and return to Vera and Natalya. Above him the ornate clock showed the time to be nine o'clock.

His phone vibrated in his pocket. 'Yes?' he answered abruptly.

'Get rid of the police and walk two hundred metres straight ahead, and wait. Make no calls,' the Irish voice instructed. 'That the pigs are here, I'll let slide for now. But if I see them again, there'll be no meeting and you would have outlived your usefulness. Got it?'

'Yes.'

Setting off, Michael tripped over a loose shoelace. He bent down and retied it. Straightening up he continued along the Kramgasse. The seconds wasted had allowed the Swiss plain-clothes police to get to the new rendezvous point. Michael tried to recall the voice on the phone, but drew a blank. Could be anyone of Niall's lackeys.

Reaching the new location his phone vibrated.

'Take a right. And easy does it. We're watching you.'

Michael turned into Keuzgasse and scanned the area for signs of danger. All clear. At the next corner, about to cross the Junkerngasse, a black Audi slowed down next to him. The rear door opened.

'Get in!' a voice shouted.

Unperturbed, Michael crammed his large body into the back seat, coming face to face with two pistols aimed at his head.

'Your phone, shoes, and your *toys*. Careful or this meeting won't last long.'

He handed over the few items.

The Audi slowed to a crawl. A white delivery van pulled up alongside. Framed in its open side door, two men waved their semi-automatic rifles at him to switch vehicles.

'Move it, now!' the man next to Michael shouted and shoved a pistol into his side.

Resisting the temptation to crack the man's skull, Michael jumped out of the moving car and into the van. Immediately, four pairs of hands grappled him to the floor. The van's door shut. It careened forward. With the rear-windows blacked out and the front compartment screened off, he could not tell in which direction they were travelling.

'The stones!' someone demanded.

Michael retrieved the pouch containing the sample of diamonds and handed them over.

'Okay, put these on,' a young man with a clean-shaved head ordered.

'As you say, boss,' Michael replied, thinking Niall must be scraping the sewers for foot soldiers. He removed his clothes, confident his backup team was not far behind.

But he was wrong. The switch between the two vehicles had happened within a flash and on a blind spot. The Swiss

Police had missed it. And, as he still had not activated the homing device hidden in his false tooth, the drones and unmarked police cars continued tailing the black Audi in a northerly direction.

The van proceeded east across the Nydeggbrücke and Aare River and into the countryside.

Dressed in the new set of clothes, and electronically scanned for hidden devices, Michael sat back. Did he underestimate Niall? No.

Without slowing down the van's door slid open. As they threw his bundle of clothes out, Michael caught sight of a passenger jet climbing into the night sky approximately one kilometre from his location.

Klinik Beau-Site, Bern Centre

The two plainclothes Schutzpolizei outside Vera's room, watched the grey-haired cleaning lady push her trolley out of the lift. Passing the nurse's station, she mumbled a greeting to the two nurses on duty and entered the first suite on her right.

Twenty-five minutes later she presented her credentials to the two stern-faced Schutzpolizei. Having scrutinised her papers they allowed her in accompanied by officer Breneman.

Vera smiled a greeting at the old woman. Her eyes lingered a few seconds before she returned her attention to Natalya in her arms. She was on edge; she had not heard from Michael since his call from the base of the Zytglogge. And that was thirty minutes ago. She assumed everything was still under control.

No news is good news... Or was it?

The blare of the fire-alarm made her jump. Voices erupted outside her room. Running footsteps. The suite's door flung open. Four police officers stormed inside and formed a protective ring around her.

Finally, Officer Breneman broke the silence. 'Fire alarm. Nothing to worry about. Possibly a fault in the wiring, or triggered by accident.'

One of the police officers stepped out on to the terrace. His eyes swept the area. Below him the thirty-metre-wide garden was quiet. As was the lane marking the end of the clinic's property. He spotted no suspicious activity on the roofs of the three-storey buildings lining the opposite side of the narrow street.

Vera watched the cleaner lean on her mop, waiting to finish her shift. She looked worried. *Fleeing a fire at her age must be quite unnerving.*

The all-clear came seven minutes later. There was no fire. A maintenance team would investigate what had triggered the alarm. The officers nodded at Vera and left.

With the room and bathroom cleaned, the old woman walked on to the terrace. It was still spotless; exactly as the night before. Wanting to get home, she decided it could do until the morning. She closed the terrace door, drew the curtains shut, said goodnight to Vera, and left the room with officer Breneman on her heels.

Burdened by the large tool bags slung over their shoulders, the two maintenance men exited the stairwell on to the roof. Cautiously they approached the snipers next to the air-conditioning chiller-unit and standby generator. Warned of the maintenance men's arrival the two snipers waved them forward.

Five metres separated them. Greeting the snipers, the Russians' deep voices camouflaged the four cough sounds. The snipers collapsed where they lay, their skulls shattered. The assailants stepped over the bodies and continued to the corner of the roof.

Directly above Vera's suite they slipped over the eaves and landed soundlessly on the terrace. With the curtains drawn, no one had seen them. The leader, Pasha, opened the door a fraction without rustling the curtains. The cleaner had done her part; her husband would be spared.

The sound of the TV muted the soft swish of the door. Parting the curtains slightly, Pasha stared at his target. Vera.

238

Her head was tilted forward and her baby was fast asleep on her lap.

Pasha raised his pistol, took aim, and fired.

Startled by the sting of the miniature dart in her neck, Vera's hand shot up, wanting to rub the itch. But her arm went limp and dropped to her side. She keeled over. Pasha caught her and pushed her back in the chair; her head lolled to one side. Gently, he lifted Natalya off her lap and placed her in the cot.

Vadim stuffed some cushions and towels into Vera's bed, moulding it into the shape of someone sleeping. With the night light on, they lifted Vera, still fully dressed, off the chair and carried her on to the terrace.

Having retrieved the steel zipline and collapsible cross-bracing out of Vadim's bag, they fed the steel brace through the cable swage. Quickly, they rigged the brace inside the door frame and fed the cable on to the terrace, leaving the door ajar.

With the end of the cable connected to the grapple gun, Pasha peered over the rail, searching for their team in the lane five storeys below. 'Are you in position?' he whispered into the miniature mic attached to his headset.

Behind him, Vadim, the lighter of the two, fitted a buddy-harness over Vera and himself and attached it to the cable. Ready to go, he clipped Pasha's harness to the zip line as well.

'Five seconds,' the response came in Pasha's ear.

The white Citroën Dispatch turned into the lane and stopped opposite the terrace. With the van's side door open, Pasha fired the grapple gun's arrow into the van and watched the cable uncoil at his feet. Camouflaged by the city's night sounds, no one heard the soft whizz of the cable flying across the garden.

Neither did the special-ops team deployed in the area notice the zipline.

The arrow's aim was true. At 106 metres per second, its flared head penetrated the large fifty-centimetre-thick polythene foam-board inside the van. Eight seconds later the cable was hooked up to the winch and pulled tight.

'Go!' the order echoed in both Pasha and Vadim's earpieces.

Hoisting Vera's limp body over the rail happened at lightning speed. Skilfully, Vadim controlled the rate of his and Vera's descent, gliding them towards the open door.

As Pasha's feet touched the ground, he unhooked himself. Instantly his teammates released the cable and dropped it on to the road. From the time the zipline had flown across the garden until the door of the van shut, twenty-eight seconds had elapsed.

The van raced around the first corner. At an intersection three hundred metres down the road, it swung left and stopped. Behind it, an articulated truck pulled across the narrow lane, buying them precious time to get away in case someone followed.

Seven hundred metres up the road they stopped next to an Opel and Volkswagen. With Vera transferred into the Volkswagen, the team squeezed into both cars. Someone emptied a jerrycan of petrol over the van.

By the time the flames engulfed the van, the Volkswagen was already a hundred and fifty metres clear of the scene. Remaining within the speed limit, it headed towards Zurich.

Also respecting the speed limit, the Opel with its five passengers drove towards Bern Airport. As the runway came into view, they abandoned the car and jumped into a 4x4.

The team of Russian Spetsnaz troops enjoyed the private contract. The two weeks' work would reward each with a year's salary.

In the narrow lane in Bern, the Swiss Special Forces unit stared at the burning Citroën Dispatch, unsure of which direction to take.

Soon after the Citroën had exploded, Michael's van pulled up on a secluded lane twenty kilometres outside Bern.

'Right, end of the road for ya. Get out!' one man spat, and slid the door open.

Michael hesitated.

'What ya waiting for? Move it! And here's ya fecking phone. We'll be in touch. Meantime, get the rest of the stones. Cheers mate.'

Without another word they shoved Michael out of the van and drove off.

Furious, he sat in the snow and watched the van disappear. He had his phone, but it was useless without the battery. With his hands and feet cuffed he could not walk or jog anywhere. He removed the false tooth and activated the homing device as a deep sense of unease washed over him.

Why did they arrange a meeting and dump me in the middle of nowhere with not a word about Sinead?

His gut told him something was wrong, very wrong.

The news of Vera's abduction sounded too absurd to be true. But the more he heard, the more he realised it to be fact. Inspector Müller, was not spouting gibberish.

Michael exhaled in disbelief. 'How's my child?'

'She is unhurt and sleeping.'

'Thank God. Any idea where Vera is?'

'No, sorry. But the plane we watched did not go anywhere. Therefore, we must assume she's in Switzerland. We have put up roadblocks to prevent them from crossing the borders. Seems they just wanted you out of the way.'

'Yes, something like that,' Michael replied.

'Question I have. Why abduct both women at great risk? If they wanted them dead, why did they not just kill them? I know it's not pleasant to discuss now and in such a manner, but I insist. If there is anything else, any reason which could explain their odd behaviour, then please be kind enough to share it.'

Michael rubbed the red bruises on his wrist. He looked at Inspector Müller and said, 'No, there's not. As I've told your colleague, this is very personal. Niall McGuire, the man responsible, wants revenge. I'll explain. For years he had held Vera and Sinead under his control as mules in his illegal operations of drugs, human-trafficking, and illegal weapon sales. Two years ago, they had escaped and ratted him out.'

241

Michael did not care that he was knowingly withholding information. He would do this his way. Not again would he leave his wife's fate in the hands of someone else.

'Subsequently, an FSB agent who had helped them had Niall arrested and sent to prison in Cuba. But he had escaped and is now out for blood. Two days ago he had assassinated this agent's child and parents. You get the picture? So, if we don't find Vera and Sinead, this will end badly for them,' Michael said. 'Now, can we please go? I need to see my child.'

Chapter 40

Midnight, Wednesday
Norway

Boris shut his mask and breathed in the clean oxygen; thirty minutes till leaping into the night sky from an altitude of 10 000 metres. The drop zone's restrictive size of one-and-a-half-kilometre diameter did not cause him any great concern. Neither being spotted when touching down. The surrounding islets formed a natural barrier between them and the target.

Waiting, ready to fish them out of the icy water, was his support team.

Four days ago, the support team of nine had moored at Kopervik eleven kilometres west of the target with their twenty-two-metre yacht. As *tourists*, some the worse for wear, they had needed a haven to recover. After a day of *rest*, and their *energies restored*, they had ventured into the inlet to *enjoy the scenery* while scouting for a suitable temporary base.

Currently, the yacht, crewed by two men, was sailing to the next rendezvous point on the open sea. At midnight, three zodiacs had parted from the yacht and sped to the drop zone.

At the open door and with all the equipment re-checked, Boris waited for the signal. The next instant he disappeared out of the hatch and plummeted towards the infrared signal ten kilometres below. At 1500 metres altitude he deployed the canopy and drifted into the drop zone.

A ripple of splashes near the three zodiacs confirmed touchdown. Within minutes, the Torqeedo silent-outboard engines steered the fully loaded zodiacs through the ring of islets. Reaching the shore the engines cut. Two minutes later, Boris and his team raced up the snow-covered incline.

The sixty centimetre, dark-brown bats perched on top of the groundsheet with their wings stretched out, looked harmless. In the dim light, the three technicians tested all moving parts, ensuring there would be no malfunction. The wings operated smoothly; the soft flap sound hid the muffled whirr of the spinning rotor blades.

Boris was confident his men would not let him down, just as in Turkey.

'All yours, Sir,' Lieutenant Igor Yanukovych said, having meticulously checked each of the twelve drones.

'Right men, move out. Rendezvous ninety minutes. Check your watches. Time: 00h45. Go.'

Boris, flanked by four men, each carrying a "bat", disappeared into the dark. Behind them, Lt Yanukovych and the two technicians broke camp, removing all evidence.

Three hundred and fifty metres north of the Kårstø onshore gas processing plant, Boris raised his fist. The men took a knee, alert. The surrounding forest fell silent.

Dressed in Nemesis-turkey-suits, Boris and his unit were invisible to the thermal imaging devices deployed in the area. The anti-thermal layers of the suits broke up the heatwaves washing over them. The pattern of these waves blended in with the heat waves of their surroundings.

Boris checked his watch: 01h05.

Ready to fire he inspected the ASM-DT amphibious assault rifle resting on his legs. All was quiet. No one moved.

At 01h15, the first three clicks echoed in his ear. Five minutes later, four more clicks confirmed all teams were in position. Boris gave the team furthest east the go-ahead. And then the next.

Below him, the plant remained quiet.

At 01h40 he received the all-go from the first team, and ordered his four-man team to launch the drones. The timers were set to detonate at 05h00. Constructed out of low-reflective carbon-fibre composites, the drones would be invisible to the sensors guarding the plant.

Mimicking the erratic flight of a bat, the first drone lifted into the air and swept across the trees towards the installation. Its electronic "heart" radiated a metabolic heat signal as produced by a bat. Against the frosty night air, it gave the distinct thermal image of a bat. Reaching the acid-gas-removal installation, the drone flew to its designated target. As the "bat's" wings folded in, the next "bat" lifted into the air.

Eight minutes later, the last bat was in position.

Still no movement at the plant.

The anti-drone security measures had failed to detect the invasion of the twelve hi-tech drones whose timers ticked off the minutes to zero.

By 02h10, the men regrouped and retraced their steps to the zodiacs. Under cover of darkness the zodiacs slipped into the water. They had ninety minutes till Astronomical Twilight; a time when the sky would turn dark grey. At full throttle they shot forward.

On schedule at 04h30, they rendezvoused with the yacht. Thirty-two kilometres in the distance the dark silhouette of the Norwegian coastline broke the horizon.

Boris arched his back, releasing the tensed muscles, and gave his first smile of the day. He felt relaxed in his combat fatigues, glad to be out of the tight-fitting anti-thermal suit. The news of the other two missions' success at the onshore gas processing plants at Kollsnes and Nyhamna made him smile even more.

He was ready to sail home and embark on his next mission.

NATO HQ, Belgium

Stuck in the HQ operations room since 17h00, Thomas struggled to focus. The one-hour shut-eye on the settee around midnight had not been enough.

Having poured himself another cup of strong coffee, he took his seat in front of the panel of monitors.

Time: 03h50.

The Russians' manoeuvres over Sweden and Norway made no sense. Except, of course, for the obvious. And that was what bothered him. Their actions had been too transparent.

Leaving Russian airspace, the three privately owned jets with cleared flight plans to Norway had split up in three directions and overflown the main water reservoirs at Helsinki, Stockholm, and Oslo. But before reaching the reservoirs, they had dropped to a few hundred metres altitude. Once beyond the reservoirs they had shot back up to ten thousand metres. A typical pop-up bomb drop… But not quite; too many seconds had been spent on the level run.

Back at altitude they had continued to international airspace west of Norway. Having joined them over the North Sea, six MiG-fighters had escorted them across the Baltic Sea to Kaliningrad, where they had touched down two hours ago. None of the planes had ventured near their original destinations.

These actions led to one conclusion. The Russians had dropped something in the reservoirs. Most likely chemical agents, poisoning the water supply.

Informed of the threat, the three states had implemented emergency procedures and shut down the water supplies of the three reservoirs. Only when hundred per cent certain the water was clean would they open the valves. In case of an extended disruption, they had also slowed down the backup reservoirs supplies.

The military had sealed off the lakes and was monitoring the air in case of an airborne chemical substance being released. Residents in the area were being evacuated. The civil

246

defence units of these cities were preparing water trucks to ship in water supplies if need be. Special teams fine-combed the reservoirs for foreign objects.

For now, they did this in absolute secrecy, in case it was a false alarm.

As this threat had been shared too late with the Scandinavians, none of their fighters had been able to stop the three jets from re-entering Russian airspace.

And that was what niggled Thomas.

The attack on the reservoirs had all the characteristics of a smokescreen, a cover-up of something far more sinister.

The fact that all three cities had additional reservoirs able to supply a day's water in an emergency made these attacks pointless if not carried out with stealth. Which it was not.

If this was the Russian colonel's doing, which Thomas believed to be the case, then there must be something else at stake. The Russian would have been well aware that radar would have tracked their approach, resulting in immediate countermeasures, thereby nullifying their mission.

So, why bother? And why did they not turn around once they had released the cargo? Was the continuation of flights west to mislead the Scandinavians?

I don't buy it, Thomas thought.

He leaned forward and studied the routes more closely.

Plane one had crossed Lake Päijänne 120 kilometres north of Helsinki and continued west-northwest.

The second one had flown over Lake Mälaren west of Stockholm and continued westerly after regaining altitude.

And the last plane had repeated this manoeuvre over lake Maridalsvannet north of Oslo and then veered south towards the North Sea.

What else was there?

He dotted down all town and place names of interest en route to the three cities and beyond, verifying if any were of significance.

None.

Lastly, he researched the town Kårstø on the coast south of Oslo. Something struck him. Quickly he correlated the other two routes crossing the Norwegian coastline north of Kårstø for similarities.

Kollsnes… Nyhamna!

'They also plan to attack the gas processing plants in Norway!' he warned, convinced he had uncovered the Russian's real objectives.

Surprised, fifteen heads turned in his direction.

'Get Norway's HQ on the line. Poisoning the water supply might not be all. Europe's gas supply is next.'

To him, his deduction made perfect sense, as it would be in keeping with the attack on the gas compressor station in Turkey.

He checked the time: 04h17.

As soon as the call to Col Hansen was patched through, Thomas said, 'Colonel, I believe they are going to attack the gas processing installations at Kårstø, Kollsnes and Nyhamna.'

The commanding officer on duty at Military Intelligence, Norwegian Joint HQ, snapped, 'Please explain.' The fact was, they had just mobilised substantial resources to nullify a likely attack on the reservoirs. 'Are you sure, or is this just a hunch? And if you are so convinced, why did you not tell us earlier?'

Fully appreciative of his colleague's frustration, Thomas ignored his tone and explained himself. The colonel was right; they should have picked this up earlier. 'These may be the primary targets, but we cannot rule out the attacks on the reservoirs as just decoys,' he concluded.

'Point taken,' Col Hansen replied in a more conciliatory tone. 'Any other intel?'

'If correct, they would have parachuted in near the three facilities at around 0h30. For now, nothing else. But we've commenced satellite recons of the three arenas, covering a ninety-kilometre radius. If the insurgents had left, they can't be far. If not, they could be holed up somewhere close by.'

'Roger. I'll investigate and get back to you ASAP.'

After an agonizing thirty minutes, they reconvened their discussion while sharing a live satellite link of the gas plants.

'Do you have any naval craft nearby in case we have to chase down some bogeys?' Thomas asked.

'I have ordered the base at KNM Harald Haarfagre, Madla, 40km south of Kårstø into action. The other two are more remote. No naval craft in the immediate vicinity. But we've dispatched special forces units to all three plants, and… Excuse me. The manager at Kollsnes is on the line. I'll put him on speaker.'

'Good morning, Colonel. This is Knut Larsen. We have checked the facility perimeter fence and found no sign of a breach. Also, no sensors had been activated, nor any suspicious activity noticed—'

'Are you certain?' Col Hansen interrupted, hopeful that they were in time to stop a potential attack.

'Yes.'

'Good. You'll have some military units with you any time now. They will take over security and will need your full cooperation.'

'Of course. Colonel, I was trying to say that something odd happened earlier this morning.'

'What?'

'Maybe nothing. Some personnel commented that a few large bats had settled in the plant.'

'Is that unusual?'

'Not sure. Usually, no one reports any. Maybe because of the questions, people remembered things. We have a bat cave nearby. Someone might have disturbed them.'

'Give the location of the cave to the CO when he arrives.'

'Will do, Colonel.'

'And keep this line open,' Col Hansen said, and ended the call.

Having listened to the conversation, Thomas mulled the information over. A few bats disturbed during the night…? It proved nothing. 'Colonel, any feedback from the other plants?' he asked.

'I'm holding for the manager at Kårstø. Right, he's on,' Col Hansen said. 'Hello, Mr Kristiansen, this is Col Hansen, Military Intelligence. Anything to report?'

'Good morning, Colonel. No sensors tripped, no breach of security.'

Col Hansen frowned. Was his colleague's assumption unfounded? 'Nothing unusual? Anything that might indicate a disturbance outside the plant? Kollsnes mentioned some bats landing in their facility, most likely spooked by insurgents. So, anything—'

'Did you say bats, the Chiroptera type?' Mr Kristiansen interjected.

'Yes. Why?'

'Strangely, a few flew in early this morning.'

Thomas, who had been listening in silence, did not hesitate to interrupt. 'Colonel, best you check with Nyhamna. See if they also spotted some bats. I don't think they are bats. Mr Kristiansen, are any bats still present? If so, you better find them quickly.'

Three minutes later, they received confirmation from Nyhamna.

'Could be drones camouflaged as bats. In other words, bombs. I suggest you evacuate the plant and shut it down immediately,' Thomas said.

As Thomas's words hung in the air, Col Hansen's voice exploded across the speaker. 'What! You've found two and they are bombs set to detonate in five minutes! Get everyone out of the area, now!' he shouted in response to the voice of the special force's CO at Kollsnes. Cutting the call, he turned to his staff. 'Order everyone out of the other plants!'

Thomas lowered his head, furious. This should never have happened.

'Sir, you may want to see this,' Lt Dupont said by his side.

The excitement in his voice made Thomas sat upright. 'Show me.'

'We've picked up a lonely yacht 35km west of Kårstø. The body-heat-signal shows at least twenty passengers. We've checked the other plants. The same. I doubt they are tourists; a bit overcrowded. Maybe worth investigating. Too much of a coincidence.'

'Yes, you're right. We'll get—' Thomas started hopeful. But the next word froze on his lips. In disbelief he stared at the three monitors filled with a bright light.

North Sea

The sky in the east changed to a sinister orange. A deep thunder rolled across the water, causing the yacht's hull to vibrate beneath Boris's feet. His face shone in the glare of the burning inferno, highlighting his broad smile. The smile of bitter-sweet revenge.

Expecting the submarine's sail to appear at any moment, the men sat in two rows next to him, ready to disembark. Some cracked a few jokes, causing a ripple of laughter in tune with the distant rumble.

No one gave the casualties, and chaos inflicted another thought. It had simply been another mission, one which had gone as clockwork and with maximum effect. War... Killing was in their blood. What they craved. What they lived for.

And who or what the next target would be was immaterial. All that mattered was to obey orders and succeed. But before their next mission, they intend to enjoy a few hours' leave in the arms of some female company.

On schedule the grey shape of the submarine broke the surface twenty metres on their starboard side. Men jumped into action, ready to toss the spring lines to their comrades standing on the hull of the submarine. Slowly, with fenders deployed, the yacht approached against the wind for a beam-to-beam crossing.

As soon as the spring lines were secured, a gangway dropped into place. The ships' engines idled in neutral, allowing the transfer of men and equipment.

'Colonel, we have a bogey approaching from the east!' the radar operator shouted from inside the yacht's cabin.

At thirty kilometres, the AW101 helicopter of 330 Squadron RNoAF was not visible in the hazy dawn, skimming the water, racing towards them.

Lagging the chopper, two Skjold-class stealth corvettes cut through the surf at a maximum speed of 59knots. Each carried eight Kongsberg Naval Strike Missile SSMs, one x76 mm Otobreda Super Rapid multi-role cannon, and two x12.7 mm Browning M2HB HMGs Mistral SAMs.

'Move it! Go, go, go!' Boris ordered from the back of the line. 'Scuttle the yacht!'

The six men still onboard placed the explosives, timed to detonate in five minutes. Grabbing their gear they raced on to the sub. They were sitting ducks if a gunman opened fire.

Boris climbed into the sub's hatch, wondering how they had found them. And so quickly.

The submarine's propellers pushed the sleek hull forward, dipping its nose below the surf. About to shut the hatch, Boris took one last look at the approaching helicopter. Less than a kilometre separated them.

Framed inside the open door, the Norwegian door-gunner pointed the M3M machine-gun at Boris. The man's full-face mask spared Boris the hatred burning in his eyes, ready to blast him to hell.

Boris grinned and shut the hatch.

Unstoppable, the submarine vanished below the surf.

08h00, NATO HQ, Belgium

Him again! Thomas fumed, glaring at the photo of the colonel grinning from inside the sub's hatch. He wanted to strangle the man who had outmanoeuvred him at every turn.

Why did I not see this earlier? Even half an hour might have foiled the attack.

He did not lose heart despite the catastrophic attack. As long as there was still time, however little, he would do everything in his power to avert a war.

The images captured by the helicopter crew of armed men boarding the submarine the Russian government rejected outright. It proved nothing. That some of their units were on routine exercises in the North Sea in international waters at the time of these "most dreadful" attacks was purely coincidence.

NATO High Command.rejected this statement for what it was: a blatant lie.

The direct result of the attacks was horrific. More than four hundred fatalities had been reported so far. What the final tally would be, only time would tell. On site, the jet-fires still raged out of control. The domino-effect of the explosion and sub-explosions made venturing near the facilities far too dangerous.

The supply of rich gas from the Norwegian gas fields had been cut to starve the fires. Inside the network supplying dry gas to the receiving terminals in Germany, Belgium, France, and the UK, the fire was spreading. The extent of damage to this network of thousands of kilometres of transmission pipelines, no one dared to guess.

Fortunately, the automatic fire safety valves not destroyed in the initial explosion had safeguarded vast sections of transmission pipeline. Also, spared was the Draupner platform 160km offshore, a key hub for monitoring pressure, volume, and quality of gas flows in Norway's offshore gas pipelines. It connected the Statpipe lines from Heimdal and Kårstø for onward transmission.

Nevertheless, the result would be a thirty per cent loss of energy supply to Europe. Billions of euros in damages, loss of revenue, and a crippled infrastructure. It would take years before these would be reinstated.

First, they had destroyed the American gas pipeline in Turkey, and now this! Europe will depend on Russia for 90% of its energy and be at Russia's mercy.

Talk about a motive, Thomas sighed. How anyone could dissuade NATO from acting now seemed unlikely. The Russian colonel remained his only hope of finding the mastermind behind the attacks.

At last NATO knew the exact location of the colonel's submarine. Using its dipping sonar, the helicopter had initially followed the Daniil Moskovsky (B-414) – a Victor III nuclear attack submarine. And currently, the corvettes equipped with the latest anti-submarine warfare (ASW) systems shadowed the sub.

From the intel garnered, Severomorsk in Murmansk Oblast, Russia – the main administrative base of the Russian Northern Fleet on the coast of the Barents Sea – seemed to be the sub's destination.

Thomas detested their arrogance: having committed a crime which could start WW3, and then coolly sail back to port, knowing full well they were being followed. The Russian colonel had to be stopped.

Once he reaches port and slips away, who knows where he'll pop-up next? So, for now, it will be Severomorsk. That's where I'll grab you, Thomas thought.

But to succeed, he needed support. Someone to assist him and his team in locating the colonel and abduct him while in transit. The idea of trying to carry out a snatch and grab operation inside a Russian military base was sheer madness. Thomas smiled at the ludicrousness of such a notion. But then, desperate men do desperate things.

It would take the sub at least thirty-six hours to cover the 2000km to the naval base. That left him enough time to prepare.

When news of the attack would spread across Europe, an official declaration of war against Russia by NATO would be inevitable. This attack would be regarded as a first strike against Europe. An incident so great, not even the most liberal-minded citizens of Europe would ignore and let go unpunished.

The destruction of these installations and the detailed planning ruled out any theories that a splinter group or third force might be behind the attacks.

Not for a second did NATO's leaders doubt the orders came from very high, from the president himself. As far as they were concerned, there was nothing more to be said. This attack had been the final straw. Therefore, half an hour ago, they had issued instructions to all member states to mobilise their forces, however meagre.

Diplomacy had reached an impasse with all lines of communication cut.

With NATO's intelligence agencies stumped, unable to provide any information to the contrary, Thomas was on his own. He had to reach someone trustworthy inside Russia to help him unearth the facts.

Chapter 41

Geneva, Switzerland

Dressed in blue jeans, white shirt, light-brown anorak, and Timberland boots, Michael approached the Crédit Suisse AG, Place de Bel-Air in Geneva. Under his arm he clutched an empty brown-leather briefcase. It was his second visit to the bank in two days.

Entering the main foyer, he removed his sunglasses and slipped the anorak's hood off. At the lift, he greeted the two security guards and presented his Interpol credentials for inspection.

'*Bonjour,* Monsieur Mahoney. They're expecting you. Please proceed.'

Fretting over Vera had resulted in only three hours' sleep. The rest of the night he had spent reviewing his plan, as well as the footage recorded by the city's CCTV network near the Crédit Suisse. Having identified Brian Murphy in the marine-blue Volvo 4x4 – one of Niall's henchmen – he had had no more doubts.

He had fed Brian's photograph into Interpol's databank, making him a wanted man. If he showed his face in a public space covered by CCTV, Interpol's facial recognition software would alert the local police. His days of roaming free would soon be over.

With his baby daughter safely in the hands of the Klinik's staff, he had set off for Geneva at 07h30. En route he had contacted Svetlana and Ivan. Updating them on the latest developments, he had hoped they might have some news on Niall's whereabouts. But nothing.

The possibility of Niall returning to his island in the Caribbean was ruled out. The property had been sold on public auction eighteen months ago to an American billionaire-politician. And as far as they could tell, there seemed to be no connection between the new owner and Niall.

Satellite footage also confirmed that neither a plane nor boat had ventured near the island since Sinead's abduction. Therefore, it was unlikely that she was being held there.

The wall of monitors in the bank's security office displayed activities inside and outside the bank. Michael focused his attention on those covering the exterior, curious about who might turn up; the real reason for his trip to Geneva. It was not to collect more diamonds. Nor to arrange a ransom as he had told the police.

The exterior-mounted CCTV cameras panned the area. Meticulously, it scanned all parked and approaching cars, as well as the faces of pedestrians passing by or loitering on the pavement.

Thirty minutes Michael waited; his attention on two vehicles. A black Lexus 4x4 with four passengers parked fifteen spaces behind his 4x4. During this time, two men had exited the vehicle and attached what he assumed to be a tracking device – it was too small for an incendiary device – inside his 4x4's wheel well. Other than that, there had been no activity.

The second vehicle was a dark-grey Citroën Space Tourer parked a hundred and thirty metres west of the bank's entrance. It had slipped into its parking space soon after Michael had entered the bank's security office. Since then, it had not budged. Neither did any of the four passengers exit the vehicle.

None of the passengers in the vehicles looked Irish. Their features, short-cropped, fair-blond hair were military or ex-military of eastern European descent.

Must be Mafia. Niall's buddies.

So, he has changed tact after his men's failure yesterday, Michael thought. Parked out in the open, not bothered if they would be seen or not, was worrying. What are you up to? Follow me out of town, crash my car, relieve me of the "diamonds" and then bump me off. Negotiations over. Or put a bullet in me when I step outside the bank and grab the "diamonds"?

Thanking the security personnel, Michael picked up the full briefcase and left.

The three packs of Xerox copy paper and wads of soft tissues stuffed inside the briefcase gave the right effect. It should satisfy Niall's men that he was not leaving the bank empty-handed.

Not to jeopardise Vera's chances, he would let it play out the way they expected it to. Only when she would be safe would he permit all hell to break loose.

Niall's men watched the tall man in a light-brown anorak with the hood pulled over his head exit the bank's main entrance. He clutched a full briefcase under his arm. A pair of sunglasses, blue jeans, light-brown boots completed his attire. Purposefully, he strode towards the Mercedes 4x4 parked at the rear of the bank.

As the Mercedes pulled out of its parking bay, the Lexus and Citroën followed, maintaining a discreet distance. A few minutes later, the Mercedes turned into Geneva's train station's underground parking garage. Reaching the first available space close to the shopping arcade's entrance, the Mercedes pulled in. The Lexus and Citroën continued to circle the carpark, searching for vacant spaces.

The driver of the Mercedes got out and entered the shopping arcade, linked to the ticket office and train-platforms.

Six men jumped out of the moving vehicles. Following the driver to the ticket-sales hall, they were oblivious to the four undercover police officers stationed along the length of the arcade.

Exiting the ticket hall the driver glanced left, right, and hurried up the ramp to the platform. He boarded the train to Bern, due to depart in three minutes. Having located his designated seat, he sat down opposite a couple in their mid-thirties. He took out his smartphone and typed a message.

Before the train's doors closed, Niall's men scrambled on board. Four of them sat down in the same carriage and two positioned themselves in the doorways at either end. None of them noticed the four Interpol agents watching them.

Michael looked at his phone and smiled. The trap had been set. This time, no one would escape or go free until Vera and Sinead were safely home.

Also, knowing that Svetlana was processing the images of the men following him lifted his mood considerably. If they were the Russian mafia, their details should be on file and would lead to the ringleader. Most likely the same man who had murdered Svetlana's family. And in turn this person would lead them to where Niall was hiding.

Chapter 42

NATO HQ, Brussels

Thomas replaced the receiver. Encouraged by the information shared by Maj Gen Luik, he contemplated how to enter Russia undetected. But he faced a problem. Two hours ago, all commercial flights to and from Russia had ceased.

The thought of travelling as a diplomat on a last-minute mission to avert the impending war crossed his mind. Whether he would succeed was questionable. If his real identity as senior officer in the Bundeswehr Intelligence Corps were to be discovered, he would be trialled as a spy.

And if he tried to sneak across the border – a border currently crawling with troops – and caught, there would be no trial. They would shoot him on the spot. But he may have no choice unless the call he expected delivered an alternative.

Major General Ivan Lukyanov, Deputy Director FSB Counter-Intelligence, who are you? Why would you risk...or rather, want to meet? Wonder what you have to say?

It was in the early hours of Thursday morning when the scrambled call came. With identities confirmed, arrangements were made for a face-to-face meeting on Russian soil. Both men knew the risks if caught. Neither had hesitated.

Thomas cleared the details of the meeting with his superior. Their way in would be as a Russian intelligence unit returning from a recce in the Ukraine.

Without delay he commandeered an eighteen-seater military Gulfstream 650 jet; wheels to be up in two hours. Destination: Sumy, Sumy Oblast, North-eastern Ukraine. Forty kilometres from the Russian border. A Ukrainian special-ops unit would escort them to the border. Including a stopover in Calw to pick up his men, Thomas estimated three hours to complete the 2 140km journey.

ETA at the border: 23h00.

Thomas wished he had a few hours' reprieve to go home, rest, and clear his head. And see his wife. But it would have to wait.

He missed their time together. Holding her close. Sitting under the tall oak next to their home in the Baden-Wurttemberg countryside. Watching the sun set over the Blackforest Mountains with her head on his shoulder. Of times like these when there was no need for words.

Realising just how much he missed her he touched her bright shining eyes in the image on his phone.

Chapter 43

Kursk, Russia

The funeral arrangements were in place for tomorrow. And if she were to die, then so be it. Although she had no such intention. If people thought she had nothing to live for, they were wrong.

There was Ivan…

There was revenge…

Numbed with her emotions in tatters, she tried to focus on the monitor at the FSB HQ in Kursk, hoping for a hit.

Methodically, the computer searched the FSB's extensive database for a match of the men who trailed Michael in Geneva. But three hours and still nothing. She was worried. The suspects might not be the Russian mafia or even Russians. If so, then their efforts in finding Niall's connections in Russia – the men responsible for the murder of her family – would fail.

Thirty-five per cent of the search remained.

Tired of staring at the screen she got up and wandered down the corridor to Ivan's office. On the way, she poured two coffees.

Outside his office suite, two men stood guard. They held the door open and let her into the reception area where Marina was typing a report.

'Is the General free? I need to discuss my findings with him,' she asked.

'I'll check, Major,' Marina said and smiled.

Entering Ivan's office, he jumped up and relieved Svetlana of the two mugs, placing them on the desk. He pulled her towards him.

'I needed a break… Hope you don't mind me barging in?'

'Barge in as often as you like,' Ivan said, 'And I can do with a break myself.'

Standing at full stretch she draped her arms around his neck and kissed him. A sob escaped her lips. She needed him. She did not want to let go.

He stroked her hair and whispered, 'Any luck with your search?'

'No, nothing… I'm sorry. I can't do this…'

'It's okay. Shh…' Holding her close, he ignored the stifling surroundings of grey walls, cabinets, and bookshelves cramped with files. Relics of the old USSR.

Finally, Svetlana dropped her arms to her side.

'Come, sit down and let's have that coffee before it's ice cold,' Ivan said.

Svetlana wiped her face with a tissue and straightened her hair. 'As I meant to say, I'm worried our search may be a waste of time.'

'Let it run. I'm sure they're in there somewhere,' he reassured her while silently sharing her misgivings. It might have been far more productive to have circulated these images to all FSB branches. But that he could never have allowed. If the wrong people would have discovered their investigation, it would have meant the end of Svetlana. 'Any news from Michael?' he asked.

'Spoke to him a few minutes ago. He's expecting a call from the abductors. Poor man. Can't imagine what must be going through his head. I'm glad I'm not the abductors. When he gets hold of them, he'll show them no mercy.'

'Good. I really hope so.'

'According to him, it's going as planned. Interpol's agents and the Swiss are watching them. Hopefully, they'll lead them to where the girls are. Michael suspects Vera's in Switzerland and Sinead in Morocco. I must help them. I feel so guilty—'

'Stop blaming yourself. It's not your fault,' Ivan cut her short. 'How could you have prevented Vera's abduction when she was protected as if she were the president?'

'I know…'

'I'm sure we'll find them,' Ivan said confidently.

'I'll try…'

'Now, another matter. Regarding this pending war, I may be on to something.'

'What…' Svetlana asked, glumly.

'I'm to meet someone tonight. He has information which might help unravel this mess.' Ivan saw his words did not reach her.

'Sorry… What was that?'

Patiently, he repeated himself. 'I have a meeting tonight which might be very fruitful.'

'That's good… Where?' Svetlana asked, struggling to pay attention.

Ivan did not give up, trying to guide her out of the dark labyrinth she had slipped into. 'Can't tell. Don't want to compromise the meeting, or you.'

'Take me with you.'

'No. I need you here in case something happens to me.'

'Please don't say that…'

Ivan disregarded her protestation, however insensitive, and said, 'If something happens, you must contact my friend, Major General Jakob Luik – retired, Military Intelligence – and update him on the situation. Speak to no one else. I've lost four agents during the last five days. Men who had asked too many questions. You understand how bad things are? Why I need you to stay?' Ivan cautioned, and scribbled the general's contact details on a piece of paper.

'I won't need it. You'll be back.,' Svetlana said stubbornly, fighting back the tears.

'Yes, I shall,' Ivan replied, knowing his words were of no comfort.

'Please, can we go for a walk, get something to eat? Or are you too busy?' Svetlana asked.

'Let's do that. Give me five minutes.'

Returning to her office, she hoped the computer had by now spouted out the names of Sinead and Vera's abductors.

Chapter 44

The spacious room felt bare. The king-size sleigh bed, matching bedside lockers, chest of drawers, two-seater couch, and full-length pivot floor mirror did nothing to change that.

Three large paintings in ornate frames depicting scenes of winter hung on the walls: a sunset over a frozen lake; a fog-covered hill with a lonely tree and a yellow moon; a family of deer crossing a vast snow-covered plain. The subdued tones of blue, silver, and grey made the room feel cold. The stone floor, covered by a generously sized oriental rug in light-blue hues, added to the gloom.

The winter's sunlight pouring through the two stained-glass windows did not calm Vera, who wondered why she was not in the clinic holding her baby.

Groggy with the lingering effect of the heavy tranquilliser, she slipped off the bed and walked over to the door. It was locked. Next, she tried the window. To her surprise, it swung open.

Facing her was an expanse of snow-covered forests and mountains. On her left, a tall tower. That of a castle. On her right, nothing. And five storeys below the forest floor. It would be a simple escape if she was a spider or wanted to end it all. Well, a spider she was not and the latter she had no intention of doing.

266

Her body shuddered. She shut the window, turned around and glared at the single long-stemmed red rose in a crystal vase on top of the chest of drawers.

A red rose. How banal. You missed me; can't live without me, Vera mused angrily.

She picked up one of the three neatly stacked books next to the vase. Yama: The Pit by Alexander Kuprin. She knew the story well. Life in a brothel owned by Anna Markovna in St Petersburg. 'Niall, you are so hilarious,' she sighed and replaced the book.

The thought of being subjected to Niall's psychotic mind once again repulsed her. The awful memories of her working for him as a sex-slave and drug mule resurfaced. Up to yesterday she had lived her life contently under the misguided notion she was rid of him for good.

As incomprehensible as the news had been that he was alive, so was it awful.

And now captured by him…

Unthinkable!

She knew what lay ahead for her and Sinead. Months of torment and abuse before he would blow their brains out.

In your dreams. You'll never touch me again, she vowed to herself.

But she knew the chances of her preventing him from doing his worst were pure fantasy. Nothing short of jumping out of the window would stop that from happening. And would she? No. She had too much to live for.

What puzzled her was how they had managed to abduct her from the clinic. The last thing she remembered was sitting in her chair with Natalya asleep on her lap. And then, staring at the ornate ceiling and wooden chandelier.

Is someone in the Swiss Police or Interpol, someone close to Michael helping Niall? Must be. How else could they have managed? And Michael most probably trusts this person…

Horrified, she realised Michael had walked into a trap. He would die.

The thought of Natalya alone in the world, the same as she used to be, frightened her.

No, not her, please, not her…

She must escape. She got up, entered the bathroom and splashed her face with cold water, trying to clear her head.

The creak of the bedroom door made her jolt upright. Quickly she dried her face and returned to the room.

Two men in black. One held a tray, the other a pistol.

'Dinner. Eat, you'll need your strength,' the man carrying the tray ordered in Russian and placed it on top of the chest of drawers.

'Where am I? Where is my child?' Vera shouted and lurched forward, wanting to rip their faces to shreds.

'Shut up!' the one nearest barked and punched her in the stomach.

She doubled over and collapsed on to the floor. Stunned, unable to move, she watched them leave. Before the door shut, she saw a tall man in the dim-lit archway, standing with his feet apart, his face cold, soulless.

The man's glaring eyes haunted her. They were familiar. Dark. Sinister. Evil. They were the eyes which belonged to someone else. To a man she loathed with every fibre of her being.

16h00, Thursday

The heavy door creaked open. Two men in black jumpers and jeans entered, pulling someone into the room. Annoyed, Sinead snapped, 'What do you want?'

'We brought you friend,' one said in broken English and shoved his victim inside, tripping him up.

The man, his hair and clothes dishevelled and torn, rubbed his head and sat up. Stunned, Sinead looked at his blood-covered face and the dark bruise on his forehead. Her mouth dropped open, speechless.

Crammed inside the doorway, the two men, their pistols drawn, watched Sinead's face change from shock to disbelief.

'Brendan!' she cried out.

'Enjoy you…self, lovebirds,' the one said and laughed as he retreated into the corridor.

'Sinead, thank God! Are you okay?' Brendan asked, sitting up, trying to wipe the blood off his face with a torn sleeve. 'I was so worried about you.'

'Yes, I'm fine. But you, your head… Your face. What have they done to you?'

'It's nothing,' Brendan said, got up and embraced her.

'What happened?'

'They must have watched you. Knew about us. They phoned and said if I wanted to see you again, I must come to Geneva and bring one-million-euro. I didn't hesitate.'

'You shouldn't have. You have no idea who you're dealing with. They are very dangerous. You'll never be allowed to leave. They'll kill you. I'll be spared for now. They have other plans for me.'

'Yes, I know. But what do you mean they have other plans for you?'

'They'll force me to whore for them. And when I'm of no further use, they'll bury me somewhere in these woods.'

His gaze held hers as he spoke, his voice firm, 'No, that will not happen. We'll escape… We'll find a way out. And remember, Michael and the Swiss Police are looking for you. They won't give—'

'I'm in Switzerland…?'

'Yes. But where exactly? I'm not sure. They brought me here by car from Geneva. Once past Zurich, they had blindfolded me. I reckon Zurich is only half an hour's drive. If you can get away… There must be people nearby.'

'Yes, if I could fly it would be easy,' Sinead said and stared at the windows. Her face relaxed. She smiled. 'You're right. I'll try to get out before it's too late.'

'That's better. There's always a way.'

'Yes… And how are Michael and Vera? Did you speak to them?'

'To him, many times. I offered to help. But he had told me to stay out of it, concerned I might get into trouble. Well, at least I did "find" you.'

'Yes, you did… I'm so sorry I dragged you into this.'

'Believe me, I would not want to be anywhere else than here with you. I was sick with worry. And regarding them being okay. No, they're not. Somehow, they had abducted Vera from the clinic.'

Sinead's eyes shot open, not sure she heard correctly. 'You're kidding!'

'No, I'm not.'

'Poor Michael… The baby,' Sinead sighed. 'Then maybe Vera is also here?'

'You could be right. Makes sense.'

'We must find her. Try to get away.'

'Yes, we will,' Brendan said as his eyes met hers, filled with longing. She did not resist his kiss. He slipped the straps of her dress over her shoulders and let it fall to the floor. 'How I've missed you. I was so worried.'

'Me too,' she said, removing his ruined jacket and pulling him on to the bed.

She sat up and looked at Brendan asleep next to her, at the dried blood covering the wound on his face. It needed cleaning. But she did not want to disturb him. Poor man, what have they done to you? she thought.

Forlornly, her eyes drifted towards the windows, to the darkening sky. How many hours do we have left? she wondered.

Without warning the door swung open.

Four men stormed inside and grabbed Brendan by his arms and legs. Lifted into the air, they carried him out of the room. His attempts to break free failed. His eyes met hers as she raced after him. Before she could reach him, they slammed the door in her face.

Two loud gunshots rang out from the other side of the door.

Sinead sunk to the floor with her head in her hands. As she wept, she whispered his name. Brendan was gone. She would never see his smile again.

Chapter 45

Bern

Michael lifted Natalya out of the cot as if she were made of porcelain. She gurgled softly, her eyes wide open, curiously staring up at him. Tickling her under the chin he wrapped her in a warm blanket. 'Don't worry, I'll find mummy,' he said. But he doubted his own words; up to now things have not gone his way.

After the failure by the Swiss to protect Vera, he did not want to leave his or his family's fate in other people's hands. He also hated having to sit around doing nothing. But for now he had not much choice. All he could do was to let them come to him.

And that was exactly what Niall's men were doing.

Michael watched them follow the taxi. Arrive at Hotel Waldhorn in the city centre. Enter a room on the same floor as the presidential suite, and in a room on the floor below.

Impatiently, he waited for them to make contact. To get this over with. And for news from his colleagues and Svetlana.

As for Sinead, he did not know where she was. The office in Morocco had failed to locate the plane. He felt somewhat guilty having focused his attention on rescuing his wife and not also her.

And Brendan, where was he? For two days, not a word. Did he decide to investigate, find her on his own? He hoped not. Because if he did, he would only exacerbate matters. Get himself abducted or killed.

His phone vibrated. At last. 'Hi Svetlana, any news?' Michael whispered and put Natalya back in her cot, careful not to wake her up.

'Sorry, not one hit. But that doesn't mean they're not Russian. I suspect they could be black-ops operatives employed by a private company or an individual. In that case their records won't be on our system. The military will have them locked away somewhere. And we don't want to knock on doors till we know who we can trust. Too dangerous.'

'I understand,' Michael replied thoughtfully. 'Considering their mannerisms, body language, I think you're right. They smack of black-ops: well-trained, lots of experience. That would explain how they'd pull off Vera's abduction.'

'I agree. I'll proceed on the premise that they are.'

'I trust you'll find some answers soon.'

'Let's hope so. Any luck on your side?' Svetlana asked.

'Nope.'

'Sorry I couldn't be more helpful.'

'No problem. But all's not lost, though. Can't say more in case someone's listening.'

That they had Niall's men under surveillance and eavesdropping on them, he kept to himself. These men may not know where the girls were or what the plan was, but may let slip with some useful information. If they dared to arrest them and they were black-ops, casualties could be high.

And shoved into a corner, Niall would not hesitate to eliminate Vera and Sinead.

19h30, Thursday, Kursk, Russia

As soon as the call ended, Svetlana opened her laptop. Her fingers touched the keys and instinctively started to type. In her mind's eye her thoughts clustered together like light, wispy clouds, taking shape.

Her fingers paused…

How did I miss that? Must be all this. My family, Vera, Sinead, and Niall resurfacing, she thought, realising she had been too distracted.

Other than Niall, there was another man to be feared. His ex-business associate or presently so. The head of one of the most powerful international criminal outfits.

Nicolai Baranovsky.

He was a man whose history was quite colourful in every derogative sense of the word. Someone who had exploited the collapse of the USSR to the full, empowering and enriching himself with total disregard of how many lives he destroyed. Today he controlled most of the ex-USSR's steel production, plus having a substantial shareholding in Russia's oil industry. His name never appeared on any official documents. Instead, a string of subsidiary company names represented him.

His operation was no different from Niall's defunct criminal empire. The odd thing was that at the time of Niall's arrest, Nicolai had somehow escaped prosecution.

The evidence had clearly shown that he had been a major cog in the wheel regarding the theft of Russian arms and secrets. So why did nothing happen to him?

And his friend… General… General Andreyev? Yes, that's him. Who helped them? They must have had powerful friends.

They all should have been locked up, if not executed. Instead, they had escaped punishment. Except for the general, forced to retire early with some medal thrown in for his loyal service to the motherland.

How banal! Who are your friends? Military black-ops perhaps? Time to find out. Ivan, you better come home. I need your help.

The thought that they all had been in cahoots from day one worried her deeply.

Off-the-books, black-ops missions, were they financed secretly by selling weapons to countries blacklisted? Countries prepared to pay over the odds for hardware and military secrets? And those secrets sold, were they of any real value? Come to think of it, most probably not. Were they financing something off the record? Something much bigger than limited subversive operations here and there. Something like what is currently unfolding, she wondered.

She was entering treacherous waters, far beyond her skill set. She had been marked. The slaughter of her family was the first warning for her to back-off.

At the time of her success in catching Niall and his co-smugglers, it would have been an unwanted interference at best. But someone in authority must have sanctioned her mission, someone genuinely concerned by the arms and secrets stolen from Russia. How ignorant these individuals had been, oblivious to what was really going on.

Also, the investigation of the murders in Cuba, and her insistence on uncovering the facts, had not been welcomed. They did not like loose ends, as it might lead to events not meant to be found.

What are you hiding? Who are you?

If she and Ivan dared to continue down this path, the risk of them being killed was very real. Well, she did not care. She had to stop them.

So, number one priority.

Where are you, Nicolai?

She needed to map his every move since then. Find out everything about him and his associates. The facts and not the flowery reports on file. It would be a mammoth undertaking; one she could not hope to achieve on her own. She needed help. But who?

Diligently, she began her report, dreading where it might lead. What she would unearth? Finding Nicolai would be the simple part.

Then something else dawned on her. Why did they only lock Niall up? She smiled.

Yes, Niall, they made you the scapegoat. First opportunity I get, I'll tell you.

But she knew that could only happen if she found him.

Chapter 46

Sumy, Ukraine

Guided by radar, the plane descended into the dark, snow-covered countryside. The pilot struggled to stay on course; the jet thrown from side to side by the strong crosswinds. To the north, Sumy's lights flickered. Suddenly, the runway's edge lights sprung to life, guiding the pilot in. Silhouetted on the edge of the runway were six Boeing C-17 Globemaster III transporters.

The plane came to a stop. The runway of the provincial airport went dark.

Stepping on to the asphalt, the icy wind pounded Thomas's jacket. Above the noise of the wind the drone of military vehicles hummed as men and machine arrived at the North-Eastern Ukrainian front.

The capital of Sumy Oblast was preparing for war.

Marching towards the terminal building, a squad of soldiers blocked their path. A voice ordered in German, 'Papers, please.'

Wearing snow-camo fatigues with no insignia, and a head shorter than Thomas, the Ukrainian held out his hand. Dutifully, Thomas handed over his unit's IDs and clearance papers. The soldier studied them and shone his flashlight into each German's face.

Satisfied, he said, 'Welcome Colonel. I'm Colonel Maxim Sokalov, commander of the Special Forces, Sumy Oblast. We'll escort you to the border and remain in support until you leave.'

'Thank you, Colonel,' Thomas replied. 'Just hope our numbers won't spook the Russian.' He would have preferred a more low-key approach. But uncertain of what lay ahead, he was grateful for the additional men.

'Not to worry. He, or they, won't know we're there. Come,' Col Sokolov said. As his sinewy face cracked into a smile, he added, 'Just a warning; it's going to be a bumpy ride. The roads are terrible. But just be glad there are any.'

'Fine with us. Grateful for the ride and for watching our backs.'

Ten minutes later, four camouflaged vehicles left Sumy Airport, commandeered as a military airbase, and closed to civilians.

Skimming Sumy town, they headed towards the border forty kilometres north-east. Approximately halfway, the KrAZ Spartan light tactical vehicle swung right on to a secondary road.

'Hold on, Colonel. Our joyride is about to start,' Col Sokolov warned.

After twenty minutes of bumping and shaking, avoiding potholes large enough to swim in, Col Sokolov checked the GPS. 'Another ten minutes and we walk. Two klicks to the RVP (Rendezvous Point). An hour ago, our intel reported the area to be clear, but this could have changed by now. The Russians are focussing their attention on the northwest, Black Sea, Donbas, and Kharkiv. For the moment, there is no sign of a troop build-up across the border here.

'High Command believes that if they attack, it will be a missile strike on all our major airfields, power plants, and communications networks. Controlling the air, their land forces will make a move on Kyiv, Kharkiv, and the south coast. Their goal would be to replace our leader with a Russian puppet like before.'

'Why invade? Why not just fix the next election?' Thomas joked. 'But seriously, you're convinced they will?'

'Yes. But it will be something they'll regret, as we will fight them to the bitter end. Their standard MO of bombing towns flat, raping women, etc., will not make us surrender. We'll never forget the Holodomor. Just because they were let off when they took the Crimea and Donbas, they must not think we'll just roll over this time.'

'A war with Russia is what we in NATO are trying to prevent. And I doubt you'll face them on your own if we fail.'

Col Sokolov smiled. 'Colonel, I would like to share your optimism. But few leaders in Europe…the West, have the will to fight anyone, let alone Russia. They would never risk a nuclear war. What angers me is that they have led our leaders and people up the garden path with all kinds of rubbish thrown at us like we're imbeciles. And if Russia attacks, they'll betray us. We'll be sacrificed. Many will die or shipped off to Siberia. When the war is over, whether we've won or lost, they'll continue business with Russia as usual. Only hope we have is for men in NATO to overrule their leaders and help us beat Russia.'

Thomas nodded his head. 'I think Russia's ambitions are more than just Ukraine. But I trust it won't get to that.'

He could not disagree with Col Sokalov's words. But as for himself, he would not stand by and watch the country of his birth turned into a mass grave.

In single file, Thomas and his men dressed in snow-camouflage uniforms followed Col Sokalov. Hugging the woodlands on their right, and with the terrain flat, they made swift progress through the fifteen centimetres of snow.

Suddenly, Col Sokolov raised his left hand, fingers extended and joined, bringing the file to an abrupt halt. He lowered his hand to waist level, his palm facing down. The men disappeared out of sight.

'Half a klick to the border,' Col Sokolov said, as he searched the frontier with his night-vision binoculars for Russian patrols.

277

Thomas also swept the terrain with his thermally enhanced night-vision binoculars. From the woodland on his left, across a clearing of three hundred metres, to the woodlands on his right. Between his position and the border, there were no impediments. Neither was there anything remotely resembling a border: a fence, guard towers, ditches, patrols, anti-tank barricades. Nothing. And neither a single living soul.

'Where's the border?' Thomas asked.

'An imaginary line just this side of those woods. There's no physical border. People can cross as they like.'

'Landmines?'

'For now, none. Not needed.'

'Good. We'll take up a position inside the Russian woods. We've one hour to rendezvous.'

'Roger. We'll be here to cover your retreat,' Col Sokolov confirmed.

Thomas and his men scrutinised the border, the woods. Half an hour they waited. Positive the way was clear, Thomas got up, and with his Heckler & Koch HK 416 assault rifle, pointed the way. Driven by the wind, a few icy drops stung his face.

The column of men split in two and disappeared in amongst the swaying evergreens, their branches heavy with snow. The men spread out and took up positions to monitor all potential lines of approach.

At precisely midnight, out of nowhere, a shadow appeared midway between the two woodlands. A blue light flashed three times.

Thomas responded with three blips of his own.

The figure stopped ten metres short. Above the howl of the wind, a voice called in Russian, 'The sun will set on all—'

'Unless the truth is found,' Thomas completed the sentence, identifying himself.

'It's safe to show yourself, Colonel. Tell your men to hold their positions.'

Facing the FSB Deputy Director, Counter-Intelligence, Thomas shook his hand. 'Glad to meet you, Maj Gen Lukyanov.' He appreciated the Russian's precarious position. If caught conversing with armed insurgents, it would be the end of the line for him.

'Likewise, Colonel. I think we can skip the rank. Call me, Ivan.'

'Thomas... Best we take shelter. Are you alone?'

'Yes.'

'Must admit, I didn't spot you in the open.'

'This anti-thermal camouflage sheet works well,' Ivan said, and tapped the white camo tarp draped over him.

Thirty metres into the trees, two of Thomas's men waited next to a rigged tarpaulin, providing shelter against the sleet. Both soldiers nodded in acknowledgement of the Russian's presence before fading out of earshot.

'Coffee?' Thomas asked and pulled a flask out of his backpack. 'Should be warm. Made it before we touched down.'

'*Spasibo*,' Ivan replied, grateful for something to alleviate the cold which had crept into his bones while lying in the snow. It had been a while since he was last in the field; sitting behind a desk had made him soft.

Holding mugs of coffee, the two men, roughly of equal stature, studied each other in the white glow of the Phantom Warrior light.

'How do you know our mutual friend?' Ivan asked.

'Met him when I was a young intelligence officer. My senior had introduced us. Over the years, we had built a mutual understanding. I trust him with my life.'

'That was quite convincing,' Ivan replied, having heard enough. The determination in Thomas's eyes had revealed far more than his words.

'And yourself?'

'The same. He was my mentor. If anyone else had suggested this meeting, I would not be here,' Ivan said.

Quickly, Thomas recapped the weeks' events. Turkey. The Georgian general's doomsday scenario to be unleashed upon

Europe within the next few days – this intel visibly stunned Ivan. Current activities at the military black-ops base west of Moscow. The destruction of the gas-filtration plants in Norway. The saboteurs escaping by Russian submarines. And the one person involved in all these incidents: Col Polyakov.

'Just as I had suspected,' Ivan groaned. 'And who knows who's involved? Is it a group in our military trying to start a war and wanting to overthrow the current regime? Possibly. But considering the president's recent statements, I suspect he could be giving the orders. Best we find Col Polyakov and hear what he has to say.'

'If you can establish his location, my men and I will pick him up and bring him to you.'

'Hmm, you should blend in. But how's your Russian?' Ivan asked.

In perfect Russian, Thomas recited from memory an excerpt from the novel Eugene Onegin by Alexander Pushkin. The book, with its eponymous protagonist, considered a national classic, had served as the model for many Russian literary heroes.

'I think there's a lot you have not told me, Thomas. And, I suspect that's not your real name either,' Ivan said, realising the man facing him was as Eastern-European as he was. 'For now, I'll not ask any more questions. I hope one day we'll be able to share our stories.'

'So do I.'

'If I track him down, when can you be back here?'

'We're ready. Came prepared.'

'Sounds like you have it all planned.'

'Yes,' Thomas replied. 'Two of my men – both fluent in Russian – will join me. We have the necessary documents and clothing. The rest of my unit will wait at the border as guests of the Ukrainians and guard this route. Any safehouse where we can lie low till you have the intel?'

'Of course,' Ivan said. 'Best you stay in Kursk. I must attend to some personal business for a day and then return to Moscow. Thomas, you grab him as soon as he steps on to the quay in Severomorsk, Murmansk Oblast. Seems the most logical destination.'

11h00, Friday, Sokol'ye, Kursk Oblast, Russia

The house was filled with flowers, their scent heavy in the air. Since ten o'clock, family and friends had quietly filed through the door into the lounge and dining room where the three closed-caskets lay on top of a table.

Her parents' coffins overshadowed Dasha's small white casket. Next to the wreath of pale pink roses and carnations with a teddy bear and banner was a framed photograph, a reminder of a life taken too soon. Hidden inside the coffin were the burned and crushed remains of an innocent child.

The well-wishers paid their respects and filtered into the kitchen, where, in subdued voices, they continued to express their grief.

Svetlana shook hands, received kisses, smiled meekly at the sorrowful faces while fighting back her tears. Controlling the urge to flee and run into the open field, she did not dare look at the little white casket.

Ivan stood by her side, his face grim, suppressing his anger. Seeing her like this infuriated him. He must remain calm. She needed him to get through the day... And the next. And when the house would be empty. When Dasha's rippling laughter would only be a distant memory.

As the priest spoke, people hoped for some miracle to resurrect the love which used to dance inside these walls.

Slowly, the procession made its way to the graveyard she visited twenty-four months ago. Her sister's grave. And here she was again, to bury the last of her family. She walked without seeing in a world of her own.

Ivan supported her by the arm. His eyes swept the quiet road. In his periphery he saw his men flank the procession. Concealed in the surrounding fields and forests, a ring of armed men secured the area. In the grey sky three drones circled, combing the area for snipers. Ivan's earpiece stayed silent. It seemed the killers had not taken the bait. He hated the risk she was taking – the vest would stop a bullet aimed at her chest, nothing else. But she had insisted. She wanted them caught, no matter the risk.

With the last visitor gone, Ivan shut the front door of the empty house. He did not lower his guard. Neither did he tell his men to stand down. They would remain till Svetlana was back in Kursk. Someone targeting the house with an RPG from outside the village could not be ruled out. Or an ambush on the way back to town.

He took her hands in his. 'Svetlana, do you need more time?' He wanted to go, eager for an update on Col Polyakov's location. The looming war would not wait for anyone.

She squeezed his hand and smiled. 'I'm ready. Let's go. I want to find the men responsible for the murder of my family. And help stop this war from happening.'

'Am I that obvious?'

'Yes. Shall we go?'

'Yep. Pity we didn't get them. My men most likely scared them off. But to be honest, I'm relieved nothing happened. A confrontation with so many bystanders could have—' Ivan stopped in mid-sentence, interrupted by the loud ring of Svetlana's phone.

Not recognising the number, she hesitated. 'Wonder who it is? It's not local.' She swiped the screen and said, 'Yes?' as she put the call on speaker.

'Sorry about your loss. I'm sending you a video which might cheer you up. I'll call again in a minute,' an unfamiliar voice with an Irish accent said.

Her phone beeped. The video started. Stunned, her hand shot up and covered her gaping mouth, recognising the person in the video. The smiling face. Dasha!

On the thick oriental rug, surrounded by toys, Dasha played in the sunlight pouring through two tall windows. It was a large room luxuriously furnished with expensive paintings, an ornate mirror, rich tapestries. The walls were of smooth stone. An attractive, fashionably dressed young woman stood to one side. The camera panned from Dasha to her and zoomed in on the newspaper in her hand. On the date. February, 18th!

'No, it's not possible... Is this some sick joke!' she cried out. 'Did they not punish me enough...'

In disbelief, Ivan stared at the recording a second time.

Her phone rang.

With a trembling finger she swiped the screen. 'How could you, you bastard!'

'Now, now. I'll have none of that. However, I'm a bit shocked that you think so little of me. Did you honestly think I would murder a child? I thought you knew me better than that, *dearie*. Not my style to kill children,' the voice ridiculed. 'Anyway, I thought you'd be delighted to know it was a hoax. A teeny-weeny punishment for your sins.'

As the realisation that Dasha was still alive dawned on her, she smiled and gripped Ivan's arm. 'Dasha's alive!'

Regaining her composure, she returned her attention to the phone. 'And my parents?'

'Sorry. No such luck. I said, "Not my style to kill children", and nothing about adults. Now, be a good girl and return the little one to the morgue in Kursk. I'm sure the parents must be frantic by now.

'Okay, here's the deal,' he continued. 'You want to see your child again, then you better jump on a plane. Oops, forgot, flights are cancelled. But seeing you're such a brilliant spy, I'm sure you'll find a way out of Mother Russia. Be in Geneva, Switzerland, tomorrow 14h00 local time. I'll give you instructions from there. And don't worry, as you can see, I'm taking good care of your child. Cheers.'

Seated in the back of the speeding 4x4 with its blackened windows, her head rested on Ivan's shoulder. They hardly spoke. They both knew she had no alternative. She must do as ordered. A terrible foreboding haunted them, knowing she might never return.

Ivan's mind was in turmoil, dreading not seeing her again; she could not take the killers on by herself. He must go with her. But duty called. He had to do his part in stopping the pending conflict.

Svetlana looked at his tormented face. 'Don't worry, I'll be fine.'

'I can't let you go on your own. I'll deal with—'

'No, Ivan. If this war is not stopped, there will be nothing to come home to. I'm sure Michael has enough resources to help,' she interrupted, knowing her words were wishful thinking. Michael had his own problems. Watched, and held at ransom, he may not be able to do much. 'Please, let's not discuss this anymore.'

'Fair enough, but I don't like it,' Ivan replied.

'Nor do I. But I have no choice,' Svetlana said wearily. 'Any idea how I can get there?'

17h00, Friday, Kursk, Russia

'The first sub's ETA in Severomorsk, Murmansk Oblast, is 23h00. You better get there ASAP,' Ivan said. Establishing the routes and schedules of the submarines returning from their "manoeuvres" off the Norwegian coast had been easier than he had expected.

Opposite him, his back straight, Thomas listened attentively. 'How many subs?'

'Three. Having to cover the most klicks I suspect his should arrive last.'

'I agree. Any intel on flights out of there?' Thomas asked.

'Not yet. I'll establish that while you're in the air. I have arranged the necessary items for your team: IDs, orders, uniforms, hardware, and a tranquilliser gun in case he resists. You work for the FSB with orders to escort the colonel back to Moscow for a debriefing. At least that part is true.'

Ivan knew full well what would happen if this mission failed, but it was a risk he was prepared to take. 'An Antonov An-12 troop carrier is waiting at Kursk airport. It will also be your ride to Moscow, where I'll meet you. Once you're on the plane, you're on your own.'

'Good. As soon as we're kitted, we're set to go.'

'It's in the 4x4,' Ivan said, and added hesitantly, 'Thomas, one more thing. I need a favour.'

'Shoot.'

'It's a private matter.'

'Fine. If I can help, I will.'

'A colleague of mine must be in Geneva, Switzerland, tomorrow 14h00. It is a matter of life and death. One problem though. As she's a major in the FSB, the Ukrainians might not be keen to help. Or they might, and then hold her as a spy to extract intel from her. Can your unit escort her across the border and get her on a flight out of Ukraine?'

'Understood. By your expression, I gather she is more than just another colleague.'

'You're right. She means a great deal to me.'

'I think she means much more than just a "great deal",' Thomas said with a smile. 'As she is also in the same corps, I can treat this as a military mission and fly her out on our plane. I'm sure I can convince the Ukrainians to take her to Sumy airport. Can you "arrange" a German passport for her? We'll land in Germany. From there, my men will drive her across the Swiss border. Will she need help in Geneva?'

'Thomas, I'm most grateful. And, yes, some muscle in Switzerland will be welcomed. She'll be facing extremely dangerous killers who have abducted her child. She has a contact at Interpol who might be able to help. Whether he can, remains to be seen. I want to go with her, but can't.'

'Don't worry. She won't be alone, I guarantee you.'

Twenty minutes later, Thomas put his phone away. 'It's arranged. The Ukrainians are cooperating. They think she's working with me and has valuable information she must present to NATO HQ in Belgium. Be at the border by 22h00. Lieutenant Bernd Schmidt and his unit will meet you.

'The lieutenant is hundred per cent trustworthy. An excellent soldier. He will be by her side until she is safely in Germany. From there, a twelve-man special-ops unit will escort her.'

'Trust this never comes to light, or there'd be hell to pay. You'll be court-marshalled,' Ivan warned. Despite his concern for this stranger, he felt as if a world-size boulder had been lifted off his shoulders. The knowledge that Svetlana would not be alone was of great comfort.

'You and I'll have to cover each other's backs,' Thomas said. 'We can report this as a joint covert operation to find the men who started hostilities. And the major is a vital cog in this, as her actions will hopefully help to prevent a major conflict.'

'She might very well be.'

'What do you mean?'

'She came up with a hypothesis, which is starting to make sense. Especially after what you've told me. The men who abducted her child and murdered her parents may be black-ops with potential links to Col Polyakov. And could be temporarily employed by a private individual named Nicolai Baranovsky – the ringleader of one of the biggest international criminal syndicates. According to the major's findings, this man has gone missing. Disappeared off the radar. Very sinister.

'Or, they are in the military and did this dirty work as a "favour" for someone. If so, then some senior officers are involved. This may go back a lot further. As they say, the plot thickens. No point dwelling on that. It will only distract us. Let's just find this colonel and squeeze the truth out of him before we are all blown to hell,' Ivan said.

'If the major's theory is correct, then the paperwork will be easy. Her report should do it,' Thomas said. 'And believe me, if this colonel turns up on the Kola Peninsula, I'll get him.'

Chapter 47

Burg Reinhardt
Switzerland

Yes, Svetlana, you should have killed me when you had the chance. It's too late now, Niall thought, savouring his success in meting out punishment.

He turned up the volume of the eight o'clock news on the TV. With glee he regarded the images of the ambulances and fire engines filling the street in front of the burning hotel in Bern. Twenty-three people had perished in the explosion. He felt no guilt. Unfortunately, they were people in the wrong place at the wrong time. Their deaths he laid at Michael's door; a traitor who had sided with the two whores.

At least I'm rid of you. Pity about the kid... Upside: I've saved her from growing up an orphan and ending up a whore like her mother.

Niall studied the eight coloured A4 photographs in his hands as he arranged them in sequence and placed them inside the envelope – a record of Michael's last movements before he had died.

The one on top was of Michael leaving the clinic carrying his child. The next one, Hotel Waldhorn still intact. Then of Michael entering the hotel. One of him framed in the bedroom window on the top floor minutes before the explosion. Next, the blast laying waste to the hotel, engulfing it in flames. The Ambulances arriving. And the one at the bottom depicted the stream of firefighters carrying out body-bags.

That will do nicely; cut you down to size. And with you single again, maybe we can rekindle our lost love...?

He recalled laying eyes on Vera for the first time in a strip club in Brussels. Of her floating down the stairs in a revealing evening dress, her deep-blue eyes filled with pride. Immediately, he had lost interest in the dance routine on the stage – a blonde lustfully writhing around a pole – and had focused his attention on her. Not wasting time, he had paid off her traffickers and invited her to Ireland. Soon they had become lovers.

But Niall was Niall.

After three months he had craved his freedom, bored with her hanging around his neck. This rejection had nearly destroyed her, especially when forced to continue where she had left off in Brussels. To work as a sex-escort in Dublin.

Soon he had used her as a drug-mule, slipping in and out of countries in Europe, dealing with customers on his behalf. It was a risk, but one which had paid off. She had never double-crossed him. The extensive list of those killed who had defied him had been enough for her to live by his rules.

But her subservience had evaporated soon after she and Sinead had become friends, resulting in them stealing his diamonds. Well, he would teach her a lesson she would never forget.

In the background the TV droned, reporting on the growing hostilities between Russia and NATO. Not interested, he picked up the envelope with the photographs and left the lounge on the upper floor of his private quarters.

Two suites occupied this level. Besides the spacious bedrooms and bathrooms, each contained a lounge, dining area, and a balcony with views over the Alps.

His private quarters were located on the top two floors of the castle and covered an area of one thousand square metres.

The double-storey entrance level consisted of a large living and dining area. In the south wall a series of tall French doors led on to a wide roof terrace. The billiard room, home theatre, gym and spa with a twenty-five-metre two-lane pool were tucked in under the upper level. The entrance, a set of large double oak doors, was sited in the south-east corner. To its right, a lift and staircase linked the two floors.

Niall enjoyed his new home.

While incarcerated in Cuba, he had lost his manor house outside Dublin, the Caribbean Island, the planes, the luxurious yacht, along with a string of other properties scattered around the globe. All were sold off at auction.

But he had retained this castle, the chalet east of Bern, and his private game ranch in the north-east corner of South Africa. No one knew about these as he had never ventured near them till after his escape from Cuba.

Bought four years ago, an agent had overseen the redesign and refurbishment of the old castle. At the end of the project this agent had met with an unfortunate accident with all records of their dealings erased. If anyone had discovered this castle, he might not be the proud owner today.

Even his most trusted employees did not know of its existence. Nor had they seen him since his escape. As far as they were concerned, he lived somewhere outside Geneva.

Niall shut the door to his quarters. He turned towards the tower on his right, accommodating the main stairs as well as Sinead's suite one floor up.

Not bad for a prison, he thought. She should count herself lucky. She could have been in a hole like the one in Cuba. She better behave, or she might find herself in a seedy brothel somewhere in Spain.

Ignoring the lift, he jogged down the stairs to Vera and the child's rooms, crossed the lobby, and walked to the end of the stone-arched corridor. He knocked on Vera's door, slipped the A4 envelope under the door, and hurried to the security room located one floor below.

TV screens lined the one wall of the security room, displaying all habitable rooms inside the castle, except of course for his own.

'Evening. Everything okay?' Niall asked.

'All good, *da*,' the one security guard replied.

'Right…' Niall said and looked at the screen showing Vera's room. He was just in time to see her pick up the envelope, return to the bed, and sit down.

Warily, she slipped the pictures out of the envelope.

Confused, she looked at the picture of Michael leaving the clinic, their child in his arms. Quickly she looked at the next one of him entering the hotel… Suddenly, she dropped it on the bed and grabbed the one showing the hotel's top floors destroyed in the blast. Her hand froze in mid-air. The palm of her left hand slammed against her forehead.

She did not scream. Instead, she sank on to the bed, and in a state of shock stared at the next few pictures. The ambulances, the firefighters, the body bags. The photographs drifted to the floor. She got up and walked to the window. Her hand reached out for the latch. She swung the sash open…

'That will teach you to double-cross me. Now jump,' Niall coaxed the figure in the live-feed. But Vera did not move. She merely stared out of the open window.

Losing interest in her, Niall turned his attention to Sinead's monitor. Sinead was sitting on her bed with her knees pulled up under her chin, her arms wrapped around her legs, and staring into space.

'Maybe I should go and comfort her. What do you reckon, lads?' Niall ridiculed. With their English limited, the men on duty had no idea what he meant.

He looked at the next monitor.

Seemingly without a care in the world, Dasha sat in bed, listening to the bedtime story read to her by the babysitter. Niall found the scene quite entertaining, considering only a few metres away the two women suffered mental agony. One ready to jump to her death – if she had not already. And the other trapped in a world of her own.

Fortunately, being used to be separated from her mother from time to time, the young child had without a fuss believed the lie that her "mummy will be home soon".

But Svetlana would never hold her child again. She would die knowing her child was happily playing somewhere nearby. The camera in Dasha's room would ensure that.

The cell prepared for Svetlana was a replica of the Cuban hellhole he had rotted in for six months. It came with all the trimmings: the putrid stench of raw sewage, bugs, and lice. Living in that muck, she would see her child day and night, but never talk, hold, or touch her. Her only salvation would be the bullet he planned to fire into the back of her skull. He could already smell the sweet taste of revenge, the metallic odour of her blood seeping from her wound.

20h15, Friday, Bern, Switzerland

Next to Michael's bed, Natalya was fast asleep in her tiny cot, unaware of the turmoil which had welcomed her into the world.

He paced the room, exasperated, not having received a word from Niall or his men. The news of Dasha's staged "death" had only enraged him more. He wished he had rid the world of Niall at the time, cursing the laws he had to live by. This killer had no right to be alive.

The video sent by Svetlana was being analysed in Bern by the forensics lab. Dasha's room was possibly in a castle, chateau, large manor house. And with Svetlana's destination, Geneva, it must be somewhere in Switzerland. Then again, it could be anywhere within a hundred-kilometre radius. Niall would have ensured nothing in the video could lead them to Dasha.

For the fourth time since the dull explosion had rattled the clinic's windows an hour ago, he tried the Swiss Police commander in charge. Finally. 'Herr Röthlisberger, Michael here. I lost the video-feed from the hotel. I guess the explosion was aimed at me?'

'Hello. Correct. The top two floors of the hotel were destroyed.'

Michael did not reply.

'Are you there?' Commander Ben Röthlisberger asked.

'Yes, I am. Any casualties?'

'Except for the building, no. We evacuated your double, the hotel guests, and staff in time. Not to alert the killers that we had discovered the bombs, we escorted everyone out through the back. As far as they are aware, you both died along with everyone else.'

'Thank God. How did you discover the bombs?'

'When all the chatter in their rooms stopped, my men knew something was wrong. Checking the bedroom near your double's, they had found a bomb with a time delay of twenty minutes. There were two more devices on the floor below. But we could not disarm them in time. Michael, who are these people? Obviously, they are trained professionals.'

'Yes, seems to be the case. Any idea where they are?' Michael asked. It was a question he already knew the answer to.

'No. They slipped out one at a time. Didn't return to the rooms. We're checking the city's CCTV footage to establish their escape route, their mode of transport. I believe—'

With the phone to his ear, Michael stopped listening. They had lost Niall's men. And so, Vera. And, for all intents and purposes, he had been "killed". This assassination attempt confirmed one thing. He was never supposed to meet them, nor survive. This whole charade had been a decoy – retrieving the diamonds were immaterial. Vera and Sinead were never to be exchanged. And Svetlana was heading towards the same fate.

He was furious, having walked into the trap.

Vera had been right. He should have listened.

'Herr Röthlisberger, I'm truly sorry for all the trouble. I'll call back in a few minutes.'

'I understand. Call when you're ready. We'll do everything we can to track them down. I have not given up hope,' Commander Röthlisberger said, trying to sound encouraging.

Michael walked over to the cabinet and took out a bottle of Jameson whisky. He poured himself half a glass and took a large swig. Allowing the smooth warmth of the amber liquid to spread through his body, it eroded the stress. He sat down and placed the tumbler on top of the coffee table. Enough for now; he needed to keep a clear head.

Well, at least I'm still alive.

And being "dead", he could move in and out of the shadows unnoticed. And if Svetlana arrived with a unit of special-ops soldiers in support, Niall's men would not see him till it would be too late.

Chapter 48

Friday Evening
Murmansk Oblast
Russia

Colonel Andriy Rebroff, Lieutenant Petro Fedorov, and Staff Sergeant Mikhail Romanov found themselves in the middle of an airbase on high-alert at the northern tip of Russia. The three German special-ops members looked out of the porthole and then at each other. They smiled and raised their shoulders, knowing what had to be done.

'No turning back now. Let's get this over with,' Thomas, alias Col Rebroff, said.

Disembarking the Antonov An-12 troop carrier, a Lada 4x4 pulled up. The driver jumped out, saluted Thomas, and asked him and his fellow officers to join him.

At exactly 22h20, they entered the guardhouse and presented their travel orders. The officer on duty – a junior captain – examined each document. Satisfied, the captain relaxed and said, 'Welcome to Severomorsk, Colonel. Please proceed. Hope it's not too cold for you.'

'I think we'll survive, Captain,' Col Rebroff replied good-heartedly. 'By the way, we should be back in about three hours, tops. We may have company. And then we'll head south for some *warmer* weather.'

'The Lada is at your disposal. Do you need a driver?' the captain asked.

'Not needed. We'll take it from here. Issue is too sensitive. You understand.'

'Yes Sir, of course,' the captain said and saluted sharply. The clearance papers as presented by Col Rebroff stamped "Top Secret" required no further clarification.

En route to the naval base they passed through two more security-checks. Having found a vantage point close to the quays, but not too close to draw attention, they settled back into their seats.

At 23h25, as the cold arctic wind shook their vehicle, the first submarine berthed.

First to disembark was a twelve-man unit of black-ops soldiers. In less than fifteen minutes they had loaded their equipment and three inflatable zodiacs on to a truck. With all men boarded the truck drove off, leaving no trace of their presence behind.

In the mooring the submarine continued preparations to set sail again.

A heavy silence filled the Lada. Sergeant Major Chris Koch frowned and said, 'Colonel, run that by me again. How do you intend to kidnap the Russian colonel with twelve heavily armed special-ops Ruskies watching? The distance from the quay to that truck is only fifteen metres. So, no chance of banging him on the head and carrying him away.'

'I know it won't be easy. See the three-storey building, Port Control?'

'Yes…' Sgt Maj Koch replied, intrigued, wondering what scheme his commander had dreamed up. Filled with trepidation he studied the old building with its wrap-around veranda.

One hundred and twenty metres separated them from the building. Between the docking-station the first submarine had occupied and the port control were three more double-docking stations with four submarines moored, preparing for sea. The two moorings closest to the first U-boat were vacant. Most likely reserved for the two other subs returning from Norway. The over one-kilometre quayside was crawling with military personnel and vehicles.

'This is what we'll do. When the third sub approaches, we'll move to the other side of the Port Control. I'll call the colonel as soon as he sets foot on the quay; an urgent phone call from Moscow. You'll wait for him at Port Control, zap him with the tranquilliser, and dump him in the Lada. From there, it will be a race to the plane and out of here,' Thomas said.

'No disrespect, Sir. That sounds like a bunch of baloney. Way too many eyes about to zap anyone.'

'Yes, you're right,' Thomas said, knowing such stunts as he had in mind only worked in movies, never in real life.

'Pardon for butting in,' Corporal Hans Krüger said. 'I watched the truck head into town. Didn't get far. Pulled up next to that watering hole.'

Thomas and Sgt Maj Koch's eyes followed the direction Cpl Krüger pointed in.

'Looks like it. So, are you suggesting we take him after he had a few drinks?' Thomas asked, rubbing his chin.

'Yes Sir. Might be an alternative. They all seem to stop there for a few before proceeding to the airfield.'

'Mmm… Luring him away from his men won't be easy. It will be thirty-six, minimum, against us. And with them intoxicated, they'll be on edge. They won't like strangers waltzing in on their soirée. Especially FSB officers,' Thomas said. 'You're up for it?'

'Sorry Hans, that's even crazier than the colonel's plan,' Sgt Maj Koch said, unconvinced.

'Not like you to back out of a fight. Why the change of heart?' Thomas asked.

'You nearly bought it a few days ago, Sir. Don't want a repeat of that. Must be another way… Maybe your suggestion is not so crazy after all. Anyway, it's a thousand times better than Hans's. We'll have to find a way to convince the port staff to escort him to the phone. If he becomes suspicious, he won't be any the wiser. And we'll take him once he has finished his call,' the sergeant explained.

'Yes, I believe you're right. Gen Lukyanov can telephone with some *bad news*. Something along the lines that his wife had a heart attack and is in hospital,' Thomas said. 'And if he reappears with some company, we'll put them to sleep as well. Risky, but doable.'

By the time the second submarine sailed into port thirty minutes later, their plan was in place. Ivan would make the call as soon as the Russian colonel showed up. Scouting the area outside the harbour master's building they picked a spot for the abduction.

The three Germans waited for the Victor III nuclear attack submarine to open its hatches. It had arrived two and a half hours after the second sub. For a while they had been worried their intel was flawed.

Thomas shifted uncomfortably in his seat, watching the crew disembark. None looked like special forces. Fifteen minutes elapsed with no sign of the colonel and his men.

'Back in a sec. If not, go to the plane and leave,' Thomas ordered and jumped out of the Lada.

With purpose he marched on to the docking station where the Russian colonel was supposed to have been. The first officer he encountered, Thomas asked, agitated, 'Lieutenant, I'm trying to locate Col Polyakov. There is an urgent call for him at port control. Is he still on board?'.

For a few seconds, the lieutenant seemed puzzled. His face brightened. 'Oh yes, sorry Sir. Couldn't place the officer; don't know his name. But a chopper airlifted him and his men off the sub last night.'

'Any idea where he went so I can tell the caller?' Thomas asked, his face expressionless.

'No Sir,' the lieutenant replied, and shrugged his shoulders. 'Not sure the captain knows either, as these guys keep to themselves. We're just a taxi service and know better than to ask questions.'

'Of course. Well, no point bugging the captain; he's got enough on his plate as it is. Carry on, Lieutenant,' Thomas said, hiding his disappointment at having reached another dead end. He returned the junior officer's salute and hurried back to his men.

Getting into the Lada, he grumbled, 'Let's go. He's not here. Nor will he be. They were picked up earlier and are heading somewhere undisclosed.'

02h30, Saturday, Beregovaya Gas Processing Plant, Black Sea Coast, Russia

The mission carried out with military precision was a repeat of the attack on the Norwegian gas processing plant at Kårstø. But with a distinct difference. This time the all-weather drones had not been altered. They were American made and retrieved after their lethal ordnance had been delivered at their designated targets.

The sea was calm despite the slight breeze.

In unison the special-ops soldiers dipped their paddles into the surf, pushing the three six-person inflatable rubber boats forward, away from the coast. The cloud cover was light but sufficient to block out the glare of the moon and stars. They were invisible to the naked eye.

At four kilometres the lights of the Beregovaya compressor station, located at an altitude of three hundred metres and surrounded by heavy forests, were visible. To the east, the lights of Dzhubga flickered. And to the west, those of Arkhipo Osipovka.

The hike up to the plant, launching the drones, delivering the explosives with their timers, and sprinting back to the beach had gone as planned. The evidence of footprints and boats dragged across the sand had been erased. But not completely. Nor did they pick up the few Marlboro and Newport cigarette butts discarded near the road.

After ten minutes of paddling, Boris's twelve-man team donned their scuba gear. Without a sound they disappeared overboard and scuttled the inflatables. Two of the six drones deployed at the plant were also destroyed. The rest of the gear they secured in dry-case containers and tied to their waists.

Submerged below the sheet of silver-black they steered their underwater scooters towards Arkhipo Osipovka, nine kilometres north-west. It was the maximum distance the Aquarobotman MagicJet scooters' batteries allowed them to travel at 6,5km/h. The oxygen tanks they kept in reserve for the last stretch to be completed underwater.

At 05h15, Boris's head rose out of the shallows. To his left was Arkhipo Osipovka. He signalled three blips with his infrared flashlight towards the deserted beach.

Immediately, three red blips responded. Holding his position, he watched his team emerge from the surf and race through the ankle-deep water. Crossing the narrow pebble beach they stepped in each other's footprints.

By 05h25, the Ural-4320 general purpose off-road 6x6 military vehicle rolled up the slight incline. In the back, the men changed into their battle fatigues. Following the country lane, the truck veered northerly and down the slope into Arkhipo Osipovka. The driver accelerated out of town toward Gelendzhik Airport.

At 06h00 the transporter's wheels cleared the runway. In the distance, six bombs detonated, destroying the Beregovaya compressor station. As the plane climbed higher, away from the mayhem, a massive ball of flame and smoke rose into the dark sky.

Boris sat back, thinking this should wake up anyone who still resisted their plan. The people will never forgive the Americans for this attack on Russia.

The vein supplying Russian gas from the compressor station at Pochinki via the compressor station at Beregovaya, across the Black Sea to Turkey and onwards to Europe had been severed.

08h00, Saturday, FSB Headquarters, Moscow

'Rubbish!' Ivan growled and slammed the mahogany top. Seated behind his desk in the FSB Headquarters he glared at the computer screen, at the message marked urgent:

DEFCON 1

For the attention of Deputy Director, Maj Gen Lukyanov.
Special Emergency Meeting: The Security Council of the Russian Federation.
Time: 13h00, Saturday, 19th February.
Venue: Kremlin Senate Building.
By Order: The Director of Counter-Intelligence, Igor Kozlov
Agenda: American maritime attack at 06h00 on Beregovaya gas compressor station. Facility destroyed. Casualties: 18. Regarded as a retaliatory strike in response to Russia's alleged attacks on installations in Turkey and Norway. Your presence is required to deliver evidence to the contrary.

Ivan, knowing full-well the events leading up to the attack, was doubtful the Americans were involved. Being the same MO as employed in Norway, it could only be the elusive colonel's handiwork.

If you think you'll drag us into a war, then you're mistaken. No, not while I'm in this chair, he fumed.

It was up to him to convince the few leaders who were still undecided or not involved to avoid a conflict no one could win. But believing their own propaganda that Russia's military was all-powerful and NATO dysfunctional, it would be difficult without absolute proof. And the only proof he had was Thomas's account based on circumstantial evidence.

He needed more time. Five hours would not suffice.

If he dragged Col Polyakov in front of the security council not knowing who issued his orders, it would be suicide. As whoever did, had to be very senior and would not take kindly to accusations levelled against their executioner.

After Thomas's call in the early hours, confirming the colonel's disappearance, Ivan's attempts to establish his location from the time he had been airlifted off the submarine till now had been futile.

Throwing caution to the wind, he had contacted 14-BOPS Corps. The CO, Colonel General Vladimir Coshenko, had refused to indulge him. Ivan's senior position in the FSB had made no impression on the general, who had growled at him like a rabid dog, defending his territory from interfering outsiders. The officer's tone had confirmed Ivan's fears; the call had been a mistake. He could not rule out a surprise visit by a few special-ops soldiers.

Since the call, he had checked his pistol twice, making sure it was locked and loaded. He had also raised the security level inside the FSB building. As long as he stayed indoors, he was relatively safe. But this meeting would force him outside. Under normal circumstances, the short walk to the Kremlin would be of no concern. But now it would be like crossing a ten-kilometre war zone. Plenty of opportunities to take him out.

The only option left to him was to discuss his findings with his superior, Colonel General Igor Kozlov. Fourteen years his senior, he was a relic from the USSR's old school. Ivan hesitated, unsure whether he could trust him. What was the alternative? None.

'Thomas, time to leave Russia,' Ivan said into his phone; the call scrambled.

'Why the urgency?'

'Situation has taken a nasty turn. There was an attack on a Russian gas compressor station earlier today. The country is on lockdown.'

'For God's sake! Any idea who's responsible?'

'Initial report. America.'

'Uh-huh. And?'

'The MO indicates it to be Polyakov. Would explain why they were airlifted off the sub.'

'Hmm, probably. Any idea where he is?'

301

'No. I enquired at his base. As expected, the CO did not appreciate my call.'

'Understood… Where did this attack take place, and at what time?' Thomas asked.

'06h00, Beregovaya, Dzhubga, Black Sea coastline. What have you in mind?'

'I'll instruct my office to review naval and air traffic in and out of the area around that time. Our satellites are monitoring Russian waters and airspace. Considering the time and distances involved, he must have travelled by plane. If he did, we can establish his route. Pinpoint his current location. What's the distance from his base to this plant?'

'My guess, 1 700km. If a military transporter, then three and a half to four hours flying. He could still be in the air. But no need for you to investigate. Too risky. Where are you now?'

'With our mutual friend.'

'Good. Wait there. And now you must excuse me, I have to attend a security meeting. Try to convince them not to go to war,' Ivan said.

'Are we close?'

'Yes. If I fail, we'll be at war within days.'

Ending the call, Ivan contacted the FSB spy satellite unit to track down all planes in and out of Beregovaya during the past twenty-four hours.

Fifteen minutes later he received a positive ID.

A military transporter had landed at 21h00 at Gelendzhik Airport, fifty kilometres west of Beregovaya. And had departed at the exact time the plant had been destroyed. At present, it was in the air 300km south of Moscow, en route to the colonel's base.

It was the break he had hoped for.

One slight problem. How to catch the colonel? Does he force the plane down before it reaches its destination? Or drag him back to Moscow as soon as he lands? But considering his call to the CO, he doubted he'd be allowed to set foot on the base.

He rang Thomas again. 'I need him arrested as soon as he touches down. It's the only option. Not sure how.'

'Prepare orders for me to visit the base. I'll abduct him.' Thomas volunteered. 'You have no one else you can count on.'

'Are you sure? You realise where you're heading?'

'Into the lion's den. The base should be relatively empty with most troops shipped out.'

'Not much of a comfort. There'd still be thousands present.'

The warning elicited a smile from Thomas. 'I'll need an excuse to visit.'

'Observing war preparations. You'll represent the FSB as Col Rebroff. But spying on my department's behalf, you won't be liked. That's the best I can think of unless you have an alternative in mind.'

'No, that will do. By the way, I'll be going alone. Can't risk my men. Too dangerous.'

Chapter 49

Orbe, Switzerland

On the outskirts of Orbe, west of the E25 motorway, Hôtel des Mosaiques had been picked for the meeting. The busy highway linked the northern and eastern cantons with Geneva.

Michael had finished his recce of the hotel's grounds. As expected, he had encountered no one of interest; only his colleague knew his plan.

Someone rapped on the door. Michael got up and opened it a fraction, pistol in hand.

'Hi, Michael,' Svetlana greeted with a smile. Behind her, two young men nodded.

'Hello, Svetlana. Come in.' Michael slipped his pistol back in its holster. 'You as well,' he added, letting her escort in.

'Glad to see you and thank you for helping,' Svetlana said, and gave Michael a hug.

'No trouble. Remember, we're in this together. Again, my sincere condolences. How're you holding up?'

'Just fine,' she replied, her eyes drained. 'And I'm sorry for not warning you in time.'

'Not your fault. Fact is, we knew and still couldn't stop her abduction... By the way, when last did you sleep?'

'On the plane. That'll do for now. Next time I sleep will be when I have Dasha by my side.'

'Hmm…' Michael acknowledged. She did not realise how exhausted she looked. 'Please, make yourself comfortable while I order breakfast.'

He turned his attention to the two soldiers who were looking out of the window. 'Apologies for not introducing myself sooner. I'm Michael.'

'Roger, Michael. Please to meet you. I'm Lieutenant Karl Hofmann, German Special Ops,' replied the one soldier standing 1.85 m tall. His eyes were pleasant, bright blue. His full head of black hair was neatly combed in behind his ears. 'This is Corporal Günther Krause. The rest of my men are deployed in the area. Keeping an eye out for hostiles.'

'How about you? Breakfast?'

'Won't say no. Thanks.'

'Please tell your men the three lads in the white Peugeot Boxer van are with me. Interpol.'

Munching their croissants, pain au chocolats, and cold meats, Michael checked his watch. 'One hour and fifty minutes, and we move out. Taking the back roads, Geneva is a two-hour drive. All okay with that?'

'Yes,' the others agreed.

'Well, here's the plan. Svetlana will be taken…'

As Michael wrapped up the briefing, Svetlana asked, 'You're sure this will work? They won't be able to detect it…?' She was not sure, sceptical about the freshly applied nail polish.

'Yes, it's undetectable and works up to a range of five kilometres. That was the maximum I got when testing it earlier.' To ease her fears, Michael swept the scanner over her. Nothing.

'In simple terms, it functions like the active sonar of a submarine. This device here sends out a super high-frequency microwave signal which bounces back once the specific metallic compound of the nail polish is picked up. Watch,' Michael said and switched on the large shoebox size device.

On a handheld screen, a light blinked, showing Svetlana's exact location on an interactive map.

'Good. Just hope they don't know about this,' Svetlana said.

'Except for my colleague Jacques, no one does. It's a prototype, brought straight from our laboratory, so to speak. The other two agents don't know what we're up to. Have faith, Svetlana.'

'If you say so…'

Not deterred by her slight scepticism, which was not totally unfounded, he continued, 'Don't forget, we'll be watching you at all times. This is an additional precaution. And I'll be in the background, listening in on your conversations till such time they'll confiscate your phone. Neither my colleague nor I will lose you. He also has one of these,' Michael reassured her and pointed to the monitor in his hand.

'And I'm convinced neither will Lt Hofmann and his men. Lieutenant, these images are of the men who trailed me and blew up the hotel in Bern. I presume they'll be the ones who'll take Svetlana.'

'Roger,' Lt Hofmann said. 'Major, we'll stay in the shadows till we've established the location of your child. We'll only act when we're certain there'll be no friendly casualties. Just don't try to do anything on your own.'

'And as I'm supposed to be dead, I'll hang well back; don't want the mission blown,' Michael added. 'I admit this is not much of a plan, but there is nothing more to go on. Oh yes, one last thing. If you spot this guy, let me know,' he added, and gave them some colour photographs.

'Who is he?' Svetlana asked, studying the photographs with some apprehension.

'Brendan, Sinead's fiancé. He turned up in Geneva two days ago. This photo is by courtesy of Geneva Airport security.'

'You think he may be involved in this?' Svetlana asked.

'Not sure… I ran a check on him, and he came up smelling of roses. Way too sweet for my liking.'

'And…'

'After Sinead's abduction, he had phoned non-stop. Then suddenly he had just stopped. I tried to reach him, but couldn't. His phone was off. Concerned, I had run his image through Interpol's live facial recognition software to see where he may pop-up. And voila, surprise, surprise, he turns up right here.

'Three probable reasons could have brought him to Switzerland. One, he's on a lone crusade to rescue her. Two, coerced. Three, he is involved. But which one, I'm not sure. Could be any. So, if you see him, don't make contact, just let me know. Okay, that's a wrap,' Michael said.

Chapter 50

Special Ops 14
Russia

The captain gave a lame salute and shouted to make himself heard above the chopper's noise. 'Follow me, Sir!' His face was hard, emotionless. He dropped his arm to his side, turned around and marched towards the parked jeep, not bothered whether the FSB colonel followed him.

Thomas refrained from reprimanding the captain for his insolence and climbed out of the Kamov Ka-226 military helicopter. With cold fury the arctic wind stung his cheeks. Warned to expect a frosty reception, he was not surprised. Well, he was getting one literally and figuratively. Thankfully, the Russian overcoat was warm enough to ward off the natural elements. As for the human element, he'd let it slide.

As the jeep sped off, his eyes swept the airstrip, searching for the colonel's transporter.

Except for twelve fighter jets and six long-range bombers prepared for action, there were no other planes. The trees on either side of the asphalt restricted his view. The transporter could be hidden away, although that was doubtful.

Two hundred metres in front of him the roof of the old manor house jutted out above the trees. Except for several auxiliary vehicles trundling about, the base seemed deserted. It was as he had expected.

The main reception area at HQ was exceptionally plush for a military facility. Persian rugs covered the tiled floor. Large oil paintings in gold frames. Gold chandeliers, leather couches, polished dark-wood furniture. Leftovers of the Tsarist-era, having survived the Bolsheviks' plundering of the bourgeoisie.

Ushered through reception, he headed upstairs to the office of Colonel General Vladimir Coshenko, CO.

The CO's secretary greeted him. Her full lips smiled politely. As she spoke, her beauty did not conceal the agitation in her eyes. 'Sorry Sir, Col Gen Coshenko left two hours ago for Moscow. Capt Petrov will be your guide. If you have questions, he will assist you as much as he can. If not, please let me know.' Her voice was as *warm* as the arctic wind outside. 'I'm sure you'll find everything to your satisfaction and your report will be most favourable.'

'I assure you, my report will be more than glowing. Reflecting the efficiency, strength, and loyalty your men's exemplary reputation demands,' Thomas smiled, his sarcasm lost on the young woman.

She raised her eyebrows a fraction as if caught by surprise and expressed her gratitude in an uncertain voice, 'Thank you, Sir. Col Gen Coshenko will be very pleased.'

The massive underground hangar was half empty as Thomas poked his nose into every corner of the concealed warehouse. After two hours he gave up. There was no sign of the colonel. It had been a waste of time, time he did not have. It was already 15h30.

Traversing the airfield on foot, Thomas noticed a new arrival: a large AC-130 troop carrier. Its propellers choked to a halt. The hold's rear door lowered to the ground. It was the same make and model Col Polyakov was travelling on. He veered in its direction.

A truck rolled out of the hold, followed by men in fatigues. That they were returning from a mission was a definite. He approached the plane.

Two soldiers paused, stared at him, and shouted into the plane's hold. He could not hear them, neither the response hollered from inside. The next instant they dropped their gear and raced towards him.

'Sir, this is a restricted zone. Please turn around and vacate the area,' the one soldier said, and saluted. The salute was a challenge not to be ignored.

'Why? I have clearance to visit any part of the base,' Thomas scowled, not pleased to be ordered about by a soldier.

'Other areas, not this one. It is out of bounds.'

'By whose orders?'

'My CO. Sir, this is not a request. I will not repeat myself. Captain, escort the colonel out of here. I have my orders.' The soldier did not stand down as he aimed his rifle at Thomas's head.

The threat left Thomas under no illusion that he would be shot if he did not obey. 'Understood, soldier. And take note, your CO will have some explaining to do to my superiors at the FSB,' he said without moving, hoping to ID the colonel amongst the men piling into the truck.

'Divert your eyes and turn around. Now, Sir!' the soldier barked, his face glowering. The point of his rifle inched forward.

Thomas turned away as ordered. He had spotted the man joining the truck driver in the front cabin. It was the man he was looking for. Desperate not to lose sight of him, he followed the truck, thinking, if ever there was a black-ops unit in the worst possible sense of the word, then they were it.

Having lost sight of the truck, Thomas's eyes flitted from one barrack to the next. Striding through the vast base was a wild-goose chase. Daylight was fading fast. He changed tack and headed towards the HQ.

At the main reception he introduced himself to the lieutenant on duty. 'I am Col Rebroff, FSB. I need to know who do Col Polyakov answer to?'

'The CO.'

'Is he available?'

'Unfortunately, not, Sir. Is it urgent?'

'Yes. I would like to report an incident. Is the XO in?' Thomas asked.

'Yes, but he is busy and cannot be disturbed.'

'Right. Then where can I find Col Polyakov? The matter involves him.'

'In his quarters, but he's not available either. He has a plane to catch.'

'So, no one can talk to me?' Thomas said, feigning exasperation. 'Lieutenant, I'm glad you are following orders like a good soldier should. A commendable attribute which I might add to my report. That's if…'

'If I cooperate. Understood, Sir.'

'You took the words right out of my mouth.' Thomas smiled. 'Any idea where the colonel is going which is so important that he has no time for a senior officer of the FSB?'

'Sorry Sir, I don't know. And even if I did, I may not divulge such information without proper authorisation.'

'What time is his flight?'

'Sir, I cannot say,' the lieutenant said. The colonel opposite him was FSB; his world might not be the same after today. 'Anything else I can help you with, Sir?'

'Yes, where is a desk and phone I can use?'

'First floor, second door on your left, Sir.'

Without a word Thomas turned towards the stairs.

'He's leaving in thirty minutes. The main runway.' The lieutenant's words were hardly audible behind Thomas's back.

Pretending he did not hear, he kept on walking and, with the tip of his finger, tilted his cap back in acknowledgment of the young man's cooperation.

'Reception was as expected. Saying it was hostile is putting it mildly,' Thomas said, marching towards the helicopter. 'Anyway, the target's flying out in twenty-seven minutes. Destination unknown. But I'll try to establish—.'

'No, don't. Best you get out of there,' Ivan cut him off.

'You sure?'

'After my meeting at the Kremlin, we have no alternative. Suffice to say, you must leave Russia,' Ivan said, his voice filled with apprehension.

Thomas understood. 'I gather we've crossed the line. No turning back now…'

'Afraid so. I could not convince them. Sorry, my friend.'

'How much time do we have?'

'Three days max.'

'Then all is not yet lost. Wherever the target is heading, we must intercept him,' Thomas said, infuriated by the damning news. 'And you were right; the CO gives the orders.'

'I was afraid of that. He was also at the meeting and pushed for war. Anyone who had challenged him were quickly silenced. He's part of the problem. My subsequent enquiries confirm his hard-line views, shared by most of the council, including the Marshal of the Russian Federation, and my boss. If anyone resists them, they'll be eliminated. With the military set on war, nothing can stop them. Maybe the president can be reasoned with…?'

'Well, at least we now know who we're dealing with. And you were right not to trust anyone. So, I'll see this through to the end,' Thomas said, and asked, 'By the way, what's the latest on the major?' He needed to know when he could expect his men back at base.

'Last word fifty minutes ago confirmed your unit is in position. They are about to make contact. For now, the major is safe.'

From inside the helicopter Thomas had a clear view of the main runway. An Airbus A320neo touched down and rolled to a stop. Two trucks pulled up and led by the infamous colonel, thirty-six men jumped out.

Standing at the top of the steps, a man waved the colonel and his men to board. Carrying a large duffel bag and semi-automatic rifle each, the unit disappeared into the fuselage. Another truck rolled up and transferred more equipment on to the plane.

The fact that there was no military insignia visible on the plane meant it was preparing for a clandestine mission.

'I'm sending you a photo of an Airbus A320neo. The target plus thirty-six men, armed and equipped, have boarded. All in civilian clothes. Nobody disembarked,' Thomas said.

'Instruct the pilot to take off immediately. I'll establish the plane's details, original airport of departure, and its cleared route. Should have that by the time you're back,' Ivan said.

The turbine roared, lifted the chopper into the air, and turned towards Moscow. As they increased their speed, a burst of energy pumped through Thomas's veins, spurring him on not to give up. He had risked life and limb to find the colonel, the one man who might reveal all. It was a matter of *carpe noctem* (seize the night) or there might not be a tomorrow to seize the light.

Chapter 51

Geneva, Switzerland

Seated upstairs in Starbucks with her back against the wall, Svetlana observed activity on the floor, the lift, and the stairs. She refitted her phone's battery, switched it on, and placed it on the table next to the mug of coffee. The time: 14h00.

Other than Lt Hofmann and two "friends" installed at a table next to the stairs, enjoying a light lunch, she did not recognise anyone. The Germans spoke in subdued voices not to draw attention.

Two women in their late twenties appeared at the top of the stairs and hurried over to a vacant table. Plain-clothes police? If so, I hope they don't blow our plan, Svetlana fretted, not knowing how many eyes were on her and the eatery.

The deception arranged by Michael for her to arrive in Geneva via the baggage hall at the airport had paid off. On her way to the train's platform, she had spotted three Eastern European men matching those in Michael's photographs. All had boarded the same train, shadowed her from Geneva's train station to Starbucks, and now occupied the table ten metres in front of her. Not once did they look at her.

So far, everything was going to plan.

Her pistol fully loaded and tucked inside the unzipped flap of her parka; the presence of Niall's men did not bother her. She was not alone either. But what worried her was whether Dasha would survive the rescue attempt.

Her phone rang. 'Yes Niall,' she snapped.

'Good guess. So, my voice didn't fool you.'

'No, nothing to do with your voice. Only person who can stoop so low is you.'

'Okay, you've made your point. Now drink up. Time to go. See the three men at the table on your right?' She turned her eyes in the direction as told. 'Yes, them.'

'So, you're watching me. Good for you. Why don't you show yourself like a man instead of hiding behind your hoods? Or are you too scared of a little me?' Svetlana taunted, dragging the conversation out. Giving Michael a chance to locate him.

'Patience, *Irina*. Trust you don't mind me calling you that. After all, it is the name I knew you by,' Niall mocked. 'I understand you can't wait to see me again, but you'll just have to keep your legs closed for a bit longer. We'll have lots of time to get reacquainted. Must admit I'm looking forward to that as I'm sure you are too,' Niall laughed, baiting her. 'So, here's the deal. I'll let your daughter live if you become my lover again.'

'I will not even answer that.'

'Okay, enough chatting. Now, go with my men and tell those two *lovely ladies* to disappear or Dasha will vanish for good. Remember, there are many unfortunate parents in the market for brats,' he said, his voice humourless. 'Jeezus, pity my aim wasn't truer. I should have blown your fuckin' head off at the time!'

'So, you missed. Live with it. And which two "lovely ladies"?' she asked scathingly, pretending to search the faces of the thirty-odd customers.

Across the room, Lt Hofmann and his friends left their table. One man slapped the lieutenant on his back, laughed at some joke, and traipsed down the stairs.

'Irina, you know who I'm referring to. And if I see anyone I don't like, kiss your child goodbye.'

His words puzzled her. How could he see her? None of the three men nor anyone else pointed anything in her direction. So, no hidden cameras. Was he watching from a window on the opposite side of the street? No, not possible from where she sat. He must have hacked into the coffee shop's security cameras. If so, he could also have accessed the city's surveillance cameras in the area.

She had to warn Michael, listening in on the conversation.

'I gather you hacked into the coffee shop's CCTV. And, I suppose Geneva's as well. You went through a lot of trouble. I'm flattered. But I'm alone. Niall, I'm not scared of you. Maybe you are the one who is scared. And as far as the two women are concerned, I don't know them.'

'They know you. Lose them. Now move your butt. Remember, I won't tolerate any tricks. I'm watching,' Niall warned.

Niall's men got up and locked eyes with her. One tilted his head for her to follow. Svetlana got to her feet and pocketed her phone, left on for Michael's benefit. She paused next to the two women and spoke softly. 'He knows you're here and instructed me to "lose" you. He has hacked into Geneva's surveillance cameras and is watching us. Please inform your superiors.'

The one started to protest. Svetlana stopped her. 'I really appreciate your help, but my child's life is at stake. Please.'

'We understand. Sorry,' the woman said in broken English and heaved her shoulders apologetically.

Reaching the three men waiting at the bottom of the stairs, they demanded she hand over her weapon, phone, handbag, and jewellery.

Leading her into the street via the side entrance, they dumped everything into a bin except for the pistol. They turned right, crossed at the end of the street, turned right again, and after fifteen metres turned left into a side street. At the next T-junction they crossed the near-empty street, and aimed for an apartment building next to a pulled-down roller-shutter covered in graffiti.

The few people going about their business took no notice of them. An attractive woman surrounded by men who seemed to be Russian mafia automatically made people look the other way – a prostitute escorted to her next client.

Certain no one was following, they opened the building's front door and entered. The concierge behind the glass window paid them no attention. Two men seated in the semi-dark foyer nodded and pointed at the lift.

Outside the apartment building, two young men with backpacks slung over their shoulders strolled past the front door. One had longish blond hair; the others was short, reddish. Both wore blue jeans. One a brown parka, the other a black one. At the corner they turned left and continued their recce in search of the back entrance to the building Svetlana had entered.

Minutes later, seated inside a coffee shop, the one with reddish hair spoke into his mic. 'Have eyes on the rear. Only one vehicular entrance. Over.'

'Roger. The monitor indicates she hasn't left the premises. I'll let you know if the situation changes. Out,' Michael replied.

'Strip off and put these on,' the leader of Svetlana's escort said, and threw a bag at her.

Inside were panties, blue jeans, a long-sleeve T-shirt, beige turtle-neck, socks, runners, a brunette wig, and a black burqa. She averted her eyes to block out their stares and undressed. Naked, she grabbed the panties.

'Stop!' the leader snapped.

He took out a scanner and swept the device over her body. Hovering over the bullet and knife scars, he said, 'You've dodged death a few times. Well, your luck is about to run out.'

But the scanner did not respond. She was clean.

'Get dressed!'

The burqa was the last item she slipped over her head, concealing her identity.

Next to her, some men were also transformed into Arabs. Two darkened their faces with fake tans, false beards, and full-length white tunics with red and white chequered headscarves. Sunglasses concealed their blue eyes. Two of them slipped into black burqas. Underneath the robes they carried semi-automatic rifles.

Accompanied by her "Middle-Eastern family" she reached the ground floor and exited the building at the rear. Two minutes later, their car – a plain white Renault Grand Scenic with clear windows – joined the one-way traffic system.

The leader pretended to be a nervous driver in a foreign city, unsure of which direction to take. He circled the same block twice, then got "lost" by driving into a dead end. Feigning frustration, he threw his hands in the air before continuing. Reaching the lake, he swung on to Quai De Mont Blanc towards Lausanne.

He was confident no one shadowed them, except for their two backup cars trailing further back.

Svetlana said nothing, trusting Michael and the Germans had not been outmanoeuvred and that the nail polish worked.

The instant Svetlana's blip had moved on Michael's monitor, he had alerted the Germans, reporting each change of direction.

At the eatery, the two men had spotted the white Renault Grand Scenic with its Muslim family exit the parking at the precise moment Michael had reported it in. A few seconds later, a black Audi sedan with tinted windows had raced past. Immediately, the details of the two vehicles had been forwarded to Michael.

With the details of the vehicles noted, Michael had swung out of the parking bay. At that exact moment, a silver Toyota Landcruiser had pulled up next to the apartment building and picked up two men and a suitcase.

Michael smiled, his eyes on the white Renault one kilometre up ahead. The ruse by Niall's men had failed.

Further back, the Interpol control-and-surveillance van brought up the rear.

The restricted view annoyed Svetlana. She craned her neck and peeked through the mesh screen, trying to establish their location. But in the twilight she saw very little. Thirty minutes ago, the sun had dropped in behind the ridge of mountains on her right.

Before leaving the vicinity of Lake Geneva hours ago, the white Renault had been switched for a light-grey Opel. Since then, the drive had taken them through snow-covered hills.

'I need the bathroom,' she demanded a third time. 'I really must go.'

'You can wait. We're nearly there.'

'How long?'

'Stop whining. If you can't hold it, piss yourself.'

'If you say so,' Svetlana moaned. She did not need to go, but had hoped to stall their progress for Michael's sake.

Finally, the car left the motorway and transited a small town. Once back in open countryside, it sped towards a forest in the distance.

Ignoring the exit the abductors had taken, Lt Hofmann continued towards Bern, as did the three other cars. Behind them, Michael monitored the route of the light-grey Opel Mokka X4.

Turning off the motorway, he wondered if it was another detour to see if anyone was following. The distance between him and Svetlana was at the scanner's maximum range. He pressed down on the accelerator while updating Lt Hofmann.

Cautiously, Michael approached the treeline, slowing in sync with the blip on the monitor. The blip made a sharp left turn and picked up speed. On the screen, the satellite image displayed a lane bisecting a large forest. Beyond lay a farmhouse, barn, and buildings resembling stables. Except for the farm's network of roads, it seemed to be a dead end.

Not slowing down, Michael sped past the farm's entrance, not knowing where the two backup cars were. For all he knew, one of them could be monitoring the entrance. Reaching the far side of the forest, he reversed in amongst the trees.

'They're at a farmhouse,' Michael said. 'Her movements indicate she must be on foot. I'm approximately one klick from her position. We'll have to trek through the woods; vegetation's too dense for cars. Best we move in after dark... Hang on, something is happening.'

The blip was moving, and fast, heading straight for the barn.

'She's in the car again... No, wait. Went through the building... She's in the air,' Michael said. What he had dreaded was happening. They're flying her out. A scenario which could foil their plan if they did not act fast.

The Airbus H155 helicopter cleared the barn's pitched roof. Inside the cabin, Svetlana was the only one still in disguise.

They had scanned her four more times since taking her, in case some hidden tracking device had been activated remotely, or by her. By now they were a hundred per cent sure no one was tagging along.

As the chopper tilted forward and changed direction, Svetlana wondered where Michael was. When she had raised the possibility of flying, he had been adamant he had that covered. But by now they must be well beyond the five-kilometre range of the scanner. Unless Michael could perform a miracle, she was on her own. And it wouldn't be the first time.

'Does anyone have eyes on the chopper? Michael asked. 'Should be over the trees.'

'Negative.'

'Jacques, launch the drone, now!' Michael instructed his Interpol colleague in the control van parked on the other side of the woods. With one eye on the monitor, he raced to join them. The chopper flew north and veered east.

By the time he cleared the woods, the Vulcan XX Unmanned Aerial Vehicle catapulted into the air; the second tracking device secured inside its light frame.

The jet with a three-metre wingspan – which had unfolded the instant the catapult had rolled out of the control van – increased its speed to 350km/h and raced after the helicopter. The distance between the two craft was seven kilometres, two kilometres beyond the scanner's range.

They had lost Svetlana.

Bertrand's fingers nimbly rolled the remote steering control – the ground control systems (GSC) – inside the "cockpit", flying the drone to the last point of contact. Four klicks out the blip made a welcome return on the monitor.

'Got them, Michael!' Bertrand exclaimed as he zoomed the UAV's camera in on the helicopter's flashing taillight. With a flying time of eight hours and a range of three hundred and fifty kilometres, he would not lose Svetlana. That was if they did not leave Swiss airspace and the drone did not malfunction.

'Get the chopper's details. Search who the owner is,' Michael said. However tempting, he resisted contacting Swiss Air Control to monitor the chopper's progress, or the Swiss Police to issue an APB. With Niall involved, they might be compromised – he had too many friends.

'Okay, we're moving out. Jacques, lead the way,' Michael said.

'Best you and the lieutenant go ahead. We cannot drive too fast. Don't want Bertrand to crash the drone. I'll direct you,' Jacques replied as they returned to the E25 motorway. Towards Bern.

Chapter 52

Moscow

The sixty-seater steakhouse on the outskirts of Moscow, three hundred metres from Ivan's home, was relatively quiet. He had frequented the steakhouse more than he cared to remember and knew the proprietor well. So much so that he had put him on his department's payroll – always useful to have some extra ears where people relax and tongues loosen.

Five minutes before entering, the premises had been swept for bugs. In addition, the security camera covering their corner table had been switched off and would remain so till they left.

"Reserved" signs on the two adjoining tables ensured no one would occupy them. In the background, the cello's deep rich sound – Bach's Complete Cello Suites performed flawlessly by Massimiliano Martinelli – resonated through the air, masking the three male voices.

It was still early. Ivan planned to be gone by 20h00, allowing the proprietor to benefit from his usually busy Saturday evening trade. And to get Thomas to the border.

'Georgia could be their destination, but it's too soon to tell. And as the mission is classified, no flight plan is available. But the instant they deviate, I'll know,' Ivan said.

Opposite him, Thomas swirled some red wine in his mouth and swallowed. 'If it is Georgia, then to Georgia I go,' he said determined, and cut another piece of medium-rare ribeye steak. He was famished and craved the sustenance only red meat could provide for a big man like himself. The succulent, richly marbled meat melted in his mouth. Just as well as his injured tongue made chewing a rather unpleasant experience. 'Must admit, this steak is good. It will keep me up all night, which may not be a bad thing.'

'Agreed. Food is excellent. Thomas, have another steak. You'll need all the energy you can get to help you through the next twenty-four hours,' Maj Gen Luik said with a genial smile.

Addressing Danylo as Thomas, the general found awkward. In private he either called him by his real name or son. He regretted not being able to do so now. For the safety of Danylo, his wife, sister, and parents, that's the way it must be. Too many intransigents of the old days were still in power. To forgive and forget was not part of their psyche.

'A thought regarding the colonel's route. They could be heading to Turkey, change the plane's details, and continue to their designated targets in Europe,' the retired general suggested.

At the soft beep of his phone, Ivan quickly diverted his eyes. 'Sorry, have to check.' Next instant he raised his hand, pausing the conversation. 'Or once over the Black Sea, they head straight for Europe. The plane is registered in Rome. Belongs a company somehow connected to the Vatican. This means no one will intercept them. The power the Vatican wields is not to be challenged.'

'Who the hell are we dealing with?' Thomas questioned, annoyed.

'At least we're getting closer to who is orchestrating this conflict,' Maj Gen Luik said. 'Could be the sinister *Holy Council* running our world. Or someone on the inside operating behind their backs.'

'Svetlana's theory is becoming more plausible by the minute. I'm not a conspiracy theorist, but it seems very likely that a global cabal which includes several Russian officials, may be our enemy. If I can get my hands on this Nicolai, he'll talk,' Ivan grumbled, worried about the mess he was trying to unravel inside Russia. Also, about Svetlana, alone at the mercy of a brutal killer.

'Thomas, as soon as we've finished our meal, you must leave. They are shutting all borders within the next few hours. Sneaking into Ukraine will become impossible. Are your men still in position?'

'Yes, they are,' Thomas said. Noticing the unease in Ivan's eyes, he added, 'Don't worry, we'll beat them.'

'I know we will. I'm just concerned about the major. They've taken her. Now it's up to my Interpol friend, Michael, and your men... Very frustrating being stuck here,' Ivan said, slightly embarrassed for having slipped his mask of confidence.

'Ivan, you do what you must. I'll keep digging. Establish how deep the military is infiltrated. I have a few friends in the service. Trustworthy men. Well, now is a good time to see just how strong these friendships are,' Maj Gen Luik said.

'General, if you have the slightest doubts about any of your friends, walk away. Do not risk it,' Ivan warned.

Chapter 53

Switzerland

'Captain, divert to location C, now! You're being followed.' Niall seethed. Was it not for his contact, he would not have known.

'*Nyet*, no one follows,' the Russian captain piloting the helicopter to Zurich, retorted. 'Sorry, my mistake. *Da*, I see flying man in cape waving us to stop.'

'You think it's funny? Well, it's not. There's a bloody drone on your tail! Do as I say and shove your smart-ass comments. Got it?' Niall said, his words controlled. He needed these men. Riled, he rubbed the twelve months' old scar concealed within his hairline.

A bloody drone… And Michael still alive! What a cock-up! And blowing up the hotel for nothing. Next time, he'd kill the bastard himself.

'*Da*, understood,' the Russian captain said, wondering how Svetlana's team had located them. 'Must have drone in sky in Geneva? Our tactics…no good.'

'Yes, that about sums it up. By the way, your mark you had supposedly blown up in Bern is alive. He's the one controlling the drone following you. I won't ask how you missed him. We can discuss that another time. Let's focus on losing the drone, please,' Niall implored the Russian, hating to even pretend to be asking nicely.

'What, he's alive!' the captain blurted out, and swore in his mother tongue. He knew there would be consequences. A failure like this was unacceptable in anyone's book. Especially in that of his superiors.

'I presume you're asking if you heard correctly. Then, yes, you did. He's alive. As is his child. Slip-ups happen. So, make the detour and lose him.' Fortunately, he had taken precautions for just such an incident.

'*Da*, no problem.'

'You better be right,' Niall said and hung up. He was in a hurry. It was half-past seven. His guest would arrive at any minute.

Svetlana would have to wait till after tomorrow's meeting. *And I was looking so forward to seeing you again and swipe that smile off your face*, Niall simmered.

Dressed in a black tailored suit, white silk shirt and matching thin black tie, he picked up his black wool coat. He took another look in the mirror and smiled at the stranger staring back at him. Pleased with himself, he dashed down the stairs and hurried to the security control room to monitor progress and ensure things would go according to plan.

With his faith in the Russians severely marred, he would not leave matters in their hands. They were far too callous. Neither did they care much for tactics, believing if things go wrong, one blasts one's way out. Way too heavy-handed, even for him.

Svetlana moved in her seat, keen on catching what her abductors were mumbling after the chopper's sudden change of direction. In the dimmed light of the cabin, none seemed happy. And none more so than their leader. In fact, he looked like he was about to put a bullet between the eyes of the first one to annoy him.

Something was wrong. Must be the reason for them puffing vigorously on their cigarettes. As annoying as the stench of the tobacco was, it was the least of her problems.

The possibility that her backup was nowhere near was far more worrying. But there was nothing she could do as they raced towards the dark shapes of the Alps. The lights of a large city lit the evening sky on her left. Zurich.

Infuriated, Michael listened to Jacque's report, informing him of the chopper's change of direction, flying south towards Lucerne. It would be impossible to keep up. Traversing the low, mountainous region meant a massive detour for him and his team.

'All we can do is keep going. I'll get the local police to watch them when they land, wherever that might be,' Michael said.

'Agreed. We'll stay in the air as long as the fuel lasts and keep an eye on her. Should be a few hours, no problem,' Jacques replied.

'Wonder why this sudden change? Could they have picked up on the drone... Spotted it by any chance?'

'No, it's too small. With no lights and stealth technology, it's invisible to radar and the eye. Something else made them deviate. Or, they are heading in the direction they had intended to?'

'No, doesn't make sense. They would have made a beeline straight there and not flown to Zurich; an unnecessary detour. Something happened.'

'What are you saying?'

'How many people know what we're up to?'

'Quite a few, I imagine. Why? Are you thinking they got tipped off?'

'Maybe. Compile a list of those who are aware of this operation. Jacques, tell Phillipe to do some digging. Knowing this Niall character, it won't surprise me if he has friends at Interpol. Won't be junior either. Oh yes, any news on the ownership of the chopper?'

'Yes... But no luck. Private charter. Leased by an Italian company.'

'Hmm, right... Why am I not surprised? And it's most likely a subsidiary of ten other companies, etc. etc. Will take

327

weeks to unravel. Okay, park it for now,' Michael said as he focused on the road sweeping towards the mountains and Lucerne. The chopper was seventy kilometres ahead and could land at any moment. Or continue further south to Italy.

The hangar's emergency lights cast a dull amber glow on the walls and floor as the chopper sidled into the empty space and landed. The noise of the screaming turbine was deafening. It fell silent. The rotating blades stopped.

Without warning, they shoved Svetlana out of the chopper, and into one of the four parked cars; all were of different make with their windows tinted. Resigned to her fate, she sat back and folded her arms. It couldn't be much further till she would face Niall…and hold Dasha. What lay ahead would not be easy. But whatever that might be, it did not matter, as long as Dasha would be free and untouched. As for herself, she would find a way back to her child and Ivan.

The hangar doors slid open. The cars drove into the night; and left the airfield. At a large intersection they split in different directions. It was impossible for the drone to follow each one. Nor could it determine which car Svetlana was in.

Circling high above the airport at the south-eastern tip of Lake Lucerne, the drone's cameras zoomed in on the cars. The images were near perfect.

'Michael, the convoy broke formation,' Jacques said, watching the live-feed. 'Where are you now?'

'Few kilometres south of Lucerne. Any sign of the police?' Michael asked. The decision to involve the Swiss did not sit well. If Niall did have friends at Interpol, as he suspects he does, then he also has friends in the Swiss Police.

'Five unmarked patrol cars are heading to the airport.'

'Thanks. I'll get them to shadow the Niall's men. Copy me images of the cars.'

'Coming up in a sec.'

'Anything happening at the hangar?'

'No, the situation is unchanged.'

'Okay… That can only mean one thing: they're waiting for the drone to take the bait and disappear. So, let's call their bluff. Follow the cars but don't venture too far; keep an eye on the hangar. Mind if we talk privately?'

'You can talk,' Jacques said, and swivelled his chair away from Bertrand seated next to him.

'Do you trust your two colleagues?' Michael asked.

Surprised by the question, Jacques hesitated before replying. 'One, yes. The other's still young. I think his heart's in the right place. So, yes. Why?'

'Don't want to find out one of them played us,' Michael said thoughtfully, concentrating on the road. 'Is Phillipe driving?'

'Yes.'

'Do me a favour. Keep him behind the wheel and call head office. Tell them we've reached a dead end and are storing the drone. But make sure Phillipe hears you. On the quiet, tell Bertrand to continue the surveillance. Then pull over for a pit stop and send Phillipe outside for a smoke break. In short, I don't want him near the monitors. And let's see if anything changes.'

'Of course,' Jacques said, his curiosity piqued.

Niall read the message on his phone:

"They're pulling the drone out. The mission's over. They've lost their target."

He texted back: "Good. Is it clear to proceed?"

"Yes."

"Thanks. Stand by. May need your help again. Cheers," Niall responded.

He rang the Russian captain. 'You can proceed. Take her straight to her cell. Friendly warning, she is extremely dangerous.'

'Da, no problem. We take good care of her,' the captain said, amused. The Irishman gave this young woman far too much credit. She can do nothing he and his men could not handle. He'd gladly add a few more scars to the ones she already had.

329

Exiting the hangar, the captain craned his neck out of the car window and said, 'See if you can spot the drone in case it is still somewhere above us.'

But all they saw was a heaven filled with twinkling stars and some low clouds to the east.

'Sorry, Major, your friends are gone. No one is going to rescue you. So, to save yourself and us a lot of trouble, try nothing stupid. We'll soon have you *home.*'

'Fine. I'm not complaining, am I?' Svetlana scoffed stubbornly from behind the mask.

As the silver Audi 4x4 slipped on to the Zurich motorway, the drone changed direction, its main lens trained on the car. Hugging the ridge of the valley's eastern mountain range, it followed the blue blip on the monitor.

Chapter 54

Ukrainian Border

It was well past eleven by the time Thomas parked the rented car in the dark lane, fifteen minutes' walk from the border. Guided by the GPS, he trudged his way through the snow.

With the image of the massive military convoy making its way to the Ukrainian front fresh in his mind, he picked up the pace. Col Sokolov had to be warned in case NATO spy satellites had missed this last-minute advance. The colonel and his High Command's assessment of the situation were wrong. The Russians were going to drive through Sumy as well!

The thousand-vehicle convoy of tanks, armoured personnel carriers, 9A52-4 Tornado universal multiple rocket launcher missiles, trucks, and the usual array of ancillary vehicles were only fifty minutes from the border.

Notwithstanding the urgency, Thomas did not run, mindful of units patrolling the border. And dressed in civilian clothes, armed with a fake FSB ID and standard FSB service pistol — by courtesy of Ivan — he did not want to draw attention to himself.

Two hundred metres from the border, he slipped in amongst the trees, keeping the forest in view where his men were concealed. Twenty minutes he waited. All was quiet, unnervingly so. Finally, he broke cover and continued to the border.

After thirty metres, three men stepped into the open and blocked his path, ordering him to halt. He placed his hands on top of his head.

'Papers!' a voice snapped. A Russian corporal.

Having presented his ID, the corporal inspected the document in the flashlight's glow. 'Colonel, this is a restricted area. Where are you going?'

'Corporal, I cannot share that with you. It's classified. Contact your CO. He'll clear me.'

'Yes Sir,' the corporal replied, not sure what to make of the colonel creeping around in the dark. 'It may take a few minutes.'

'Carry on, Corporal,' Thomas said, wondering how many men were watching him. Hoping Ivan's message had reached the corporal's CO. The moment he had passed the convoy outside Kursk, he had alerted Ivan of possible problems and had furnished him with the division's details.

Avoiding eye contact with the corporal and his men, he waited. He did not make light conversation either; the less said the better. Less chance of a slip-up or an incorrect response to a seemingly harmless question.

'The CO, Major General Kandinsky, Sir,' the corporal said, handing the phone to Thomas.

'Good evening, Sir. I am Colonel Andriy Rebroff of the FSB. I believe my superior had informed you of my mission.'

'Yes, Colonel. Your superior's name? And, "On Deribasovskaya weather always good...",' the CO, irritated by this interference, barked the agreed password for Thomas to complete.

'Maj Gen Lukyanov. And, "It always rains on Odessa beach".'

'Colonel, give the phone to the corporal. Good luck with your mission,' the general said, his voice edging towards a hint of civility.

As soon as the corporal ended the call, he saluted Thomas. 'Colonel, you may proceed. We'll cover you from here... Make sure you don't walk into an ambush.'

Thomas left without looking back. Only when he reached the trees on the Ukrainian side did he glance over his shoulder. Clear. No one was watching or trailing him. He entered the woods and after a five-minute walk, whispered, 'Lieutenant, you can show yourself. No lights.'

'Yes Sir,' Lt Schmidt's voice responded five metres on his right. 'Glad you've made it.'

'Thanks. Was close enough though. Is Col Sokolov nearby?'

'This way,' Lt Schmidt replied and handed Thomas a pair of night-vision goggles.

Marching southwest, Thomas briefed Col Sokolov of what was about to hit him, his men, and the Sumy Oblast.

FSB HQ Moscow

'They had changed direction over the Black Sea and are currently crossing the Transylvanian Alps in Romania, en route for southern Hungary...Austria. They could land anywhere in Europe. Most likely the targeted nuclear plants,' Ivan said, bringing Thomas up-to-date.

Staring at their monitors, the operators' faces manning the satellite live-feed remained indifferent, having no interest in their superior's conversation.

Routing this colonel was like a game of chess, one Ivan intended to win in as few moves as possible. 'We can either keep tracking them, or NATO can force them to land, impound the Airbus, and arrest everyone on board. But that would be counterproductive.'

'Yes. We don't have many options. Best see where they're going. Let them lead us to whoever is calling the shots. Then we'll arrest the lot. They're merely hired hands,' Thomas said.

'Agreed. What's your current location?'

'Overflew Kyiv twenty minutes ago. Do you have their current coordinates?'

'One moment… At 01h14 it was 45.552732 by 24.688014. They have not deviated direction since turning west over the Black Sea. We have protracted this route to the Austrian border. The point of entry into Austrian airspace will be 46.928517 by 16.019108. Their current airspeed is 955km/h. Unless they deviate, your operators should be able to calculate their position and you can intercept them.'

'They're forty minutes ahead of us. We should have radar contact before they reach Austria. And when we do, I'll contact you for confirmation,' Thomas said, and signed off.

Good luck my friend, Ivan thought as he left the control centre. He had to place a private call to Michael. But first he needed a boost of caffeine and a brisk walk to shake off the creeping lethargy.

With a disposable mug of steaming coffee in his hand, he nodded at the guards on duty at the FSB HQ's front door and aimed for Lubyanka Square across the road.

Not deterred by the snow and freezing temperature, the square and sidewalks crawled with late-night revellers. This did not surprise him. Who would not take advantage of the fragile peace? They had six-and-half hours left to enjoy a visit to a club, bar, hotel, or spend a few moments with a loved one. All available men and reservists had to report to their units by 08h00.

Waiting for the line of taxis and cars to pass, Ivan took a sip of coffee. As the traffic broke he crossed to Lubyanka square. Continuing his walk he took a deep breath, allowing the oxygen to seep into his blood.

The heavy clouds blotted out the stars. It was going to be a cold night, most likely well below -15C. He was glad for the detour to his office and for having geared-up appropriately. His gloved hands pulled the scarf tight around his neck. Four attractive young women blocked his path. Giggling, they offered him all kinds of pleasures if he cared to join them. He smiled and declined politely.

'Don't worry, she still loves you!' one teased and kissed him on the cheek.

Behind him, singing replaced their giggles. Not bad, he thought, impressed by their melodious voices. He shoved the frivolity aside as the thought of Svetlana, captive and alone, plummeted his mood.

With some dregs of coffee left in the mug, he threw it in the nearest bin. Spotting a vendor selling hot snacks at the other end of the square he changed direction. Not breaking his stride he took out his phone and dialled Michael for news.

Last he heard Svetlana was being held at a farmhouse in the Swiss mountains. Michael was not sure whether this was to be her place of captivity, and was to investigate. The good news was the drone had recorded her escorted inside. Meaning she was alive.

'Hello, me again. Any developments?' Ivan asked.

'No. She's still at the farmhouse. I assume it will be her place of captivity. Doubt the others are there. We're about to carry out a recce. Should have more intel within the hour. Before we'll do anything, I'll run it by you.'

'Appreciate the gesture, Michael, but no need to.'

'No, you're part of this. Your input is vital.'

'Okay, call me as soon as you—'

Thwack! Thwack! Thwack! Thwack!

Ivan's words ended in mid-sentence as a whoosh of air escaped his gaping mouth. The sound of a man exhaling his last breath. That of a dying man.

The force of the four 7.62 mm bullets striking him in the back catapulted his large body forward, sending him sprawling face down on to the concrete pavers. Next to him, his phone smashed on to the ground.

Loud screams cut through the night as bystanders rushed forward to where he lay. Two men and a woman flashed their FSB badges for them to keep their distance, while blocking the body on the ground.

'Ivan! Ivan, are you there?' Michael asked, confused. 'Can you hear me?'

The sound of the bullets striking and Ivan's breath escaping his lungs repeated itself in Michael's ears. He knew something terrible had happened. The fast repetitive beep noise emitted by his phone confirmed the connection was cut.

Crushed, he sat down.

'What's wrong?' Jacques asked, observing his colleague.

'Someone shot him.'

'Who? Who got shot?'

'Ivan. Svetlana's friend. Damn!'

'That's terrible,' Jacques whispered, and shook his head in disbelief. 'And we were so close to rescuing her. Her child… Your wife. I'm sorry.'

Michael did not respond and got up.

Stepping out of the van, he looked up at the clear night sky. Having to deal with the abduction of someone he loved and of his newborn baby alone was getting to him. Facing danger, fighting the odds when it affected only him, he could deal with any day and all day. But not this.

The night was cold, crisp, unlike his hometown in Ireland, which was humid, damp with moss growing faster than you could say knife. He shrugged off the frosty air and kept pacing. The thought of having to share Ivan's death with Svetlana hung over him like a cloud, shadowing his every step.

Well, my boy, you better get a grip or more will die, including Vera.

Each stride he took lifted his mood. With his eyes bright and the frown smoothed away, he popped his head into the Peugeot van. 'Right, what have we got? And not a word to Svetlana about Ivan. I'll tell her when the time is right.'

Chapter 55

Switzerland

Sinead ignored the dinner tray. She had not eaten anything since Brendan's execution outside her bedroom door. Her mind was in turmoil. She did not see how she could survive. She did not want to…

Locked up in the tower of the seven-hundred-year-old medieval castle at the Burg Reinhardt estate, Sinead had no interest in the world around her. The 2 650 hectares estate was thirty kilometres east of Zurich near Fischenthal in the Töss Valley. During the summer months, a mottled green blanket of coniferous and deciduous trees covered the slopes of the Schnebelhorn Mountain. And during the winter months, virgin-white-snow transformed the estate into a fairy-tale landscape.

The bedroom door swung open.

Sinead did not bother to look up; not interested in what they wanted.

'You seem very upset,' someone said.

She immediately recognised the voice. Puzzled, she turned her head to the door. 'Brendan…?' As her eyes met his, she repeated, 'Brendan, you're alive! Thank God!' She jumped off the bed and raced towards him. 'I thought they…'

Noticing the grin on his unharmed face, she swallowed her words, froze on the spot, and stammered, 'Your wound, it's gone… I don't understand… What's going on?'

'Oh, the wound and blood. Makeup. Came off easily. And the gunshots… Some theatrics to wind you up,' Brendan said. 'Sorry to disappoint you like this, but it had to end. It never would have worked between us. An upstanding citizen marrying a prostitute. What would my parents have said…? One thing, I must admit I enjoyed every minute of our "engagement". You really are a good lay. I now understand why clients were so ecstatic about you. Especially Paul.'

Hearing the name of the man whose eyes she had nearly scratched out, Sinead stuttered, her voice filled with dread. 'Niall…?'

'Yes, it's yours truly. Surprisingly enough, laryngoplasty and plastic surgery works. To be honest, I had my doubts when I had first met you in Dunnes. Wasn't too sure I'd pull it off… Come on now, don't be so upset. You're not the only one who got tricked,' he said, and gave one of his charismatic smiles.

'Well, we're back in business, dearie. And this time you're not going anywhere. So, enjoy your new room. Ain't bad, what d'ya reckon? Quite grand… Suitable for you and Vera to apply your trade in. Just like the good old days. Slight difference though. No more freedom. No opportunity to escape. And no diamonds to steal. Cheer up, you're still alive. Tell you what. As the wedding is off, you may as well keep the ring. Regard it as payment for services rendered.'

She wanted to scream, do anything to not hear his voice. But she could not. The room spun. She collapsed to the floor.

Desperate fool, falling for the first guy who came along, Niall thought. Believing every sweet word whispered in her ear. Even the plastic surgery scars attributed to a fatal car accident with the loss of a fictitious wife and child. That must have been it. Stupid woman, thinking with her heart, throwing all caution to the wind in a blink. He had enjoyed playing her, using her. But he had meant what he said. She was good in bed, very good indeed. And even more so when in love.

Well, you're staying right here. I'm not sharing you with anyone. Don't fancy picking up some disease, he thought, and locked the door behind him.

'Great to see you again, my friend,' Nicolai greeted as they walked towards the castle's Gothic front door. 'Though it'll take time to get used to your new face,' he said and laughed.

Niall towered twenty centimetres over his guest. But Nicolai's small stature, a sinewy body exuding a limitless energy and strength, was not to be tested. At fifty-six, he headed the biggest mafia organisation in Russia. Relying on his phenomenal intelligence, he outwitted his enemies to remain in control. Though his lethal tongue was measured equally by his deadly hands. The few who had dared to challenge him never survived the brutal encounter.

The six hours of sleep during the flight from Cuba in his customised Boeing 737 had restored his energies. He was ready for the days ahead. 'Did you receive the parcel intact?' he asked.

'Yes. Thanks for helping with my little *domestic problem.*'

'Always glad to assist an old friend. Especially one so generous.' Nicolai smiled and averted his eyes.

Entering the castle, six men traipsed in behind them – Nicolai's security.

The meeting of the Council would commence at eleven in the morning, eighty kilometres south of Burg Reinhardt. The venue, Camp Wägitalersee, a spa-resort of sixteen luxurious chalets and a central banqueting facility. Most delegates opted to stay there for the night, with others due to arrive in the morning. What puzzled Niall was why Nicolai had asked to visit him instead.

Seated at the bar on the ground floor, Niall enjoyed a whisky, Nicolai a vodka. The attractive young brunette, serving their drinks, busied herself in preparing finger food and snacks. As the conversation drifted, Niall lapsed into the tale of Svetlana's abduction and how she was now once again safely in his fold.

'You realise you're in love, or rather, infatuated?' Nicolai said.

'What are you on about? Can't stand the bitch—'

'No, you don't. You're in denial. Why not try to win her over? Forget this witch-hunt,' Nicolai cut him off. 'But then, as you've killed her parents, it may be a bit late. If I had known how you felt about her, *Uncle* Nicolai would have given you some sound advice.'

'Yes *Uncle*,' Niall said with a lame smile.

Nicolai heaved his shoulders. Like a door slammed shut, his expression turned foul. His piercing eyes glared at Niall.

'Niall, as a friend, and having known you for years, I'm concerned about you. Your craving for revenge has clouded your judgement.'

'No need to be. But thanks all the same.'

'Don't be cute,' Nicolai warned. 'If you're wondering why I'm here, it is to instruct you to let the major go. The council is not impressed with today's events, as your actions may lead the police to us.'

'Really no need to worry. We've lost the police. They have no idea where she is.'

'We cannot leave it to chance. Get rid of her. And I don't mean kill her. Set her free.'

An uncomfortable silence settled between them. After a minute, Niall spoke. 'Yes, of course.'

'Good. Just don't say you'll do and then don't. Remember, you're surrounded by Russians. Do not think they are loyal to you just because of the money. They're not. Their loyalties are with their unit and its code. If there's a weak link, they'll cut it out, whether it's you or me. You get the picture?'

'Understood.'

'Also, let the child and women go immediately. This Interpol agent won't give up until he has found his wife. Drop them off far from here. If you don't, we'll do it.'

'Let me think about it.'

'I'm not asking, I'm telling you. And do not kill them. You can do that another day.'

Niall did not respond, wondering whether his friend was bluffing. 'Right, will do,' the measured replied, spilt out convincingly.

Nicolai's eyes were cold, hard. If Niall thought he could take advantage of their friendship, he was wrong. He had his orders and would not hesitate to execute them. 'One more thing, your security team is pulling out tomorrow evening. Monday morning latest. They're needed elsewhere.'

'Fair enough. With Svetlana gone, I won't need them anymore.'

'Okay, my friend, I think we have exhausted the topic of your *domestic problem*. Shall we move over to the fire?' Nicolai suggested.

Seated in comfortable armchairs they faced the stone fireplace. As Nicolai was about to speak, Niall's phone signalled an incoming message.

'Excuse me,' he said and read the condemning words. His face turned dark with anger. If Nicolai finds out, the evening won't end well.

'What's wrong?'

'Nothing.'

'Sure?'

'Well, not quite. I lost ten million dollars on a property deal in China. Buggers ran off with the deposit. Was a bloody scam,' Niall lied straight-faced.

'Not like you to get swindled. Told you your judgement is clouded. Come on, my friend, wake up. Once this war is over, we'll find the crooks and make them pay. I have more than enough friends over there who owe me. And it will be my pleasure.'

'And how much is that "pleasure" going to cost me?'

'Come on, what's a few million between friends?' the Russian laughed.

'Hmm, I'm sure we'll come to an arrangement which won't be cheap,' Niall said good-humouredly, hiding his anxiety. 'Let's put that on ice for now. So, back to business.

341

My American friends, are they ready?' The question masked the news he had just received from his mole at Interpol.

So that's how they did it!

He had to act quickly, or things might spiral out of control. One thing he could not afford was to disobey them. If he did, he would die. There would be lots of time for revenge once the war was underway.

Chapter 56

Austrian Skies

'No luck, Colonel. Can't reach Maj Gen Lukyanov,' Lt Schmidt said.

'Damn! Wonder where he is? We need confirmation we have eyes on the target,' Thomas said, frustrated.

'Must be them. HQ confirmed the plane's details,' Lt Schmidt replied, trying to placate his CO. The colonel looked bushed, not having slept more than a few hours in the last three days.

'Yes, you're right. I am more concerned about the general. Something's wrong. He would not cut communications without reason or without warning. Get Karl on the line. Maybe he knows more?' Thomas said. It was only logical that Ivan would have stayed in touch with the Interpol agent in Switzerland regarding the Russian major.

A few minutes later, Karl transferred the call to Michael. With introductions out of the way, Michael shared the news of Ivan's death.

'Are you sure?' Thomas asked, stunned.

'I can only tell you what I've heard. The impact of bullets was unmistakable.'

'Is there any way you can get verification of his death?' Thomas asked. As appalling as Ivan's assassination was, it confirmed they were on the right track. But of more concern, without Ivan, finding those responsible for the destruction of the energy installations would be impossible.

'No, I cannot. Do you have any contacts in Moscow who can?'

'Yes…' The thought of asking the general did not sit well. If he got involved, he would implicate himself as being complicit and possibly meet the same fate as Ivan. Other than the general, he could ask one of NATO's deep undercover agents in Moscow.

'As you can appreciate, I'll hate to share the wrong information with Maj Nikolaeva,' Michael said.

'Understood. What is the current status?'

'We're still watching the farmhouse east of Zurich where she's being held and are trying to establish whether the others are also present,' Michael said. As an afterthought, he asked, 'Do you know why they killed Ivan?'

'He was helping my investigation regarding the attacks on the gas installations. Damn thing is, with him gone, I may not be able to complete my mission and stop this war from happening.'

'I see… How much time do you have?'

'Russia could invade Ukraine or Europe at any moment. So, a few days at most. D-Day could be as early as Monday.'

'Bloody hell!' Michael cursed. 'You sure?'

'That's according to the last intel I got.'

'Anything I can do to help?' Michael asked. He needed to rescue Vera before hostilities began or he might never see her again.

'Yes. Can I reach you on a secure line?' Thomas asked, prepared to risk sharing information with a relative stranger. Ivan trusted Michael, and with his options limited, that was good enough.

'Of course. Give me a minute.'

Reconnected, Thomas said, 'We're following a Russian, a Col Polyakov. He carried out the recent attacks. Seems he's heading to Switzerland. If I cannot get authorisation to operate on Swiss soil, I may need your help.'

'Understood. Send me his details. I'll help as much as I can and monitor the situation.'

'Michael, a warning. His friends most likely infiltrated NATO, Interpol, and Europol. If he discovers we're on to him, he'll disappear. I can't lose him.; he's our last chance,' Thomas reiterated.

If Thomas's words were correct, then his rescue mission was hopeless. With the world blown to hell they would all end up dead. Michael smiled to himself, thinking, well, you better get to it then; rescue Vera and help find this Russian colonel. And all by the end of the day...

Eight hundred metres from Michael's position, confined in the cold basement of the old farmhouse, Svetlana paced the cell-size room, trying to stay warm. The stench of excrement was unbearable. A few centipedes crawled in and out of the cracks in the mouldy, damp walls. She did not sit down on the filthy mattress lying on the floor; she could only imagine what crawled inside. Neither did she wrap herself in the grubby blanket; the burqa would have to do.

No, she'd rather stand, having no intention of overstaying. She would escape soon enough.

Fixed to the wall out of reach, the TV showed Dasha asleep in the same room as in the video clip she had received.

Niall had outsmarted them. He was holding Dasha captive somewhere else. Their entire operation had been based on the premise that she would be brought to her. A huge oversight, as that was never Niall's intention. No, he wanted revenge. To make her pay. She would never come near her child.

It was going to be a long night. Her legs ached. Finally, she gave in and tore a strip of cloth off the burqa, cleared a patch of ground and sat down.

Once more she looked at Dasha, vulnerable and alone.

He most likely plans to sell her to a childless couple, she thought. But then another ugly possibility dawned on her. Or he might adopt her himself. The thought of Niall cuddling Dasha was unbearable. No, that would never happen...

The door's lock clicked.

Four men entered, their pistols pointing at her.

The 4x4's engine purred softly as it crawled out of the walled kitchen yard and followed the narrow lane through the trees.

'Michael, a marine-blue Volvo 4x4 is on its way to you. Four passengers. All male. No sign of her.' Lt Hofmann's voice reverberated in Michael's ear.

'Roger. I'll put a tail on them. Svetlana's still in the house; signal hasn't moved,' Michael replied, wondering where they were heading. Getting supplies... Or were they no longer needed with her securely locked up?

'We have eyes on three hostiles in the yard. Five cameras and six tripwires neutralised. Could be more. I suggest we deploy the hornet for a recce inside the house.'

'Should be with you in a few minutes. Hold your position.'

Fifteen minutes later, Lt Hofmann's voice, barely a whisper, reported, 'Two cars moving out. Total seven passengers. Again, only males. No sign of the major. Where is the hornet?'

'A slight hiccup. Should be a few more minutes.'

'Copy. But I suggest we investigate before the cars return. Most likely a few bogeys left to guard her.'

Michael hesitated, wondering if he should wait. But the hornet was malfunctioning. 'Right Lieutenant, move in.'

Lt Hofmann signalled his three men to break cover. Doubled-over, they raced across the forty metres of open space.

The sudden explosion knocked them off their feet.

The ground shook as a massive ball of fire reached into the sky.

Stunned, Lt Hofmann watched his men stagger to their feet, and unsteadily retreated to the safety of the trees.

'Lieutenant, what happened?' Michael asked.

'They blew it up!'

'Jeezus! Are you okay?'

'Yes. If we had gone in a minute earlier, you would not be talking to me now. None of us would have survived the blast.

We must assume the major, and whoever else was inside, is dead. Sorry.'

'You sure?'

'Yes,' Lt Hofmann replied.

Another death. Unthinkable, Michael groaned. The scanner had shown Svetlana inside the building at the time of the explosion. That signal was now gone. It had vanished along with her. Not only did he lose her, but also any chance of finding Vera. He had failed. He had been too cautious. Too slow.

A feeling of defeat washed over him, wondering whether Vera and Dasha were also in the farmhouse at the time of the explosion. He felt powerless. All he could do was wait and see what the wrecked building would reveal, or for Niall to phone and make more demands.

'Sorry to interrupt,' Jacques said by his side. 'I think you better take this call. It's Sergeant Franz Strauss who's following the Volvo. It's urgent.'

Michael took the phone. 'Yes, Sergeant.'

'They've dumped a body in the woods.'

Niall's Castle

Staring out through the glass pane, Sinead again tried the ornate handle of the French door and shook it violently. It did not budge. Futilely, she banged her fists against the unbreakable laminated safety glass. She wanted to flee. Throw herself off the balcony to the forest floor below so the maggots can eat her rotting carcass. She deserved no better.

How could I have been so pathetic? So desperate, blinded by love. Dear God, please let me die, she sobbed.

Niall had expected as much after revealing their romance as a big hoax. He knew Sinead would crumble into a pile of misery. Therefore, as soon as she had drifted off, the men had secured the windows, doors, and removed any articles which could assist suicide. If she thought she could escape her punishment, she was wrong.

He had carried out Nicolai's demands in his own way in ridding himself of his hostages, except for Sinead. Having convinced his friend that she was a nobody, with no one to come looking for her, Nicolai had given his consent for him to keep her as his plaything.

When Niall had shared Sinead and Brendan's *romance* with Nicolai, the Russian had been in stitches. Although unable to imagine Sinead cheerfully becoming his lover. But Niall had assured him that a diet of drugs would make her a very pliable sex slave.

This small *victory* did not lessen Niall's anger, not impressed being dictated to. But he knew the men he was dealing with were not to be challenged. They would not tolerate any sign of disobedience, especially if their operation was threatened. He would not survive.

Well, time to change that and bring Larry and the lads back into the fold. The Russians had overstayed their welcome.

The message received from his mole at Interpol had been in the nick of time. Nicolai would not have forgiven him for such a slip-up. At least that problem had been taken care of.

01h45 Sunday, Austrian Night Sky

'Michael, I can confirm there was a shooting outside the FSB HQ in Moscow. My friend is making further enquiries. Sorry, that's all I have at this stage,' Thomas said as the plane flitted through the night sky over Austria, trailing what he believed to be the colonel's jet.

'Understood. Some more bad news. Svetlana was killed in an explosion. Having evacuated the farmhouse, they had blown it up with her inside. There may be more victims,' Michael said.

Thomas sighed. 'Are you sure?'

'Yes.'

'Michael, I know it's not a good time to ask, but any news on the plane we're chasing?'

'Of course. The Airbus A320neo's details match the one which left Moscow. Its route to Geneva is via Salzburg, Friedrichshafen, and Basel. Continuing north of the Jura Mountains, they'll turn south to Geneva before reaching Besançon. What puzzles me is how does he think he can waltz into Switzerland armed to the teeth?'

'Geneva's probably a refuelling stop. We suspect they are heading further west.' That the route made no sense, he did not share.

'Understood... Thomas, we're not quite finished here and I don't know how long it will take. But as soon as I'm free, I'll head over to Geneva. In the meantime, a Maj Huber of the Swiss Special Forces will accompany you.'

Geneva, or was it? And why the detour? Thomas wondered. Too many times the Russian had slipped away. Best to arrange a boarding party and inspect the plane during refuelling at Geneva. That should confirm who is on board. If anyone at all.

He turned to his men. 'Sarge, you and Cpl Krüger pick four men to join me in Geneva. Lieutenant, gear up the others for a HALO jump. I think the colonel's about to repeat the same tactics as in Norway. They're avoiding the mountains, so I estimate they'll bail out somewhere between Basel and Besançon.'

'Roger, Sir.'

'Try to establish likely landing zones, Lieutenant.'

'Yes Sir. We'll rule out heavily forested areas. Should narrow down their options,' Lt Schmidt replied.

'I'll request some French choppers to assist,' Thomas said.

Far below, the lights of Salzburg flickered, its inhabitants fast asleep.

Farmhouse, Switzerland

Flanked by Lt Hofmann and Jacques, Michael concluded his briefing. 'We cannot stop now. I suggest—'

The loud buzz of his phone stopped him mid-sentence. 'Yes?'

'Michael, Cpl Burmeister. I'm with the body they've left behind.'

'Yes, Corporal.'

'It's a female. Thirties.'

'Is she alive?'

'Yes. In bad shape and heavily drugged.'

'Can she talk?' Michael asked.

'Yes. But she's mumbling incoherently. Sounds Russian.'

'What colour hair?' Michael asked, anxious to know who it was.

'Brunette… Light. Difficult to say.'

'Thanks, Corporal, that will do. Keep her awake. Don't let her drift off. We're on our way.' It does not sound like Vera. Can't be Svetlana with her remains scattered all over the rubble behind me, Michael thought.

Twenty minutes later he swerved into the woods where Cpl Burmeister stood over a body propped up against a tree. He dipped the car's headlights. With an emergency kit in hand, he raced to attend to the victim. The corporal moved out of the way. The face smeared with blood looked familiar.

'Svetlana?' he asked. 'It's not possible…'

He bent down for a better look.

More cars stopped. Doors slammed shut. Men jumped out and joined him.

In the LED's bright light she seemed far worse than merely in "bad shape" as Cpl Burmeister had put it. She was covered in blood. Michael searched for the wound. Her pulse was extremely slow. He laid her flat on the ground and asked for a stretcher.

He raised her left arm. It was soaked in blood. 'How the hell did they manage to slip her…' Michael's words froze on his lips. 'Jeezus, they pulled her nails out! I don't think she's

350

drugged. She's delirious. Lost a lot of blood.' He checked the other hand. The nails were intact with the polish removed.

'That explains it, doesn't it, *mon ami?* That's how they got her out,' Jacques said.

Wiping her face clean, looking for other injuries, Michael asked, 'Svetlana, can you hear me?'

Her eyes opened slightly. 'Michael?'

'We'll take care of you. Did they give you any drugs?'

'Hmm…' she moaned.

'I repeat, did they give you any drugs?

'No.'

'Good. I'll give you a sedative to ease the pain. You'll be okay.' Without warning, he popped a Fentanyl OTFC 800g tablet into her mouth. 'Don't chew. It will dissolve. You'll soon feel better.' He did not want to knock her out for too long. Her recollection of what she had seen and heard while in captivity was vital to help find the others. Or to establish whether anyone else had been held hostage at the farmhouse.

Forty-five minutes later, Svetlana, recovering on the stretcher with her hand cleaned and bandaged, opened her eyes. Seated next to her in the control van's swivel chairs were Michael, Lt Hofmann, and Jacques. They were deep in conversation. Touching Michael's arm, she whispered, 'Sorry, Michael, I've blown it. Now you won't find her.'

Relieved at hearing her clear and lucid, Michael said, 'No, you haven't. I did. I underestimated him. Should've known better. He must've found out what we did. My department has a mole. Anyway, how you're feeling?'

'Fine, thanks.'

'Then maybe you want to get rid of that burqa and stained clothes?' Michael suggested and gave her the backpack she had brought from Russia.

'Can't wait to get out of this rag.'

Svetlana climbed out of the van, unsteady on her feet. Michael grabbed her by the elbow. 'Easy there. Best you sit down. You lost quite a bit of blood. Here, have some juice, it will help. How's the pain?'

'I'll live.' Sitting on the floor of the van with her feet resting on the ground, she asked, 'What now?'

'We're trailing the Volvo which dropped you here.'

'Where?'

'West of Zurich, heading towards Bern. Svetlana, before we get into that, something we need to know. Did you see or hear anyone else at the farmhouse?'

'No, not that I can recall. I was locked up in the basement, in a disgustingly filthy cell. I'm sure it was a replica of Niall's cell in Cuban. Sorry, I'm digressing.'

'It's okay. You're sure there was no one else?'

'As sure as I can be. The place was dark when I arrived. No lights on or people anywhere.'

'Right,' Michael sighed, relieved. Vera and Dasha must still be alive.

'What happened, Michael?' Svetlana asked.

'They blew up the farmhouse fifteen minutes after you left. But why would he do this to you? He could just have scraped the polish off, transferred it on to something else. We would not have been any the wiser.'

'You know Niall. He had it all planned. Was going to keep me there for as long as he could. To teach me a lesson. Even had a TV hooked up to Dasha's room so I could see her day and night. I don't understand why he did not leave me inside to die in the explosion. He must have known I would not give up until I find Dasha.'

'Well, he has his ways. I'm sure there's a reason which will reveal itself.'

'Michael, any news from Ivan? How is he? He must be worried sick by now.'

'Last we spoke, he was fine. He's not reachable right now, but I'm sure he'll phone as soon as he's free,' Michael said, straight-faced. He hated himself for lying. But under the circumstances, he felt it best. He needed her alert.

'I see… Hope his enquiries are more successful than ours,' she replied. 'Where did you say the Volvo was?'

'On its way to Bern.'

'I thought that's what you said.'

'Why?'

'It's odd. Why keep me here and then the others a hundred kilometres away? No, Niall would not like such inconvenience.'

'True. Though it may be safer for him.'

'Hmm… However, the Russians mentioned that he was to pop over in the morning and not last night as planned. Meaning he could be nearby.'

'Makes sense. The Volvo did initially drive east, and after five kilometres had suddenly changed direction to Zurich. They must have spotted the tail and are now leading us as far away as possible from Niall.'

'Yes, I think you're right,' Lt Hofmann interjected, having listened in silence to the conversation.

'Any word from the lab regarding the video?' Svetlana asked.

'Not yet.'

'Watching the TV-link, I studied Dasha's room in detail. It had a heavy solid-wood door with a pointed arch and stone surround. Most of the walls were made of stone. The ceiling was exceptionally high, curtains long. Old wooden chandelier. I'm not that knowledgeable about castles, but it looks like the inside of one. And I'm sure there can't be that many in the direction the Volvo initially drove.'

'Good point. Although it could be fake. Worth a try though,' Michael replied. 'Jacques, tell HQ to search for castles, palaces, manor houses, or similar structures in a forty-kilometres radius. We might get lucky.'

Chapter 57

Region Besançon, France

'Total, twenty-four, Colonel,' the co-pilot said, having counted the number of men jumping out of the plane up ahead.

'Thanks, Oscar,' Thomas replied, and turned to face the pilot.

'Captain, take us to the drop zone seven klicks north, coordinates 47.359450, 6.230427. Drop to 700 metres altitude for bailing out. I'll confirm with the French DZSTL (drop zone support team). DZ is marked with a red flare. By the time the men bail out, the Russians should already be on the ground and on the move.'

'Roger, Sir.'

Returning to the cabin, Thomas briefed Lt Schmidt and his unit of six, who had discarded their gear for the HALO jump. With the French cooperating, jumping from high altitude was no longer required. 'The French officer in charge is Major Claud Boucher. They're monitoring the Russians' descent and will have eyes on them at all times. Choppers are at your disposal. This time, they won't slip away. Or blow anything up. You have eight minutes. Any questions?'

'No Sir.'

'Good luck, Bernd,' Thomas said and slapped his second-in-command encouragingly on the back.

Seated on his own, Thomas rang Maj Gen Luik in Moscow. If irrefutable proof were to be found, he would need the general's support when presenting that to NATO and world leaders. After twenty rings, he gave up. He would try again later.

Sweeping in at an altitude of seven hundred metres with the cabin lights off, the exterior red, green, and white navigation lights glowed dimly in the dark. On the ground a marker indicated the drop zone. Within seconds, Lt Schmidt and his unit vanished into the night through the open cabin door. The jet accelerated and turned south towards Geneva.

At Geneva International airport the Russian's Airbus received clearance to touch down, having circled over Lake Geneva. By the time Thomas's plane landed, three minutes separated them from the Russians.

Dressed in combat fatigues and fully armed, he and his men entered the Private Jet Terminal. A young Swiss officer at the head of a twelve-man unit approached Thomas and introduced himself as Major Leon Huber, Swiss Kommando Spezialkräfte Offizier (Special Forces Command Officer).

'Please, follow me,' he said.

Standing on the mezzanine floor of the arrival's terminal they had a perfect view of the deserted Baggage Hall. The one-way glass ensured anonymity.

'Wonder what's keeping them?' Thomas asked.

'They haven't disembarked. We've delayed the aircraft's steps to allow us time to get in position. They'll be here shortly. We have another unit on the asphalt watching the plane in case they try to sneak off in the dark.'

'Good. Just hope the Russians don't spot your men. We must be discreet. Everything depends on our success,' Thomas cautioned. 'If we fail, the world will be at war within the next few days.'

Showing no emotion, the Swiss officer considered the information. 'Roger, Colonel. You have me and my men's support. We'll get this done, I—' He stopped mid-sentence as an irate Swiss brigadier general accompanied by a platoon of forty-four men marched through the Baggage Hall towards the underground passageway leading to the boarding gates.

'And this!' Maj Huber exploded, dumbstruck. 'Hope they don't intend to arrest the Russians. I better stop them. Excuse me, Colonel.'

The double doors swung open. Behind Maj Huber was a lieutenant and twelve armed men. Addressing Thomas, the major's expression was blank. 'Sorry, Colonel, I've been ordered to stand down.'

'What do you mean, Major?' Thomas asked, baffled.

'The general has taken over the operation. He and his men will escort the Russians off the plane and to the military base in Geneva. I have tried to explain the importance of what we're doing. But he had shut me up, threatening me with a court-martial if I interfered.'

'Unbelievable! Shall I speak to him?'

The major shuffled his feet uncomfortably and said, 'No, Colonel, you can't.'

'Why not?'

'The lieutenant is to arrest you and your men as armed insurgents, having entered Switzerland without proper authorisation. There—'

'You're not serious!'

'Sorry, I have my instructions. Best you hand over your weapons and accompany the lieutenant.'

Thomas realised he had no choice. 'Roger. May I make a call? If the Russians get away, it will have severe repercussions which you, your men, and the rest of humanity will regret.' By stressing the importance of his mission, he hoped the major would reconsider.

'I fully understand. And of course, you may make a call. Again, my apologies,' the major said and added, 'I'll contact my CO. See what's to be done.'

'Right…' Thomas replied thoughtfully. 'Men, you heard the major. Hand over the hardware.'

As they proceeded along the mezzanine, the major turned to the young Swiss lieutenant sent to arrest Thomas.

'Lieutenant, you can re-join your commander. Tell him the Germans are unarmed, in my custody, and cooperating fully.'

The lieutenant stopped. 'Major, with respect, I cannot comply. I have clear instructions to accompany the Germans back to HQ.'

'Roger, Lieutenant. But I cancel your order. Your support will be needed by your commander; one can never tell what the Russians may do. Whereas the Germans are our allies and will be no trouble, especially unarmed.'

'Yes, but—'

'Lieutenant, you heard me. You and your men are dismissed.'

'Yes Sir,' the lieutenant replied and led his men away.

'Let's go—' Maj Huber said. Stopping in mid-sentence, he blocked Thomas's path with the palm of his hand. On the floor below, the Russians entered the Baggage Hall flanked by the Swiss platoon. The brigadier general was deep in conversation with whom Maj Huber presumed to be the Russian colonel. What struck him most were the broad smiles they shared. 'I'm not comfortable with this. They are too cosy.'

'Not what I would've expected. By the way, the one he's talking to is not the colonel. The colonel is the tall, bald guy to the left. Whoever this Russian is, he's more senior, and it seems they know each other well. No wonder your general wanted us arrested. They must have discovered someone was tracking them and had arranged for an escort out of here. Mind if I snap this Russian. Will be good to know who he is.'

'Go ahead. When you're done, we'll shadow them,' Maj Huber confirmed.

'As I've thought. The Russians are not going to the base,' Maj Huber said, and instructed the driver to follow the four civilian 4x4s which had peeled away from the military convoy. The four Swiss special forces unmarked vehicles trailed behind them.

Seated in the back of the major's 4x4, Thomas acknowledged his observation with a nod and answered his phone. 'Yes Lieutenant, I can talk. Go ahead.'

'Rendezvoused with French on the ground. Pursuing insurgents. Direction Dijon. Total number, thirty-six in nine vehicles, split into three groups two klicks apart. Don't have eyes on the leading three vehicles. Two unmarked police cars are following them. We're bringing up the rear in two 4x4s and four vans.'

'Lieutenant, any chance of you catching up with the leading group? I'm not comfortable with the current situation.'

'I'll see what I can do, Sir.' After a brief silence, Lt Schmidt said, 'We'll break formation. Should have eyes on the lead group in a few minutes. I'll contact you as soon as we have, Sir.'

'Roger and out,' Thomas replied.

The time was 03h55; sixty-nine minutes since the lieutenant had jumped out of the plane.

Trying to catch the Russian colonel was like Groundhog Day, and an unpleasant one at best; hoping to succeed but constantly failing. With the Russian colonel finally in his sight, he had no intention of losing him... No, not this time.

Informing Lt Gen Beck of the situation, the general cursed like a drunken sailor. Calming down, he undertook to prepare a suitable plan of action with his NATO colleagues in case the Swiss refused to cooperate.

With the support of the general and NATO, Thomas remained optimistic of success. His phone buzzed. 'Have you got eyes on them, Lieutenant?' he asked.

'Negative, Sir. Neither do the French. The Russians and the two French units have disappeared. They left the motorway further back. All we've found so far are the five abandoned vehicles. Sorry Sir,' Lt Schmidt apologised. 'The French are setting up roadblocks in the vicinity. But they had a fifteen minutes' head start; could be anywhere by now.'

'Understood,' Thomas said, suppressing his raging anger. The French were also infiltrated!

The Russians had allowed for any and every conceivable eventuality. They could not have known they were being followed until he had contacted the French for assistance, and therefore, organised this deception in under an hour. No, they had everything in place long before they left Russia.

'Not your fault, Bernd. No need to apologise. They have *friends* everywhere. Don't trust anyone. No one. Where are the other cars?'

'We have them in our sight. What do you want us to do?'

'For now, you stick with them. I'll get HQ to investigate the matter – try to establish where they've disappeared to. Report in if the situation changes, and watch your back,' Thomas said, signing off.

With his eyes resting on the vehicles skirting the north shore of Lake Geneva, he called Lt Gen Beck, expecting a tirade of expletives to rain down on him yet again when sharing the latest setback. First the Swiss, and now the French. And who else? No, he would not be impressed.

What hope is there to win a war when they have infiltrated all one's allies? Thomas fretted, wondering who was still on NATO's side.

Chapter 58

Switzerland

'Michael, look at this,' Jacques said, pointing at the map on the screen. 'We're here... And these pins mark the thirty-seven manor houses or castle-type structures in a forty-kilometre radius. Should not be too difficult to find them if our assumption is correct.'

Studying the map, Michael said, 'We can disregard those in built-up areas. Knowing Niall, it would be private, secluded and very grand. The bugger just can't help himself. Let's prioritise properties accordingly.'

'I agree. If you've seen his hideout in the Caribbean, you'll fully appreciate his vanity,' Svetlana concurred. She was exhausted. Her hand felt like it had been through a meat mincer. 'I think I need another painkiller. Any left, Michael?'

'Of course. Come,' Michael said. Stepping out of the control van he headed towards his 4x4.

'Where are we going?'

'To find you a place to sleep.'

'No need, Michael.'

'You think.' He ignored her protestations, opened the back door of his 4x4, folded the seats down, and rolled out a sleeping bag. He switched the engine and heating on. 'Now, in ya go. And here, take this. It will knock you out for a few hours, which you need. No arguments. In the meantime, we'll continue the search and when we've narrowed it down to a few options, I'll wake you. We won't do anything without you. You have my word.'

Inside the control van, Michael and his team sat poised to eliminate targets from the west to the east. And those ticking most of the boxes would be left till daylight for more detailed reconnaissance.

'Bertrand, how's the drone?' Michael asked.

'She's ready. Enough power to inspect each location.'

For the next three and a half hours they studied the video-feed captured by the drone hovering over each site. Quickly, they eliminated the first thirty buildings. These were deemed too public, had no visible security, cramped inside a suburb, no sign of activity, family cars in the driveways, or were too limited for Niall's needs. But more telling, none of the external door's shapes and finishes matched the Gothic, solid-oak door with its natural stone architrave and stone walls as described by Svetlana. All these properties were finished in plaster and paint.

The three older Interpol agents were feeling the strain of being up for the past twenty-four hours. Phillipe was asleep in the front. Michael got up and arched his back. 'Time to send the troops in and do a live recce of the rest. Back in a sec.'

Sheltered in the woods, the early morning light was soft with the air freezing. He clasped his hands together and rubbed them briskly. After a clear night, he could not have expected anything else in the Alps. He peered through the 4x4's frost-covered window, left slightly open for ventilation. The engine had been turned off hours ago. Svetlana was still fast asleep. Was it not for the goose-down sleeping bag, comfortable at -29°C, he would have been worried.

Reaching Lt Hofmann's 4x4, he rapped on the window.

'*Guten Morgen*, Michael,' the lieutenant greeted and smiled.

'Morning Lieutenant. You're well-rested?'

'Yes, ready to go. Any progress?'

'Covered a lot of ground. Narrowed the search down to seven. We need your help.'

The nearest castle was twenty kilometres from their position, in the direction Svetlana's abductors had initially travelled. And twelve kilometres further along a minor road, another castle had caught their attention.

'Bertrand, let's get this show on the road. Hit the first one,' Michael said with optimism in his voice.

'*Bien sûr*,' Bertrand replied.

Inside the control van, four pairs of eyes concentrated on the monitor displaying the surrounding snow-covered forests and mountains as the drone soared into the morning sky. On the lower slopes, a scattering of chalets and five settlements were visible. At three thousand metres altitude the drone was inconspicuous to the naked eye. As the onboard cameras panned out, a bank of clouds rolled in from the east.

'There she is, Bertrand. Zoom in.'

With the image in focus, they studied the building with its well-maintained gardens. Surrounded by forests, it was located midway up the slope. A solid gate, gatehouse, and wall with electric fencing secured the estate. The half kilometre driveway ended in front of the castle. Three men idled about on the steps.

'Hmm, what have we here?' Michael hummed. 'Any sign of more guards? Anyone?'

'*Non.*'

'Negative.'

'Definitely of interest,' Michael confirmed.

After fifteen minutes of more fly-overs and zoom-ins by the drone, permitting them to study the terrain, Lt Hofmann confirmed a position overlooking the castle, easily accessible for his team.

'Good. Next one,' Michael said, eager to narrow down the search.

The castle, high up on the slope, looked formidable. Its stone walls seemed to have been chiselled out of the mountain face. Far below, the long, cleared driveway twisted its way through the snow-covered woodlands, crossed a narrow moat, and disappeared underneath a stone battlement. Two black 4x4s were parked in the forecourt. In the north corner, an entrance led to an underground parking garage. A wide set of steps swept four metres up to the next level. Parked on the upper terrace were two more black 4x4s and a helicopter. In the southern corner, a vehicular ramp connected the two levels.

'Crooks, they just can't live without their black 4x4s,' Michael commented. 'And a helicopter… Six men present… The turrets look fortified. I know it's a castle built to repel invaders with pitchforks and bows. But these are far more sinister.'

'And more men in the woods,' Lt Hofmann added. 'I suggest I recall my men and we move in on this target as first priority.'

'I agree,' Michael said thoughtfully. His instincts told him this was Niall's lair. 'Lieutenant, find a place as close as possible for your team. If he's there, it's going to be a bugger getting inside without raising the alarm. Best to wait till nightfall. Excuse me a sec, time to wake up Svetlana.'

Fifteen minutes later, Svetlana watched the drones live-feed. Not much had changed since it had first zoomed in on the castle.

As she watched, the castle's front door opened. Five men stepped into the morning sunlight. With purpose, they strode towards the two parked 4x4s.

'Svetlana? Anyone familiar?' Michael asked.

'Not that I can recall. Can we zoom in on the faces and copy them? Best to do a facial recognition.'

'Yes,' Bertrand said obligingly.

'Can you get a better angle on the short guy? Can't see his face clearly. He looks familiar,' Svetlana said as the two vehicles drove down the ramp on to the lower level and joined the other 4x4s.

'Can we see who's inside?' Michael asked.

As the lens of the drone's camera zoomed in on the other vehicles, the tinted windows denied them access.

'Best we tag along; may have nothing to do with Niall. Who knows? Lieutenant, can one of your cars oblige and establish where they're going?'

'Yes, of—' the lieutenant started and stopped, interrupted by Svetlana.

'It's Nicolai Baranovsky! The short guy. And if he's there, then Niall must be as well.'

The men in the van turned and looked at her.

'You sure?' Michael asked.

'Yes, hundred per cent. If you check your database, you'll have a thick file on Baranovsky. Head of the most dangerous criminal syndicate in Russia.'

'Hope you're right. Okay, let's start the recce,' Michael said.

'Lieutenant, get as close as you can to the castle before deploying the hornet. We need to save its power for the recon of the interior,' Jacques said. Wanting to make sure it won't malfunction this time, he put the mechanical hornet on the table. The next instant, its wings whirred with incredible speed as it zipped into the air. An interior image of the van appeared on one monitor. With the control in his hand, he deftly manoeuvred the hornet, adjusting the view. 'Seems to be fixed. Lieutenant, once it's in the air, head back. We'll control it from here.'

Pulling Michael to one side, Svetlana asked, 'Any word from Ivan?'

Caught off-guard, and unsure whether to tell her now or wait till he had the facts, Michael hesitated a second.

'Michael, has anything happened to him?' she asked, realising something was wrong.

'I don't know. Last I spoke to him, the call was interrupted. I haven't been able to reach him since. However, I've asked Col Bauer to make some enquiries. I'm sure he's okay. If not, the colonel would have contacted me by now. Russia might have shut down the network.'

'Yes, maybe that's why there's no word yet…' she replied, unconvinced. 'Michael, so your earlier story was not quite true. And now, are you sure you're telling me everything?'

Caught out, he spoke frankly. 'Svetlana, I don't know the facts. And sorry for not being quite honest. I thought it best.'

'I understand. But please, don't lie to me. I'm not a child.'

'Right… Well, let's hear what Col Bauer has to say,' Michael said, refraining from telling her what he had heard. That could wait.

'Yes, Michael, we can do that. Or, I can phone my office. Someone's bound to be there and able to locate him. I just find it strange that he hasn't rung you,' she said. 'Big favour, can I use your phone? Mine's smashed.'

With the phone on speaker the ringtone was loud and clear. After three rings, a female's voice answered in Russian, 'FSB, good morning. How can I help you?'

'Can I speak to Maj Gen Lukyanov?'

'Who may I say is calling?'

'Major Svetlana Nikolaeva.'

'Please hold, Major,' the voice responded mechanically.

Facing Michael, she said, 'Seems he's fine. Just busy dealing with the current situation. I feel silly pestering him. Maybe I'll wait for—'

'Maj Nikolaeva, this is Capt Simonov. Unfortunately, Maj Gen Lukyanov is not available.'

'Good morning, Captain. Yes, I understand he is very busy, but I must speak to him as a matter of extreme urgency. Please tell him.'

'That's not possible.'

'Why not?'

'Because he has been shot.'

'Shot…?'

'Someone assassinated him in Lubyanka Square eight hours ago. Anything else I can help you with?'

'No…'

'What urgent matter did you want to discuss with Maj Gen Lukyanov?'

Without replying, Svetlana ended the call and whispered, 'They killed him…'

For the second time the castle's front door swung open. Five men appeared and approached the helicopter parked on the lawn. Michael studied them. One man, slightly taller than the others, stood out.

'Do you know him?' Michael asked Svetlana.

'No. No, I don't. He has a similar build as Niall… Can we get a closer look at his face?' she asked, struggling to pay attention. The death of Ivan had shattered her resilience. He was gone. She kept reminding herself that her child needed her; Dasha had to be saved. Mourning Ivan had to wait.

As the man's face filled the screen, Michael hissed, 'That's Brendan, Sinead's fiancé!'

'Are you sure?' Svetlana asked, mystified.

'Yes. See this?' Michael scrolled through the images on his phone. 'Here ya go. Never met him. Spoke to him several times. Something about him bugged me. Supposed to be a lawyer in Dublin. Yeah, right, like hell he is!'

Svetlana watched the man climbed into the helicopter, talking animatedly to the four men by his side. 'His movements seem familiar… Maybe I'm crazy and my eyes are playing tricks on me. I'm sure that's Niall.'

This time it was Michael who reacted even more surprised. 'You're kidding!'

'No, I'm not. He must have had reconstructive surgery. Also altered his voice; he did not sound like Niall when I spoke to him. No wonder he'd tricked Sinead. Poor girl. She'll be heartbroken when she finds out.'

'That's for sure,' Michael nodded. 'At last, we've found his hideout. Jacques, can we get the hornet inside, see if they're there?'

'Will do, as soon as the lieutenant is in position,' Jacques replied. 'In the meantime, shall Bertrand follow the chopper?'

'Yes,' Michael said, watching the helicopter lift into the air and swing south.

Scrutinising the castle's blueprints, downloaded from the local council's planning department's website, Svetlana commented drily, 'Nice place. He hasn't given up on his luxuries. Still has lots of money.'

'Wonder how he managed that?'

'That's Niall; always prepared. Trust, he enjoys it. He won't be for much longer,' Svetlana said, and studied the castle's layout. 'Seems the top two floors are his quarters. One below has several guest suites… And one grand one in the tower. The lift and stairs next to the tower connect all floors. We need to access this foyer, preferably near the top where these suites are. If they're in the castle, they're most probably there.'

The hornet flew through the open window on the top floor, its electronic eye scanning the hallway. Empty. Halfway along the left wall, a set of double doors; Niall's apartment. On the right, the tower, main stairs, and lift. The hornet flapped its wings and continued up the stairs. Outside the suite's door, it dropped to the floor, crawled underneath, and flew up, circling the room. Empty. Tidy. And no light on in the en-suite.

It flew down the stairs, past Niall's level to the floor below, and landed on a chandelier in the hallway. The miniature camera scanned the area. A door opened. Two men. Russian. Each word they spoke was received in the control van. Svetlana translated the dialogue:

"We have six hours to report to our CO. Our ride is waiting in Geneva. Let's get out of here. Job's over."

"I'll miss the money. Where's the CO now?"

"Not far… Apparently at some meeting. We can…"

Svetlana stopped, unable to hear more with the lift's door shutting behind the two men.

'Wonder who's their CO? Does this have anything to do with the man Col Bauer is hunting?' Svetlana asked.

'Perhaps, but let's leave that for now. Jacques, see what's on the other side of that door,' Michael said.

The empty corridor was lined with doors on both sides. Recognising the stone gothic arches over the doors, Svetlana said excitedly, 'She must be there!'

The hornet sneaked into the first room, its camera sweeping the interior. Nothing. No one.

Svetlana could not hide her disappointment. 'Please, try the next one.'

But it was empty, as was the third one.

However, the fourth suite brought their search to an end. The scattered toys on the floor confirmed Dasha was being held there.

'Where is she?' Svetlana asked. 'Maybe she's in the kitchen, the garden…'

'We'll find her, don't worry. Let's proceed,' Michael said as his gaze shifted to the monitor showing footage relayed by the drone trailing Niall.

'Michael, as soon as Dasha, Vera and Sinead are safe, we'll go after him,' Svetlana said, seeing him distracted.

'Yes, of course,' he replied and returned his attention to the hornet's images.

By the time the hornet finished scanning the floor below, they started to lose hope. There was no sign of Vera, Sinead, or Dasha. Other than the security personnel and kitchen staff, there was no one.

'They're not there,' Svetlana whispered, crestfallen.

'They must be nearby. Couldn't just have disappeared. Damn! Bertrand, how much longer can the drone stay in the air? With the Russian security leaving, it makes Niall's immediate return to the castle unlikely. We cannot lose him.'

Vera sat up and stared at the bare walls, the unmade bed. The soft daylight filtering through the high-level window brought back a memory she would rather forget. The hour spent in the workshop in Mykonos, tormented by men she had hated. Was it not for Michael, she would not be here today, having rescued her from certain death.

The thought of him…of their baby murdered by Niall plummeted her mood. A heavy sigh escaped her lips. After a long night of sorrow, she thought she had no more tears left. But the memory of them drew emotions from deep inside, like a windmill drawing water from an arid plain.

She wiped her cheeks and touched the photograph of them entering the hotel in Bern. It was beyond her how anyone could be so cruel, so bitter, killing an innocent baby not even two days old.

'I will not let him live. Without you, I will not continue. No, I won't,' she whispered, vowing to kill Niall, even if she died trying.

She did not know where she was.

In the middle of the night they had plucked her out of bed, slipped a thick anorak on her, and pulled a bag over her head. With her hands tied behind her back, a rope wrapped around her body, she had been marched out of the castle and shoved into a car.

Approximately an hour later she had found herself standing in the freezing snow; the smell of the pine forest overpowering. Unable to rid herself of the hood, she had placed one foot in front of the other and followed the sound of the disappearing car.

Soon another vehicle had arrived. She had shouted for help, hoping it was someone friendly. But hearing men's mocking laughter and Larry's scratchy voice, she had choked on her words. 'We meet again, dearest Vera. Come, let me help you,' he had scorned and pushed her into the snow. Grabbing the hood and a fistful of hair, he had dragged her off.

Again, the journey had not lasted more than an hour. Finally propelled into the room, they had untied her and shut the door before she could remove the hood.

Her future would be nothing other than nonstop harassment with the odd punch thrown in for good measure. And them, taking turns in raping her.

Not long after her arrival, there had been a commotion outside her room; muffled voices. This was repeated a bit later.

She did not touch the tray of food left on the bedside table; eating was the furthest from her mind. Inside a chest of drawers were some clothes for her, and stacked on top, a few books. An old chair. Other than that, the room was empty. Empty as her world felt without Michael and Natalya.

Chapter 59

Switzerland

Cast in deep shadow, the Wägitalstrasse meandered gently up the narrow valley from Siebnen towards lake Wägitalersee. Patches of black ice forced Maj Huber's convoy to slow down. With snow piled up on either side of the road and covering the minor roads, they were not concerned about losing the Russian colonel; the Wägitalstrasse had become a dead-end.

At the edge of Vorderthal village, Maj Huber ordered the driver to pull into a cleared parking area.

Three men – their firearms concealed – strolled into the sleepy town with most of the buildings' shutters closed; a typical wintry Sunday morning.

Despite his mind being in turmoil, Thomas did not miss a thing. At least he now knew the identity of the colonel's companion at Geneva airport. He was the man he had failed to meet at the base in Russia. The man who gave the colonel his orders. Colonel General Vladimir Coshenko, CO of Unit 14-BOPS Corps, and the 21st Airborne Division's Rapid Deployment Unit.

There were too many questions still unanswered. Where were the Russians going…? Who were they meeting? Where was the unit who had disappeared on the French motorway, and what were their targets? Even if he catches Col Polyakov, would there be enough time to avert the war? And then more on a personal note: Ivan… Maj Gen Luik, were they safe, alive? And how were his men coping in tracking down Niall to rescue the three hostages?

The news of what had befallen Svetlana infuriated him immensely; disgusted by the barbarity of the Russians. He rang Lt Schmidt. 'Lieutenant, SITREP.'

'We're tracking one unit, direction Paris. The other had veered off to Reims. Two units are following them. No news on the third unit. Doubt we'll find them. Sir, I suggest we pull over the unit I'm following and extract the information we need,' Lt Schmidt suggested.

'Not yet. We'll move in as soon as the first Russian unit is in position. They might just bite a capsule rather than talk. Then we would have lost not just one, but two marks. Best to concentrate on the ones we have eyes on,' Thomas said.

'Roger, Sir. I'll contact you as soon as we have reached the target.'

Next, Thomas contacted Lt Hofmann. 'Lieutenant, when I can expect you back.'

'Still searching for the hostages. Found evidence where they're being held, but they are not present. Don't know how long we'll be, Sir.'

'Roger. Anything else?'

'Sergeant Franz Strauss is following a convoy of 4x4s, south-eastern end of the Obersee, direction Siebnen—'

'You said, Siebnen?' Thomas cut him short.

'Affirmative, Sir. Why?'

'I'm currently twenty minutes south of Siebnen,' Thomas said thoughtfully. 'Any idea who they are?'

'Yes. Maj Nikolaeva confirmed the occupant of the second vehicle to be Nicolai Baranovsky. Russian mafia. An associate of Niall McGuire.'

'Patch me through to Franz. I think his heading our way.' Holding on, Thomas turned to Major Huber. 'We can expect more company. Russians.'

As the three Swiss soldiers returned from their recce, Maj Huber wound down his window. 'Anything to report, Lieutenant?'

'Manned roadblock, private security, one klick beyond the town on the Wägitalersee road. They allowed our mark through. No hostiles in town.'

'Thanks, Lieutenant,' Maj Huber replied as he studied the map on the monitor. 'There's no alternative route bypassing the roadblock. Anything else?'

'No Sir.'

'Understood,' Maj Huber said and pointed at the map with a gloved finger. 'If passable, we'll swing into this lane and rendezvous in the woods there. Lieutenant, instruct the men.'

Thomas, dressed in a white hooded anorak, snow pants and boots, edged his way towards the treeline. He hunched down behind a tall fern covered in snow. The view was not perfect but sufficed to observe the roadblock and narrow road winding up to the lake.

Twelve heavily armed men manned the barrier, and three 4x4s blocked the road. Five hundred metres further up, another two 4x4s sealed the lane off. Six men carrying assault rifles stood about smoking and chatting.

'They don't want uninvited guests barging in on whatever they're doing up at the lake,' Maj Huber commented. 'Shall I arrange air support to carry out a recce? No point in hiking up there only to walk smack into an unsanctioned Swiss-Russian military exercise.'

'Doubt it's an exercise,' Thomas said. 'I suggest we play it safe and carry out the recce ourselves. I'll link up to a NATO satellite.'

Combing the woods opposite, Maj Huber replied from behind his binoculars, 'Two snipers. Could be more. Wonder why my people are colluding with the Russians?'

'I've asked myself the same question,' Thomas remarked. 'Maybe it's simply an isolated incident with the general having gone rogue. Well, nothing we can do about that. Once we know who gives the orders, we'll deal with them.' As his words drifted up in the fresh morning air, his eyes fixed on the four black 4x4s rolling to a stop at the manned roadblock. 'And here they are. Mafia. The theory that some third force is involved is gaining credence by the minute.'

Maj Huber whistled softly by Thomas's side, studying the live footage of the holiday retreat on the east shore of lake Wägitalersee.

Fourteen helicopters, thirty-nine vehicles, and a hundred and twenty armed men were visible. Thirty held VERBA 9K333 MANPADS – portable infrared homing surface-to-air missile launcher.

'We're outgunned and outnumbered at least six to one. And some of them are Russian Spetsnaz. Not going to be easy,' Maj Huber said.

'Bit of an understatement. Have you got any spy-drones at hand?'

'Yes, but won't be of much use. The clouds will force us to fly low. They'll spot them.'

'Only alternative is to get eyes inside the main chalet. You up for it, Major?'

Sheltered by heavy foliage and banks of snow, in single file the seven Germans and fifteen Swiss followed the animal track up the mountain towards the Wägitalersee. Ten men had remained at the vehicles as backup.

Feeling his phone vibrate, Thomas fished it out of his pocket and shot his fist into the air. The column halted and took a knee. Conscious of the short distance separating him from the armed men across the ravine, Thomas answered with a whisper, 'Yes?'

'Thomas, it's me,' Maj Gen Luik's strained voice replied.

'General! That's a relief. You had me worried. Everything alright?'

'With me, yes,' Gen Luik replied. 'Sorry, I missed your call. Had my phone off by accident.'

'Gathered as much. I can't talk right now. In the middle of a recce.'

'Understood. I'll be quick. My source confirmed Ivan was shot. No one is prepared to divulge more information. But I'll keep digging.'

'Real shame…' Thomas sighed. 'General, with him gone, we'll need you to present our case to the Russian president if this mission is successful. Will you do it?'

'Of course.'

'Then it's best you leave Ivan's death for now. Too dangerous. Members of the FSB, Russian and Swiss military, Interpol, and French Police are involved. Can't trust normal circles.'

'That bad?'

'Yes. As soon as I'm free, I'll send names of those you can trust. Got to go. Be careful,' Thomas said and pocketed his phone.

11h00, Sunday, Wägitalersee

Rows of stuffed deer heads welcomed visitors to the main chalet. Their glass eyes stared vacantly into space. In the righthand corner of the spacious reception area, a wide wooden staircase swept up to the mezzanine level. A roaring fire blazed in the gigantic fireplace in the opposite wall. Adjacent to the reception desk, through a solid wood-panelled screen, two doors gave access to a banqueting hall.

Ten guards occupied the mezzanine level. Like hawks they scrutinised the clusters of resolute faces seated around the six fully laden eight-seater tables in the banqueting hall. Two men watched the reception area for any new arrivals. A nervous twitch, a sudden move by a visitor would result in immediate ejection and interrogation.

The locked doors in the banqueting hall's south-facing wall led on to a wide terrace, ideal for entertaining during the summer. But not today. Outside, the murky sky cast a dull light on the vacant chairs and tables, with clouds building up

375

against the surrounding mountains. Adjacent to each door, armed men stood guard.

Seated, the forty-eight attendees – council members, their assistants, and advisors – listened to the chairman, bringing the meeting to order. Overhead, three wrought-iron and deer-antlers chandeliers, suspended from heavy solid oak beams, emitted a soft glow over the sinister proceedings.

Among those present were the representatives and heads of some of the most powerful business syndicates and political and military leaders in the world. A mixture of greed, revenge, ideological and religious beliefs, and a raw hunger for power had brought them together. They stood on the threshold of their dream which had taken years of meticulous planning.

Niall sat next to Nicolai. Sharing their table to his right were Boris and his commander, Colonel General Vladimir Coshenko. Whereas Niall seemed relaxed, the opposite could be said about Boris, who looked worried.

In a reassuring voice the chairman expressed his satisfaction with the operation to date, carried out with military precision. The few lapses in security had been dealt with and were of no further concern. In an operation of this magnitude these were to be expected. But most importantly, they were on schedule. Nothing could stop them now... Except for the last item on the agenda: a final vote with no abstentions.

A unanimous yes was required to safeguard the fruition of their plan. If passed, then by tomorrow the world would be a very different place. If not, the years of planning would have been in vain. The operation would cease immediately... For now.

The chairman was not concerned. He knew each member was committed to the bitter end. The vote would be a simple formality. All had sworn an oath, one which would cost them their lives if they had a change of heart. Of course, some might be plagued by uncertainty as the blood of untold numbers would be on their hands. Nevertheless, it was a small price to pay for taking control of the world. Tomorrow, the Council's motto of *libertatem aut mortem* (liberty or death) would be tested to the full.

Conspicuous by their absence were members of the world's leading banks and WEF. The enemy. The Council had every intention of wrenching away control from them. Change was long overdue. The world's central banks, the media, and politicians would be *set free* to carry out their duties, but under a new master.

The Russian armed forces were destined to be the sword to sever the demon's head. When hostilities begin, the first strike would be against NATO and US communication and spy satellites, and seventy-five per cent of all intercontinental ballistic nuclear missile installations across the US, Europe, including all major power plants. In deterring the enemies' roaming stealth nuclear fleets from joining the fray, the UK and French aircraft-carrier fleets would be eliminated.

During the past five years, Russia had launched twenty-four new weather and communication satellites, replacing the outdated systems floating in space. *Harmlessly*, they circumnavigated earth at an altitude of five hundred kilometres more than the US defence meteorological satellites.

Many in Washington had expressed serious concerns regarding the true nature of these satellites; their size exceeded by far that of standard meteorological satellites. Not willing to entertain any scare-mongering, the US president had brushed aside these fears. However, the military did investigate these floating monsters but had failed to identify their actual function.

Camouflaged by an array of radar dishes, solar panels, and camera lenses, were six independent nuclear-powered energy laser-beam firing systems. It was technologically the most advanced attack system ever perfected, capable of destroying every missile site or enemy target on earth or in space. And any projectile fired at Russia.

For years, America had struggled to perfect their much-maligned Star Wars program. But twelve years ago, they had finally succeeded in destroying an in-flight ballistic missile with a high-powered laser gun.

The ALTB moving at a speed of 7200km/h off the Central California coast had been no match for the superheated, high-energy laser beam approaching at over one billion kilometres per hour. Blasted for a few seconds by a football-sized beam, it had caused a stress fracture to develop, resulting in the target disintegrating into a million fragments within seconds.

Mounted on a Boeing Jumbo jet – converted at a cost of US$1,5 billion – the weapon had tracked the missile racing over the ocean off Point Mugu Naval Warfare Centre by employing two low-energy lasers. And when acquired, had fired a megawatt-class Chemical Oxygen Iodine Laser (COIL) at the target.

Notwithstanding its success, the programme which had seen billions in cost overruns, had suffered a sharp budget cut by the defence secretary, calling the concept "fatally flawed". Therefore, the airborne laser program had continued on a drip-fed basis.

But the Siberian hinterland hid a frightening truth. Two years before the American's first success, the Russians, having stolen their research, had already succeeded in its first laser experiment. Manufacturing of their own "Star Wars" system was well on schedule.

Therefore, having deployed their laser weapons, NATO would find itself powerless against the Russian armed forces. With its nuclear arsenal intact, including the intercontinental ballistic doomsday weapon, Satan 2 (the RS-28 Sarmat), the success of their intended "Blitzkrieg" was guaranteed. This belief Colonel General Vladimir Coshenko, representing the Russian consortium, had repeated unequivocally.

For Russia not to be named the aggressor at the end of hostilities, Col Gen Coshenko and Col Polyakov had played their role in stoking the fires of war. But their work was not quite done. The colonel and his unit would continue until Europe would strike first.

Therefore, by Monday evening, with their last operation completed, NATO would declare war against Russia. The "imminent attack" as ordered by the Russian president would be delayed until NATO would strike. Only then would the Chief of the General Staff of Russia issue the final command to proceed in self-defence.

As discussions centred around current affairs in Europe, with most countries reeling economically as a result of the two-year Coronavirus pandemic lockdowns and restrictions, brewing racial and religious conflicts, their timing could not be more opportune.

The deployment of a 40,000 American expeditionary force seven days ago in Europe, bringing the total of US forces to 70,000 did not deter them.

But the most crucial part of their plan, to be executed during the next eighteen hours, they did not discuss. This knowledge was for the ears of only a chosen few. Even Col Polyakov was excluded from this group. Unknown to him, some of his men were not. Men who answered directly to Col Gen Coshenko.

Niall listened to the rumble of voices debating the agenda. He felt at home amongst men who created their own destinies. Like him, they feared nothing and no one. Nor did any of them jump about hysterically bellowing fascist ideologies. They were not fanatical. They were in full control of their faculties, sharing a common goal. Power and greed, camouflaged as a "change for the greater good of man"; their own "Reset" of the world.

The minimum the Russians wanted was full control of Europe's energy supplies and the reinstatement of the old Soviet Union's borders; the blocking of the West's decay and decadence. Other members wanted control of the energy and mineral resources of the third world, and the central and world banks.

Each cartel stood to gain untold amounts of wealth and assets by the time this would be over. New puppets, controlled by the Council, would be installed in key positions. The rebuilding of large parts of Europe would be a mammoth task; contracts worth unimaginable sums funded by loans granted by the Council's banks and repaid by taxpayers as throughout the centuries. Shares would crash overnight and transfer into the hands of the Council's members. It was a win-win situation for them.

However, if they failed in their grab for power, they would slip back into their roles as before and reap the benefits of rebuilding a post-war world; from the biggest money laundering operation in history. The blame for the war would rest solely on the shoulders of current leaders and their administrations.

A smile tugged at Niall's lips. He had been fortunate to have been included. Was it not for his American friends who he had introduced to Nicolai and the Council, he would not be there. Thus, forced to change his plans regarding the hostages had been inconsequential.

The amplified sound of the male voices picked up by the directional microphone pointing at the patio's glass door echoed in Thomas and Maj Huber's earpieces:

"It's unanimous. We'll proceed as planned. Let's raise our glasses and toast to our imminent success."

Immediately there followed the scraping of chairs on the floor. Glasses clinked. After a moment of silence, the same voice announced the meeting concluded and that lunch would now be served.

'We're too late!' Thomas fumed. It was 12h30. The seven-kilometre hike up the valley had taken too long. Numerous times they had to detour around sentries patrolling the woods. 'Major, any theories regarding their plans?'

'No. Maybe we learn something during their lunch.'

'Let's hope so,' Thomas replied as he contacted Michael and spelt out what he needed. 'Our satellite cover is poor; too much cloud to carry out a detailed recce. Do you have your drone overhead?'

'Yes, we do. Have the same problem though. If we drop any lower, they'll spot us. We'll have to clear the valley and track them once they exit the mountains. Problem is, we're running out of fuel; max half-an-hour flying time left.'

'Understood. They'll have lunch soon. Should give you a couple of hours to recharge the drone. The Swiss are watching the road and will follow the two marks. We have a visual on the carpark and Niall's helicopter. We'll ID their cars and update you on any new developments.'

'Thanks, Thomas. Any luck eavesdropping?'

'No. Caught only the end of the meeting. But whatever they're planning got the final go-ahead. I'll discuss the situation with my chief.' As tempting as it was to arrest those present, it would be premature. They lacked evidence.

'Niall, we could snatch on grounds of kidnapping. That's it. But gate-crashing the party with an arrest warrant for one of their men would not go down well. They may have— Michael, I must sign off,' Thomas said as the major indicated for him to end the call.

'We have an incoming bogey, two hundred metres east-northeast. Time to relocate,' Maj Huber whispered, storing his gear, preparing to move out. They could not afford to get caught up in a shootout. It would be a slaughter.

An hour later, having circumvented the south end of Wägitalersee, they once more directed the microphone and thermal-imaging camera at the Wägitalersee resort from across the lake. The additional nine hundred metres compromised reception, although the images were clear enough to establish movement inside the walls. Attendees were still seated with lunch underway.

'Major, best if you and your men return to the TPB. As soon as we've photographed the conspirators, we'll join you,' Thomas suggested.

Having to stay clear of the road and tunnel connecting the lake with Vorderthal village, the trek down the valley would be a minimum of fifty minutes. Hopefully, the major should be in position to follow the Russians by the time they drove past.

Two cameras zoomed in on the entrance of the main chalet. Patiently, Thomas and the six men by his side waited.

And so did Gen Beck's team at NATO HQ in Belgium. As soon as the images of the leaving delegates would pour in, each delegate would be identified and picked up en route or at their destination. Lt Gen Beck was adamant that the conspirators' plans would be snuffed out before the next sunrise.

Chapter 60

Russia

The room was dark with the curtains drawn. His body ached. The drip attached to his arm was not a good sign. The room was sparsely furnished. Someone's body armour lay on a coffee table; flattened bullet rounds embedded in it. A chair creaked.

'Glad you're awake. Trust you're not too sore. Wasn't our handiwork. Your colleagues' doing,' a voice sounded close to him; the fluent Russian spoken with a slight accent.

Ivan tried to sit up. The pain in his chest stopped him. 'Who are you? Where am I? What day…time is it?' he asked.

'John Smith. And that guy at the window with a face only a mother can love is Peter Smith. My second-in-command,' the man on the chair replied and stood up.

The man called Peter smiled and nodded his head in return.

'Here, have some water,' John Smith offered. 'And it's ten past two, Sunday. You haven't been out that long.'

A leggy brunette entered the room; her hair tied in a bun. A slender neck protruded from her V-neck blouse. Her movements were smooth, catlike. Her black attire, offset by her milky-white skin, was completed by a string of natural white pearls. Quite chic, Ivan thought, studying her heart-shaped face.

'And, let me guess, you are Sarah Smith,' Ivan said without smiling.

'Close enough. Normally we call her Anne, but Sarah will do,' John corrected him, eliciting a genial smile from Anne. John was in his late forties, lean and muscular. Blue eyes with a full mop of blond hair. Firm jaw.

'I gather you know who I am. So, what does the CIA want with me?' Ivan asked, weary of the chitchat. 'And where the hell am I? How did I get here?'

'Luckily for you, Maj Gen Lukyanov, we just happened to be around when they tried to take you out. I'm curious though. What's with the body armour? Were you expecting trouble?'

'Rubbish, why were you following me?' Ivan replied.

'Okay, first, you're in a CIA safe-house outside Moscow. Secondly, we've been watching you for the last few days, wanting a friendly chat. That's why we were three metres from you when you were shot. And when bystanders had rushed forward to help you, we had flashed our "FSB" badges, picked you up, and hustled you into our car cruising next to us. Before the shooters realised what had happened, you were gone. And we had jabbed you with a sedative to avoid any resistance.'

'So, I guess I owe you a thanks. But why this urgency to speak to me?' Ivan asked.

'An asset of ours had picked up a lot of interesting chatter between you and a Colonel Thomas Bauer – NATO, German Intelligence.'

'Uh-huh,' Ivan acknowledged, not impressed by his office's lack of security.

'Considering your discussions with the colonel, we felt you were approachable. Maybe willing to share what you know about who is stirring trouble. How far up this reach? Is it the president? His wealthy friends? Someone inside the military? Or all of them? Therefore, we had hoped to meet. The fact that your own people tried to kill you confirms you were getting too close to the truth. Any idea who sanctioned this hit?'

'I suspect I do.'

John tried again. 'Please, do tell.'

'Not so fast. Before I share any intel, can you show me some proof other than your fake FSB IDs,' Ivan demanded as lucidity returned with the drug wearing off.

Grateful to be alive, he was glad to have donned the vest before wandering outside; his fears had not been unfounded. Although, the pain in his chest he could do without. Some ribs must be bruised or broken. He won't be much use in a fight. Well, not for a while. He'll have to cooperate with the Americans and find a way out.

'Do you have a medic?' he asked, curious to know how bad his injuries were.

'I am,' Anne replied. 'I examined you while you were out. Two fractured ribs. So, best you rest for a day or two.'

'Thanks Anne. Now IDs please?'

'Here you go,' John said, showing him his CIA badge.

'Could be fake as well.'

'Sorry, it's the only one I have. Maybe you can get your friend, Col Bauer, to verify our identity through his connections. Shall I get him on the line?'

'And how do you propose to do that? You have his number?'

'Yep. By the way, your phone's busted. However, we retrieved your sim.'

'How about you put a video call through to the director of the CIA and I can have a word with him? I know him.'

'If you insist.'

'I do.'

Eight minutes later, the CIA Director had verified the CIA's agents' identities.

Sticking to what had been uncovered regarding Col Polyakov's involvement since the explosion of the gas filtration plant in Turkey, Ivan gave them a rundown. But the decision to go to war within the next twenty-four hours, he did not share, not prepared to compromise his country. If the Americans found out, they might launch a first strike.

'Best I call Col Bauer for a SITREP. Last I heard, he was chasing Col Polyakov towards Austria. Mind if I use your phone?'

Holding John's phone to his ear, Ivan waited. No answer. After three more tries, he gave up. 'Must be too busy to take the call. Can you please check another number on my sim?'

'Do you mind if I call you Ivan?' John asked.

'Please do.'

'Right, who am I looking for?'

'Hello,' Michael answered, unable to recall the number with the Russian country code.

'Michael, is that you?'

'Yes, and you are?'

'It's me, Ivan.'

'Ivan…'

Seated inside the control van next to Michael, and hearing the name, Svetlana looked up. 'Please, may I?' she asked and reached for the phone. 'Ivan, is that you?'

Chapter 61

Switzerland

'That was good,' Niall lauded the four-course meal, putting his empty wineglass down. 'Time to get the hell out of here.'

'*Da*, and quickly.' Nicolai nodded.

Placing the conspirators and their representatives in one place on the eve of hostilities had been downright crazy. Convinced nothing could stop them with enough security present during the meeting, senior members of the council had brushed aside his concerns. More crucially, they were amongst friends, in a country where money bought loyalties. And their power reached far above and beyond world political leaders. The small group heading the organisation was not present. The chairman was the only contact between the two tiers.

At the reception desk, Niall exchanged the receipt for his pistol, ammunition, smartphone, and coat. 'Please take this. You must wear it when you exit the building. Your men already have theirs. It's merely a precaution,' the attendant advised.

Retrieving his belongings, Nicolai received the same article. Exiting through the front door by his side, Niall asked, 'Are you heading back to Russia?'

'Not for now. I'll lie low in Switzerland for a week or two. See how this special operation pans out?'

'Maybe not a bad idea. Where will you be staying?'

'Sorry, rather not say.'

'Of course.'

'I suggest you do the same. Disappear,' Nicolai advised.

'Was my intention. No need to return to the castle right away; nothing there to entertain me. I think I'll head back to Ireland. One place no one will bother to invade,' Niall lied. The last place he would return to was his country of birth.

'Very cute!' Thomas exclaimed. He was livid. 'Damn! So much for taking pictures.'

In disbelieve he watched the first delegates make their way to the cars and helicopters. All wore Guy Fawkes masks. And with each and everyone in a black suit, there was no telling them apart.

With us gone "missing" from the airport, why am I even surprised? They were expecting us. Well, if they think they've got us beaten, they can think again, Thomas thought.

'Major, please instruct your men to photograph each car before they reach Volderthal. We need the make, colour, and registration. And if possible, pictures of the passengers. I'll ask Michael to use his resources and trace the registered owners. If they are rentals, which they most likely are, we'll follow the money. Might take too long though. Any alternative suggestions, Major?' Thomas whispered into the small mic.

'If I had the authority, I would stop them from leaving the tunnel. Seal it off on both ends and arrest the lot,' Major Huber's voice sounded in Michael's earpiece.

'Would be the better option. But without your government's permission, you, your men, and mine would be put against the wall. I have no problem facing the music, but I cannot ask that of you.'

'Thank you, Colonel.' The relief in the major's voice was palpable. As a junior officer with his entire future ahead, he had a wife and two young children to consider. He already had some serious explaining to do for disobeying orders and disappearing off the radar.

Thomas's eyes did not stray from the chalet's entrance. 'That looks like the colonel and the general clearing the steps. Tall, baldy and his merry men. Numbers match. And bingo, same 4x4s. You agree, Sarge?'

'Affirmative.'

'Major, can your men follow the colonel and we'll grab him once he's cleared the valley?' Thomas said into his mic, taking photos of the two 4x4s' registration plates the Russian officers climbed into. 'And we need a chopper. Can you organise one?'

'I'm sure that can be arranged on the QT.'

'We also need a forensic team to comb the banqueting facility. Should be enough evidence to link most to this group once we've rounded them up. Right, I better inform my CO – we'll need your government's permission to snatch them on Swiss soil.'

Just as Thomas reached for his phone, it vibrated in his pocket. Same number as before; better take it. 'Col Bauer speaking.'

'Thomas, it's Ivan. Can you talk, or is this a bad time?'

'Ivan, you're alive! What happened?'

'Got shot—'

'What! Are you okay?'

'Yes, I'm fine. A few bruised ribs. Fortunately, I had my vest on or we would not be having this conversation. An American CIA team snatched me from the scene. I'm with them in a safehouse.'

'CIA?'

'Yes. It seems they're the only allies I have left over here. I cannot go near my office. Though I will present the evidence to the president when you're ready. Can you give me an update?'

'Of course. Our situation—'

'Thomas, do you mind if I put you on speaker? John Saunders, Peter Macmillan, and Anne Lewis from the CIA are here with me,' Ivan interrupted. 'I've verified their credentials with the CIA Director. You can speak freely.'

As soon as Thomas finished his report, John spoke. 'Hi Colonel, John here. That was most informative. I'll convey this intel to my boss. Anything we can do to help? We have assets in Zurich.'

'Thanks, John, I'll take you up on that. Any chance of a safehouse in Switzerland?'

'Yes, we have a house near Bern. I'll contact our head there. Richard Meier. By the way, if you need manpower, just say the word. Right, I'll be back in a few minutes,' John said, leaving the conversation.

'Thomas, can you do me a favour?' Ivan asked.

'Of course.'

'Please inform Gen Luik that I'm fine. I don't want to risk contacting him in case they tapped his phone. Be careful how you put it. I need to remain "dead".'

'And what about Maj Nikolaeva? Shall I contact her?'

'No need. I spoke to her a few minutes ago.'

'Have to go. Target's on the move,' Thomas said, signing off.

Immediately he rang Michael. 'Niall's clearing the ground. Heading down the valley, north. You've got him?'

'Yes,' Michael confirmed. 'We'll take it from here. Good luck.'

The view from the drone was hazy as it followed the chopper racing over Volderthal and along the narrow road through the valley.

Niall was not the only one escaping the mountains; three more helicopters and a convoy of vehicles were visible. Michael ignored those and focused his attention on Niall's midnight-blue Augusta Westland AW109 helicopter.

Seventy-three kilometres into the flight, beyond Baden, the chopper slowed, hovered a fraction before settling on an open field. Four men jumped out. Seconds later, a silver Audi

4X4 sped off towards Baden. The chopper cleared the lawn and flew in a northerly direction.

'Which one do I follow, chopper or car?' Bertrand asked.

'Lets' see,' Michael said, replaying the footage of the men disembarking and zooming in on their faces. He cursed out loud as they all wore Guy Fawkes masks! There was no telling whether Niall was in the car or helicopter.

Svetlana considered their options. 'The car. He's trying to throw us off track. He cannot know we're watching and is playing it safe. One can trace the helicopter, but not the car once it reaches town where it can easily disappear.'

'You're right,' Michael agreed. 'Bertrand, the car.'

The drone's thermal imaging camera showed five occupants inside the Audi racing east. Direction Baden.

'Thanks buddy. Much appreciated. For sure, I'll look after you,' Niall said into his phone. Just as he had thought. He was being followed. His informants have proved themselves to be very useful assets. People to look after, as he had promised he would. He needed their loyalty.

'Right then. Time to leave you chaps. Pull into the basement carpark,' Niall ordered as the train station came into view.

The parking garage was full. It did not matter. The Audi circled the carpark twice and stopped at a spot not covered by security cameras.

Getting out, Niall said, 'Leave the car in the Zurich main train station's carpark; the rental company will pick it up in a few days. Here's something extra for your services. Your salaries have been transferred to your bank accounts.' He handed each man an envelope containing five thousand euros. 'I believe your commander is expecting you. There's an express train. Should get you to Geneva airport on time.'

Niall donned a cap and sunglasses. The simple disguise won't fool anyone, but it did not matter. No one was watching.

At the first men's shop he saw, he bought a pair of black jeans, a casual white shirt, a dark blue jumper, a pair of comfortable black sneakers – in case he needed to run – a scarf, sunglasses, and a heavy charcoal anorak. Paid for in cash, he changed clothes and placed his old suit and shoes in the shopping bag. Leaving the shop, he strode towards a ticket-machine and bought a return ticket to Zurich.

At a leisurely pace he made his way to the platform, cognisant of the cameras recording his every step. Passing by a large bin he shoved the shopping bag inside.

The platform's overhead screen showed the next train to arrive in ten minutes at 16h11. He bought a Sunday tabloid, a cappuccino and sat down on a bench occupied by an old lady. He greeted her with a nod and opened the newspaper.

'Who got out of the car?' Michael asked. It was a question no one could answer. The thermal imaging camera showed only four passengers in the car leaving the railway station's carpark. 'Come on. Any guess?'

'Niall, perhaps…I think,' Svetlana said.

'Or not. Possibly a decoy,' Jacques added.

'As always, he has every angle covered. Makes me wonder.' Michael rubbed his chin. Or he knows our every move, tipped off by the same bugger as before. Or by someone much closer: Jacques, Bertrand, Phillippe? Michael fretted, unsure.

'Have to agree with Svetlana. So, let's presume he got out. Jacques, can you access the CCTVs at that station? Should show whether he's there. In the meantime, Bertrand, stay with the car, but only as far as you still have a visual on the station. I want to have eyes on the next train out of there.'

Assisted by the young technician, Phillipe, the French Interpol agents did as instructed. Svetlana and Michael kept their attention on the video showing the Audi slowly making its way through the light afternoon traffic.

Michael turned his head, looked at Svetlana's hand and pulled a face, as if suddenly remembering that she must be in incredible pain. 'I better change your bandage while we have a moment. Come.'

Having retrieved the first-aid kit from his 4x4, he gave her a painkiller. 'We'll give it a minute before I get to work. Okay with you?'

'That's fine, thanks. I gather you don't only want to change my dressing. What's worrying you?'

'You are quick, ain't ya?' he smiled. 'I think we might have a rat amongst us. Have you noticed anyone sending secret messages, anything odd? I have been too distracted. I don't suspect the Germans, as they're outside Niall's reach. But my colleagues, not so sure. What do you reckon?'

'I haven't noticed anything suspicious.'

'Yeah, nor me. Maybe I'm just paranoid at this stage. Well, I reckon we'll soon know. I'll ask Lt Hofmann to keep an eye out as well,' Michael said, removing Svetlana's bandages.

With the wound redressed, they entered the control van.

'Train is pulling out of the station. Direction Zurich,' Jacques said.

'And the Audi?' Michael asked.

'Lost visual in Zurich. Hope your hunch is correct, or he's gone,' Bertrand replied.

'And the CCTV?'

'Still trying to access the circuit. Will take a while,' Phillipe cautioned.

Reaching the next station, Killwangen-Spreitenbach, the train stopped. In silence, five pairs of eyes watched. Again, there was no view of the platform. Six people exited the station. Three backpackers headed for the bus stop across the road. A woman turned right. The last two, both males, turned left. One entered the open carpark, the other walked towards a blue Mercedes.

The man standing next to the blue Mercedes looked up at the stranger approaching him. Recognising Brendan, Sinead's fiancé, Larry asked, confused, 'What are you doing here?'

'Relax, Larry. *Ce'st moi*, your boss,' Niall replied.

'Fecking hell! Niall?'

'Okay, enough of *introductions*. Now take me to my two favourite whores. By the way, how are they?' Niall chuckled. As he got into the car the first drops of icy rain pelted down.

'Zoom in on that guy next to the Merc,' Michael asked. His voice tingled with excitement. 'Larry! Got ya, you bugger! And who else do we have here... Of course, our beloved Brendan. Or rather, Niall.'

Seventeen kilometres southwest of Lucerne, the blue Mercedes turned left into a long driveway. Two hundred metres further it drove through a security gate. Slowly, the car continued towards a large chalet and entered a barn. Moments later, Niall and Larry stepped out into the dull afternoon light, crossed the forecourt, and entered the chalet. It was nothing too grand. But as to be expected of Niall, it was neither modest.

'Finally!' Michael exclaimed excitedly, knowing they had found Niall's lair. 'Right, let's hit the road. Bertrand, how much power's left in your toy?'

'Hour, at the most.'

'Hmm, okay. Keep her over that house as long as you can. We should make it.'

Svetlana's eyes shone with expectation. She could not wait to see her child.

'Jacques, you bring up the rear. Svetlana, come with me,' Michael said. 'We'll rendezvous in the church carpark in Schwarzenberg. By that time Lt Hofmann should already be in position at the chalet.'

'*Bon chance!*' Jacques wished them good luck as Michael and Svetlana left the van.

Michael estimated that by the time they would reach Niall's hideout, there should be sufficient time to carry out a proper recon and formulate a realistic rescue plan. Being a Sunday, the roads should not be too busy.

Turning the ignition of the 4x4, Michael saw Phillipe leave the Peugeot Boxer with phone in hand. Michael paused, his hand resting on the gearstick. He opened the door, got out, and covered the ten metres to where the young Interpol agent was typing a message on his phone.

'Do you mind?' he bellowed and grabbed the phone out of the startled man's hands. He read the half-written message. His right fist shot up and hit Phillipe under the chin, lifting him clear off the ground. The force of the punch was as if there had been nothing in its path.

Having witnessed the incident, Lt Hofmann raced over, glad he had not been on the receiving end.

'Here's our bloody mole,' Michael growled and handed the phone to Lt Hofmann. 'Read this.'

Other than the number, the message contained no information about who the recipient was. Although no name was needed. It was self-explanatory:

"Tell our friend they have him pinpointed. He must get out of there right away and not return to the castle, either. They know its location. He's got less than an hour. I'll try—"

The message ended in mid-sentence.

'You can thank your lucky stars you did not send it!' Michael snarled, wanting to break Phillipe's neck.

Jacques read the message and glared at the motionless body on the ground. 'Looks like he's dead.' He checked for a pulse. After a few seconds, he got up. 'He'll live. Pity, now he'll cost the taxpayers a lot of money for having to put him up for a very long time.'

'Jacques, find out whose number that is. Perhaps it's another colleague... Or an outsider. But whoever it is, we'll make sure the two will share a cell till the day they die,' Michael said, glad he had stopped the message in time and caught the mole.

Without a fuss, Lt Hofmann flipped Phillipe over, cuffed his hands and feet behind his back, and taped his mouth. Assisted by one of his men, they picked him up and asked, 'Michael, where shall we throw him?'

'You sure you want to know?' Michael said. 'Chuck him into the back of the van. We'll deal with him later.'

Chapter 62

Switzerland

The Swiss military helicopter swept over Lake Zurich's west bank. Flying dead west, it aimed to intercept Col Polyakov's convoy on the E25. The colonel who had a seventy-minute head start was currently five kilometres west of Zurich. Two of Maj Huber's vehicles were shadowing the Russians.

Thomas had the abduction of the colonel planned out. If it went his way, it should be low-key with no guns blazing. Well, that was the theory. But he needed the go-ahead to proceed. When he spoke to Lt Gen Beck an hour ago, the general had had no qualms about abducting the Russians. Although he could not authorise such action on Swiss soil without their permission.

Seated next to Thomas, the major appeared nervous. If his superiors did not agree, then these unsanctioned actions might blow up in his face.

'Yes Sir, what's the verdict?' Thomas answered his phone, eager to conclude his mission.

'Thomas,' Lt Gen Beck said. Addressing him by his first name did not bode well. 'You must call it off. The Swiss are not impressed that we did not clear our actions with them first. Neither at the prospect of being drawn into a diplomatic feud with Russia. They value their relationship with Russia as too important to jeopardise. Also, they want to keep their neutral status. Therefore, they refused to cooperate. In fact, they insist that you and your men must be out of Switzerland by 22h00. They felt that would give you ample time to gather your men, wipe your tracks, and disappear back to Germany.'

Thomas did not interrupt his superior.

'I take your silence as an indication of how you feel. Sorry, Thomas. Even our chancellor and the head of NATO failed to convince them. This makes me believe some of their senior members are also connected to this rogue council. Our hands are tied.'

'Understood, Sir. What about Maj Huber?'

'He will not be charged. He had acted in good faith as expected of any true Swiss soldier and, therefore, will be commended for his actions. On one condition, he returns to his base immediately. If not, he will be court-martialled. That's the best I could do.'

'Copy that, Sir. I'll tell the major.'

'Well, you have six hours to leave. Maybe you want to do some *sightseeing*, pick up a few *souvenirs?*' General Beck suggested.

'Yes, why not? Sir, inform the Swiss we'll be out of here by 22h00.'

Facing Maj Huber, Thomas repeated the general's words and asked to be dropped off in Bern. From there, they'd make their way back to the jet in Geneva. Next, he messaged Richard Meier, head of CIA in Bern, requesting assistance and transport.

The race was far from over.

At 16h45, the chopper hovered one metre above the carpark at Bern Bümpliz Nord railway station, Bern. Thomas and his men jumped out and raced in under the railway station's canopy.

'Right men, you heard what I told Maj Huber. Well, forget that. We're not leaving without the colonel.'

'As we thought, Sir,' Sgt Maj Koch smiled. 'What's the plan?'

'American CIA should be here any minute with transport and backup. We have a war to stop and less than twenty-four hours to do so.'

Ten kilometres west of Bern on the E25 motorway, the Mercedes 4x4 suddenly lost power. The driver pressed the accelerator to the floor. It made no difference. The power faded away. 'Useless German car,' he grumbled in Russian. He flicked on the emergency lights. 'Sorry Colonel. Must pull over.'

'*Da*. Be quick!' Boris snapped. 'Germans don't make cars as we do in Russia. These are for women to shop in city. Off-road car, my arse!'

The convoy of four 4x4s slowed down and switched to the inside lane. As the colonel's 4x4's engine finally cut, they drifted on to the hard shoulder and stopped twenty metres beyond the exit ramp. Boris got out, and ignoring the rain, walked to the 4x4 behind him. The rear passenger window rolled down. 'Yes, Colonel, what is the problem?' Col Gen Coshenko asked.

'Engine died. Sgt Smirnov is investigating. Best you keep going and we'll rendezvous at the airport. No good for you to sit here out in the open. If we can't fix it, we'll order another car. Bern is only five minutes from here,' Boris said, confident the problem would be solved quickly.

'Roger, Colonel,' the general replied and instructed the convoy to proceed.

With the bonnet open, Sgt Smimov tested the wiring. All felt secure. Irritated, he mumbled to the soldier beside him, 'To be expected of a rental. Most likely been across the Alps and back.' He fiddled some more with the wiring, got back in behind the wheel and tried the engine. It started without a problem. Before engaging the gears, he revved the engine and felt the power of the turbo kick in. 'Good. Seems okay.'

The 4x4 jolted forward and after seven metres the engine stalled again. This time all four soldiers got out. Boris waited in the car. They popped the bonnet open. As the men investigated the problem, Boris consulted the driver's manual. Trying to find the relevant chapter was too much trouble. Fed up, he shut the manual and searched for the rental company's emergency number.

About to dial the number, he noticed a white Mercedes Sprinter pull up behind them. The driver got out. There was no one else visible in the van. Smiling, the stocky man approached him and rapped on the window with his knuckles. Boris rolled it down.

'Good afternoon,' the man dressed in a slightly stained light-brown overall and a black beret greeted in German. 'What seems to be the problem?' Slung over his shoulder was a tool bag with a three-pointed star logo.

Boris looked suspiciously at the man, touched his sidearm underneath his jacket and shrugged his shoulders. 'Not understand,' he said, his English limited.

'Ah, you speak English,' the German said haltingly. His English did not sound much better. 'Me mechanic for Mercedes… Bern. Maybe I help.'

'No. I phone rent company. They fetch junk. Bring new car,' Boris replied.

'You sure. Maybe only something little wrong?'

The two Russian soldiers on Boris's side of the bonnet straightened up and moved closer, alert. One faced the German, the other stared at the snow-covered rise next to the motorway, his submachine gun at the ready. Nothing moved. The other two kept fiddling with the engine. One was in front of the 4x4 and the other on the driver's side.

Boris's eyes shot open. Too slowly he reached for his pistol as the taser hit him in the chest, immobilising him instantly.

Shouting in agony, the two Russian soldiers beside Cpl Decker fell to the ground, the silenced snipers' bullets having shattered their legs. At the same instant, the Russian in front of the 4x4 collapsed where he stood, also eliminated by a bullet to the leg. The snipers' shots had been perfect; at forty metres they could not miss. On the roadside, a loud bang confirmed a super-sock bean bag impact round fired, felling the fourth soldier. The Russian never saw Thomas, wearing a balaclava, sneak up on him and discharge the 12-gauge shotgun at eight metres, incapacitating him.

The skirmish had lasted three seconds.

Five Germans, wearing balaclavas, joined Thomas and Cpl Decker. Like a pack of hungry wolves, the Germans fell upon the wounded Russian soldiers and disarmed and cuffed them.

Thomas grabbed Boris and jabbed the point of the needle into his neck, injecting a strong tranquilliser. 'Got you!' he growled. His elation in having finally caught this elusive adversary was measured in equal amounts by the fury in him. Controlling his anger, he concentrated on the mission.

A few cars slowed down. The passengers stared at the Germans. Sgt Maj Koch pulled out a Swiss military flag and waved them on.

Without delay they shoved two Russians into the back of the 4x4. Boris and the other two were carried to the van.

Having cleared the scene of any evidence and retrieved the Swiss Police warning triangle from the side of the road, the van's doors shut. Cpl Decker reversed towards the exit ramp. In the back, the Russians' feet were secured, their mouths taped, and their shattered legs dressed. The four Germans glared at them, itching to shoot them, punish them for the number of people they had killed.

Thomas slipped in behind the wheel of the immobilised 4x4. Next to him, Sgt Maj Koch strapped himself in, his pistol aimed at the two sedated Russians propped up in the back.

'All clear. We're good to go,' Thomas said into his mic.

He waited a few seconds before turning the ignition. The engine engaged and with the emergency lights on he backed the vehicle up to the exit. The remote GPS immobilisation system had performed as expected. Once the vehicle's engine management system had received the initial code – obtained by the CIA by hacking into the car rental's database – the 4x4 had slowed down to a crawl and stopped. Switching it on and off was then in the hands of the CIA agents who were watching the 4x4 from the same position as the three snipers.

At the top of the exit ramp Thomas turned right and followed the Mercedes van. Two kilometres north of the E25 he pulled in amongst a cluster of trees and got out. In the back of the 4x4 the heavily sedated Russians grunted. Pity, they needed to feel the pain, Thomas thought.

'Well done, men. Finally, we've got them,' Thomas congratulated his unit as he joined them in the white van. 'Let's get out of here.'

With the van's registration plates changed, they drove east along the quiet, tree-lined lane. In the fading light, visibility was further impeded by the sleet blotting the windscreen. They were in open country with not a building in sight. After three kilometres they swung into a clearing.

Time was ticking; the Russians would soon come looking for their comrades. And they would not be alone. The Swiss would also be out in force. From their current position the nearest Swiss-French border crossing was seventy kilometres north-northwest. An hour's drive, minimum. Possibly a few minutes too many.

At 17h45, three 4x4s pulled in next to them. Six passengers got out.

The mood amongst the men was upbeat. They had reason to be, having pulled off an extremely tricky abduction without any fatalities. The operation could easily have gone the other way.

'Hello, Richard. Couldn't have done it without you and your men,' Thomas said. 'We have been chasing them across Europe for days. Their warring days are over and we can now hopefully stop this impending war.'

'You're welcome,' agent Richard Meier bellowed in his American southern twang. 'Was quite a show you guys put up. German efficiency at its best! A pleasure to have watched. Anytime you need us, say the word.'

'Will do. All being well it won't be necessary. Right, we better get moving. The key is in the ignition.'

'Take those two SUVs,' Richard said, pointing at the Audi and Peugeot 4x4s. 'We'll get rid of the van and keep you posted if we hear anything.'

Four minutes later, Thomas, his men, and the three heavily sedated Russian captives headed for the border. Officially, the minor crossing was unmanned and, with luck, would remain so for the next two hours. Worst-case scenario, they would go off-road to avoid any Swiss border checks. Once inside France they could rely on the French who were currently assisting his men in hunting down the Russian insurgents in France.

The latest SITREP from Lt Schmidt confirmed the missing Russian-unit still at large. The second one was holed up in a hotel in the centre of Paris. And the third was just about to cross the English Channel.

This information did not make sense. If they were to hit the nuclear power plants, why sit around in Paris? Or was that a decoy? Will they move out in the middle of the night and join their cells at the power plants south of Paris? And where in the UK were they heading? Those two attacks they might stop. But the third one, most likely not. Unless the colonel tells all. And so he shall, Thomas vowed. For once he had the upper hand.

But the questions did not go away. Why attack the nuclear power plants and render most of Europe uninhabitable? Why kill millions if you wanted to rule over the survivors? People who would not rest till they had their revenge. It did not add up.

Chapter 63

Switzerland

The village of Schwarzenberg was quiet. The church carpark empty, except for the Interpol van and Michael's 4x4. The drone was folded away in the back, cramping the van. And Phillipe locked up in the police cells in Zurich, to be dealt with later.

Neither Michael, Svetlana, Jacques, or Bertrand spoke, studying the images on the monitors. Niall's hideout, surrounded by snow-covered mountains. The forty-acres estate was 4.5km south of their location.

In the dark sky, the 30cm diameter drone hovered. Far below, five hundred metres separated the old chalet from the regional road.

From an elevated position two hundred and fifty metres east of the cluster of buildings, Lt Hofmann and his men watched the chalet. This was the closest they could get, having circumvented the three-meter-high electrified fence. The skull-signs, annotated in German, French, and Italian, warned people to stay away.

Inside the perimeter fence was a fifteen-metre-wide cleared strip of land. Beyond, mature woodlands stretched towards a cluster of buildings. Forty metres of tarmac and snow-covered lawns separated the buildings from the woods. It was impossible to approach the chalet undetected.

'Not going to be easy. Reckon the woods are littered with motion sensors, silent alarms, security cameras, and enough booby-traps to blow us all to hell,' Lt Hofmann said cynically. 'Right, let's see if there's a way in. Hornet deployed.'

The tiny electronic hornet sped across the treetops, the lawns and tarmac, and circled the chalet. Halfway along the front it landed on a top-floor windowsill next to an open window. Inside, two men sat smoking, watching a bank of TV monitors. The security control room.

'Michael, that must be the Irish luck I've heard about,' Lt Hofmann said into his microphone. 'Shall we proceed?'

'Looks like it,' Michael laughed. 'Don't enter, we don't want to push our luck too much. They're sure to hear or see it. Zoom in on the monitors.'

The top row of monitors showed the interior of the house. The corridors were mostly empty. The common living areas and kitchen showed a few men and women looking relaxed, chatting. But no sign of Niall. The next row down showed the interior of the ancillary buildings. And the row of monitors at desktop level covered the exterior; the perimeter fence, the woodlands, the open grass area, the main house, the smaller annex, the barn, plant room, and store.

'Try the ground floor again. We might have missed a window,' Michael said.

The hornet lifted off the sill and dropped to ground level. Flying from one corner to the next its electronic eye scanned the semi-basement's obscured windows. All were shut. Turning the last corner; an open stairwell leading down to the semi-basement. An old solid door. No window.

'See if there's a gap under the door,' Michael said.

The hornet landed on the ground and crawled along the threshold. A crack. It sneaked inside. On the opposite side of the hallway, another door. The hornet slipped through. The camera lens swept the area. A corridor. Empty.

'Take her up.'

The hornet flew past a few closed doors; the dimmed bulkhead lights masked its flight. Halfway down the passage it past an opening in the left wall; a staircase. At the end of the passage it turned around.

'Good, all clear. Let's try the rooms,' Michael urged.

As the hornet returned towards the entrance, Svetlana perked up. 'Did you hear that?' she asked

Everyone remained quiet, their ears pricked. Bertrand turned up the hornet's microphone.

Not a sound.

Lt Hofmann landed the hornet on the nearest doorhandle. The whirring noise stopped.

A child's soft sobbing.

'It's Dasha!' Svetlana exclaimed, recognising the cries.

Quickly, the hornet landed on the next doorhandle. The weeping came from behind the door. The hornet dropped to the floor, crept underneath, flew up and scanned the room. On the bed Dasha cried into a pillow.

'I'm coming, Dasha. Don't worry,' Svetlana whispered.

Michael wrapped his arm around Svetlana's shoulder. 'We'll get her. I promise.'

A minute later, the hornet circled the adjoining room. On the bed Sinead lay with her eyes wide open, staring blankly at the ceiling. The hornet sat down on the pillow next to her head. She did not blink, her breathing faint, hollow.

'She's alive, but her mind's a mess,' Lt Hofmann stated. 'We may have to carry her out.'

'Yes, you're right. Okay, next room,' Michael urged, impatient to find Vera, convinced she was there as well.

Vera looked upset. Her usually bright blue eyes were bloodshot. The hornet flew up to her. She swiped at it but missed. Michael smiled, seeing his wife untouched. Sad, but full of fight.

'Bertrand, can we communicate with her?' Michael asked.

'No. There's no speaker. Maybe I can get her attention with the hornet. Hopefully, she doesn't wreck it. She's angry enough.'

'You're right about that. Okay, Lieutenant, approach her again and try to communicate.'

Out of reach, the hornet hovered near Vera's head. Her eyes opened wide, concentrating on the insect emitting a soft whirring sound. Lt Hofmann flew closer and landed the hornet on the bed and switched it off. Curious, Vera reached out and picked it up. An uncertain smile spread across her face. Suddenly, the wings whirred once and stopped.

'Can anyone hear me?' she whispered.

The wings whirred again.

'Is that a yes?'

Again, the wings whirred. Her smile spread wider. Her eyes lit up.

'Are you here to help?'

The hornet's response was as before.

She nodded. Keeping her voice down, she asked, 'Are you from Interpol?'

"Yes."

'Are Michael and Natalya alive?'

"Yes."

Unsure whether to believe her eyes, she repeated the question. The answer was the same. Staring into the hornet's camera, she whispered, 'Michael, is that you?'

When the reply came, she asked with tears in her eyes, 'Is Natalya safe?'

"Yes."

'Michael, we have to get out of there before we lose power,' Bertrand interrupted.

Without giving another signal, the hornet flew towards the door and crawled into the corridor. Five minutes later it was back with Lt Hofmann.

'How long before we can go back in?' Michael asked.

'Twenty-five minutes to recharge. Shall I attach a note to Vera?' Lt Hofmann asked.

'Too risky. We need another recce to find a way in.'

'Roger, Michael.'

The mood amongst the team had improved dramatically with the discovery of the hostages. But they remained cautious, not wanting to trip over the last hurdle.

For the second time, the hornet entered the building via the basement door. Quickly, it checked all the other rooms. There was nothing of interest except for the one in the southeast corner. It had no windows, and its proportions seemed wrong. Michael noticed the floor tiles sailed in underneath the end wall.

'Wonder if anything is behind that wall?' Michael asked.

'Service pipes…' Jacques suggested.

'In a basement? Why bother?' Michael said, doubtful. 'Okay, let's leave it for now. Lieutenant, next floor.'

By the end of the recce, they had counted seventeen men, including Niall. However, for fear of running out of time, they had not accessed all rooms in the chalet. Nor had they entered the annex to the back which looked like staff quarters.

In addition, there were six salacious young females – clearly there for entertainment – five kitchen staff, and the two men in the security control room.

Niall had been in the main lounge, seated next to a roaring fire with a drink in hand. Accompanied by Larry, three men, and two women, they were discussing the imminent war. Niall had barely contributed to the conversation except for stating that everything was under control. The war-noises being nothing more than sabre-rattling by the superpowers to manipulate markets.

Chapter 64

Switzerland

'Colonel, we've picked up some chatter. The Swiss have an APB out on you and your men. All border crossings in your vicinity are being manned. They suspect you'll try to slip into Germany or France from there,' Agent Richard Meier warned.

'Thank you, Richard. We should make it. I'll contact you once we're across,' Thomas said as his eyes scrutinised the valley below with only a few kilometres left to the border. At their current speed and with the roads scraped, they should be there in a minute or two.

Southeast of their position, five flashing blue lights sped through the dark. 'We've got company. Go, go, go!' he urged Cpl Decker behind the wheel. Turning to Cpl Baum in the back, he asked, 'How far to the intersection?'

'Three klicks! They're about the same distance away,' the corporal replied, monitoring progress on his phone's GPS.

The racing blue lights disappeared.

'Damn, woodlands!' Thomas said, having lost sight of the flashing lights. He had no way of telling where the Swiss were. 'Corporal, how far to the dirt road?'

'Two klicks, Sir.'

'That's the way then. They may already have men at the border crossing.'

Cpl Decker slammed the brakes and made a sharp righthand turn on to a snow-covered lane. He dipped the headlights, engaged low-range, and crept through the woods.

Two kilometres to the border...

But with each metre gained the condition of the lane deteriorated, shaking, and sliding them from side to side. Branches screeched against the bodywork. In the back, the Russians groaned their discomfort.

'We couldn't have picked a worse road,' Thomas said. 'At this rate, we may as well walk.' What worried him was not knowing where the Swiss were.

Persevering, and with the chassis scraping on boulders, they slowly gained altitude.

'That's it, we've crossed the border,' Cpl Baum announced. 'According to this, we're in France.'

'Trust that gadget is right. Though I doubt the Swiss care much about a line on a map,' Thomas cautioned. 'Once we're well clear, I'll permit myself to relax.'

Two hundred metres into French territory, the helicopter's searchlight hit them full on. The forest lit up as a mortar detonated in the lane, blowing a large crater in their path. Cpl Decker swerved around it.

'Jeezus, they mean business!' Cpl Baum shouted.

'Keep going, Corporal,' Thomas ordered. 'Number one, we're in France. And two, they would not want to hurt the Russians.'

'Halt! Evacuate your vehicles!' the German voice blared over the speaker above them.

'Decker, don't stop!'

'This is your last warning. We will fire if you continue!'

'Decker, keep going,' Thomas repeated.

The 4x4's bonnet flew up, raked by bullets. The engine cut out and burst into flames.

'Okay. Game's on. I'll deal with the colonel. Bring that one. And keep up,' Thomas said and jumped out. He opened the back door and grabbed Col Polyakov. Bullets slammed into the ground next to him. Pulling the colonel out of the 4x4, he slung him over his shoulder like a bag of potatoes. Turning, and weighed down by 110kg of deadweight, he ploughed through the snow in amongst the trees.

The men bailed out of the second 4x4. With only one Russian to deal with they returned fire. The chopper's spotlight disappeared; the sergeant's bullets obliterating their target. Using the trees as shelter the Germans hurried further north, staying parallel to the track.

The second helicopter's light combed the woods.

Bursts of gunfire erupted behind Thomas. Bullets whizzed past him. But something was different; the sound of the gunfire originated at ground level. They must have dropped a unit, most likely equipped with night-vision goggles. Their situation was becoming more precarious by the second. Burdened down by the Russian colonel, Thomas kept going. Progress was slow, too slow to outrun the Swiss.

A bullet zipped past his head and slammed into a tree, exploding its bark. Those were not warning shots. They meant to eliminate him, his men, and the Russians. He had miscalculated: his prisoners were no safeguard. If the Russians could not be rescued, then their leaders wanted them killed. Dead men don't talk. It was that simple.

To his right, a cry of pain.

Carrying the Russians, and with some men wounded, it would be impossible to escape the Swiss. Suddenly, he tumbled forward. The colonel slipped from his grasp and, with a loud groan, slammed into a tree. Hurting the colonel was the least of his concerns; as long as the man was alive was all that mattered.

Thomas's left foot was firmly lodged between two boulders. He gritted his teeth and pushed himself upright. The ankle was broken or badly sprained, with possibly some torn muscles or ligaments. Ignoring the pain, he freed his leg, turned on to his back and checked his ankle, lower leg, and knee for broken or protruding bones.

Nothing. He swivelled his ankle from side to side. It hurt like hell, but his foot was mobile. Lying flat in the snow and

410

sheltered by a boulder, he pulled out his pistol. Squinting into the dark he searched for a target.

Eighty metres from his position the 4x4's flames lit the woodlands. To his left, the chopper's searchlight combed the trees – some men must have split in that direction. A flash erupted thirty metres in front of him. The bullet ricocheted off the boulder next to his head. He returned fire, having no hope hitting his intended target.

Four metres to his right, three shadows broke cover and stumbled through the dark. 'Baum, Decker,' Thomas whispered. It must be them carrying the other Russian; they had been right behind him less than a minute ago.

'Yes Sir. Where are you?'

'To your left. Can I have a rifle? I'll cover you. You think you can manage the colonel as well?' Thomas asked as his men dropped down next to him.

'Yes Sir. But best you get out of here. I'll bring up the rear,' Cpl Decker said.

The corporal was right. He could not be captured or killed. Not now. As much as he hated to, he had to go. The chances of Cpl Decker surviving were slim.

'Thanks, Decker. Give us two-minutes and then you get out of here. That's an order,' Thomas said as he hoisted the injured colonel over his shoulder and struggled to his feet. His leg buckled slightly under the weight.

'You injured, Sir?' Cpl Decker asked.

'No. Only a sprained ankle.'

'Sure you can do this, Sir?'

'Affirmative, Corporal,' Thomas replied, struggling to keep his balance. 'See you at the road.' It was going to be hell getting there. No point complaining, Thomas thought, and set off.

Accompanied by Cpl Baum, they continued in the dark, following the gentle slope down to the road. Must be about three hundred metres more, Thomas thought. Each step was agony. He doubted if he would make it. Behind them, more rapid-gunfire…getting closer.

The two choppers circled out to the flanks and raked the perimeter with sporadic fire, herding Thomas and his men like cattle into a pen. Escaping the Swiss was impossible. Ignoring the flying bullets, he struggled forward. A broken branch raked his cheek, drawing blood. He ignored the pain. Sweating, his breathing heavy, his heart struggled to pump oxygen to his aching muscles. Under normal circumstances he would have sprinted the few hundred metres at full gallop. But with an injured leg, the colonel's weight, and his age, the odds were heavily stacked against him.

The explosion was deafening.

One moment the chopper hovered in mid-air, its machinegun spitting death. The next instant, it had erupted into a ball of fire. The second chopper dived right and sped back to the safety of the Swiss border. Two Dassault Rafale fighters roared over Thomas's head and immediately turned for a second sortie.

The loud noise of helicopters filled the air. Four H225M rapid deployment attack helicopters swooped in on the woodlands. Hovering overhead, each chopper fast-roped sixteen men to the ground. Fully equipped, the French special forces raced past Thomas towards the border, firing at the Swiss.

As the skirmish continued, the Swiss retreated over the border.

There would be hell to pay, Thomas thought, approaching the nearest chopper sitting in the open field next to the road. He could not recall the Swiss and French ever shooting at each other in modern times. Nor the Swiss shooting at Germans. Someone powerful in Switzerland must be in the pocket of this mysterious council.

Two soldiers approached, their rifles pointing at him.

'Evening, I'm Colonel Thomas Bauer, German Intelligence,' Thomas said in fluent French. 'Please take me to your CO.'

Thirty minutes later, four helicopters lifted off the ground and raced towards the French air force base, Aerienne 116, sixty-five kilometres north. Behind them, French firefighters extinguished the flames of the 4x4 and the crashed helicopter.

Any repercussions the incident might have, Thomas left to the diplomats to resolve. As soldiers, he and his men had done what they were trained to do.

Sgt Maj Koch required immediate surgery to remove a bullet lodged in his chest. Two more men had received superficial wounds. Thankfully, no one else was injured.

A walking boot secured Thomas's ankle. His knee was intact except for some bruising; the icepacks should help to reduce the swelling. The cut on his cheek had been cleaned and taped. Another *trophy* to add to his extensive list of memorabilia received in the line of duty. Still, he counted himself lucky. If it had been two centimetres higher, his view of the world would have been severely limited.

Maybe he was too old for these hero-antics. A fact his wife kept reminding him of. She had had enough of worrying. She was not prepared to lose him as well. The years did not erase the loss of their baby girl, stolen by the Soviet Union. Neither of them had ever come to terms with the fact that their child might still be walking the earth… Somewhere.

Thomas shook off the melancholic feeling which had taken him by surprise. He must remain focused. A long night lay ahead, one never more important.

His meeting with Lt Gen Beck at the Special Forces Unit's base in Calw, Baden-Wurttemberg, was set for 22h00. Giving him an hour and a half to prepare for the colonel's interrogation.

Chapter 65

Switzerland

Niall read the message on his phone: "Unable to reach asset."

"Explain?" he replied.

"Asset failed to supply SITREP at 19h00 as agreed. I regard him compromised."

"Should I be worried?" Niall responded.

"Yes."

"Thanks. Keep me posted."

They could be anywhere. For all I know they are watching me right now, Niall thought, somewhat distracted by the young woman's cleavage opposite him. He gave a vacant smile, slipped his phone in his pocket, and took another sip of whisky. With the lights dimmed, the orange glare of the roaring fire bounced off the walls in the lounge.

The woman with the voluptuous breasts got up, sat down next to him, and caressed his thigh. 'Anything I can do to make it go away?' she asked in her sultry voice.

'Maybe later. Now excuse me,' Niall said and got up. He was not interested in frivolity. Agitated, he could transform into a murderous psychopath within seconds if he lost control. He knew the warning signs. There was no need to subject this woman to his temper; she was a harmless hussy. He had killed many girls like her within a blink for having said the wrong thing at the wrong time, as she just did. Well, he did not need such unpleasantness right now.

Ignoring the young woman's feeble attempt at looking disappointed, he walked over to his righthand man. After all, the only reason the girl was there was for the money. A real whore.

On the coffee table next to Larry stood a bottle of Evian water. He was in deep conversation with Brian Murphy and two other minions. Good, Niall thought. He would not have appreciated his men indulging themselves at a time like this. 'Larry, can I have a word with you,' he said and walked towards the main stairs.

'What's up, boss?' Larry asked, struggling to come to terms with the new Niall, known to him as Brendan until a few hours ago.

'Noticed anything strange outside?'

'I checked with the lads upstairs about ten minutes ago. Cameras showed everything to be okay. Why?'

'Come.'

Niall did not wait for a reply. Taking the steps two at a time, he ran up to the security room with Larry on his heels.

'Right lads, let me have a look,' Niall grumbled and viewed the footage of the external CCTV feed.

All cameras worked perfectly, showing the perimeter fence intact. No triggered alarms in the woodlands. Nothing strange in the immediate area of the barn, stores, and staff quarters. No footprints in the snow. The interior footage confirmed the same.

'Are we expecting visitors, boss?' Larry asked.

'Maybe...' Niall replied. 'Okay, let's check on our guests. And you two, you see anything odd, call me.'

With Larry by his side, he raced down to the basement, issuing instructions. 'Post men outside. Make sure they've enough firepower. Michael, maybe watching us as we speak.'

'Right you are, boss.'

The light was on in Dasha's room. She was fast asleep, curled up on top of the duvet as if in her mother's womb. She had not touched her dinner, nor the chocolate bar. Niall moved the lock of hair out of her face. She looked like her mother. The memory of Svetlana, her head on the pillow next to him, returned.

Maybe Nicolai is right; maybe I am not over her…? Am I doing this to punish her, or because I'm still in love?

Without thinking, he tucked Dasha into bed and moulded the duvet around her slight frame.

Next to him, Larry stayed silent. It was the first time he had seen his boss showing any form of kindness to anyone. Not wanting to be caught gawking, he stepped into the corridor.

A minute later the light went out in the room. The door closed.

Sinead did not respond as they entered. Neither did she react to Niall's comment. 'Nothing new here. Stupid whore.' He switched the light off and locked the door behind him.

In the next room, they found the opposite.

'What do you want?' Vera scowled, her eyes burning with hatred. She got off the bed fully dressed. Only then did she recognise him.

'Brendan?' But as she spoke his name, she understood. 'You're with Niall! Do you know what you've done? Where is he? Doesn't he have the guts to face me? And you, how could you!' Vera shouted.

Poor Sinead. If she ever finds out she had been played…

Vera lashed out.

Niall did not budge and grabbed her arm. 'Still have your good old fighting spirit.' He laughed. 'Always liked that about you.'

'You don't know me,' Vera snarled, furious.

'Believe me, I know you intimately. Remember the diamond necklace I gave you in Brussels?' Niall said, and laughed at the expression on her face.

'Niall…'

416

'Yes, my sweet Vera. Amazing what they can achieve with the knife these days.'

Vera stepped back and sat down, crestfallen. 'You sick bastard.' She shook her head in disbelief. 'Please leave… Just go…'

'That's better,' Niall said. 'Thought I'd check on you, see if everything is up to your standard. And of course, to introduce Sinead's fiancé.'

Standing next to him, Larry could not help himself and laughed like a brainless hyena.

'Oh, you're hilarious,' Vera seethed as the shock of seeing the new Niall vanished. If she could kill him, she would. But she knew she was no match for him. She had to stay alive. Michael and Natalya were waiting.

Niall looked at her suspiciously. 'Why are you dressed? Are you going somewhere?'

'To where? Some club nearby? Moron. Just maybe I feel safer dressed in case one of your pigs waltzes in here to rape me. At least this way they'd have to fight to get me.'

'Yeah, of course. Suit yourself,' Niall replied, tempted to clout her. But he did not want to give her the pleasure, knowing she got to him.

He locked the door, puzzled by the look in her eyes. They were not that of someone mourning the loss of a loved one. Facing Larry, he said, 'I don't trust her. She's up to something. Put a guard outside her door.'

The paraglider's soft flutter high above Michael's head was nearly indiscernible. He craned his neck left and right. In the dark sky, five hundred metres below him, the square ram-air glider of Lt Hofmann drifted towards the chalet. Silently, like an eagle swooping down on its prey.

Above him, at an altitude of four thousand metres, eight more men sky dived out of the Swiss Police helicopter at one-minute intervals. The German soldiers operated as members of Interpol; their real identities kept secret from the Swiss Police.

The jump was the simple part. But steering their gliders undetected and touching down soundlessly on the chalet's snow-covered sloping roof would test their skills to the limit. Fortunately, the weather favoured them. No rain, snow, or strong winds. But the clouds accumulated again. The chance of more snow was very high. They had to act quickly.

North of the woods, Michael saw the dark shadow of the parked M-ATV SFV (all-terrain/special forces vehicle) of the Swiss Police. Two more SFVs covered the main road near the turnoff to the chalet, another one to the south, and one to the east. Added to the SFV's units were twenty-four men in support.

With the estate surrounded, Niall had nowhere to run. His only way out would be by air – possibly a helicopter parked inside the barn? But if he tried, and without a hostage, it would be a very short flight.

Hiding inside the treeline, Niall's four sentries watched the chalet. If anyone ventured near the building, they would see them. And if they looked up, they would also see the parachutes coming in fast.

The four Swiss snipers on the high ground had spotted the guards the moment they had stepped outside the chalet. They had eyes on three. A tree sheltered the fourth. It did not matter. They were not their priority, not yet. Covering the escape with the hostages was.

Two metres above the ground, and at fifteen metres distance, the silenced armed drones hovered. Controlled by the Swiss and Interpol joint-task-force, the dart-guns' scopes lined up the necks of the four Irish sentries. Seconds later the guards flopped to the ground.

The images relayed by the drones confirmed them all neutralised. The jumpers could proceed.

'Touching down,' Lt Hofmann said into his mic. His chute lost its rectangular shape and drifted down on to the roof. 'Steady does it. Reeling in. Snow well-compacted,' he reported. Fifty seconds later, with the chute stacked against one of the four large chimneys, he gave the all clear.

Michael did not hesitate. He circled in, stalled his flight, and dropped on to the roof. The teeth of the crampons attached to his size fourteen boots gripped the compacted snow. He tilted forward on to his hands and knees. The roof's substantial snow guards stopped the frozen snow from breaking off and plummeting him to the ground.

His canopy drifted down. Lt Hofmann grabbed the lines and reeled the lightweight fabric in. Michael nodded his thanks, released the harness, and scuttled over to the chimney.

Behind him, the next soldier touched down.

Having secured the abseil rope around the stone chimney stack, he waited for the last man to land. Steading himself against the chimney he unclipped the crampons, and with his silenced pistol in hand peered over the lip of the roof, searching for guards in the yard.

Hidden in the undergrowth, two of them were barely visible. From his position he could not see the other two. No one else had ventured outside. Neither was there any noise from inside the chalet.

Seven minutes later they were ready to move in.

Directly above the security control room, Derek and Walter lay stretched out, their abseil ropes tied around the central chimney stack. Controlling the miniature tactical camera on its flexible arm they lowered it towards the open window.

The ten-millimetre diameter plastic tube tied to the extended flexible arm sneaked through the window. The Germans fitted their masks, signalled to Michael and the lieutenant to get ready, and opened the gas canister. The odourless, clear sleeping gas seeped into the security room.

Five minutes later the all-clear came.

The rescue team slipped over the roof's edge and dropped to the ground two and a half floors below.

Derek and Walter dropped to the security room's open window and entered. Protected from the gas by their masks, they locked the door, deactivated the sensor alarms to the basement's external door, the woodland's motion sensors, and the electrified perimeter fence.

Three floors below, Niall walked up to the large panoramic window of the main lounge. The mood of his men and their female companions were muted. Something was up. Niall felt it in his bones as he stared out at the driveway leading down to the main security gate. It was quiet. He checked his pistol. Loaded. He had three extra clips in his jacket pocket.

Larry and two men manned the other windows.

Ken, a youngster in his early twenties, was the first to spot something amiss and hurried over to Niall. 'Think you better have a look at this, boss,' he said, his voice raised a notch.

'Where?'

'At the trees. On the ground. It—'

'Got it,' Niall cut him off. The body was barely visible, half-hidden by a pile of snow. 'Ken, take another lad and check what's up. He might have collapsed from a bloody heart attack for all we know.'

As Ken scurried off to investigate, Niall walked over to Larry. 'We have company. Any word from the guards upstairs?'

'Nope. I'll check.'

'Right. Meet me in my study. And if I'm not there, wait for me. I have something to attend to.'

'We have two bogeys outside. Front, heading east,' Derek's voice sounded in Michael, Lt Hofmann and the other seven men's earpieces. 'They're approaching one of the eliminated lookouts.'

'Roger,' Lt Hofmann replied.

On the monitor, Derek saw four of his men, clad in black, sprint after the two Irishmen. Next, he gave the all-clear to his commander. 'Alarms deactivated. We have one bogey in the corridor... Correction, two. I repeat, two bogeys in the corridor.'

'Someone's coming,' Walter whispered to Derek. On the screen in front of him, a man sprinted up the last flight of stairs to their floor.

Immediately, Walter and Derek propped up one of the unconscious guards in a swivel chair and shoved him in front of the bank of monitors, his back to the door. Derek took up a position next to the gun-safe, his silenced pistol aimed at the door.

'Open up!' Larry shouted and hammered on the door.

Walter unlocked it and stood aside. It swung open.

In the security room's dim light, Larry did not see or register the movement of Walter's arm, knocking him unconscious. With his hands secured behind his back and his mouth taped, he would next wake up surrounded by four white walls.

Walter and Derek locked the door and returned their attention to monitoring the fast-unfolding situation in and around the chalet.

The two Irishman crouched over the body in the shrubbery. They nodded their heads vigorously, turned towards the chalet and ran. After five paces they sagged to the ground, immobilised by the tranquilizer darts impaled in their necks. Immediately, four dark shadows hoisted the bodies off the ground and disappeared in amongst the trees. Moments later the four men re-joined their unit.

'We're set,' Lt Hofmann said into his mic. 'SITREP, basement, over.'

'One bogey. Second one on the first floor, over.'

'Roger,' Lt Hofmann replied as he signalled to Michael and the four men flanking the basement door. He counted down, 'Three, two, one, go!'

At that precise moment, two loud explosions erupted along the property's perimeter fence. The rumbling noise masked the dull thud at the basement's door with the shaped charges blowing the door off its hinges. Silenced gunfire aimed at the inner door splintered it off its hinges. Michael's

421

boot kicked the door open. Lt Hofmann's pistol coughed twice, making two perfect holes on the Irish guard's forehead.

Michael stepped over the broken door, gave five large strides, and unlocked Vera's room. Behind him, four men raced down the corridor.

In disbelief, Vera looked at Michael. She flung herself into his arms and burrowed her face in his chest, her arms wrapped around his neck.

'Thank God,' Michael whispered.

Their lips touched, erasing the hours of separation.

'How is Natalya?' Vera asked.

'She's fine, unhurt. Sorry, I allowed this to happen.'

'It's not your fault. Michael, please take me home.'

Carrying Sinead like an invalid, Lt Hofmann stopped Michael and Vera as they entered the corridor. 'The child's not here. He must have taken her.'

'Damn! Stop the Swiss. They can't move in till Dasha is safe.'

'Roger, Michael. Can you take Sinead? I'll find her.'

'Of course,' Michael said, and lifted Sinead into his arms.

'Is she drugged?' Vera asked, concerned.

'Not sure. Could be shock.'

'Will she be okay?'

'Yes, I'm sure she'll be fine,' Michael reassured her as he cleared the short flight of stairs to the yard. He paused and spoke into his mic, 'Control, is it clear to proceed?'

'Affirmative, you're clear to go,' Walter replied.

Sinead stirred in Michael's arms. Her eyes fluttered. 'Where am I? What's happening... Michael?' she asked, confused.

'Welcome back, Sinead. Do you think you can walk?' he whispered.

'Of course... Vera!' she exclaimed. As her feet touched the ground she reached out and embraced her friend.

'Sorry to have to break this up. We must go. Now,' Michael interrupted, grabbed Vera's hand, and led her to the safety of the woods.

In his earpiece, Walter's voice continued with the situation report. 'They're arming themselves. Three hostiles advancing towards the basement. Four at defensive positions. Lounge windows. Also, activity on the upper floors. No sign of Niall and the hostage. He was last seen in the company of one female entering the room in southeast corner, ground floor. No coverage inside. Hostiles approaching control. Out.'

The Germans, outgunned two to one, needed all the help they could get. Using the treeline as cover, Michael hurried towards the compound's main entrance where the Swiss Police were waiting. As soon as they would be safe, he would return to help apprehend Niall – Thomas wanted him alive for interrogation. Also, he had promised Svetlana he would rescue Dasha.

If Vera finds out, she'll most probably murder me before Niall's punks can.

Gunfire accompanied by loud shouting erupted behind him. The chalet's front door burst open. Five screaming women stormed outside. Ignoring them, Michael continued. By the time he reached the Swiss Police the gunfire had ceased.

'Michael, they have surrendered. You can send the police in,' Lt Hofmann reported.

'Have you got him and the child?'

'Negative on both counts. He has fled with her.'

'Damn! Any casualties?'

'Three dead. Four wounded. No friendly losses.'

'Good,' Michael said. 'I'll send the chopper to search the woods. He must be somewhere on the estate.'

'Roger. We're combing the chalet. I suggest the police clear the other buildings.'

Four ambulances followed the two M-ATV special forces vehicles and six patrol cars through the gate. The Interpol control van also arrived and pulled up next to Michael. Svetlana's anxious face stared at him. She jumped out, and ignoring Vera and Sinead, grabbed Michael's arm. 'Where is she? Is she okay?' she asked.

'He took her. They are not in the building. But the place is sealed off. He won't be going anywhere.'

'Please tell me it's not true,' Svetlana begged, shaking his arm.

Michael did not respond. Meaningless words would only insult her. No apology would suffice. He had failed her; the second time in two days. 'I'm going back. Are you coming?'

'Yes,' Svetlana said without hesitating. She turned to the two friends looking on in empathy. 'Sorry about that, Vera... And I'm really glad you are safe. But now you must excuse me.'

Chapter 66

Schwarzenberg
Switzerland

While the police handcuffed Niall's men, the paramedics tended to the wounded and removed the dead. Having smashed his way into the southeast corner room on the ground floor, Michael faced Niall's empty study.

'He was last seen entering this room,' Lt Hofmann said by his side. Noticing the open window, he added, 'Must've escaped through here when the fighting started.'

Michael stuck his head through the open window. The drop was about two and a half metres. 'Possibly. It's low enough.'

'We'll check the ground and snow for prints,' Lt Hofmann said.

'No, that's too convenient,' Svetlana commented, having joined them at the window. 'Not Niall. He most likely used the door and fled through the kitchen or some other room.'

'Or from inside this room,' Michael said, recalling the basement's southeast corner room, directly below them. His eyes combed the walls lined with bookshelves.

'What's on your mind?' Svetlana asked.

He did not reply. The built-in wooden shelves on either side of the open window ended in full-height cupboards. He opened the one in the righthand corner of the room. A large drinks cabinet. He looked down. The floor-skirtings were neatly spliced in the corners. 'Nothing here.'

Next, he opened the cupboard in the far-left corner. A toilet. Did the wall in the basement conceal pipework? Possibly, but why bother? He flushed the toilet. It worked. The basin on his right also worked. He felt the corners of the mirrored panel supporting the basin. Nothing. It was solid. Didn't budge. But the tiled floor had no neatly spliced skirtings, only butt joints. *Interesting.* Michael noticed the same detail to the covings of the low ceiling. He bent down and checked underneath the basin. Soon he found what he was looking for. He pulled the tiny lever. A soft click.

'I think we have found his way out,' Michael said, and pushed the panel. It swung open. 'Yes, so we have.'

He flicked the light switch on inside the cramped space. A narrow, steep staircase. At the bottom of the stairs was a doorhandle on his right. He tried it. The panel moved. He was inside the small room in the basement.

Did Niall hide in here and slipped out once the fighting had ceased? Michael wondered.

He banged his fist against the other walls of the stairwell. The hollow sound of the one wall confirmed his suspicion. A quick searched revealed a release button hidden underneath the last tread of the stairs.

The wall panel slid open. Steps led down into a tunnel. On his right was a light switch. He ignored it and using his flashlight entered the tunnel. The floor, walls, and ceiling were made of concrete. It was just over a meter wide, more than a door's height high, and ran off at right angles to the chalet's external wall.

'It leads dead south. Lieutenant, get some men to search the woods in that direction. Must be an exit located either inside the perimeter fence or beyond. The latter would seem the most likely. Svetlana, let's go.'

'Right behind you,' she said, her voice light, quietly optimistic. She was grateful for Michael persevering and finding the tunnel. And for not losing his temper with her after her unacceptable behaviour towards him. That Niall had taken Dasha was not his fault.

One hundred metres. Two hundred… Three hundred… Six hundred metres…

Finally, a set of stairs.

A door.

Michael pushed it open and stepped outside. He swept the flashlight from side to side. They were in a lightly wooded area; must be beyond the perimeter fence. He searched the snow for footprints.

'Halt. Don't move!' a heavily accented voice ordered on his right.

'It's us, Michael and Svetlana,' Michael replied, raising his hands, palms open. 'Who's this?'

A bright beam of light lit Michael's face and swung to Svetlana's. 'Walter. Sorry about that Michael, Major. Had to be sure.'

'It's okay. Glad you checked before shooting,' Michael said. 'Can't see any footprints. He could have covered them up… Any where you are?'

'Negative.'

'He couldn't have just vanished. Maybe he didn't use this tunnel,' Michael said thoughtfully.

'No, he did. But there may be another way out. I wasn't looking for one. Were you?' Svetlana asked.

'Me neither,' Michael replied as his eyes drifted up to the surrounding hills. High ground to the left, road somewhere to the right. 'Walter, any idea how far the road is from here?'

'Six, seven hundred metres.'

'Any buildings nearby?'

'A chalet and a barn next to the road.'

Three flashlights appeared from the direction of Niall's compound; Lt Hofmann and two of his men. 'Found anything?' he asked.

'Yes, and no. He didn't come this way. Must be a second exit. Can someone search the tunnel for a false door or panel?'

'Roger, Michael,' Lt Hofmann replied. Seconds later, two men entered the tunnel.

Michael turned west down the hill and headed towards the road. Calling the Swiss Police, he requested three patrol cars as backup, warning them to approach the isolated chalet by stealth. He also requested roadblocks in all directions.

In the chalet a light was on upstairs and one downstairs. The barn, twenty metres to the south, was dark. Beyond the chalet, the regional road was empty.

'Any idea how we're going to sneak up unnoticed? If Niall's in there, he'll spot us, for sure,' Michael said, staring at the chalet across the open field.

'Maybe there is a tunnel which—'

'Yes, continue. Over.' Lt Hofmann's voice cut Svetlana off. 'They've found a second tunnel.'

'Svetlana, how do you want to play this?' Michael asked. It was her call.

'We'll flush him out. Tell them to wait for me. I can still hold a gun in my right hand and my aim is not too bad,' Svetlana said, playing down the fact that she was a top marksman. She had won international gold and three silver medals in the 25m pistol and 50m rifle, three positions competitions. As lethal as she was with her hands, so was she with a rifle, even when handicapped.

Entering the sealed second tunnel, the lasting whiff of perfume confirmed someone had been there recently. Following the curved wall, Lt Hofmann, Michael, Svetlana, and Walter probed their way forward. The fear of a hidden trigger-alarm was foremost in their minds; a blast in the confined space would be lethal.

Back at the chalet, the rest of the German unit and twelve Swiss Police had it surrounded. Two snipers covered the front and rear.

'There must be an alarm or camera somewhere. Or did he think no one would find this tunnel?' Svetlana whispered behind Michael.

'Doubt that. On the other hand, he is extremely arrogant and might think himself too smart to get caught.'

Three hundred and eighty metres into the tunnel, Lt Hofmann pointed with his flashlight at a spot on the wall 60cm above the floor. Embedded in the concrete was an infrared laser-alarm unit. The only tell-tale sign, the narrow slot in the cover, allowing the beam to shoot across the corridor to the receiver unit directly opposite.

Lt Hofmann shone the light up and around. There was no sign of additional lasers.

Michael cleared the beam with ease. Reaching out to help Svetlana over, she hesitated. 'We're doing this all wrong. It won't work. If he's expecting us, we'll die in this tunnel. I have another idea.'

The car drove along the empty road through the sleepy valley, the driver hoping to avoid the threatening snowstorm. Suddenly, the engine stuttered and stalled. The driver turned the ignition. On the fourth attempt, it kicked in. The car moved ten metres and stopped again. The noise of the engine trying to start grated on the driver's nerves.

The driver, a young woman dressed in jeans and a thick anorak, got out. Irritated, she kicked the tire and looked at the chalet.

She covered her head against the cold and took out her phone. Having punched in the number, she jumped on to the car's bonnet, the phone to her ear. After a few seconds she stared at the phone in disgust. The battery was flat. Losing her temper, she threw the phone on the ground. It was not her day...

With a heavy sigh, she slipped off the bonnet, picked up the broken phone, and glanced helplessly at the chalet. Having decided, she shrugged her shoulders and approached the front door. It was late, but she had no choice.

The doorbell chimed.

She waited.

No one answered.

Confident she had seen some movement downstairs while picking up the smashed phone, she rang the bell again.

On the third attempt, footsteps.

The door opened.

A woman in her eighties yawned and pulled the belt of her nightgown tight. Half-asleep, she greeted in German and asked what she wanted.

I must have woken her. Svetlana's mood plummeted; the tunnel does not lead to the chalet.

'I'm sorry for disturbing you. My car broke down and my phone's battery is flat. I was wondering if I may use your phone if you have one?' Svetlana implored in broken German.

'Of course. Come in,' the old lady said and stood aside.

The hall was spotless and neatly furnished. To the right was a wooden staircase. Displayed on the antique sideboard were framed photographs of the old woman and an old man, a few young adults, and some children – presumably her husband, children, and grandchildren.

'Through here. Please, come.'

A male voice called from upstairs, 'Marta, who is there?'

'Just a young girl. Her car broke down. You can go back to sleep, dear.'

'I'm really sorry for disturbing you,' Svetlana apologised, regretting having misread the situation and having to go through with her plan. Every second spent in the chalet was a second wasted, giving Niall more time to get away. 'Have you been living here long?' she asked, making polite conversation, continuing her role as a stranded driver in the middle of the night.

'No, we moved here ten months ago. We were fortunate to have found this lovely place. Our children live near here. Now we can see the grandchildren all the time. We used to live in Zurich and the travel was too much for Ewald. Ah, here's the phone.'

430

Svetlana dialled Michael's number. As she explained the situation, he did not respond in case someone else in the chalet was listening. 'My friend will be here in fifteen minutes and tow me in. I'll go and wait in the car,' Svetlana said, putting the phone down.

'Nonsense, it's too cold. I'll make you a cup of hot chocolate. I can do with one myself. The doctor said I must be careful with my blood sugar. He's wrong. At my age, I might as well enjoy myself,' Marta said and smiled conspiringly.

'No, that really won't be necessary. Thank you.'

'My dear, it's no problem and it will do you the world of good. If you don't mind me asking, what happened to your hand?'

I will not leave here soon. You better hurry, Michael, Svetlana fretted, smiling feebly as she accepted the offer of a hot drink. 'Was a clumsy accident. Cleaning the blender, I forgot to unplug it first. They said the stitches should hold it together.'

'That's awful! Well, we all make silly mistakes. I cannot even count the many I've made.'

'Oh yes, I just remembered. The barn door is open. I meant to tell you.'

'Strange… I'm sure it was shut when I checked earlier,' Marta said, surprised. 'We don't use the barn. Don't even have a key for it; the landlord's car is in there. I better have a look. Do you mind coming with me?'

'Not at all,' Svetlana replied. The news of the landlord's car piqued her interest.

Marta covered her head with a woollen hat, threw on a heavy coat, exchanged her slippers for some sturdy snow boots, and grabbed a flashlight. In the hallway, she unlocked a tall cupboard and pulled out a 12-gauge shotgun. 'In case there's a thief, best to take her along,' she sniggered. The weapon seemed wrong in the old lady's frail hands. If she squeezed the trigger, she would most likely fly further than the pellets.

431

The flashlight's beam lit up the inside of the barn. 'My goodness, it's empty! Someone must have stolen the car. I better phone the police,' Marta said, alarmed. She opened the barn door wider, entered, and flicked the lights on. 'It was here when I peeped through the window before I went to bed.'

'Do you know what make of car it is?' Svetlana asked, taking in every detail of the barn.

On the far side were two stores, a large petrol drum, a pump, a long workbench, and some tools hanging on the wall. Half of the exposed roof-tie-beams had floorboards nailed to it, creating a usable storage area. A steep, narrow staircase gave access to the deck.

As Svetlana walked over to the stores, Marta said, 'I know the make and registration number. Should be easy to find. But maybe best you don't walk around too much in case the police want to look for prints.'

'Do you mind if I call you Marta?' Svetlana asked, her eyes holding the old lady's.

'Of course you may. And your name?'

'Svetlana.'

'You're Russian… Ukrainian? I thought you might be Czech or Slovakian. Why are you here?' Marta asked suspiciously, aware of the threat Russia posed.

'I am Russian. And I'm trying to find someone dear to me. Do you mind pointing the shotgun the other way, please?'

Marta lowered the shotgun. 'Sorry, I am a bit nervous. So, who are you? Remember, I'm old and have met many liars over the years.'

'I am Major Svetlana Nikolaeva of the Russian FSB, Moscow. I am here with Interpol, the Swiss Police, and the military. We are trying to find my child who has been kidnapped. And we suspect your landlord and the kidnapper are one and the same. His tracks lead right to this property.'

Marta turned pale.

'And there's nothing wrong with my car. In fact, four armed men are hiding inside as we thought the kidnapper might be in the chalet,' Svetlana added. Smiling disarmingly at Marta, she spoke into her anorak's lapel. 'Lieutenant, you can come in.'

'My goodness,' the old lady sighed.

'Marta, please don't be alarmed when they come in. They are heavily armed. And more men will follow. I apologise for the deception. But now, I have to look in those stores.'

On cue, Lt Hofmann and three of his men entered the barn, their assault rifles sweeping the room.

'*Guten Abend*,' Lt Hofmann greeted in German from under the black balaclava. 'Forgive the intrusion. We have to search the barn, if you don't mind. Also, can you please give us the description and details of the car?'

'Yes, of course,' Marta replied and backed up against the wall. 'I'll have to get the details in the house. Come with me.'

'Thank you, Ma'am. Walter will go with you,' Lt Hofmann said.

Silhouetted in the open door by the flashing blue lights, Michael introduced himself and the Swiss superintendent by his side. Reassured by the official's presence, Marta relaxed visibly.

'Any sign he was here?' Michael asked, having joined Svetlana busy inspecting the lock of the largest store.

'Nothing yet. But I'm sure the tunnel's entrance is behind this door. The lock seems clean. Best we vacate the barn. I don't trust Niall. He would not have fled without leaving us one of his "parting gifts".'

'Agreed. I'll see to that. Lieutenant, please secure the area and check the inside of the store and barn for explosives. The major and I will try to find the missing car.'

The first sign that they were on the right track was the discovery of the detonator's release switch fixed to the top of a wall-shelving-unit. It took the Germans five minutes to disarm the booby trap and another five to remove the panel.

'Michael, we have found the tunnel's exit,' Lt Hofmann said into his mic.

'Good. Meet me at the control van.'

It was all fine, but Niall had at least an hour's head start. By now he could be anywhere, Michael thought. Ignoring this concern, he supplied the superintendent with details and photographs of Niall, Dasha, and the young woman, required for a nationwide APB on them.

Despite Vera and Sinead's rescue, Michael felt like he was back to square one with Niall having escaped. As much as he wanted to get back to Vera and Natalya, he could not leave Svetlana to find Dasha on her own.

'Svetlana, any idea where he could have gone?' he asked.

'To be honest, I don't. But it won't surprise me if he has returned to his castle. He may not be aware we know where it is unless Phillipe had told him. Anyway, it's a good place to start; we may find some useful clues. I'll head over there rather than sit around here hoping someone may spot him.'

'You're right. We'll do so.'

'No need, Michael. I'll do this on my own. Take Vera to Bern. She must be dying to see Natalya... And I know you are too,' Svetlana said. 'Please, you have done more than enough. I'll manage if Lt Hofmann and his men can back me up. I mean it.'

'True, I can't wait to see Natalya. But sorry, can't do. Boss's orders. Vera told me to help you until Dasha's home. Not that I would have it any other way myself. Vera and Sinead are already on their way to Bern,' Michael replied. He refrained from sharing the one condition Vera had insisted on; he had to keep out of trouble and not try to be the hero.

Chapter 67

Germany

Inside the interrogation room at the KSK (Kommando Spezialkräfte), Calw, Baden-Wurttemberg, the atmosphere was tense. Thomas stood opposite Colonel Boris Polyakov, separated by a table bolted to the floor. The clock on the wall indicated 02h30. Real time, 22h15. A slight deception for the benefit of the Russian.

Thomas's voice dripped venom as he spoke. 'Welcome to Germany. Hope you have recovered after your *extensive* travels. Must have been quite something, all business morning, noon, and night. Impressive for someone your age,' he said. 'Well, you can relax. Your job is done. But before you retire to your *dacha* outside Moscow, we, on behalf of our government and other interested parties, need to ask you a few questions. If you cooperate, you'll be free to return to your lovely wife, Ludmilla. And of course, also to your pigs and geese in the woods. You don't mind; shouldn't take long.'

Thomas's accent-free Russian took Boris by surprise, the biting sarcasm not lost on him. He turned his head and spat on the floor.

'I'll tell you nothing,' Boris said, and stared with disdain at the tall German boasting a fresh wound below his eye and one leg in a walking boot. He feared nothing, no one. Least

435

of all this overgrown German who thought he knew what real Russians, like him, were about.

'Just because you speak our language doesn't mean you know us. *Nyet,* you don't. You are nothing like us. Whoring pig! So, do us both a favour, take your queer boyfriend and jump off a fucking cliff. Stop wasting my time. As an officer in the Russian armed forces, I have my rights. I don't have to tell you anything. But I'll gladly tell you one thing; you're too late,' Boris said stubbornly, having noticed what time it was.

Yes, you fool. There's nothing you can do to stop the war. Many things have already happened which will change the world forever, Boris thought. But despite his defiant words, he did not feel well. He was sleepy, lethargic. Not interested in anything the German had to say. Neither in the old man seated beside the TV screen.

He tried to scratch his aching head. His hands jerked back, handcuffed to the table. He stared down at his feet, secured by an iron ring to the tiled floor. On the metal table in front of him was a notepad, pen, microphone, and a glass of water. The room was sterile, tiled from the floor to the ceiling. No windows. The room was lit by a double fluorescent bulkhead light, protected by a wire-cage. One door. A tap with a hosepipe in the corner and a drain under it. A chain with arm clasps dangled off the one side wall.

Two armed guards, one to his left and one to his right, their faces concealed, watched him. Most likely the same bastards who jumped us on the motorway, Boris thought.

'Let me introduce myself and my superior. I am Col Bauer, German Intelligence. And this gentleman who you had so respectfully referred to is my superior and head of NATO Intelligence. Rest assured, we do acknowledge your rights and will respect them the same way you had respected the lives of the innocent people at the gas filtration plants in Turkey and Norway. Not forgetting your fellow countrymen killed at the Beregovaya gas processing plant. Not sure your countrymen will be pleased when they find out. There goes your retirement plan…' Thomas paused.

Boris did not blink and stared challengingly at Thomas. 'Don't know what you're talking about,' he said, undaunted, not interested whether they were bluffing or not.

'Or as new *friends*, we can keep it between ourselves. As I've said, you tell us what we want to know and you'll be free to go. So, a few simple questions. Who gave you your instructions? Who was at the meeting you attended in the mountains? And what is this group's ultimate objective? In short, everything you know about this grandiose scheme to blow us all to hell. But first, before you entertain us with your colourful confession, tell us what your men are doing in Paris and London. And your third unit, where are they?'

This time Boris's Adam's apple bounced up and down. The knowledge Thomas shared was like a painful kick in the groin.

'We can offer you a deal. You cooperate fully and you will not be named as a source. I'm confident Lt Igor Yanukovych or Cpl Alexei Volkov, being lesser men than your good self, will confess by the time we've finished with them. That should put you in the clear, don't you think? No repercussions in Russia. No looking over your shoulder. You'll be able to live out the rest of your days in peace,' Thomas said, throwing the proverbial carrot at the colonel. Although if accepted, it would be a deal neither he nor the general would honour. The man in front of them will pay for his sins.

Boris sat back in the metal chair. He laughed and clapped his hands. 'Very good. You should have joined the circus, Colonel. You're a natural clown. Well, my friend, you can shove your carrot where the sun doesn't shine. I'll never betray my men. And if I'm right, neither would you. So, you understand my position. You'll have to do better than that.'

'Suit yourself. But before we continue, we have someone who wants to have a word with you. You mind?'

'Go ahead. You're in charge.'

Boris's tone revealed his disregard for Thomas. And that was exactly what Thomas wanted; put him at ease, make him think he was in control.

Thomas flicked on the TV. 'Hello, Ivan. You see and hear us? Then let me introduce you to the elusive Colonel Boris Polyakov.'

The face on the screen was stern. 'Thank you, Thomas. Good morning, General. Picture's perfect. My connection any good?' Ivan's deep voice rumbled through the interrogation room.

'As if you were here. You may continue.'

'Col Polyakov, I am Maj Gen Lukyanov, Deputy Director, FSB.'

In disbelief Boris's mouth dropped open.

'You seem surprised to see me. Thought I was dead. Well, as you can see, they missed,' Ivan scoffed. 'I gather you have been explained what is required of you. I suggest you comply with my colleagues' request and you do it right away. If not, I'll tell them to proceed. Not my colleagues in the civilised West, but here in Moscow.'

'I don't talk to traitors. I spit on your mother's grave!'

'Have it your way,' Ivan warned.

The camera panned out and moved to an adjacent room.

It was an empty shed or store of some sort with no ceiling. The exposed steel girders supported a flimsy metal roof, the corrugated sheets visible – no insulation. Some of the clerestory windows stood open, allowing the freezing air in. The room was well lit.

In the centre, a middle-aged woman dangled by her arms on a meat hook, her hands tied together, her bare feet thirty centimetres off the ground, her hair and dress soaked.

As the camera moved, it zoomed in on her swollen and bleeding pulverised kneecaps. Next, the lens focused in on her blood-smeared, bruised and bloated face with her eyes nearly shut.

A loud groan escaped Boris's lips.

'I take it you know her,' Ivan said. 'To be sure, we have the right person, mind telling us who she is?'

'Let her go, she has nothing to do with this!' Boris shouted and continued with a succession of expletives as only a man in the military could string together. Spittle flew in all directions with every word he uttered. He tried to break the cuffs, tried to climb over the table. But there was nothing he could do to rescue his beloved wife. She was at the mercy of Maj Gen Lukyanov. Boris knew the cruelty the FSB was capable of. What they have done so far to his wife was only an interlude of what was to come. Hours of more torture, keeping her on the brink of death before they would kill her. Unless, of course, he confessed; do as they ask.

'Ludmilla, can you hear me? It's Boris.'

His wife turned to the sound, unable to see where it came from. 'Boris?' she muttered. 'Please help me... Why am I here?'

'I'm sorry... Don't worry, I'll do as they ask.'

'You must—' she started. The audio link cut.

'Enough,' Thomas said. 'Good. Continue.'

Boris nodded his head. He had no fight left in him. Helplessly, he looked at the monitor with his wife suspended in mid-air and the two masked men threatening her with rubber truncheons. One pulled her head back by the hair. Her mouth opened. He could not hear the scream. 'Stop!' he shouted and grabbed the pen and paper on the table.

'Good. First, you tell us the objectives of your units in Europe. We'll move on from there. Step at a time. You can write the details down once you've finished your confession.'

Boris whispered, 'Yes. Now please lower her to the floor.' He could imagine her arms pulled out of their sockets by now, as she was too heavy.

'Ivan, give her something to sit on. I think he got the message. See how simple it is? You cooperate, we cooperate.'

As Ludmilla settled on the stool with tears streaming down her cheeks, Boris spoke. 'The targets in Europe are the Euronext Paris, London Stock Exchange Tower, and the Luxembourg Stock Exchange. To be destroyed one hour after trading begins today.'

The camera recorded every word.

'You sure about that?' Thomas asked. These objectives made sense – someone stood to make a fortune – however, it did not tally with the nuclear plant scenario. 'We believe you have far more destructive targets in mind. Something to do with nuclear power plants.'

'Misinformation. Whoever told you does not know our real objectives. We're not crazy. What sense is there in rendering Europe uninhabitable?'

'Point taken,' Thomas nodded. It was as he had thought. No one could be that mad. But if they failed in their objective, they might do desperate things. Therefore, he did not discard the nuclear plants as targets. 'Humour me. What are the names of these "decoys". No harm in sharing them, don't you agree?'

Boris rambled off the plants' names: Sizewell B and C, England; Nogent and Saint-Laurent, France; Emsland plant in Lower Saxony, Germany.

'And how were they supposed to have been sabotaged?'

'As you've said, they were decoys. We never investigated how,' Boris said and looked at his wife. Her head rolled from side to side. He turned away and stared back at the men glaring at him. They don't believe me. So, what – I won't survive either way. And Ludmilla is beyond help, he fretted.

'Do you have sleeper cells in the cities you are to hit? We need specifics of the planned attacks,' Thomas asked. *We'll soon know if he is toying with us, taking us for fools.*

For twenty minutes, Thomas kept up the questions. Some were answered promptly, other replies were vague.

The room fell silent.

The clock on the wall showed the time to be 03h30.

Lt Gen Beck, not having made a sound till now, got up, cleared his throat, and motioned for Thomas to follow him.

In the adjoining room, he pulled up a chair and sat down. 'My view is, he is playing us. He'll say anything to ease his wife's suffering. But he won't crack because of her, whether or not she dies. I suggest we bring in his men in Paris and London and get to work on them. It's eleven. We have time.'

'I agree,' Thomas concurred. 'His explanation of the attacks was vague and showed a dire lack of intel. I'll instruct the men to move in. Best we step up security at all nuclear plants. They will have a Plan B and C in place. Therefore, whatever he believes to happen is no longer relevant. They would move on to the next set of targets, using other assets. He has played his part and will be sacrificed. All he can offer us now is a confession, including the names of his superiors.'

Fifteen minutes later, Thomas and Lt Gen Beck confronted the colonel again; their faces stern. The earlier *friendly* overtures were gone.

'Your confession. Write it down. Names, dates, places. Every detail. From those who issued instructions to those who carried out the attacks in Turkey, Norway, and Russia. And how these were carried out. The sooner you finish, and we are satisfied with your statement, the sooner we'll release your wife and treat her injuries. If you don't, she will continue to suffer,' Thomas said, in no mood for games.

'And we need the names of those who attended the meeting at Camp Wägitalersee. Especially the chairman's name. The man who served you your lavish lunch.'

Thomas's words stunned the colonel. In disbelief he gawked at the German.

'We watched you arrive and leave in your cavalcade of 4x4s, as well as the fourteen helicopters transporting your co-conspirators. Currently, they are all being arrested. Do I need to continue? I don't think so. Now, start. Remember. we know far more than you think.'

Picking up the pen, Boris said, 'The chairman is known as "The Chairman". And I am familiar with only two members. Some of those present represented members who had regarded the meeting too risky. They are Chinese, Americans, Russian, and Europeans. That's all I know.'

'Understood. The two names then.'

'Nicolai Baranovsky and Colonel General Vladimir Coshenko. Nicolai represented the Americans and the general, the Russians. You'll have to speak to them to find out who's in charge. I am just a donkey doing the dirty work. My knowledge is limited.'

'Yes. Now your statement. You have half an hour,' Thomas said. He did not expect the Russian colonel would be able to reveal much more. However, the news of the Americans' involvement took him by surprise. Who were they?

'Any progress tracking down the delegates?' Lt Gen Beck asked, drinking a cup of coffee.

Not having slept enough, Thomas appreciated the caffeine boost of his own drink. There would be no rest for him until this was over.

'They rented the cars at Geneva and Zurich airports. Our search has led nowhere. And ditto with the helicopters. The Russian, Nicolai, has disappeared. As did his business partner, Niall McGuire, an Irish criminal who had also attended this secret meeting. This man was last seen near Lucerne. He is holding a Russian FSB officer's child hostage. The mother, Major Svetlana Nikolaeva, is a lethal asset and is currently hunting him down. According to Ivan, it's only a matter of time before she'll resolve the situation.'

Lt Gen Beck raised an eyebrow and said, 'Assume she brings him in, would he know more than the colonel?'

'Doubt that. He has been out of circulation for a while; was in prison. The Russian major's handiwork.'

'Interesting. We'll deal with him once he is in cuffs. Our best bet is the colonel. As soon as we have his confession, we'll present it to the Russian president and NATO leaders. Trust none of them are part of this coup. What's the situation regarding the Russian cells in Paris and London?'

'Not good news. They've slipped the net.'

Lt Gen Beck's face sagged. It was not what he had wanted to hear. 'How?'

'Via basement passageways.'

'Clearly well planned.'

'True. But with sniffer dogs following the scent from the hotels and the CCTV footage of the areas, I'm confident we'll find them. Our teams are watching the stock exchanges and will move in as soon as the Russians show up.'

'Then there's not much more we can do for now. Let's hope our men find them,' Lt Gen Beck said.

Facing the TV monitor and camera, Thomas translated Boris's statement for the benefit of his superior. 'Questions, anyone?' he asked as he put the document on the table.

'Send us a copy and we'll get back to you. I'll get our friend to arrange a meeting with the president. So, please keep that piece of filth alive for the call. He can explain to his boss what he did and why. Should be interesting to watch. And Boris, as a sign of goodwill, we'll take good care of your wife.' Ivan walked over to Ludmilla and pulled out a big knife.

'Don't you dare touch her!' Boris shouted, already seeing the blade slide across her throat.

Ivan ignored him and rammed the knife into the stool Ludmilla sat on. He picked the cloth up off the floor, next to a bowl of water. Patting her face, he wiped the streaks of blood clean. He picked up the knife and started on her face. His body blocked the camera.

Boris shouted as Ivan threw lumps of skin on to the floor. He was beside himself, watching his wife mutilated in front of him.

Finally, Ivan picked up the cloth once more and wiped her face again. He stood aside and inspected his handiwork. Her face was untouched. There were no bruises. The swollen eyes had disappeared, as did the smashed knees. Satisfied, Ivan discarded the makeup putty into a bin and continued to rinse her face with clean water.

'Amazing this stage makeup, don't you think so, Boris? Say hello to Ludmilla. She may not respond too well as the drug has not quite worn off.'

Ivan unclipped the transparent nylon cord tied to her hands' bindings and the leather belt strapped around her waist, having carried her while suspended in mid-air.

Furious, Boris banged his fists on the table.

'To be frank, no apologies for the deception. You deserve far worse. Did you take us for animals, beating up a helpless woman?' Thomas said, affronted by the mere suggestion. 'Have some water. You'll need your strength.'

Chapter 68

Switzerland

Above the trees, Burg Reinhardt's snow-covered roof and turrets projected into the night sky. Ominous, silent. One kilometre west of the castle's drawbridge, the five vehicles pulled up and cut their engines.

At 01h00, the quadcopter lifted off the ground and skimmed the trees. The images relayed by its camera were not encouraging. The castle looked deserted.

Svetlana heaved her shoulders, disappointed. It seemed her hunch was wrong. Then again, if she were Niall, would she have advertised her presence? No. The castle was the perfect sanctuary. He could hide inside its walls for months. No one would know.

The drone cleared the bailey.

Darkness.

On the upper terrace the helicopter sat idle.

Not a car in sight.

The view shifted higher up the south face of the castle.

Nothing.

The drone continued up and over the roof and dropped into a service yard between the cliff face and the keep.

Finally, a light on the ground floor!

Was someone in… The caretaker, perhaps?

The drone flew around the back. Another light, also on the ground floor. Gaining altitude, the camera recorded a slither of light shining through a gap in the curtains on the top floor.

As the atmosphere in the control-van lifted, Michael broke the silence. 'Someone's home. And whoever it is, might be able to tell us where to find Niall.' His words echoed what everyone thought. 'Right, let's find a way in.'

'If we can get to the top of that cliff, we can abseil into the courtyard. Michael, can you organise a chopper?' Lt Hofmann asked, pointing at the monitor.

'I'm sure the Swiss will oblige. Just a sec. Have to take this call,' Michael said, interrupted by the ring of his phone. The Swiss Superintendent.

Pocketing his phone, Michael smiled. 'They have traced Niall's car in Lucerne, then Zurich. The last image of it was just over an hour ago, fifteen kilometres from here, travelling in this direction. He's home. And Lieutenant, your ride will be here in half an hour. Best you rendezvous a few klicks down the road.'

Svetlana sighed. She had been right. It won't be long till she would hold Dasha again. But along with her optimism, was the nagging feeling that Niall could escape as soon as they move in. Like at the chalet. 'How do we stop him from slipping away this time?'

'We'll get the Swiss to seal off the area, block all roads in and out. He's not going anywhere,' Michael said, adamant.

'Lieutenant, while you sneak in through the back, I'll ring the front doorbell. It's me he wants. Of course, he might shoot me on sight, though I doubt that's his plan. It won't be that simple... No, not with him. But wearing body-armour may be a good idea,' Svetlana said.

Staying within the cars' tracks, Svetlana followed the lane to the castle. By the time she reached the moat, it was 02h30. As expected, the drawbridge was up.

Fitted on a pedestal to the left was the intercom. For a brief second she hesitated, not sure this would work. But with no alternative, she reached out for the button.

The sudden sharp squeal of metal made her pause. She pulled her hand back. With a loud creak, the drawbridge slowly dropped across the deep, ice-covered moat.

Headlights appeared in the arched entranceway.

She stepped in behind a tree.

It was an Opel sedan. The same car Niall had used to flee from Schwarzenberg. She did not recognise the driver. As soon as the car had passed she sprinted across the drawbridge. With her eyes on the archway and the squeaking gate, she lifted her knees and increased her speed. The gate was almost closed. Three more metres… The next instant she squeezed through the narrow gap.

She was in, but whoever operated the bridge and gate must have seen her. Then so be it, she thought.

In the deep shadow of the archway, she crept towards the bailey. Reaching the far corner she stopped and observed the dark windows, doors, and walls of the courtyard. To her left, a tower, at its base an entrance leading up to the battlements. On her right, the guardroom.

She peered through the guardroom's window. No one. The chair was empty. A blue desk lamp cast an eerie light over the open magazine, the smouldering ashtray with a cigarette tilted on its rim, and a mug. The monitor showing the gate and drawbridge confirmed these to be firmly shut. Another monitor showed images of the bailey and battlements.

About to open the guardroom's door, a man entered, concentrating on fixing his belt. No wonder he did not see me; he must have been in the bathroom. If she proceeded, he would spot her immediately.

She took aim and squeezed the trigger.

In the night's silence, the soft cough of the pistol and tinkle of glass sounded like a cannon smashing through a shopfront window. The guard toppled forward. She opened the door and rushed inside.

'Michael, man down. Gatehouse. Needs medical attention. Lieutenant, you can enter via the main gate if you're not in position yet,' Svetlana said into her mic.

'We'll be with you in a minute. Can you hold your position?' Michael asked.

'Affirmative.'

With one eye on the monitors and the other on the wounded guard, Svetlana operated the drawbridge. The screeching noise of the swinging gate was hardly noticeable inside the guardroom.

Thirteen men darted across the bridge. Michael's head appeared in the doorway, followed by the lieutenant and three men. The rest of the unit secured the bailey.

'How did you get in?' Michael asked.

'Luck. I'll tell you when we're safely home,' Svetlana replied. 'Don't want to jinx us. Okay, I'm going in.'

Svetlana, Lt Hofmann, and six men raced through the snow along the bailey's outer wall, following its sweep towards the ramp and six-storey keep – the main part of the castle. The others remained in the forecourt.

Using the shadows as cover, Svetlana sprinted up the ramp in search of a window or door. The keep's south wall connected to the main battlement forced her to slip past the front door and helicopter. At the next corner she turned right.

A covered walkway blocked her path with a door to the keep. At the other end, a series of steps led on to the north outer wall. Centred was a double gate. Beyond it lay the service yard where a light was on during the recce.

In less than three minutes, Lt. Hofmann had picked the two locks of the keep's door. Searching for a sensor, he found one fitted in the top corner. Temporarily *blinding* it with a strong neodymium magnet, he opened the door. Without activating the alarm, and with everyone inside, he shut the door.

'Michael, we're in. Proceeding to the upper floors,' Svetlana whispered into her microphone.

'Remember, he's not expecting anyone and may shoot before asking questions,' Michael warned.

Guided by the flashlight's beam, Svetlana hurried along the narrow service corridor. The north-facing external wall was on her left. She entered through another door into a lobby. Four doors.

She ignored the door on her left and opened the first one on her right. The great hall. It was empty. She closed the door. Behind the fourth door were the ancillary rooms and kitchen; the source of the light.

Voices.

They stopped and listened. Two males and a female. Joking, flirting. Not Niall.

Having committed to memory the blueprints of the castle, Svetlana entered through the second door on her right into a spacious foyer. She hurried towards the lift and staircase connecting the upper floors.

On the fourth floor they crossed the dark hallway.

She opened the security room's door a fraction. It was empty... Most of the monitors were switched off except those covering the exterior; the only source of light in the room.

Where were the guards? Why was no one monitoring the live feed? If anyone had been watching they could not have missed them. They had gained access too easily. She pulled the door shut and whispered to Lt Hofmann, 'We've walked into a trap.'

He said nothing, just nodded.

Filled with apprehension, she proceeded to the next floor, wondering what Niall was up to. A soft glow of light spilled from under the door into the corridor. Her heart raced. Was Dasha in there?

The Germans spread out. She bent down and peeped through the keyhole. It was too dark to see much. Without a sound she opened the door.

A young woman lay on the couch. Stuffed dolls cluttered the floor beside her. The unmade double bed was empty. Svetlana crossed the room, covered the woman's mouth with her bandaged hand and pushed the pistol against her temple, shaking her gently.

Terrified eyes stared up at her.

Svetlana whispered, and in English said, 'Sssh... I will not shoot you unless you give me a reason to. Where is my daughter?'

The woman mumbled under Svetlana's hand and tried to turn her head towards the bed.

Svetlana removed her hand.

'She's in her bed, sleeping,' the woman said with a strong Russian accent.

'No, she's not,' Svetlana replied in her mother tongue.

Surprised, the woman smiled unsurely.

'Where is she?'

'I don't know. He must have taken her while I was asleep.'

'How long have you been sleeping?'

'Not long... Twenty...thirty minutes, I guess?'

'Where's his bedroom?'

'On the next floor. But you won't be able to enter. The door is always locked.'

'We'll find a way in. Why do you work for him?'

'I was trafficked and can't go anywhere. They watch me all the time.'

'What's your name? Where are you from?'

'Aleksandra... From Odessa. Can you please help me?'

'*Da.* Get dressed and wait here. First, I'll get my daughter and then I'll come back for you. And not a sound.'

'*Spasibo.* Be careful, he must know you are here. That's why he took Dasha. He's very dangerous.'

'Yes, he is. And so are we. Don't worry.'

The door to Niall's quarters was unlocked. She pushed it open and in the semi-dark noticed a movement behind a couch.

'*Irina*, welcome. I was expecting you. Although, a bit sooner than what I thought. Just show how much you missed me,' Niall mocked. 'You and one of your friends may enter. The rest have five minutes to get the fuck out of my house

449

and off my land. If not, I'll blow us all to hell. See that package in the hallway next to the planter? There are many such "presents" scattered around the place. They have four minutes and forty seconds.'

'Evacuate now!' Lt Hofmann ordered his men. 'And take Aleksandra. Warn the kitchen staff. Go!'

Svetlana had never doubted the outcome of her journey to Switzerland. She had known it would come down to this.

'I'll do so, but on one condition, you let my child go,' she said, entering the large space and holding her pistol by the tip of the barrel. Her eyes did not shift from Niall, hiding behind the couch with Dasha asleep on it. In his right hand he held a pistol pointed at her. In the other, a detonator. Her heart sank, wondering what he had done to Dasha; the urge to grab her child and flee was overwhelming. But she knew she would not leave with Dasha. That would not happen. Not now.

She put the pistol on the floor.

'Good girl. Now kick it over here,' Niall ordered, and gave one of his charming smiles.

His transformation had not changed his smile, one she had grown to hate while living with him during those dreadful weeks.

'Thought you'd never see me again. Come to think of it, you're not,' he said and touched his reconstructed face as if touching some iconic statue sculpted by the hands of Michelangelo. 'Do you like the new me? Well, it doesn't matter if you do. You'll learn to like it. We'll have lots of time to get reacquainted. And by the way, in case you were wondering, I must confess I missed you. Yearning to repay you for your kindness, arranging that *lovely hotel* in Cuba. Irina, you should have killed me when you had the chance. Okay, enough chit-chat. Tell your friend to take Dasha. You're staying in case you haven't worked that one out yet.'

'Of course,' Svetlana replied, careful not to antagonise him. One wrong word and he would not hesitate to act irrationally. 'What have you given Dasha?'

'A mild sedative. Couldn't have a screaming child on my hands now, could I? You may come closer and say your bye-byes.' Niall harried her and motioned her forward with the barrel of the pistol. 'Come on, don't be shy.'

Svetlana's fingers touched Dasha's face. She swallowed and fought back her tears. Tears of joy at seeing her child unharmed. Tears of anger, wanting to kill the man in front of her. Tears of defeat, unable to do anything other than do his bidding.

She kissed Dasha on her forehead. 'Go now, they will take good care of you. I will be with you soon.' Her vision blurred, marred by her tears. She looked up at Lt Hofmann. 'Please take her to Michael and Vera.'

The young lieutenant's eyes burned with rage. Where was the justice in this? If he had things his way, he would put a bullet between Niall's eyes. But as a trained soldier, he knew the man behind the couch would press the detonator long before he could raise his weapon.

Svetlana saw the fury in the German's eyes, and said, 'Lieutenant, it's okay. I'll be fine. Thanks for your help. I will never forget—'

'Jeezus woman, give it a break or you'll have us all in fucking tears!' Niall scowled. 'Okay Lieutenant, you heard her. Now get out. Tell Michael if he, you, or anyone else I don't like comes within a hundred kilometres from here, I'll blow miss Muffet's brains out. Roger that, Lieutenant?'

Lt Hofmann did not reply and lifted the sleeping child into his arms. He saluted Svetlana, turned, and left. Svetlana's eyes followed him out of the room.

Facing Niall, she said, her voice filled with hatred, 'I'm all yours. Do with me as you please.'

Holding the detonator in one hand and the phone in the other, Niall tried to worm his way out of his predicament. With each passing minute, the precariousness of his situation became more evident. If he remained in the castle for a few days, he would be relatively safe. If he dared venture outside, a sniper would undoubtedly end his life.

And with her in the same room, he had no guarantees either. Therefore, he kept his distance. He knew what she was capable of. And when hurt, incensed, she would be ten times more dangerous.

Her eyes glowered pure hatred as she spoke. 'So, you're happy now, finally having me at your mercy? What shall we do, jump into bed and have some fun? Pretend you did not murder my sister and parents and rip my nails out? Why not? After all, they were only my family. And the nails will grow back. Well, I'm prepared to forgive and forget if you are. Locking you up and destroying your *kingdom* in Ireland was purely business, nothing personal, as they say.'

He did not budge, nor did he fall for her baiting. 'As always, you're still full of it. A warning, though. Things are changing as we speak. Believe me, in a few days you'll be begging me for help. To save you and your child. If you behave, I might just consider that. But don't expect me to help your friends.'

'Poor Niall. I suppose you're counting on your Russian friends, who must have "wonderful" plans for you. Something like two years ago. Not so? Sorry to disappoint you. That will never happen. They'll do nothing for you. I think it's time you know why you were locked up.'

'Please enlighten me. I'm all ears.'

Svetlana's stare cut through him; her voice void of humour. 'I was sent to catch you because someone outside your circle of friends had discovered the selling of Russian intel and weapons by you, Nicolai, and Gen Andreyev. These concerned citizens had been ignorant of the fact that your racket had been orchestrated by your friends, paving the way for something much bigger than pure greed. It was for this coming war. But these individuals kept on digging. And to stop them, they had made you the fall-guy; the so-called mastermind behind the thefts. And with you out of the way, the case was closed.

'Illegal sales had continued under the auspices of your "best" friend, Nicolai. Surely you must have wondered why nothing ever happened to him. And what about Gen

452

Andreyev? Fact is, he had retired in luxury to the countryside with a medal thrown in for his loyal service to the motherland. And you…'

Svetlana's words engulfed Niall like a freezing Siberian fog. But he did not blink, his throbbing temple the only sign of his anger consuming him.

'Niall, you have no idea who you are involved with. Their loyalty is to themselves, to Russia, and the cause you naively support. Whatever they've promised, they are not going to rescue you in case you were hoping.'

'If so, I may as well push this tiny button,' he threatened, his finger hovering over the detonator.

'One thing, I must admit, I didn't take you for a loser. Wouldn't you much rather see them locked up and be the hero who saved the world? I'm sure the powers that be may overlook your sins if you help them avert this war. Catch the men orchestrating this conflict. That's if you know anything useful.'

Niall looked at her, uncertain. 'Interesting. Say I consider that. How can you arrange a pardon?' he asked sceptically.

'I can try. Depends on what you have to offer.'

'Their main objectives, for starters.'

'That's it?'

'And the names of the main players.'

'Better. That may work.'

'And what about you?'

'What about me?' Svetlana asked.

'Yes, they might pardon me. But will you forgive me?'

'No, I never will. If you do get a deal, you better disappear and hope I never find you. I'm sure I speak for Michael as well.'

'Right then, why don't you just kill me now? Get it over with instead of offering me a deal. Come on, do it. I'll even give you my gun,' Niall taunted. 'And you know why you can't? Because deep down, you care for me and refuse to accept that. What we had was something special. I'll never believe yours was merely a big act to trap me. No, your eyes

453

did not lie. That's why you took your daughter's place. To be with me.'

Svetlana nearly burst out laughing. He truly was insane.

Instead, she replied, 'Niall, think what you want. For now, we are irrelevant. Let's focus on what I've said. Do you want me to arrange a deal or not? If so, we must be quick. And if not, you will not leave here alive. They will kill you.'

Niall did not respond.

Svetlana's eyes held his.

The man she had known, who thought he always had the answers, was always ahead of others, now looked lost, vulnerable. The long, lonely months of isolation in prison had taken its toll. Yes, he still reeked of bravado, but he had changed. He had become weak.

When he spoke, he sounded like a man lost on a sea of ever-shifting sand. 'Okay, call them,' he said and put his phone on the coffee table between them.

'You'll have to dial. I can't do it with one hand.'

Niall picked up the phone and put down the detonator. 'Give me the number.'

Svetlana quoted Michael's number.

Concentrating on his phone, he did not see her arm shoot out. With a perfect knife hand, she struck the left side of his exposed neck next to his Adam's apple, hitting the Vagus nerve. His brain instantly received a spike in blood pressure and immediately dropped the pressure again. His phone slipped out of his hand. He toppled forward on to the floor. Unconscious.

She grabbed his pistol and the detonator.

And picking up the phone, she completed the number Niall had started to dial. She took three steps back and with the pistol trained on Niall, said, 'Michael, you can come up. He has been neutralised.'

'Yes, Niall, you have become weak,' she said to the unconscious body on the floor.

'Mummy, there were so many toys. There were—' Dasha jabbered happily, cradled on Svetlana's lap in the back of the 4x4.

Squashed in next to them were Sinead, Vera, and Natalya. Aleksandra sat in the front. With the utmost care Michael drove along the road from Bern to his house in Lauenen.

With large eyes Dasha continued recounting her time in the castle. As far as she was aware she had visited one of her mummy's friends. However, with regards to her time in the chalet's basement, she did not talk about. She did not want to upset her mummy, tell her how much she had cried. How much she had missed her. Her mummy looked tired.

'Aleksandra, thanks for taking care of Dasha. Keeping her happy,' Svetlana said, knowing how she must have missed her freedom. Notwithstanding, she had put on a brave face for Dasha's sake.

Aleksandra smiled. 'I'm very happy she is safe.'

'We'll contact your parents as soon as we can and get you home,' Svetlana said.

'But till then, Aleksandra, you'll stay with us,' Vera said, and turned to Svetlana. 'Michael and I want you and Dasha to be our guests till this is over, or for however long you want. We have plenty of room and it's very peaceful. Also, there are lots of things to do. Our home will be yours,' Vera said. Her tone made it clear she won't have it any other way.

'You're both very kind and we'd love to. But I must return to Moscow. Ivan needs me.'

'Hmm, sounds like someone's in love,' Vera teased.

In the dark interior of the car, Svetlana could feel the flush of her cheeks. 'He's a wonderful man,' she admitted.

'Svetlana, having spoken to him a few times, I believe you are right. Ivan sounds like a great man,' Michael added, his attention fixed on the road, the impending war, and what needed to be done. He hoped Thomas, Ivan, and the CIA could deliver sufficient evidence to a receptive audience. And on time.

As soon as the women – and there were quite a few of them: Svetlana, Sinead, Aleksandra, and his wife – were settled in, he'd *escape*.

Michael was never comfortable in the company of a lot of women. Thankfully, he had a good excuse to disappear; an extremely lengthy report had to be filed. And with Lt Hofmann escorting Niall to Calw, Baden-Wurttemberg, where Thomas was ready to hear his "confession", the four women would be safe; there was no Niall to hunt them down.

If NATO offered Niall a deal, then he better not set his foot in Switzerland again. He would watch him day and night, year in year out. Of course, he could not control what Svetlana or Ivan might do…

Niall was a marked man. In Russia, he was wanted for the abduction of Dasha and the murder of Svetlana's parents and sister. Not forgetting the Swiss, the Cubans, and the Irish who also wanted their pound of flesh for a string of infringements, murder being one of them.

Chapter 69

Germany

Filled with the utmost contempt, Thomas glared at Niall secured to the metal table; the mutual dislike had been instant when Lt Hofmann had brought Niall into the room.

Both were tall, well-built, healthy, fit, highly intelligent, and roughly the same age.

Thomas, virtuous, compassionate. Someone who would stop at nothing to help his fellow man. And, sitting opposite him, the personification of evil. A psychotic psychopath whose world centred around himself and his perverted self-gratification. A man who would stop at nothing to get what he wanted.

Thomas faced a slight dilemma. Did this man deserve anything even smelling like a deal? The minimum he deserved was to be locked up for good if a death sentence was not possible. When he thought of a life-sentence, he understood it to be just that. And not in a European modern *hotel*. No, he deserved an isolation cell in a gulag as the one his wife had been in.

'Apparently, you told Maj Nikolaeva you would like a deal in return for the ringleaders' names of this coup and their objectives. Correct?'

'Yes.'

'But an agreement was never reached as she had neutralised you before she had spoken to us. Therefore, we are not bound by anything she might have said or inferred. Any arrangement depends on what you have to offer. And your role in this coup. Is that clear?' Thomas warned.

'Yes.'

Lt Gen Beck was resting and had left the questioning of Niall up to him. There was not much time left to squeeze whatever he could out of his prisoner and prepare for the conference call. A call which could end this conflict or finally ignite it.

'What do you hope to get? That's if we agree.'

'A full pardon for my role in this coup, and a new identity. I will have to "disappear" or else there is no point. They will kill me if word gets out. Which undoubtedly it will.'

'What is your role in this coup?'

'Minor. Therefore, I'm not acquainted with most council members. Only know a few. My involvement was limited to introducing certain individuals to the council who are now part and parcel of the operation. Names which might surprise you. As a reward, I was promised lucrative construction contracts during the rebuilding phase.'

Thomas rubbed his chin, wondering whether he should give Niall the benefit of the doubt. Lt Gen Beck had authorised him to proceed with an agreement if he thought Niall's information was of any worth. If this were true, then it might add great value to the evidence they had.

'Who are they? Where are they from?' Thomas asked, hating to have to negotiate with the criminal.

'Americans. Politicians. That's all I'll say for now.'

Not surprised by Niall's allegiance with the Americans, he said, 'Yes, we can arrange a pardon, and for you to "disappear". I must warn you; we cannot guarantee your safety. The actions of the Russians, Swiss, Irish, Interpol, and Cubans are outside our control. Be under no illusion, they will try to find you.'

'I can live with that. Colonel, you put that in writing and I'll be delighted to cooperate.'

458

Niall's tone irked Thomas. He said nothing and left.

Thirty minutes later, he returned with three copies of a freshly typed document dated and stamped with a NATO letterhead. Behind him were two officials. He placed the copies in front of Niall. 'Read and sign.'

'And if I don't like what I read?'

'Then tough. Listen, you either sign it or there is no deal. Then we hand you over to the Russians. Not your friends, but ours.'

With two ratified copies in his hand and Niall holding his, Thomas said, 'You have thirty minutes to finish your statement. I leave you with my colleagues and trust for your own sake you'll be frank or the document you hold will be worthless. Remember, we already have some of your Russian friends in custody who have made statements. So, no lies Mr McGuire.'

By 07h30 Thomas slipped in behind his desk. Preparing for the conference call, his men in France and England were foremost on his mind.

So far, in collaboration with the local governments' intelligence agencies and military, they had failed to find the Russians – no one had ventured near the targets specified by Col Polyakov. There had been no suspicious activity detected at any of the stock exchanges. If they did plan to blow up these, they would have to sneak trucks loaded with explosives into the basements, or crash them into the foyers, or deliver a deadly cargo by drone.

Nor was there any sign of the Russian unit supposedly in Luxembourg.

Furthermore, all European nuclear power plants and their immediate surroundings had been placed under military lockdown. Only essential staff were allowed on to the premises, each under the watchful eye of two guards. No one was to be trusted.

The question remained. What and where were these targets?

Col Polyakov's information seemed to be outdated, or he was playing them. The team of interrogators had failed to uncover anything useful. The fact was, neither he, Ivan, nor the general put much credence in what he had revealed so far. Killers like him did not give up information at the sight of a woman in distress, even a loved one.

Thomas picked up the framed photograph of Klaara taken six months ago. The lines on her face and hint of sadness in her eyes did not diminish her beauty. To him, she still looked the same as the day they had bumped into each other thirty-five years ago. He wondered if they would ever be able to take the world trip they'd been dreaming of. Or retire to a cottage overlooking the sea, somewhere warm.

Returning his attention to the problem facing him, he once more studied the colonel's "confession", trying to see if there was anything which could give a hint of what was to come next. Nothing. His phone rang. Distracted, he answered with a cool, 'Yes.'

'Colonel, it's me, Michael. It sounds like I caught you at a bad time. Can you talk?'

'Oh, hello, Michael. Of course. Apologies… Been a bit preoccupied.'

'You better sit down. We're receiving reports of a string of assassinations, murders. Not that it's anything unusual, except the victims are the wealthy and powerful. Individuals with one thing in common: banks. More specifically, central banks worldwide, as well as the Bank for International Settlements (BIS) in Basel.'

Thomas did not reply.

'You're there?'

'Yes… Who are they? CEO's, managers, staff?'

'Main shareholders. Heads of the old banking syndicates. What's emerging is that all family members had been targeted: spouses, children, and board members. The families who had controlled our world's finances for centuries had been eradicated.'

'Impossible…'

'As outrageous as it sounds, it happened.'

For a few seconds, Thomas digested the news. 'We thought they were going to take out the stock exchanges. But they did nothing as crass. They were far more clinical. This is the first salvo to replace those who thought they were in charge. Stocks will plummet and will be snapped up. Control of the central banks will transfer to this group, whoever they might be. Governments will fall, new puppets will be put in place. And the Russian military will ensure this comes to pass.'

As Thomas spoke, it all became clear. They did not hit the stock exchanges and for a very good reason; they needed them to keep trading. A bad sign of what was to come.

And who or what the next targets would be was obvious.

'Michael, as terrible as this is, your call might have saved many lives. I'll tell you later. Now you'll have to excuse me.'

It was time to wake up the general. They needed to act quickly.

Halfway down the corridor his phone rang. Ivan.

'Morning, Thomas. The general arranged a conference call for noon your time. The president and some advisors will be present.'

'Good. We'll be ready,' Thomas replied, not sure whether the conference call would ever happen once the news of the murders of the rulers of the world surfaced.

'And again, thank you for helping Svetlana and rescuing Dasha.'

'Ivan, it was a pleasure.'

'Trust you won't get in trouble.'

'Not at all. She caught a murderer and co-conspirator. How are they?'

'In great form and are staying with Michael and Vera till this blows over. The mountain air will do them a world of good, and they'll be safe there. Oh yes, she wants to thank you in person. Can I give her your number?'

'Of course, would be great to meet the woman who has knocked you off your feet. What I've heard, she's a wonderful person. Glad for you, Ivan.'

461

'I'm very lucky,' Ivan said, his adoration of Svetlana evident in his voice. He cleared his throat and asked, changing the topic, 'Any progress with Niall?'

'Yes, he may have some useful intel. Names of Americans involved. We'll soon find out whether it's true or not. But something else happened.'

'By your tone, it doesn't sound good.'

'According to Interpol, the oldest banking families had been eliminated. Those who have controlled the world and its finances for years.'

Stunned, Ivan said nothing.

'Governments will fall. This may include your own. Unless, of course, they are the problem…'

'Understood,' Ivan replied.

'Ivan, best you don't reveal your current location to anyone, including your president. Can you also please warn the general and his wife? Watch your back.'

Chapter 70

Brussels
Belgium

The 18-tonne Scania freezer lorry pulled into the demarcated delivery yard at the European Union Parliament building's east service entrance in Brussels. Not feeling well, suffering terrible stomach cramps, the driver got out, locked the truck, and with his paperwork in hand went in search of a toilet. The deliveries of Monday's fresh produce were on time, as per the approved schedule for 10:45 AM.

Another 18-tonne delivery truck stopped and parked 267m west in Rue de Tréves. Its driver got out and popped into a café down the road for a quick cup of coffee. They also abandoned a similar truck in a delivery zone 250m to the north, and a fourth in a loading bay 250m to the south.

Five hundred metres further north, an 18-tonne Mercedes freezer lorry pulled into the delivery bay of the European Commission Building, Berlaymont on Rue de la Loi. The driver of the lorry suffered the same affliction as the driver at the EU Parliament Building and hurried to clear the area.

Lorry number six slipped into a delivery bay near the Council of Europe's building. Truck number seven was left in a loading bay in the Rue Archiméde, covering the east flank of the European Commission Building. And the last truck parked in Boulevard Charlemagne, covering the west flank.

At the time the doors of the trucks shut, the special session of the EU parliament was already in session, its members listening intently to the words of the EU president. The message of doom delivered moments ago cast a cloud of uncertainty and misgiving over the delegates. Not all were convinced, having never believed the rhetoric of the mainstream media.

At exactly 11:00 AM the timers inside the eight trucks ticked their last millisecond. Each truck's cargo comprised twenty tonnes of TNT combined with PETN, precisely placed for maximum effect.

The combined destruction of the eight simultaneous explosions was the same as that of a nuclear bomb, but controlled and without the nuclear fallout.

First, the external walls of glass and cladding of buildings in the blast's path were obliterated from the ground up. Unobstructed, the force continued, blowing away support columns and structures, collapsing buildings like packs of cards. Anyone inside had no chance of survival. An area of thirty hectares had instantly been laid to waste. Most of the surrounding buildings in the immediate vicinity had been spared the same devastation.

London, England

Approaching from opposite directions, four black crows flapped their wings and flew over the rooftops, gliding towards the long rectangular building with its many pinnacles and turrets. Below these scavengers, the usual Monday morning commotion of traffic, pedestrians rushing to work like ants, and boats gliding up and down the river, continued unabated. The water of the Thames was murky, the sky over London grey.

The doors to the Palace of Westminster were shut.

Armed police and military had cordoned off the premises to all pedestrians. The only people who had been allowed in

464

were members of parliament and MSM. Hastily erected anti-tank barriers blocked all roads leading to the famous gothic structure. Overhead, four British Army Air Corps' Agusta Westland Apache helicopters swept the area. The emergency parliamentary session called by the prime minister would be conducted in safety. Behind the closed doors, the prime minister was to deliver his sombre message. The nation must prepare itself for war.

As Big Ben struck 10:00 AM, two crows dropped into Peers Court and settled on the east corridor's flat roof adjacent to two of the tall ornate windows of the House of Lords. The other two crows landed on the flat roof of the East Division Lobby between the Commons Court and the House of Commons, also next to two clerestory windows.

At the same time, two groups of four drones each approached the palace from the north and south. Their dull-grey, 45cm diameter bodies blended in perfectly with the dull murky river as they glided two metres above the water surface at 120km/h. By the time the crows landed, the drones cleared the roof of the palace's outer library wing. A fraction of a second later, simultaneous explosions blew out the four clerestory windows. Glass and debris cascaded on to the seats below with smoke and dust filling the large gaping holes.

People screamed.

The eight drones shot towards the openings in the clerestory windows. Sniper bullets fired from the helicopters exploded two of the drones. The other six continued inside. Seconds later, a series of explosions rocked the old building. Rubble, glass, roofing material and timbers flew in all directions as two huge plumes of smoke drifted into the grey morning sky. Most of the upper walls of the House of Commons and the House of Lords were gone, as were the roofs.

Paris, France

Within the Palais Bourbon on Rue de l'Université, the French National Assembly's extraordinary session was in progress. Anxious voices debated the news delivered by the president.

France had to prepare for war.

At precisely 11:00 AM, four large pigeons landed on the seventeen-metre diameter, semi-circular glass roof over the main chamber.

Seconds after the pigeons had detonated, four drones flew through the large hole in the roof. The subsequent explosions rendered the ornate semi-circular chamber with its impressive mural and elegant columns obsolete. Four drones had been shot down in flight by defensive fire, exploding them harmlessly in mid-air.

The warning of an imminent terrorist attack issued less than an hour ago by NATO High Command to the parliaments who had scheduled extraordinary sessions for the day had been acted on with the utmost urgency. All available military and police personnel had been rushed to the parliaments in London, Paris, and Berlin.

Less than a week ago, anticipating new developments unfolding over the coming days, the leaders had called for sittings to be held on this day.

The security forces scrambled at the last-minute had done their best in safeguarding these buildings and the people already inside, allowing the meetings to "continue". But they had failed to stop the attacks.

As the dust settled in Paris and London, more military, accompanied by an endless stream of emergency services, arrived at the scenes of destruction.

Thirty minutes later, the leaders of each country, together with all parliamentarians, officials, and media personnel, were escorted out of the underground bunkers. No one was hurt. These two attacks orchestrated by Col Polyakov's unit had failed.

466

But the attack in Brussels had been devastating. The members of the European Commission, Council, Parliament, and those of the 33,000 officials, staff, and special advisers present at the time had been exterminated. The heart of the European Union had been ripped out.

With dread, Thomas read the transcript, precising the attacks. His written warning that "ALL" government institutions in Europe, including that of the European Union, must be safeguarded as a matter of extreme urgency and without delay, had gone unheeded.

No action to pre-empt an attack in Brussels had been taken.

What the hell have they been doing for the last few hours? Analysing the intel over a mug of hot chocolate while munching fresh croissants! Whoever is responsible for this shall pay dearly, Thomas vowed, filled with rage.

He and Lt Gen Beck had notified NATO High Command three hours before the attack had occurred. But the fact was, many lives had been lost, far too many. Nothing he could do would bring any of them back.

Thomas looked at his watch. Twenty minutes until the conference call with the Russian president. He was not ready for the call. He needed time to compose himself. Clear his head. He feared he might lose his temper with the Russian leader if he found the man uncooperative. And that would be the end.

Also present, Lt Gen Beck glared at the large, blank monitor. The events of the past twelve hours made any comment in defence of Russia by its president untenable. The only words he wanted to hear from the president were, "Russia, nor I had any part in these horrific attacks, I guarantee you. I shall not rest till the men responsible for these atrocities had been caught and punished", or words to that effect. Nothing less. If not, he saw no way forward and all hell would break loose.

Seated on his right was Thomas, armed with what he believed was sufficient evidence to make NATO's case. He aimed to expose the third force and negotiate a truce, a stand-down of Russian troops and a return to normalities. Whether America and the rest of Europe would capitulate and continue with business as usual, he doubted. The fragile trust which had taken decades to nurture was gone. The minimum demand would be massive financial reparations, to apply crippling economic sanctions, and for the immediate reduction of Russian troops on the western front and Ukrainian border.

But how President Maxim Fedorov would respond to the allegations levelled at members of his elite military unit remained to be seen.

Down the hall from the interrogation room, Niall and the Russians were kept in separate cells. The information extracted from the four prisoners was condemning enough. Only Niall would be allowed to go free once this was over.

The large monitor came alive.

Seated behind a desk was Ivan. Next to him the American CIA agent, John Saunders. The walls behind them were void of any pictures or symbols, as was the desk. The screen split into two. NATO's Supreme Allied Commander Europe, Gen William Oswald looking browbeaten, appeared seated next to two military generals. The screen divided into three with the director of the CIA, Terence Russell smiling confidently at the camera. He was flanked by two men.

Ivan, the youngest present, was the first to speak. 'Good morning, Gentlemen. Thank you for joining us. Hopefully, this will supply us with the answers we need. But please, watch your words. If unsure, then rather not comment – we'll ask for a five-minute respite. You all have copies of the evidence and realise what we're about to do. Don't delude yourselves. These accusations, as true as they are, will not be appreciated by my fellow countrymen. We have five minutes before the president joins us. I will do the introductions and make our case. Gen Oswald, you'll be next. Trust that is in order. Questions?'

'General, I appreciate the warning, thank you. I'll go easy on them,' Gen Oswald said, trying to sound authoritative.

Those listening were not fooled: the man was in a state of shock. The attack, which had killed an untold number and destroyed a large part of Brussels, happened under his watch. Ultimately, he would be held accountable for this disaster. 'Are the witnesses ready?'

'Yes, they are,' Lt Gen Beck confirmed. 'I suggest we start with the Irishman; may soften the Russian's stance. The president better come on board or there is nothing more to be done.'

The men on all sides of the cameras continued debating the likely chance of peace. Ivan stopped them. 'Five seconds till we are going live with Moscow.'

At precisely noon, the screens facing the four groups split into four, with a close-up image of the Russian president dressed in a dark suit seated at the end of a long table. His grey hair swept back. And his familiar Armani glasses poised comfortably on his nose. His steely, light-blue eyes showed no signs of concern.

The camera panned out.

Further down the table on his left sat a man of insignificant stature with the two chairs next to him occupied. The three chairs opposite were empty.

The small man cleared his throat and introduced himself without a word of welcome. 'I am Aleks Andreyev, prime minister of Russia. This is Maxim Fedorov, president of Russia,' he said, indicating to the familiar face on his right.

The president nodded.

'The gentlemen on my left are Deputy Prime Minister Grigory Seleznev and FSB Director Counterintelligence Colonel General Igor Kozlov. As soon as—' the prime minister paused and looked to his left. 'They are here. Gentlemen, please take your seats,' he said as the three men in military uniform, all in their mid-sixties, approached the vacant chairs opposite.

The prime minister continued. 'The minister of Defence and Marshall of the Russian Federation Timur Stalin, the Chief of the General Staff Army General Pavel Orlov. And Colonel General Vladimir Coshenko, commander of our elite

469

expeditionary forces.' At the mention of their names each man nodded.

'Thank you, Gentlemen, for joining us,' the prime minister said, addressing his fellow countrymen. 'Our friends in the West, as well as Maj Gen Ivan Lukyanov, Deputy Director Counterintelligence FSB, have asked for this meeting. They would like to present evidence of an apparent third force responsible for the current hostilities and horrendous attacks an hour ago in France, England, and Belgium. Our esteemed president has agreed to this. Therefore, I hand the floor over to Maj Gen Lukyanov. Please proceed General.'

Ivan commenced with his introductions, but the mood amongst his party had plummeted. The presence of Col Gen Coshenko was most alarming. Named as the man who issued Col Polyakov's instructions, they had to assume he was responsible for the most recent attacks in Europe. The prospect of a positive outcome to this meeting did not hold much promise.

On behalf of NATO, Gen Oswald spoke first. He kept it short and to the point with each word translated by a Russian interpreter. 'Mr President, thank you for agreeing to meet us at such short notice. We believe the evidence we're about to present would be sufficient for you to reconsider the declaration of war against NATO allies and instruct your forces to stand down. As soon as we have concluded this meeting, we will present the same to the leaders of all NATO members states and advise them to stand their forces down as well. And with the help of Russia, concentrate our efforts to find and punish the people responsible.' He paused, giving the translator a chance to finish.

President Fedorov's expression did not indicate whether he was intrigued, offended, or agitated. The men flanking him showed no emotions either. The president nodded his head for Gen Oswald to continue.

'We have irrefutable proof that America had no part in the attacks on the energy installations in Turkey, Norway, and Russia. At this early stage, indications are that the same applies to the elimination of the banking cartels and the

470

attacks in London, Paris, and Brussels. All these attacks are the work of a third force whose members have infiltrated America's security services as well as Russia's. So, without further delay, I ask Lt Gen Beck and Col Bauer to proceed.'

Lt Gen Beck indicated for Thomas to address the meeting. Ignoring the fact that he was facing one of the main conspirators, he said, 'Mr President, Gentlemen, we'll bring in the first witness. Please note, you can see him, he cannot see you.'

Another screen opened on all monitors, showing Niall escorted into the interrogation room, his hands and feet chained. Shoved into a chair, they cuffed him to it.

'This is Niall McGuire, Irish national currently residing in Switzerland under the alias of Brendan Walsh. An escaped convict wanted in Russia, Cuba, Ireland, and Switzerland for murder, kidnapping, and a string of other crimes. And also by NATO for his contribution in this coup. He has without duress handed himself over and submitted his statement. He will read it out to you. For security reasons the names of some of his co-conspirators had been changed. As you can appreciate, we do not want word to get out, giving them a chance to disappear.'

In silence, all parties listened to Niall, setting out the objectives of the council as he understood them to be. The different parties involved, and the names and descriptions of those he knew. At the mention of a senior Russian officer present at the dinner the day before, the minister of defence and Col Gen Coshenko glanced at each other briefly. The Deputy Prime Minister Seleznev shifted uncomfortably in his chair. The rest of the men showed no reaction to any of Niall's claims as he explained his involvement from the beginning up to the time Svetlana had snared him.

No one asked any questions.

NATO members were appalled by the treachery of this man, while the Russians sat poker-faced without a comment.

Col Polyakov was brought in next and secured to the same chair Niall had occupied. This time, the Russians were visibly annoyed when Thomas introduced the colonel and recited his alleged crimes. He accused him of being the hand which had wielded the sword in Turkey, Norway, and Russia. And having planned the most recent attacks.

Col Polyakov read out his statement. After four sentences the Russians silenced him, not wanting to hear anymore. The Minister of Defence was the most vocal. He demanded an immediate end to the meeting as NATO's evidence was circumstantial. They had no proof of Russia's involvement. And anything the colonel and his men had confessed was extorted under extreme duress. Therefore, it was all rubbish. This meeting was a blatant attempt by NATO to lay the blame for the attacks at the door of Russia and the honourable members of its elite armed forces. He wanted the colonel and his men returned to Russia by the end of the day.

President Fedorov interrupted him. 'Timur, I would like to hear what the colonel has to say. Colonel, as your commander-in-chief, I order you to answer me honestly. Was your statement made under duress or not?'

'Yes, Mr President. It was under extreme duress. They had captured and tortured my wife, forcing me to say what they wanted to hear. I think they're still holding her. My men and I had no part in these attacks.'

'Colonel, you don't have to say anymore. We'll bring you home,' President Fedorov said, and gave a reassuring smile. 'Gen Oswald, I appreciate your attempt at expediting peace. But I must express my disappointment at your deviousness and insist you return my men to Russia at once. They had no part in this coup theory you have concocted.

'Kidnapping our men while on holiday in Switzerland is unacceptable. It seems the only "proof" you have is circumstantial at best. Plus, the word of a convicted criminal who will say anything to save himself. For all we know, this so-called coup is being orchestrated by America. It has nothing to do with Russia. May I remind you of Iraq.

'At this point, we have no other choice. We will defend our country against any further aggression by NATO. When you have evidence to the contrary, call me. My line is always open. Until then, we will not deviate from our path. We will not stand down.'

The link cut.

Boris smiled broadly. It had gone as he believed it would.

Seeing him smirk, Lt Gen Beck bellowed, 'Colonel, if you think you have won, then you're a fool. This is not over. Corporals, remove him from my sight.'

Stunned into silence by the Russian president's words, the panel of viewers gawked at the cameras. His response had been the last thing they had expected. Forewarned by Ivan, Thomas and Lt Gen Beck were not surprised.

'Gentlemen, unfortunately, that did not go as we had hoped,' Lt Gen Beck said in a sombre voice. 'And it confirms one thing; all the men in that room are part of this operation. Therefore, our hopes that the attacks were not sanctioned by the Russian leader were nothing other than wishful thinking. It would seem war is inevitable. We have done what we could. It is time to prepare ourselves and the rest of the world. This so-called "Council", this "coup", is merely a vessel to be blamed if Russia fails in its objectives. If they lose the war.'

Chapter 71

Germany

'Well, Ivan, you were right,' Thomas sighed. His fears that the Russian president had decided the time was ripe to fulfil his dream of a new USSR had not been unfounded.

On their own, with the other viewers disconnected, Thomas and Ivan confided in each other.

'I suggest you leave Russia. Please get the general and his wife to do the same ASAP.'

'Don't think we have much of a choice. This time, they won't miss,' Ivan replied.

'Have you anywhere to stay in the West?'

'I think I'll join Svetlana.'

'Of course,' Thomas said and smiled, fully appreciative of Ivan's comment. 'But you're more than welcome to stay with us. The general and his wife will.'

'Very grateful for the offer, but I'll venture further south,' Ivan said with a boyish grin.

'Good. Now to get you out. Do you think the Sumy border region it's still passable?'

'Possibly. If you can arrange with the Ukrainians to allow us in, we'll slip across. I'll let— Just a sec, I have an incoming call. Mind if I take it?'

A frown creased Ivan's forehead. He sat up, giving his undivided attention to the caller. After a few minutes, he spoke. 'Yes, understood. I will see what I can do.'

Having ended the call, he looked at Thomas. 'You'll never guess who that was?'

'Who?'

'President Maxim Fedorov.'

'I see… What did he want?'

'He came up with some explanation for what happened. Claims it was all theatrics. That he had no choice. Too many of his top echelon are not to be trusted. Worried he might be assassinated, he had played along. Apparently, he believes us and will pause all further aggression. But he will not stand down just yet. He asked if we could arrange a video call via your office.'

'Wow! Just like that. I'm dumbstruck,' Thomas hissed. His hairs stood on end; something was wrong.

'He wants the following present. The American president, director of the CIA, the German chancellor, prime minister of Britain, president of France, Gen Oswald, Lt Gen Beck, and you. It's imperative that the American president, John O'Callaghan, joins us.

'Fedorov will be supported by his prime minister, minister of defence, and head of the FSB Counterintelligence. He wants to keep this private and away from the normal diplomatic channels.'

'Wonder why?' Thomas said warily. 'Could just be a delaying tactic, putting us at ease while he continues with plans to invade Ukraine and the West. He most likely never expected us to uncover the facts and now wants it hushed up.'

'I don't trust him either. But we'll set up the meeting and see what happens.'

The conference call took place at 14h00 and concluded at 14h50.

The outcome of discussions resulted in the Russian president agreeing to stand-down all military personnel in Russia with immediate effect. NATO agreed to do the same.

Steps were to be taken against the traitors on either side.

In America, the vice president, the deputy head of the CIA, the opposition's leading presidential candidate were to be arrested within the hour. And the hunt for their co-conspirators across the globe would swing into motion. Especially those who had snapped up the crashed shares of the Central Banks and major energy companies earlier in the day.

And as for Russia, President Fedorov vowed to clean out his house of traitors. He would spare no one. He had also agreed to pay full reparations for damages caused by members of his military.

As the wheels to ease tensions got into motion, Thomas and Ivan once more shared their concerns.

Was that it?

No.

Neither believed the Russian president. It had been too easy. Were the men responsible really prepared to walk away empty-handed after years of planning, time, and money invested? And having thrown the world into turmoil with thousands killed?

No.

Had the president been that ignorant of events in his own country?

No.

And who exactly was behind this? The president and his inner-circle perhaps…?

Highly likely…

'Ivan, I firmly believe we are being played. Fedorov may be one of the key players in charge of this mysterious council. His years of preparing the Russians for this "final war" will not be cancelled just like that. As I've said before, I don't trust him.'

'Hundred per cent with you on that one.'

'I have a nasty feeling that the war is about to start. You get to the border with our friend. There is nothing more you or anyone else can do.'

Munich, Germany

Niall walked towards Munich's main railway station entrance. Armed with a new German passport in the name of John O'Reilly, and a €50 note folded inside his anorak's pocket, he had been released. They had confiscated his expensive phone, watch, wallet, and clothes in lieu of a pair of cheap jeans, shirt, anorak, and runners. For now, it would do. At least he was alive.

Having been "processed" at the military base in Calw, the military police had dropped him off outside the station. The signed copy of the agreement, which was to serve as his insurance, they had ripped up. The only part of the agreement they had honoured was to let him go free.

He had to disappear, and fast. And the only way he could, was with money, and lots of it. The castle and chalet were gone. Annoying as it was, it was not the end of the world. Most of his financial resources were still intact. He had to get to a phone.

His appearance would have to change again. He had no choice. Not only were the governments of Ireland, Russia, Cuba, Switzerland after him, but also members of the Council and his old *friend* Nicolai. And not forgetting, Ivan, Svetlana, and Michael. He felt as popular as a whore at an all-male convention for frustrated men. Everyone wanted a piece of him.

At the thought, he allowed himself a smile and ran his fingers through his hair. Well, you can try, but you won't see me again.

Fifty metres behind him, two women followed, watching his every step. Up ahead, two men turned into the train station's busy main hall and looked in his direction. The plainclothes police had their instructions and intended to carry it out to the full. Niall won't be going anywhere…

Chapter 72

Seated behind his desk, Thomas studied the young woman's face on the monitor. Attractive, auburn hair, high cheekbones. His eyes lit up. 'Hello, Svetlana… It's a pleasure meeting you…' he said haltingly in Russian.

'Colonel, the pleasure's all mine. And I cannot thank you enough for helping me, and for helping to stop the war.'

'Please, call me Thomas. And no need to thank me,' he replied, adding, 'It maybe a little premature to celebrate peace, though. Let's see what happens over the next few days.'

He was not sure his contribution would lead to anything. Evidence so far indicates that no order to standdown has been issued by the Russian president since the previous day's conference call. Instead of a withdrawal, more troops and equipment were being moved towards the Ukrainian border. His and Ivan's fears of an imminent war erupting proved to be correct.

'I have someone little who wants to say hello,' Svetlana said cheerfully, ignoring Thomas's sombre words.

'Where is she?'

'Right here. Dasha, say hello to Uncle Thomas,' Svetlana said as a smiling toddler jumped in front of the camera.

'Hello, Dasha. My goodness, you look just like your mummy! How are you enjoying Switzerland?'

'Hello, Uncle Thomas… Switzerland is very nice. Uncle Michael and Aunty Vera are very nice too,' Dasha beamed happily as Svetlana put her on her lap and gave her a hug.

For another ten minutes, they chatted before saying their farewells, promising to meet up as soon as Ivan would arrive.

Thomas stared at the blank monitor, his mind racing. He rang Michael. And five minutes later he put a call through to Ivan, preparing to flee Russia later in the evening.

Saturday, Lauenen

Sinead wrapped in a duvet, sipped her hot chocolate. The steam rose into the crisp morning air. The woollen mittens and house socks kept her hands and feet warm. She sat back on the patio's recliner and looked out over the snow-covered valley below, touched by the early morning sun's rays. The peaceful setting was in stark contrast to how she felt.

'Good morning! You're up early. Mind if I join you?' Vera asked spritely, also cupping a hot chocolate in her hands. With her blonde hair neatly brushed, and some light makeup on, she looked radiant. The chalet, the setting, suited her. She sat down on the other recliner next to Sinead.

'Morning Vera. Where's Natalya?'

'Fast asleep with daddy's eye on her. He's so protective. The poor girl won't be able to leave the house one day without an Interpol escort,' Vera sniggered.

'I'm so happy for you,' Sinead said. Leaning over, she took Vera's hand in hers and squeezed it gently.

'Yes, I'm blessed. A beautiful baby and a wonderful husband… But enough about me. How are you?' Vera asked, concerned about her friend.

'Just grand,' Sinead said. Her feeble smile did not hide her true feelings.

'Hmm… Doesn't look like it. So, don't try to smile your way out of this.'

'You're right. I'm not. Vera, how could I have been so stupid? Only a fool can be that blind,' she huffed, annoyed.

479

'Hang on. You are nobody's fool. I don't want to hear that again.'

'But how could I not have seen it was him? Was I that desperate?'

'Desperate maybe. But knowing it was him. No. He looked nothing like Niall. And remember, he was supposed to have been dead. Neither had you known him intimately. So how?'

'Yes, I guess you're right,' Sinead sighed and took another mouthful of the warm drink.

'I know I am. You'll get over this and will find someone special.'

'No thanks. I'm not looking. Don't want any man to touch me again.'

'Yes, of course…'

'Yes, really.'

'I also thought that not too long ago.'

'Well, I'm not a pushover like you. So, no. *Never.*'

'Okay…' Vera said, amused as Sinead's last "never" was not very convincing. 'Tell you what. You stay here until you feel you're ready to face the world. And the world of men. Also, don't forget, we must start putting the diamonds to good use, as we said we'll do. That will help you focus. We won't be able to rescue them all, but there are many we can.'

'You sure? Won't Michael mind?'

'No, he won't. I have already asked him.'

'Then, I would love that.'

It was past midday when the driver buzzed the intercom at Michael and Vera's chalet. Thomas and Klaara, seated in the back, wanted to make the most of the brief visit; he had to report back for duty within forty-eight hours. For the moment, they had pushed away the clouds of war.

The gates swung open. The taxi slipped through and followed the long driveway to the chalet, where Michael waited at the bottom of the stairs. He opened the door for Klaara and gave her a hug. Shaking hands with Thomas, he said, 'Glad to finally meet you!'

Hobbling on crutches, Thomas struggled up the eight steps to the front door. Neither he nor Klaara took any notice of the magnificent scenery of the surrounding mountains and valley. High above, two eagles swept through the blue sky, searching the white landscape for food.

In silence they entered. The combination of timber floors, ceilings, posts, beams, and the crackling fire, radiated a calm, relaxing ambience. In the double-height living room a small party waited.

Sinead and Aleksandra got up, smiled at the new guests, and retired to their rooms, allowing the gathering to proceed in private.

Ivan greeted Thomas and Klaara warmly. Svetlana joined him, delighted to meet the man who had not hesitated to help her rescue her child. Hugging Klaara, Svetlana was oblivious to the tears in Klaara's eyes.

'Please sit down,' Michael invited. 'Make yourselves at home. Anything to drink?'

'A strong coffee, thank you,' Thomas accepted the offer.

'Same for me,' Klaara said and wiped the corners of her eyes with the back of her hands. She was visibly upset.

As they all sat down, Ivan turned to Svetlana and took both her hands in his, and said, 'Svetlana, what I'm about to tell you might sound like nonsense, but it's not.'

Svetlana looked at him, unsure. 'What's going on, Ivan?'

'I'll tell you… May I?' He smiled.

'Yes…'

'Right. Then I'll start at the beginning. In 1985, Klaara was incarcerated in Perm-36, the last gulag for —' The chime of the bell interrupted him.

'Aha, must be them. I'll get it. Ivan, please continue,' Michael said, walking over from the large corner kitchen.

'Where was I…? The gulag. At the time of Klaara's arrest, she was three months pregnant. Thomas was the father-to-be. And now a little secret not to be repeated: Thomas's real name is Danylo Marchenko. He is a born and bred Ukrainian and not a German.'

'You're not serious?'

'Yes, I am.'

'But how?'

'Let me continue,' Ivan said patiently. 'A few months before her incarceration, Thomas, nineteen at the time and unaware that Klaara was pregnant, had fled with his family to West Berlin. But as soon as he was safe in Germany, he had started planning to be reunited with her.'

Svetlana turned to Klaara and Thomas, observing them somewhat suspiciously.

'In Perm-36, Klaara had given birth to a healthy baby and had named her Nadezhda. After a few months the government had placed Nadezhda in an orphanage. Having lost twins during a miscarriage which had resulted in a hysterectomy, a young couple had adopted Nadezhda.

'Not knowing what had happened to her child, Klaara was left heartbroken. On top of that, she had suffered incredible abuse at the hands of the prison guards and had become very ill. If not for Danylo, she would have died in prison. On his own, he had smuggled her out of the USSR. Strapping her to himself, he had flown her across the iron-curtain with a paraglider. Back in Germany, they were married. But what Klaara had endured in prison had left her unable to conceive.'

'That's terrible. I'm so sorry for you... For both of you,' Svetlana said, deeply moved.

Thomas put his arm around Klaara's shoulders. Her head rested in the crook of his neck. He would never forget those dreadful events of thirty-four years ago. The agony her parents and he had suffered as the young woman they had loved had faded away, riddled with pneumonia and syphilis. Endless hours they had spent by her side, her youthful body a skeleton, the pallid skin stretched thinly over her slight frame. For brief spells she had slept, her lips still, her eyes closed. These moments of respite had never lasted long before raking coughs would shake her body. Drained, her cries of agony had only been a wheezing-whisper. They had stayed by her side until it had passed.

Ivan continued. 'And ever since then, they've been searching for their child, but had never found her. All that

482

was left for them to do was to believe she was alive and happy. Well, that was until a few days ago when Thomas received a video call from someone he had never met. He was immediately struck by something familiar. The caller's eyes. They were exactly like his wife's. Like Klaara's.'

Svetlana did not blink, listening attentively.

'Thomas had asked Michael and me to help establish the identity of the young woman. We did. We took and tested DNA samples – hope she'll forgive us for doing so without her consent. The samples matched.

'A friend did a thorough search through the old USSR archives and traced their missing child to the family who had adopted her. The couple had lived in Kursk and had one daughter. Their name was Nikolaevi. Yes, Svetlana, the baby was you,' Ivan said, and smiled endearingly at his fiancé.

Svetlana said nothing. Her hands shook. She clung to Dasha who had climbed on to her lap and stared at her with big eyes. Svetlana took a deep breath... And then another. 'Mama... Papa...' she whispered.

Putting Dasha down on the couch, she got up and reached out for Klaara and Thomas who rose to meet her. Without a word the three embraced in the middle of the room.

Averting his eyes from the heart-warming reunion, Ivan said into his phone, 'Yes, Michael, bring them in.'

The front door opened.

Behind Michael, two couples in their eighties, Petro and Olena Marchenko, Jakob and Ina Luik, entered. A man and woman in their fifties followed: Bernd Müller and Karina Marchenko. No one said a word, their faces filled with expectation.

Thomas held Svetlana's hand and with the other scooped Dasha off the couch. He hurried over to greet the new guests and said, 'Meet your granddaughter and her little one. Svetlana and Dasha.'

Printed in Great Britain
by Amazon